CUMBERLAND'S CRADLE

The reclusive Mr Robertson owns the most comprehensive accumulation of torture instruments in private hands and lives in Lanner Castle, a highly fortified pseudo-Gothic Castle. When two of his guard dogs are killed on his own torture implements he calls in security expert Tim Lacy to install the latest security devices. Mr Robertson goes into hiding, but Lacy cannot prevent the pride of his grisly collection, Cumberland's Cradle, from being stolen. Two days later, Robertson is found gruesomely and fatally reunited with his property, and Tim Lacy's search for answers leads him into the greatest danger he has ever faced...

CUMBERLAND'S CRADLE

Cumberland's Cradle

by
Derek Wilson

Magna Large Print Books
Long Preston, North Yorkshire,
England.

British Library Cataloguing in Publication Data.

Wilson, Derek
   Cumberland's cradle.

A catalogue record for this book is
available from the British Library

ISBN 0-7505-1230-X

First published in Great Britain by Headline Book Publishing,
1996

Published in Large Print 1998 by arrangement with Headline
Book Publishing Ltd.

Magna Large Print is an imprint of
Library Magna Books Ltd.
Printed and bound in Great Britain by
T.J. International Ltd., Cornwall, PL28 8RW.

A dungeon horrible, on all sides round
As one great furnace flamed; yet from
  those flames
No light, but rather darkness visible
Serv'd only to discover sights of woe,
Regions of sorrow, doleful shades, where
  peace
And rest can never dwell, hope never
  comes
That comes to all.

John Milton, *Paradise Lost*

PROLOGUE

The boy was the first person in the village to hear the soldiers' approach. The intermittent wailing of his nine-month-old sister and his desperate anxiety to meet her simple needs had deprived him of childhood's right to deep sleep. His ears registered every unusual nuance of sound from beyond the holed thatch and the sacking-covered window.

He had not been listening—consciously at least—for the king's men, though, like everyone else in the highland villages, he knew they were coming. The king and the one they called the Butcher were not content with having massacred the boy's father and uncles along with other clan leaders in the great valley battle. They were sending troops up into the hills, slaughtering cattle, burning settlements, driving from their home the families of the freedom fighters as well as those who knew nothing of the political conflict and wished only to be left to their subsistence farming.

The boy rose from the thin layer of straw pushed into a corner of the earth-floored room, hugging his blanket around him against the cold. Three short strides took him to the window. He lifted the rough material and stood on tiptoe to peer out. Dawn was a suggestion of grey beyond the humped ridge of Old Man's Back. The nearer ground was patterned in shades of black, outlines blurring and merging. But the boy knew every tree, every earthbank and hovel. He sensed rather than saw furtive movement; intuited rather than heard deliberately-muffled sound.

Suddenly there was light. Livid flame scarred the darkness. A man stood illumined by the flaring torch he held aloft. Then there was another, and another. Rooted by fascination, shock and fear, the boy saw a line of soldiers, their hated uniforms garish with menace in the flickering brilliance. The men advanced, first slowly, then with increased momentum. Wide-eyed with terror, the boy saw first one, then another soldier hurl his blazing missile. The incendiaries arched through the blackness. Some fell harmlessly to earth; some bounced from walls and lay spluttering on the ground; but some found their targets. Within seconds the whole compound was illuminated by the yellow glow of burning thatch.

The boy heard a snapped command in the brittle English he did not understand.

The troops stopped, knelt, and raised their guns. As women, children, goats, sheep and hens ran from the blazing buildings the king's men opened fire. The next seconds were a confusion of people and animals, shrieking, bleating, blundering to and fro, falling, writhing, lying grotesquely in twisted death.

The boy turned away from the scene. He grabbed up the bundle that was his sister, and clasping her to his chest he let himself out of the back door. The distance to the boundary wall was pathwayed with shifting shadows and he stumbled over the uneven ground. He rested his burden atop the earth and stone bank just long enough to scramble over. Then he was on the move again, feet pounding the familiar path to the river.

The river. To his young mind its width and rapid movement suggested a barrier. Crossing it was all that mattered. What he would do on the other side was a distant decision. The baby, crying again, slowed him down. It seemed an age before he heard the roar of water over Blackhawk Race. He reached the bank and sank to the mossy turf. Chest heaving, arms aching, he longed to rest but dared not. His sister was shrieking her terrified protest but the boy had no time to soothe and comfort her.

He set her down in the shelter of a

boulder and ran upcurrent beside the torrent. Above the rapids the river widened and shallowed before crashing over jagged rocks to the deep pools beyond. The boy knew there was one place where he could cross waist-deep, and he searched for this now. He soon found the spot with the aid of the spreading pre-dawn. For a moment only he stared out over the grey ripples on the surface of polished black. It was here that his father had taught him to swim. Then he turned back to collect the only other living member of his family.

He was paces away from his sister when he saw the soldier standing over the screaming bundle. Deliberately the man drew back his booted foot and swung it. The baby paused to fill her lungs then howled with pain and anger. The man laughed and muttered something in English. He swung his gun from his shoulder and pointed it at the little girl.

'No!' The boy sprang forward. He had covered half the ground when the explosion filled his ears. The soldier part turned, but was unbalanced when the boy's shoulder caught him behind the knees. He staggered, throwing out his arms to steady himself. He lurched against the low boulder and fell sideways across it, his limbs flailing to grasp something. Then he tumbled without

14

a sound into Blackhawk Race.

The boy dropped to his knees beside his sister. She was not crying now. She had nothing to cry with. Where mouth and snub nose had once been there was a hole, glistening with oozed blood.

The boy turned away. He blundered blindly along the bank, waded the river, then he ran and ran until there was no more running in him.

I

A DUNGEON HORRIBLE

Wae on Culloden's bloody field!
Dark source o' mony a tear;
There Albyn lost her sword and shield,
And her young Chevalier!

O Charlie is my Darling,
traditional Scottish air

CHAPTER 1

Darkness came early, and with it the snow. Tim and George peered through the windscreen into a maelstrom of whirling white. The hire car's engine roared in its lowest gear and laboured up the incline.

'Come on!' The older man expertly varied his pressure on the accelerator and coaxed the vehicle forward. 'How much farther, Major?'

'Two and a half miles.' Tim Lacy held his torch close to the Ordnance Survey map. 'We must be on the estate already.'

The car went into a sideways drift. Gritting his teeth with concentration, George gave it more gas and steered out of the skid. 'If there are any hills beyond this we won't make it. I don't know that we'll make this one.'

'No. When we're over the top it's downhill all the way to the loch. The peak's just round this bend. You can do it, George.'

'I hope so, Major.' George habitually addressed Tim by the rank he had held when both men worked together in the SAS. 'I just hope it doesn't all turn out

19

to be a waste of time. I've still got my doubts about this Robertson character.'

Tim shared his friend's misgivings. Several years in the business of providing the technical equipment to safeguard private and public art collections worldwide had brought Lacy Security many strange clients and taken him and his colleagues into several bizarre and sometimes dangerous situations. There were hundreds of wealthy hoarders of rare and beautiful things who had excellent reasons for secrecy and were paranoid about criminals, rivals or tax authorities who might take too close an interest in their concealed treasures. Yet there was something distinctly odd about J. Robertson.

'Contact me urgently. J. Robertson.' That had been the first message to come through on the fax machine at Farrans Court, Tim's Wiltshire home which was also his business headquarters. It had appeared on Christmas Eve when the office was unmanned—Tim and his family had been in America spending the festive season with his wife's parents. By the time he returned to work on 2 January his secretary had collected a pile of faxes from J. Robertson, all equally peremptory and uncommunicative. A brief telephone conversation had added little. The voice at the other end of the line had been gruff, its

20

tone aggressive and its message downright insulting.

'Lacy? About bloody time! I want you to come and upgrade my security arrangements. And I do mean "upgrade". I need the most up-to-date system available, and I need it yesterday. I'll fax the address, together with travel and ETA details.'

Before Tim could respond the line had gone dead.

He had dismissed J. Robertson as a crank and told Sally, his secretary, to shred any more faxes that came from him. He had given the oddball no more thought for three days. Then a call from Aubrey 'Tiger' Maximian had changed everything. Tiger was a friend of several years' standing. He was also PPS to the foreign secretary. After the conventional greetings Tiger had come straight to the point.

'You've recently been approached by a potential client by the name of Robertson.'

'That's right.' Tim responded cautiously.

'Are you taking the job on?'

'No. I didn't like the sound of him. He was rude to me. That's not the kind of treatment I respond to.'

Tiger laughed. 'I can imagine. He's a bit eccentric but perfectly genuine. And I can assure you, Tim, money is no object.'

'Friend of yours, is he?'

21

'Let's just say we would be very grateful if you gave Mr Robertson the benefit of your professional services.'

'Is that the royal "we"?'

'Ministerial.'

'Which means the Tower of London if I refuse?'

'Could be.' The young politician chuckled. 'It could also mean a few rungs up the honours system ladder if you agree.'

'You know what I think about titles.'

'OK, I'm not bribing you. Just trying to dispose of your misgivings. Robertson lives on his estate in the Highlands. Wiring up his castle will be quite a big job, and profitable. It would also oblige some of my associates who have friendly relations with him. As I see it, Tim, you have everything to gain and nothing to lose from taking on this commission.'

'Let me get this straight: there's a Scottish laird who thinks he can act the *grand seigneur* with all and sundry, and when it doesn't work he gets some of his grouse-shooting chums in high places to exert pressure. I don't care for that kind of neo-feudalism.'

There was a thoughtful pause at the other end of the line. Then Tiger said; 'Look, the fact is my boss recommended you as the best in the business. If you turn Robertson down—'

'So what it comes down to is saving ministerial face?'

'If you like. Will you do it?'

'I'll think about it.'

'Tim, I'm only inviting you to do yourself a bit of good.' There was a trace of anxiety in Maximian's voice now.

'I'll have a look at our schedules and see if we can fit your chum in.' Tim almost heard his friend wince at the word 'chum'.

'I'll leave it with you then. Now it's about time I thrashed you at squash again. When are you coming up to town?' The conversation had drifted into social chat.

So here Tim was, at the end of January, with his head of installations and right-hand man George Martin, struggling through a Scottish blizzard. The weather had deteriorated steadily since late morning, when they had stepped off the shuttle at Edinburgh's Turnhouse airport. They had planned to fly to Inverness, but the field there had been closed on meteorological advice. Light rain had accompanied them most of the way northwards, and had turned to sleet as they climbed over a thousand feet beyond Aviemore. By Inverness it was snowing convincingly, flurries overtaking the car as it headed westwards along narrowing roads into the glens. The omens, Tim reflected, were not good.

George exhaled a long sigh of relief as the ground levelled out beneath the car's wheels. He brought the powerful saloon gently to a halt. 'Quick breather,' he said, rubbing his eyes, then stretching his arms. 'We ought to have hired a four-wheel drive.'

'We shan't need the car once we get to the village. If it weren't for the snow we'd be able to see the lights already. Somewhere down there is Loch Huich, with Lanner Castle on an island in the middle and Briachan on the shore facing it.'

'And a warm welcome from Mr Robertson?'

'I wouldn't swear to that—but he's rich enough to own a couple of thousand acres of grouse moor, so he should be able to run to a comfortable bed and a decent meal.'

'Well, I'm certainly ready for both.'

George settled himself again behind the wheel, let in the clutch and accelerated cautiously. As the car gathered momentum down the slope, Tim folded the map. He opened the glove compartment to put it and the torch inside, when suddenly he was thrown forward, the safety belt taut across his chest.

'What the...!' George jabbed the footbrake and the saloon went into a skid on the white surface. George plied the steering wheel to the right, then quickly to the left. He jerked the gear into first to let the engine slow the car. Still it rolled forward, so he turned it gently towards a snow-covered bank and applied the brake just before impact. With a jolt the vehicle crunched its nearside wing into camouflaged hedge and bracken.

Without a word George jumped out and started running and slithering back along the road.

Tim grabbed the torch and manoeuvred across to clamber out of the driver's side. 'What is it? George? What's the matter?' He caught up with his friend twenty metres behind the car.

'They must be up here, just beyond where the skid marks start! Can you shine the torch this way, Major?'

They found the point where the car's tracks began to slew across the road, then followed the straight tyre marks back up the hill. 'They must be about. They can't be any further back.' George peered intently into the circle of light.

Tim said, 'What exactly are we looking for?'

The older man turned to him, snow flecking his head and shoulders. 'The kids—three of them. You must have seen them. They were in the middle of the road. I couldn't have missed them. Let's look over here, along the side.'

For almost ten minutes the two men worked their way back and forward across the road and along thirty or forty metres of its length. They saw nothing but the steadily-filling imprint of wheels in the even white surface.

Back in the car George shook his head. Tim had seldom seen him so shaken. 'They were there, Major. I swear it. Three kids in ragged clothes. About nine or ten years of age. Just standing there, holding hands and looking straight at me.'

'It's the snow, George. It can play all sorts of trick on you.'

'I suppose so.' George did not sound convinced. 'But they were so real!'

'Well, they're not real now. If there had been anyone here we'd have found some trace. Come on, the sooner we get a couple of whiskies inside you the better.'

George restarted the engine, extricated the car from the bank and took it down the hill in a low gear. The two men travelled in silence, George trying to convince himself that he had been hallucinating, Tim wondering why, when he had looked up immediately before the skid, he had seen, or thought he had seen just for a fraction of a second, three small figures in the road.

The bar of the Briachan Inn was warm, brightly lit and reassuring. It was also surprisingly well populated for the time of day. Two strongly-built men in working clothes stood at the counter, and a couple of tables at the far side of the room were occupied.

'You made it, then?' The open-faced young woman behind the bar smiled at the newcomers.

'It sounds as though we were expected.' Tim eased himself on to a tall stool.

'Oh, aye. You'll be the two gentlemen from London. The castle always tell us when guests are expected. You'll be wanting something to warm you.'

Tim took out his wallet. 'You couldn't be more right. Two doubles, please.'

'You can put away your money, Mr Lacy.' She turned to the row of optics behind her. 'This round is on Angus Logan.' She nodded towards the taller of the two standing men. 'He wagered me not ten minutes since that you wouldn't get here today.'

Tim accepted his glass and tilted it towards his benefactor. 'Thank you...Angus.'

The man nodded and offered the faintest of smiles. He wore a cap set far back on his thick, curling black hair, and his rugged features suggested several years of sculpture by sun and wind. 'You did well

27

to be over Beanlaich Hill in this weather. What are you driving?'

George told him the make and model of the car.

Angus looked scornful. 'Looks as though I'll be towing you out with one of my trucks, then—unless you've a mind to stay several weeks.'

'What's your line of business, Angus?' Tim enquired.

'Construction. We're building a new road. Were it not for the snow you'd have seen our camp as you came down the hill.'

'And a terrible eyesore it is, too,' the barmaid interposed.

'Come on, Mary, don't start that old fight again.' Angus's companion—a younger, fair-haired man—spoke the words lightly, but the glances exchanged across the bar suggested to Tim that feelings ran deep.

'Who wants a new road here?' he asked.

'No one!' The shout came from a corner of the room.

Tim and George turned to see two young women in anoraks hunched over their beer glasses and glaring at the road-builders with looks that could have burned holes in hardened steel.

'Thus spake the great unwashed,' Angus retorted contemptuously. 'Students with nothing better to do than make nuisances of themselves.'

'There's a new hydro-electric plant to be built downriver from the loch.' Again it was the other man who intervened. 'We've to put a road through to take all the heavy construction traffic. It'll cut straight across to the A862 and Inverness.'

Angus, still scowling at the protestors, added, 'It'll keep lorries away from the village here, and the new dam will provide cheap power, as well as encouraging business to come to the region, thus creating jobs. Those are the facts. It's best you should hear the truth before others start bending your ears with lies and rumours. Wherever there's progress you'll always find Luddites and banner-waving protestors.'

Mary glared at him. 'That's enough of that, Angus. You know the rule. If you want to drink here you leave your feuding outside.' She turned to his companion. 'Take him away, Alan, before I do him a mischief'

The younger man drained his glass and buttoned his donkey jacket. 'Aye. Come along, Angus. It's time we were away back to the camp. Enjoy your stay, Mr Lacy, Mr Martin. Good-day, Mary.' He steered his friend towards the door.

The silence that followed was almost

tangible. At last Tim said, 'I suppose we should be moving, too. I believe we have to phone for the castle boat to collect us.'

'You'll not be going across today, Mr Lacy.' Mary stood the glass she had been polishing on the shelf and turned to him with her frank smile.

'But, as you said, they're expecting us.'

'They *were* expecting you more than an hour since—in daylight. There's no travelling to and fro after dark.'

'But, surely...' Tim looked closely at the girl, wondering if she was playing some kind of straightfaced Highland joke. 'It's no more than a couple of hundred metres of open water. Even in this weather—'

'Oh, the weather has nothing to do with it. Mr Robertson allows no one on or off the island after dark. And with those dogs of his let loose he'd be a fool who'd try to land.'

Tim frowned. Robertson's detailed instructions had mentioned nothing about arriving before sundown. In all his peremptory faxes he had repeatedly stressed urgency, demanding that Lacy Security get to work as soon as possible. Now, when he and George had travelled six hundred miles and braved a raging blizzard, Tim was in no mood to be suddenly kept waiting. 'I think I'd better have a word with Mr Robertson.'

Mary shrugged. She waved to the far end of the bar where there were two telephones on a shelf. 'It's the green one—direct line to the castle.'

Tim made the call. After only two rings the receiver at the other end was picked up.

'Lanner Castle.'

'May I speak to Mr Robertson, please?'

'You must be Mr Lacy.' The voice was rough and definitely not Scottish.

'That's right. Now, if I might speak—'

'Mr Robertson will be pleased to know that you have arrived safely. He can't come to the phone at the moment. He'll see you as soon as you arrive in the morning.'

'In the morning! But—'

'The boat will be there at eight-fifty on the dot. Meanwhile Tam McFadden and his daughter will look after you very well. Until tomorrow, Mr Lacy.'

The line went dead.

Mary's knowing smile said 'I told you so'.

Tim shrugged. 'It seems we must accept your hospitality.'

'There are worse fates.' Her laugh was a coloratura trill. 'Will I show you to your rooms? I could introduce you to the other castle guests—' she nodded towards the four remaining occupants of the bar—'but you'll meet them at dinner. For now you'll

31

be wanting to freshen up—and we must get your car into the garage before it's buried in snow.'

Any annoyance Tim had felt at at his client's offhand treatment was soothed away by a long wallow in a deep bath full of hot water and the calming decor of a surprisingly well-appointed room.

It was just after six-thirty when, in answer to a tap at the door, Tim let his colleague in. 'Hi, George, how are you feeling?'

'All the better for a bit of a kip, Major. Still can't get that business on the road out of my mind though. Those kids looked so...solid. I could've sworn... Oh well, I suppose that's the thing about hallucinations—they seem real.' He perched on the end of the bed. 'What d'you make of the situation here, Major?'

'Whoever this Robertson character is, he's certainly slipped into the role of Lord of the Glens. Obviously folk round here dance to his tune.'

'What about all this business of no one being allowed to go to the island after dark and having the place patrolled by dogs? Either he's got some incredibly valuable stuff there or he's paranoid about security.'

'Or both! He wouldn't be the first

collector we've come across who's obsessed with the fear that someone's going to steal his treasures.'

'Have you any idea what those treasures are? What does he collect?'

Tim shrugged. 'Not a clue. I've asked around a bit over the last couple of weeks. None of the top dealers or auctioneers has heard of Robertson—not under that name, anyway.'

'Hm.' George scratched his cropped iron-grey hair. 'The closer you get to it the worse it smells. You know what I reckon?'

'Let me guess. You suspect that when we finally get across to Lanner Castle, we're going to find it stuffed to the battlements with stolen art.'

'Is that such a funny idea?' George went on the defensive. 'There's a hell of a lot of missing masterpieces—paintings, sculptures and suchlike, stolen from galleries and private collections all over the world. They have simply disappeared. They've got to be somewhere. Why shouldn't some of them be here, in one of the most remote and secure castles in the British Isles?'

'I'm not laughing, George. I don't think it's a funny idea at all. The same thought occurred to me as soon as this Robertson character got in touch with us. That was one reason I wasn't keen to accept his business.'

'So what changed your mind?'

'I found it difficult to believe that a leading member of the cabinet was close friends with a major international art thief.'

'You've got more faith in the government than I have, then,' George grunted.

Tim laughed. 'I'm not a hardened old cynic like you, George—not yet, anyway. Come on, let's go down and meet our fellow guests. Perhaps they'll be able to tell us something about the reclusive Mr Robertson.'

'I can tell you something else about him.' George paused with his hand on the door handle. 'I had to go down to the car a few minutes ago. I prefer to keep my tools by me.'

Tim smiled. 'Now who's being paranoid?'

'Yes, well... Anyway, they've got a surprisingly large garage built on at the back, and Robertson uses half of it for his vehicles—a smart Merc, a powerful four-wheel-drive job and a run-of-the-mill saloon that I suppose they use for the shopping.'

'What's so surprising about that? He must keep his transport on the mainland somewhere—there's no way across to the island.'

'What's surprising, Major, is that the castle cars are all behind a really tough steel grille, *and* Robertson's got a surveillance camera in there, which obviously feeds back to a screen on the island.'

'Seems he hasn't left much for us to do. Well, doubtless all will be revealed tomorrow. Right now, I'm ready for grub.'

They found the bar under the supervision of a slight, sixtyish man with George Robey eyebrows, who introduced himself as Tam McFadden. 'Is everything to your satisfaction, gentlemen?' His accent was stronger than his daughter's.

'Everything's fine,' Tim assured him. 'I imagine you get a lot of business from castle visitors who inadvertently miss the ferry.'

The proprietor nodded. 'Mr Robertson is very strict on that score. But we also have the overflow from his business conferences. He can only sleep a dozen or so in the castle. The rest come to us.'

'What line of business are these people in?' Tim asked casually.

Tam McFadden pushed their drinks across the bar. 'They don't say and I don't ask.'

A slight frown brought the heavy eyebrows together and indicated that the subject was closed. He turned towards the couple who had just entered from the internal doorway. 'Good evening, Andrea.'

Tim and George saw a young man and woman who looked rather exotic for such homely surroundings. The mid-twenties young lady might have walked straight off the front page of *Harper's* or *Vogue*. Her dark hair was an explosion of curls that glistered in the bar's soft light. Her strong features were so exquisitely made up that they appeared untouched by human artistry. She wore an Arran sweater over tight scarlet trousers. Her companion was very tall, black and elegant. He appeared to glide rather than step into the room, so that no untoward crease marred the suit of light grey check that he wore with a magenta roll-necked jumper.

Tam made the introductions. 'Mr Lacy, Mr Martin, meet Miss Robertson and Mr Azikwe.'

'Miss Robertson?' Tim queried as he shook her hand. 'Does that mean...'

'That I'm daughter of the manor?' Andrea's grey-green eyes sparkled in a smile. 'I'm afraid so. You see, even I can't get to the castle after closing time. So, you're not being discriminated against.'

'Do you come home very often?'

'Oh, I don't think of the castle as home. My father chooses to shut himself away up here, but I live and work in London. I don't suppose I've spent more than a year here in total.'

'Surely, as a child...?'

'Boarding schools. Holidays abroad. My father's a great believer in foreign travel. So, what with one thing and another, my visits to Castle Gruesome are few and far between.'

'Castle Gruesome? Why...?'

Andrea laughed. 'You'll see. I won't spoil the surprise for you. Now, you must meet Ben, my fiancé.'

George had been chatting with Azikwe and established that he was a Nigerian diplomat. Now Tim examined him more closely. He had the subtle combination of aloofness and ease of manner which Tim had noticed before in high-born West Africans. When he spoke there was a slight drawl in his voice which suggested a transatlantic contribution to his education.

'What brings you to the frozen north, Mr Lacy?'

'A little business with your future father-in-law.' Tim was cautious by habit. He half-turned to Andrea as he spoke, and just noticed the anxious frown which flashed across her face.

She said, 'I wish I knew what his business was. It must be very important. He gets people from all over the world to come to this...' She stopped suddenly, hand to mouth.

'I hope you were not going to say "this God-forsaken hole".' Tam leaned across the bar with a look of mock disapproval.

Andrea's embarrassment was covered by the arrival of the two students. They were wearing the same loose sweaters, faded jeans and expressions of wary suspicion as earlier. They were about to sidle over to a corner table when the landlord waved to them.

'Good evening, ladies. Come and join us. Will I be pouring you a drink?'

They exchanged dubious glances until Tim insisted that this was his round, at which they agreed to partake of two small lagers.

'Are you bound for Lanner Castle as well?' George asked.

The taller and more forthcoming of the girls replied. 'Yes, we're going to see if we can persuade Mr Robertson to put a stop to the building of this eyesore.'

'She means the hydro-electric scheme,' Tam explained unnecessarily.

'That's right. It's a pretty forlorn hope; these fat cats all stick together. Robertson's picking up a cool three million for the site.'

'Isn't that media speculation?' Andrea suggested. 'As I understand it, the Scottish

38

Office has refused to give details of the deal.'

It was as though she had thrown a switch. The students—whose names, it transpired, were Carol and Steffy—took deep breaths and went into campaign mode. 'The precise figure is two million, eight hundred and fifty thousand,' Carol stated authoritatively. 'Not bad for nine and a half hectares of empty moorland. We've got someone on the inside, so we know the facts.'

'We fed the information to ITN,' the diminutive Steffy added proudly 'It made a huge impact. We've had hundreds of supporters contacting us by phone, fax and e-mail. Some of them admit that they're not committed conservationists; they're just fed up with top people—landowners, businessmen, politicians—lining their pockets without any regard to what ordinary people want.' She stared belligerently around, defying anyone to argue.

George tried to steer the torrent into a wider channel. 'Bit of a surprise that Mr Robertson agreed to see you, wasn't it?'

Carol laughed. 'Not really. Some of our people have been making life rather difficult for the construction gangs, not to mention his grouse-killing chums. We made a mess of several shoots in the autumn and we've got an ongoing campaign of disruption directed against the road-building equipment. Robertson's had to bring in the police time and time again. I'll bet the local constabulary make him pay through the nose for that. So, what with one thing and another, he must be pretty keen to get us off his back.'

Steffy underlined the self-congratulatory tone. 'Of course, we shan't settle for anything else but the abandonment of the whole obscene project.'

During their manifesto statement Tim was watching Andrea's reaction. Would she spring to her father's defence? Would she discomfit the protestors by revealing her relationship with the owner of Lanner Castle and its estate? He saw the composed young woman sip her gin and tonic thoughtfully, regarding the students with what might have been intended as indifference or disdain. She was about to make some response when Mary came in and announced that dinner was ready.

The company filed through into a large, stone-flagged, low-ceilinged room that had once been a kitchen. A single refectory table bisected it longitudinally. It would have comfortably accommodated twenty diners, but this evening eight places had

40

been laid around one end of the gleaming oak. Everyone, including the McFaddens, took their places.

Despite the oddly diverse nature of the company, the meal turned out to be a social success. Tam told some humorous local tales which had obviously done frequent service as ice breakers. Ben capped them with interesting stories about Nigeria and international diplomacy. Though the girls refused Tam's excellent venison and munched their way sombrely through platefuls of vegetables instead, a couple of glasses of Burgundy, following the beer they had already drunk, relaxed them and enabled them to drop their masks of earnestness and moral outrage.

As the meal meandered its way from a smooth salmon mousse via a succulent roast to a selection of rich puddings, Tim was able to augment the mental files on his fellow guests. The girls were from Aberdeen University where they were both studying art and design, and were the organisers of the 'Save Glen Huich' campaign. For eight months they had been launching guerilla attacks from their base in the home of a sympathiser a couple of miles away. They claimed to have over a hundred protestors maintaining constant pressure by means of a rota system. They had little support from the local inhabitants, whose environment they claimed to be protecting; the official SGH explanation was that the small population of the glen did not want to fall out with their laird, Mr Robertson.

Azikwe had studied at Ibadan and Yale and was obviously highly intelligent and cultured. Despite being a representative of his government, he claimed to be 'a cosmopolitan by conviction'. He and Andrea had met the previous summer, at a reception she helped to organise in her capacity as translator-interpreter at the Department of Trade and Industry.

They remained at the table for coffee, and Tam produced some excellent cognac which, he assured his guests, would go on the bill for bed and board which Mr Robertson was paying.

It was during a rare pause in the conversation that George asked casually, 'Are there many children in the village?'

The McFaddens exchanged glances and Tam said, 'Why do you ask?'

'Just that I thought I saw some near the top of the hill.'

Tam rested his elbows on the table and leaned forward.

'Father, no!'

The old man waved aside his daughter's protest. 'If he's seen them, where's the harm?'

'Seen them? Seen who?' George demanded.

'Some call them "the lost ones", others "the children of the fire".'

CHAPTER 2

Tim glanced round the circle of faces and smiled inwardly. The landlord had everyone else's fascinated attention, and the atmosphere could hardly have been better for the telling of a ghost story. It was a winter's night. A rising wind beyond the room's heavy curtains roared softly as it carved the snowscape into powdery dunes. Within, soft lighting from concealed spots created areas of shadow beyond the table, where Tam's captive audience, relaxed by food and wine, waited to have their spines chilled. Tim guessed that what they were about to hear was a well-practised performance often laid on for guests at the Briachan Inn.

The raconteur sat back in his chair and spoke softly. 'There's many ballads been written about the events in these parts in 1746. I'll not trouble you with my apology for a singing voice, but I can give you the words of the best known, *Ewen o' the Glen*.

This is how it starts:

> Whence cam he then, my bonny boy?
> Brave Ewen, whence cam he?
> He's from awa, far o'er the muir,
> Ask nae mair to see.

> Why cam he then, my bonny boy?
> Brave Ewen, why cam he?
> He came the children for to save,
> Ask nae mair to see.

'You'll all have heard of the Battle of Culloden?'

It was Andrea who responded. 'The last encounter of the 1745 Jacobite Rebellion, the failed attempt to put Bonnie Prince Charlie on the throne in London.'

Tam nodded. 'Folk round here still prefer the word "rising" to "rebellion". A thousand Highlanders were killed on the battlefield and a thousand more in the ensuing pursuit. Charles Edward Stuart fled back to France, and there were many, even among those who'd fought for him, who cried good riddance to the foppish, wrong-headed gallant. The Jacobite cause was at an end—or would have been if the English had displayed an atom of common sense. If they had been magnanimous in victory, they'd have won over most of the Highlands in a short time. That was not the way of "Butcher" Cumberland.'

'Who was he?' Steffy asked.

'Good heavens, girl.' Tam raised bushy eyebrows. 'What do they teach you in universities these days—or rather, what do they not teach? William Augustus, Duke of Cumberland, was George the Second's younger son, and in charge of the army sent to suppress the rising. But not to suppress the people—that was the Butcher's own idea. He was an arrogant, violent, brutal man who loved war for its own sake. He had just returned from a particularly inglorious campaign in France and was determined to vent his anger on someone. The defeated Scots provided an excellent target. Cumberland sent his English troops and his German mercenaries into every corner of the glens—burning villages, rounding up livestock, hacking down men, women and children in the most savage display of vengeance these islands have probably ever seen.'

'And who was this Ewen of the Glen you were talking about?' George wanted to know.

Tam closed his eyes as he recited.

'Who was he then, my bonny boy?
Brave Ewen, who was he?
Of clan and laird he spake nae word,
Ask nae mair to see.

45

'There are many stories told about young Ewen; stories that link him with one or other of the great Highland clans, even with the exiled Stuarts. But no one knows who he was or how a boy of no more than ten or eleven arrived at Castle Huich, the old castle...'

Tim asked, 'That was the old name for Lanner Castle, was it?'

'It was the name of the original castle, the one that was burned down. After the events of 1746 it has always been known as Daingneach Leanabh in the Gaelic, or Lanner Castle. It means "the Child's Castle".'

Three boulders lay in such a way as to make a shallow cave largely obscured by ferns. Into this the boy crawled. It gave him two of the three things he needed. It provided shade from the midday sun and allowed him a view across the shallow cleuch he had spent the last hour or so crossing. It was the way the soldiers would come. If they were still following; he had not seen any for days.

What the granite niche could not supply was food. Once, three days ago—or was it six, or maybe ten—he had come upon a nesting capercaillie. She had run off in fright but the boy had climbed a tree to wait. When the hen returned to her eggs he had dropped on her and despatched her with his knife. The same knife had cut away feather and skin and the boy had gorged on the bare flesh. Since then he had eaten grass and chewed heather and experimented with grubbed-up roots which had made him vomit. Nothing he forced down satisfied the rats which were gnawing away at the inside of his stomach—or if they were not rats they must be equally voracious creatures, for their teeth were sharp and their feeding was unremitting. The only time they stopped was when he slept.

That was all he wanted to do. If he curled up and lay very still perhaps the rats would rest and he could sleep. He rubbed a hand lightly over his concave belly, hollow within the woollen cloth of his tunic. Then he patted some earth and bracken fronds into a thin mattress and lay down sideways, knees drawn up to his chest. He still faced the valley; he would still see the redcoats when they and their horses were two miles away and more.

Why was he running from them? He no longer knew. It seemed he had always been doing it. What would they do to him if they caught him? Could it be any worse than this rat torture? Now he must be very still. Make the rats sleep. Sleep.

It was a shout that woke him. He looked up into the face of a soldier: a large, red face scarcely distinguishable in colour from the man's tunic. Sweat trickled down the face from beneath the wig slightly askew across his brow. The boy did not understand the words the soldier shouted, but his action was eloquent and unambiguous. He prodded the boy's shoulder with the point of his bayonet and jerked his head.

Wearily the boy got to his feet and stumbled into the open. The soldier motioned to him to stand with his back to the rock, then retreated a few paces through the heather. He raised his musket to his shoulder and looked along the top of the barrel.

The boy returned the gaze. The sun was bright on the infantryman's epaulets and facings. It was warm on the boy's face, his bare arms and legs. The dusty smell of crushed bracken was strong in his nostrils. The *'kuk-kuk'* of a startled grouse across the valley sounded unbelievably loud. He took a deep breath of the breeze which suddenly tousled his red-brown hair. The moment seemed endless.

Then a yelled order made the man lower his gun and turn abruptly to his left. The boy looked in the direction of the sound and saw a magnificent white horse picking its way fastidiously through the heather. The man who sat astride it had more gleaming braid and buttons on his uniform than the infantryman, and wore a white cockade in his tricorn hat. He exchanged several incomprehensible sentences with the foot soldier, then turned a string of words upon the boy. When he shook his head the man spoke again, this time in Gaelic. 'What's your name, boy?'

'Ewen, sir.'

'And your father—what's his name?'

'I don't know, sir.'

'What do you mean, you don't know?' The rider yanked impatiently on the reins as his horse put its head down to browse.

'I don't remember.'

The officer stared down at his captive. He had come across children whose minds had been badly affected by the shocks of war. He had also seen youngsters trained to play dumb. Which was this one? 'Well, Ewen, where are you from? Surely you can remember that.'

The boy pointed back across the cleuch.

'Oh, come on, boy! Don't play games!' The horseman tapped his crop on the boy's matted mass of thick hair. 'If you don't tell me the name of your village, I'll beat it out of you.'

Ewen looked up, clenching his eyes with the effort of memory. 'It's a long time, sir. Many days towards the west. I've run most of the way. I don't remember why...Ardnabreachy.' The name came suddenly into his mind, and with it a clear picture of a straggle of small thatched houses beside a track leading steeply up to a pass over the mountain's shoulder.

Ardnabreachy! The man frowned. He had ridden through its blackened remains only three days since and had heard stories in the camp of things done there. If this boy had no memory of them he was fortunate indeed. He dismissed the Hessian soldier, then turned back to the boy. 'Well, Ewen, what are we going to do with you? How long is it since you had anything to eat?'

The boy shrugged. 'A long time.'

The horseman unbuckled the flap of a saddle bag. He took out part of a loaf wrapped in a white napkin, broke off a chunk and held it out. He watched as the boy tore at it greedily. There was certainly nothing fake about his hunger. As Ewen devoured the last fragments, Colonel James Campbell made up his mind. No good purpose could be served by making this lad suffer more. If the Highlands were to have a peaceful future—and that was a big 'if' in all conscience—it would lie in the hands of such young men as this.

He held out his hand. 'Up behind me,

boy.' He swung Ewen easily to the horse's crupper. 'You'd better come to Castle Huich,' he said, and put the grey into a trot across the valley flank to where his men were mustering on the ridge.

James Campbell was no ardent supporter of George II. Though he came from a cadet branch of the great clan headed by the Duke of Argyll—who had, decades earlier, put their power and influence behind the Hanoverians and the Union—he had more in common with the majority of landowners, large and small, who were more interested in administering their estates than in the politics of distant Westminster. Ever the pragmatist, he had little patience with the current conflict, which was in many instances simply a way of perpetuating ancient clan feuds in the name of 'German George' or 'the king across the water'. If he was now riding beneath a Hanoverian standard it was in order to ensure, as far as he had any say in the matter, that the uprising remained a Scottish conflict. He had seen enough of mercenary forces in the French wars, and had been sickened by the devastation left behind when unprincipled contingents had been allowed to plunder, rape and burn their way across a defeated country. He could not stop this absurd Jacobite adventure but, by raising a regiment on his west-coast lands, he could at least ensure an important commission—and that would mean that part of the king's army would be under his control. Right now that meant preventing his commanding officer's orders being carried out to the letter.

'Where is Castle Huich?' Ewen asked.

The column had formed up again and was now moving westwards along the ridge with Campbell and his staff officers at the front. Ewen was vaguely aware that he should hate these men, but at the moment they meant food and riding instead of running through the heather, and a destination—Castle Huich—instead of uncertain flight.

'It's about a day's march. You'll be safe there—with the other children.'

'What other children?'

But at that moment one of Campbell's subordinates ran up to make a report and Ewen's question went unanswered.

Tam stood up to offer refills to his guests' glasses while Mary poured more coffee. 'There were several children brought to Castle Huich at that terrible time. As many as a hundred according to some legends, though I doubt that myself.'

'Orphans, I suppose.' Tim held up his goblet for more cognac.

'I daresay.' The narrator seemed vague

on the point. 'Many's the bairn lost father and mother to the Butcher's men.' He resumed his seat. 'The fact is, no one really knows who all the children were or why they were here. The old castle had many unwholesome secrets according to the legends.'

Carol giggled. 'Black arts and child abuse? I thought they were all good Calvinists round these parts. Anyway, if they were secrets how come they got into the legends?'

Steffy frowned at her friend, but it was Ben Azikwe who observed with almost academic detachment, 'My people have many legends—stories of history and magic. It's fashionable among educated Nigerians to dismiss them as superstitious nonsense. However, anthropologists warn us that we do that at our peril. Myth is part of us. It helps us to make sense of the world and our place in it. It gives us our identity. Without myth, what are we but eating, sleeping, defecating, procreating automata?'

Carol was not the sort of thinking modern woman to submit to being taken down a peg. 'We're rational beings making our own decisions on the basis of perceived fact, not fantastic old stories.'

Ben smiled. 'Why are you opposing this hydro-electric scheme?'

'Because no one needs it and it would be a blot on the landscape.'

'And why should there not be blots on the landscape?'

Carol leaped to denounce the suggested heresy. 'Because no one, however wealthy or influential, has the right to pollute the environment for his own ends. Rousseau said, "You are undone if you once forget that the fruits of the earth belong to us all, and that the earth itself belongs to nobody." '

'Indeed, and that is one of the oldest myths of all—the interaction of humanity with the earth. In the Bible, Adam was made from clay. It's the same in the foundation myths of most peoples. When Europeans came to my land and tried to buy it, my ancestors couldn't understand what they were talking about. How can you buy earth or sky or air or water? These things are part of all of us. Your banner-waving and acts of sabotage are just new assertions of old myth. And your campaign against the builders is creating a new mythic story. Perhaps in years to come people will sing songs about what you're doing here, just as they now sing songs about what happened two and a half centuries ago. Whatever those things were and however inaccurately they were recorded, they were seen as wrong things, evil things which became focused in the castle. That's why they're remembered and why they should be remembered.'

'I don't know whether the castle was a "focus of evil".' Tam was determined to regain everyone's attention. 'I do know what people say happened here. The laird was Duncan o'Strathfarrar, Duncan the Red. He was for King George—or more like for himself, and saw ostentatious loyalty to the English as his best road to fortune. He boasted that he would hold these lands for the crown, and he was as good as his word. Three times the Jacobites came against Castle Huich and three times they were repulsed. But not before they'd done a deal of damage to Duncan's estate and people. After Culloden he saw his chance for revenge. He rode to Inverness and persuaded Butcher Cumberland that his impregnable fortress would make an excellent base for the subjugation of the people and a particularly good detention centre for recalcitrant Jacobite prisoners. Over the ensuing weeks scores of Highland lords and gentlemen, who had sworn allegiance to the Stuart and would not unswear, were lodged in the dungeons of Castle Huich, where Mr Robertson now keeps his morbid...his intriguing...treasures.'

'And what would they be?' Tim asked.

'Oh, I'll not spoil the surprise for you. You must wait and see.'

George stifled a yawn. 'We're still waiting to hear about these children, Tam.'

'As to that, the legends differ. There were many homeless, parentless boys and girls. Something had to be done with them. Some were brought here, perhaps to work as servants in the castle, perhaps to provide for the unnatural appetites of Duncan the Red and his cronies. Perhaps for even blacker purposes.'

'Such as...' George pressed.

'Cumberland wanted information—about secret Jacobite cells, about Prince Charles's whereabouts, about spies in his own camp. Duncan was very good at extracting that information from his prisoners. But there were those who resisted every kind of torture. So Duncan—or, so some say, Cumberland—hit on the plan of putting children to the rack, the branding iron, the wheel and Cumberland's Cradle, and making the silent prisoners watch. Many a brave man, it is said, broke under that pressure.'

'What was Cumberland's Cradle?' Steffy asked.

'A portable torture implement the duke carried about in his baggage train—the most excruciating and disgusting instrument ever devised by a warped mind.'

'Where does Ewen the Brave fit into this picture?' Ben asked.

'He was a clever lad and wise beyond his years. He ingratiated himself with Duncan, and at the same time he became the leader of the children at the castle. He helped several prisoners escape. If you were staying here longer I could tell you many stories of young Ewen's exploits.'

'That would be interesting,' George said.

'If you really do want to know more, I'll lend you a little book. A few years back we had a professor from Edinburgh staying here. He collected all the local ballads and stories he could find and published them with his own notes and research into the background of the legends.'

'And nobody knows what became of Ewen?' Steffy asked.

'After the fire, no.'

'The fire?' Three of the listeners picked up the words.

'Ewen's activities were eventually discovered, and Duncan ordered him to be put to the Cradle. At that, all the children rose up. There was a commotion and, in the midst of it, the castle took fire. Some accounts call it an accident; some say it was planned by Ewen the Brave. Certain it is that several of Duncan's men died that night. Some stories say that Ewen, also, perished in the blaze. But there is one version of the tale which claims that he and a few friends rowed to the shore and escaped. They came to the village, climbed the hill, and paused there to look down on the inferno before going on their way. From time to time they come back, to enjoy the sight and warn of further disaster. You are not the first traveller to see them, George.'

It was just before a quarter to eight the following morning that Tim had his first sight of Lanner Castle. He drew back his bedroom curtains and shielded his eyes from the glare of low sunlight on snow and water. Everything was covered to a depth of about a metre; more where wind had sculpted curling drifts. The sky was clear, the only splash of colour in a landscape reminiscent of a black-and-white film. The loch had yet to suck any blue from the heavens. It lay blanched, shiny and unrippled like a sheet of art paper. The hillside opposite, featureless and anonymous beneath its frozen covering, climbed to a ridge bristling with pines.

In the midst of this achromatic study the castle was starkly solid and black. The sun rising behind it etched its irregular outline on the landscape. Seen under these conditions, Tim reflected, it was not hard to imagine why people regarded it as sinister, nor why it should be made the setting for an extensive black mythology. His mind ran over the tourist tales Tam McFadden had told, and the secrets he had hinted at the night before. But it was Andrea's description that came more readily to mind. 'Castle Gruesome' she had called it, and the title certainly seemed apt. Perhaps the Victorian laird who raised the new building upon the blackened foundations of the old had deliberately set out to give architectural expression to grim local legend. Even when allowance was made for the harsh, unflattering light, Lanner Castle was ill-proportioned, ungainly, ugly. It rose sheer from the rock and, from this angle at least, seemed to cover the entire surface area of its islet. Its confusion of towers, crenellations and round turrets possessed neither the antiquarian charm of Gothic Revival nor the humour of Romantic Movement excess. It was simply a graceless sprawl.

Beneath Tim's window there was energetic activity. Tam, in sweater, scarf and woollen hat, was clearing snow from the front of the inn. He was using a ride-on snowplough, which chugged efficiently back and forth making a metre-wide path around the building. As Tim watched, the landlord backed his machine up to the door and set off on a new ninety-degree course. He was obviously heading towards the covered jetty protruding from the loch shore some twenty metres away.

A few minutes later, Tim was outside, strolling along the newly opened pathway and enjoying the crispness of the winter air. Some of his fellow guests had also decided on some light pre-breakfast exercise.

'Good morning Andrea, Ben.' He came upon the couple standing, arms-linked at the edge of the loch. 'Beautiful, isn't it?'

The tall African's hands were thrust deep into the pockets of his overcoat. 'Charming, quite charming. But I don't think I could ever get used to it.'

Andrea laughed. 'You poor, thin-blooded thing! Well, you won't have to put up with it for long. We've just been talking with Tam,' she explained. 'He says it won't last. There's no danger of getting snowed in. We can be away in a day or two and leave Father to his precious books and documents.'

Tim looked at her closely without appearing to do so. There were lines around her eyes which skilfully applied cosmetics could not hide. 'I suppose you'll be anxious to get home to London as soon as you've done your duty.'

They turned to walk back to the inn, forced into single file by the narrowness of the path.

Andrea led the way. 'There's no point trying to hide the fact that I shall be glad when today's over.' The lack of eye contact made it easier for her to express her feelings.

'Afraid father won't approve?'

'I don't give a damn whether he approves or not!' The statement was blurted out and immediately retracted. 'No, that's not true. He's all the family I've got. Of course I want him to like Ben. It's just that...he's so... Oh, I don't know...difficult. You'll see for yourself soon enough.'

They went in to breakfast.

They were still sitting around the long table when Tam came into the room. 'Ladies and gentlemen, your transport is on its way. They've just phoned from the castle to say that the launch is starting out. I don't want to hurry you, but Mr Robertson does not like to be kept waiting.'

'Tough!' George ostentatiously poured himself another coffee. 'We've been here sixteen hours waiting his pleasure. Now he can wait mine.'

'Hear, hear! Well said, George.' Carol had obviously psyched herself up for the coming encounter.

Andrea stood. She looked around awkwardly. 'I know how you must all feel, but...well, I know my father. I'm sure we'll all get on better with him if we humour him.' She surveyed the circle of unconvinced listeners. 'Actually, its particularly important to me that he's not put in a bad mood.'

Tim said, 'Don't you think it's about time you stood up to him?'

She looked miserable. 'I don't want to appear spineless, but...well, you wouldn't say that if you knew him.' She paused, then added imploringly, 'Please!' She turned and walked to the door accompanied by Ben.

Tim pushed his chair away from the table. 'I guess we can swallow one more bit of our pride. Come on, George.'

George gulped down his coffee. 'All right, Major, but don't ask me to tug my forelock to this Robertson character. It's not my style to kowtow to rudeness and arrogance.'

Five minutes later they were all on the jetty. The crisply painted launch was a stubby, functional affair, with a wheelhouse amidships separated from a large aft cabin.

The boatman took their luggage, helped his passengers into the craft and then, without any attempt at conversation, he cast off, jumped aboard, started the engine and steered the launch out into the loch.

Tim and George stood in the uncovered stern section, leaning against the port rail. The boat steered towards the right hand edge of the island, where the main bastion, a cylindrical mass of stone, thrust up directly from the water's edge.

'Looks as though there was a bridge once.' Tim pointed to the other end of the islet where a path wound down from the castle to a concrete platform which ended abruptly in a cliff some seven metres high.

'Did it fall or was it pushed?' George muttered. He scanned the complex as the boat rounded the southern tip of the island. 'It would take a well-equipped assault force to break in there.' He pointed to the shore line.

As they came within sight of the side of the island hidden from the inn, it became obvious that the castle was built over about half of the land surface. The area facing south and east seemed to comprise terraces at different levels. Where the walls did not rise sheer from the loch, a five-metre-high fence guarded the castle's environs. Video cameras were also now visible, protruding from the rough granite façade.

'So, if you were a thief, wanting to get into Lanner Castle and, more importantly, out again with your spoil, how would you set about it?'

This was the way Tim and George usually approached professional problems: thinking their way into the mind of the criminal.

'I'd be prepared to use whatever violence was necessary. That and surprise. Come at night; cut through the wire; dispose of the dogs and any people who got in the way. Once I was inside and in control, all the security arrangements would work to my advantage. Even if Robertson managed to send a message out it would be ages before the police could get here. By then I'd be long gone by boat—or better still, by one of those.' He pointed to a spur of land protruding from the north-eastern corner of the island. Resting on its flat surface was a small helicopter.

The boatman throttled back the engine as the launch drifted into a wide bay that made up most of the islet's eastern side. He steered the craft into a large boatshed. Inside, two similar vessels were moored against a landing stage. The boatman nudged his craft into the line, saw his charges ashore, then, with a brief, 'Follow me, please—I'll bring your luggage later,' he led the way up a flight of stone steps, out of the boathouse and on to a small landing from which further progress was barred by the wire fence. He spoke into an intercom beside a tall gate, and the lock was released with a buzz and a click. From here, more steps led up to a wide terrace running along the front of the castle.

The visitors approached a massive pseudo-Jacobean porch with a heavy studded oak door. This opened to reveal a functionary in black jacket and striped trousers.

'Ladies and gentlemen, welcome to Lanner Castle.' The functionary gave the slightest of bows. 'If you will kindly follow me I will show you to your rooms.'

As they walked the length of a long, panelled hall to a wide staircase set against the far wall, Tim looked about with curiosity. The double-storey room was lined with trophies of many kinds. There were the conventional geometrical arrangements of pikes, swords and other weapons; pride of place on one wall was given to a huge nineteenth-century canvas showing, in lurid detail, the *Massacre of the Mamelukes;* below it a Roman sarcophagus depicted armed and mounted legionaries slaughtering naked Barbarians.

Another painting which caught Tim's attention looked, certainly at first glance, like a Goya. It garishly illustrated a summary military execution, typical of the horrifyingly realistic portrayals Goya made during the Peninsular War. 'Castle Gruesome' began to assume a clear meaning.

On a first-floor corridor the guide opened a door. 'Mr Azikwe, this is your room. I hope you will be comfortable.' He marched on with the rest of his charges.

'Miss Robertson, your father thought you would like the Ivy Chamber.' He turned the handle of the next door.

'Just a minute,' Ben called out. 'Are you seriously putting Andrea and me in separate rooms?'

'Those are Mr Robertson's instructions, sir.'

'Well, you can tell—'

'It's OK, Ben.' Andrea turned to him quickly. 'I did warn you about this, and it's only for a couple of days.' She smiled at the major-domo. 'Thank you, Jenkins. The Ivy Chamber will be fine.'

Tim was allocated a turret room whose circular wall was painted crimson. It set off admirably a magnificent collection of sixteenth-century German engravings. At least, the intricate detail and varied textures were magnificent. The subject matter—apocalyptic visions of slaughter, destruction and eternal torment—left nothing to the imagination and was disturbing in the extreme.

Tim turned his attention to the view across the loch through narrow windows which were made to resemble arrow embrasures. The sun, now well-risen above the distant whitewashed hills, was laying ochre striations across the breeze-rippled surface. Sky, snow and water shared a purity of colour that was almost painful in its intensity.

There was a tap at the door. Tim turned as Jenkins entered and placed his suitcase beside the fitted wardrobe. 'Mr Robertson will see you and your assistant now in the library, sir.'

Pausing only to collect George, he led the way back to the hall along a passageway, and across a large yellow drawing room, filled with light from tall windows. In an ornate cage in one corner a large, grey parrot was perched. Head on one side, it surveyed the visitors but offered no comment.

Jenkins came to a halt before a pair of tall mahogany and gilt double doors and knocked discreetly.

'Come!'

George and Tim exchanged glances at

the sound of the sharp, loud voice. Then Jenkins opened the door, stood to one side and ushered them into their client's presence.

CHAPTER 3

The soldiers stopped to pitch camp an hour before sundown. Ewen watched fascinated as bales and boxes were unloaded from waggons and pack horses and turned into tents and cooking pots and animal fodder. Colonel Campbell's tent was the biggest, and into it went a bed, a table, pieces of furniture whose purposes the boy could not guess at, and several boxes. While soldiers were carrying and arranging the officer's belongings, his cook had set up a cauldron over an open fire, and soon torturing smells were coming from it. Ewen's mouth watered as the old man stirred and chopped vegetables and tasted and added knobs of brick salt and muttered to himself It was some time before the cook became aware of—or acknowledged—the presence of his audience. He scowled at the boy, thrust a kettle into his hand and ordered him gruffly to fetch water from the stream.

Normally Ewen would have bounded down the hillside, swift and sure-footed, but today his legs felt weak beneath him. The iron pot unbalanced him and more than once he stumbled. Carrying his unwieldy burden back was almost beyond him. Water slopped out at every uncertain step, and several times he set the kettle down to rest his aching limbs. Before he was half-way up the slope the cook came looking for him, shouting, 'What's keeping you, you idle brat?' But when they reached the camp he gave Ewen an oatcake and let him stir the pot.

When the food was ready and served to Campbell and his staff officers in the tent, the colonel instructed the cook to give Ewen some. The boy sat down by the fire and greedily gobbled game ragout from a pewter dish, using his fingers and a chunk of the officers' soft white bread to convey the succulent meat, vegetables and gravy to his mouth. The next instant the plate was snatched from him.

'The colonel spent hours shooting these birds and is good enough to let you share his supper. Will you stuff it down like an ungrateful, heathen savage? Here, boy.' The cook handed back the dish together with a fork and spoon. 'Let me see you eat like a Christian!'

Ewen took hold of the implements

awkwardly and, under the cook's critical gaze, copied the other man's eating technique. He struggled to co-ordinate both hands and spilled more than a little of the precious stew. As soon as the cook disappeared into the tent to attend to the officers, Ewen reverted to the simpler method he had always used.

Afterwards he felt tired and satisfied. The rats had stopped their gnawing. The fire was warm and comforting. He lay beside it and watched the sparks spiralling up into the blackness. As he drowsed into sleep he heard Campbell talking to the guard posted outside his tent. 'Keep an eye on the boy. I don't want him slipping away in the night.'

Slipping away? Why should he do that? Something deep inside Ewen told him that he should mistrust men in red coats, but these ones were good to him and he had just eaten the best meal he could remember. Marching with the soldiers was better than running alone, pursued by ugly, half-remembered fears with only the rats for company.

In the morning he wandered around the camp. Some of the men, busy packing up their equipment, kicked out at him for getting under their feet. But others stopped to talk with him. Those who spoke his own tongue he could understand. The others seemed to mutter in harsh, guttural sentences. However, by concentrating hard, Ewen quickly picked up some of their words. One man in particular, grey-haired and, in the boy's eyes, obviously old, took some trouble to teach him. 'Sergeant Pocock,' he enunciated clearly, pointing to himself. Then, extending his finger, he asked, 'You?' The boy shook his head. 'Ewen,' he announced. 'You Ewen?' The man laughed, seeming to find both the homophony and his pupil's puzzlement very amusing. But he persevered with the lesson, indicating the English words for such items as head, hand, stone and gun, until, sighting the approach of a young lieutenant, he sent Ewen on his way.

Back in the officer's lines the cook, busy dismantling his mobile kitchen, scolded Ewen for being nowhere to be found. But at the same time he roughly handed him a dish of cooling oatmeal and the cold remains of the ragout.

That day he did not ride with Campbell, though the colonel kept a watch on his movements. He wandered up and down the column, marching alongside the soldiers, watching, asking question, and making his own forays into intriguing clumps of boulders and burned-out cottages when his grasshopper curiosity made unpredicted leaps. Most of the soldiers encouraged the boy. Getting him to walk beside them and making jokes at his expense relieved the tedium.

There was only one part of the travelling column from which Ewen was barred. In the centre, flanked by two rows of infantrymen, were six ragged creatures, stumbling along in single file and linked by a chain attached to iron collars round their necks. Ewen noted that some were wounded. One man's arm dangled helplessly at his side. Two others had heads wrapped in grubby bandages. Sometimes one of the prisoners fell, pulling his companions down to the ground with him. Then the soldiers shouted and clubbed them with their musket butts until they unscrambled themselves and continued the march. So much Ewen saw from a distance. When he tried to get closer, the guards—who, Ewen learned, were from Germany, wherever that was—pointed their bayonets at him and motioned him to go away. Once one of the captives called out to him, 'Don't let them buy you, boy! Don't betray your own people!' One of the guards struck him across the mouth. At that moment Ewen caught sight of a stag cresting the opposite hill and sank down behind a boulder to watch him.

In camp that evening some of the men

taught their young mascot a game which involved two opposing teams trying to kick a tightly-tied bundle of cloth between spaces marked out by sticks in the ground. Ewen got the hang of it very quickly. Though still suffering some of the effects of privation, he was nimble and able to avoid the lunging hands and feet of his opponents. When he scored the winning 'goal', his team roared in triumph. One of the soldiers hoisted him to his shoulders and carried him back to the lines.

Around noon on the third day, Campbell's force came within sight of Loch Huich.

The room Tim and George entered was large and semi-circular, forming part of the ground floor of the main bastion. Tall windows pierced the curved outer wall facing them, and the spaces between were filled with bookcases. Much of the floor area was occupied by items of eighteenth-century mahogany library furniture: two long tables, crisply-carved reading chairs, chart cabinets, folio stands, and a matching pair of carved steps. The only moving object in the room was a Dobermann pinscher bitch, which bounded towards them, teeth bared.

'Maggie, stand!' At the sharp order the dog came to an abrupt halt a metre away from the door, staring at the new arrivals with what might have been curiosity or thwarted malice.

'Come in. Maggie won't bother you.' The words were spoken by a man seated at one end of the library table to the right. He rose as Tim and George approached. He shook their hands in turn and motioned them to leather-covered chairs ranged along each side of the table. Beyond that there was nothing welcoming about his manner.

'You took your time.' It was an emotionless statement of fact.

Mr Robertson was fit, rugged and fiftyish. Apart from a slight over-colouring of his cheeks and nose, he gave every appearance of a man who was in excellent health and took very good care to remain so. Wearing a dark grey track suit over a scarlet roll-necked sweater, he might have just come from the gym. The first impression he gave was one of vitality. There was no suggestion of a paunch, his black hair was close cropped, his short moustache neatly trimmed, his handshake was firm and the dark eyes that unblinkingly appraised his guests were bright and intelligent.

Tim decided not to react to the criticism. 'What exactly can we do for you, Mr Robertson?'

The potential client sat erect in his

chair, hands resting loosely on the polished mahogany. Tim thought of the famous statue of President Lincoln. 'Anything I tell you is in total confidence, and that stands whether or not I decide to employ you. Can I trust you?'

Tim was not going to yield any more ground. 'Your friends in influential circles will have told you that Lacy Security is a highly specialised, highly regarded, highly successful company with an international reputation. We didn't get to the top of our particular ladder by leaking information about our clients.'

Robertson was unfazed. 'I know you're the best. That's why you're here. I don't tolerate the second rate. What I need is the most sophisticated system available.'

'You have a valuable collection?' Tim glanced around. The paintings in this room were all pre-Renaissance, and they shared the macabre feel of the items he had already seen. Pride of place was given to a semi-circular 'doom' panel that had obviously come from a church—probably, Tim guessed, in northern Germany. After several centuries the colours were still vivid and the subject matter, even in a less superstitious age, disquieting. A fierce Christ, flanked by a host of angels, welcomed the blessed on his right hand. But the viewer's eyes were compelled towards the other side of the picture, where the mouth of hell gaped like the maw of a fire-breathing monster, and grotesque demons leaped forth with expressions of maniacal glee to drag the damned into eternal torment. Other spaces were filled by depictions of Christian martyrdoms. In a fifteenth-century painting of gruesome reality, St Sebastian, bound to a tree whose angular branches emphasized his pain, succumbed to the arrows fired by his executioners. His twisted, lacerated, vermilion-streaked torso attracted more attention than the beatific smile he turned towards heaven. This picture's companion piece was devoted, with equal clarity, to St Catherine being beheaded in front of the spiked wheel which had been miraculously shattered during her tormentors' first attempt to kill her. A glass case on the centre of the table at which they sat held a death mask and was labelled, 'Donatien, Alphonse François, Marquis de Sade—Charenton Lunatic Asylum, 2 December 1814'.

'My collection is unique,' Robertson replied. 'No one else has brought together so many works of art and other items testifying to human cruelty. I've made that my life's work, my personal contribution to the sum of man's self-knowledge.'

Tim concealed his distaste for the

concept. 'Not many people can see it here.'

Robertson nodded. 'That's because it's not complete yet. When it is, or when I die, it will go on permanent public display. Arrangements exist for the establishment of an exhibition gallery.'

'Where will that be?'

'I haven't finally decided, Mr Lacy. The collection is provisionally left to a leading London museum, but other institutions in New York and Berlin would love to get their hands on it. I'm not hurrying to make a final decision.'

George shivered. He was still unnerved by the events of yesterday and did not care for the atmosphere of Castle Gruesome. 'To return to practicalities, sir, from what little we've so far seen, I'd say it would be pretty difficult for thieves to break in here, and even more difficult for them to get away with much.'

'It's not thieves I'm concerned about.' Robertson frowned impatiently.

Tim and George exchanged glances. 'Then what...'

'Murderers, Mr Lacy. Assassins.'

Tim let the words sink in, then nodded. 'I see. You believe someone may breach your security in order to kill you?'

Robertson allowed himself the faintest of smiles. 'I know what you're thinking:

77

"This crank has shut himself up for so long with pictures of death and violence that he's convinced someone wants to murder him." You couldn't be more wrong. Jack Robertson is still in full possession of all his marbles. I'll tell you the sequence of events which persuaded me to send for you. Let's get some coffee.' He picked up a mobile phone, pressed a single button and made his wishes known succinctly. 'Three coffees in the library, Mrs Jenkins.' He put down the instrument and waved a hand. 'She won't be long. Look around, why don't you!'

George took the opportunity for a preliminary professional inspection. He examined doors and casements and cast an appraising eye over the conventional infra-red apparatus. He ended up before one of the large sash windows, gazing down at the waters of the loch lapping over rocks some ten metres below.

Tim looked along the titles of the books on the crammed shelves. Within a limited field the collection appeared to be very comprehensive. There were treatises on interrogation techniques spanning the centuries from the Inquisition to the KGB. There were volumes by nineteenth-century travellers describing the customs of Islamic and pagan societies. A whole stack was devoted to crime and punishment, and several shelves to the history and psychology of sadomasochism. Tim turned to his host just as a diminutive middle-aged woman came in carrying a silver tray of pots, jugs and cups. 'You must have a considerable specialist knowledge, Mr Robertson.'

'I'm writing the definitive history of torture. Man's inhumanity to man—an eternally fascinating subject.' He nodded his dismissal of Mrs Jenkins, who retired as noiselessly as she had entered. 'Sit down and have your coffee.'

Tim was determined not to be treated as badly as the servants. He deliberately turned back to the shelves, selected a book at random and turned the pages. 'You were going to tell us what prompted you to apply for our services.'

There were a few seconds of silence, during which Robertson stared at the back of his insubordinate guest. Apparently deciding not to engage in a trial of wills, he poured his own coffee and sat back in his chair. 'Beneath this room lies all that remains of the original castle that occupied this site—probably dungeons and kitchens. I've converted them into a gallery for my collection of torture implements. It's not the largest in private hands, but certainly the best. Maggie!'

The bitch, who had been lying in the

sunlight in front of one of the windows, got up and padded obediently to her master's chair. Robertson fondled her ears. 'I love my dogs. Loyal, obedient, a hundred per cent harmless unless I tell them to be otherwise. They're like good soldiers—trained to kill but completely under control. Dobermanns are the best guard dogs there are. I used to keep—'

Tim interrupted. 'I don't see what all this has to do with our visit.'

Robertson ignored him. 'I used to keep Alsatians but I got rid of them when I changed to Dobermanns. All except my breeding pair, Brutus and Portia. I'd had them several years and I couldn't bring myself to part with them. On the third of December someone killed Portia.'

'Here?' Tim crossed to the table to pour coffee for himself and George.

'Of course, here! The dogs never leave the island. Do you want to hear this or not?' Robertson did not wait for an answer. 'Somehow some bastard got into the castle, took her down to the torture chamber and tied her to the rack. She must have been drugged—she'd have torn her attacker's throat out otherwise. Then he just... Well, you don't need me to go into the gory details. On the floor beside the rack he chalked a big number one in a Roman numeral.'

George sat down to drink his coffee. 'Why do you reckon this was done by an outsider? Surely it would be very difficult. Someone inside the castle, who knew the dogs and was trusted by them...'

'Do you suppose I didn't think of that?' Robertson dismissed the contribution contemptuously. 'Point one: I don't have many staff here and they're very carefully chosen. Point two: the staff quarters, like the guest quarters, are locked at night, which is when this atrocity was perpetrated.'

'You lock your domestics up at night?' Tim stared his disbelief.

'I'll explain my current security arrangements later. What matters for the moment is that none of them could have got into this part of the castle. Anyway, point three: that wouldn't have explained the events that followed. We carried out a thorough investigation and couldn't find any evidence of a break-in. So, though I still didn't believe my own staff were involved, I called them together and read the riot act. I told them that if anything else remotely similar happened they'd all get the sack. I reckoned that would deter anyone who was guilty and would put them all on their mettle; they'd keep an eye on each other. Well, two weeks later it was the turn of poor Brutus. Jenkins found him one morning in the iron maiden.' He clenched his fists and hammered the table. 'If ever I get my hands on—'

'And was there a Roman two this time?' Tim asked.

'Yes, chalked on the outside of the case. But there was more, a simple equation: three equals Robertson.'

'What did you do about it?'

'The first thing, Mr Lacy, was to fire the staff.'

'Just like that? Even though you didn't really suspect them?'

'I'd warned them. I had to stick to my word. They left with generous severance pay; they weren't hard done by.'

'But you didn't sack Jenkins.'

'He and his wife have been with me for twenty years. There's no way they could be implicated.' Robertson shrugged. 'Anyway, that's the story. Now you know why I want the very best security money can buy. It's not a question of protecting my property; I want to make it absolutely impossible for anyone to set foot on this chunk of rock without my knowledge. Do you think you can manage that?'

'I take it you've informed the police about these events,' Tim said.

'And what good do you think that would do?'

'They have pretty sophisticated forensic

equipment. If the intruder left any trace they could probably find it.' Tim helped himself to more coffee.

'And while they're checking their data-bases the assassin is planning his next visit. For my money, prevention is better than cure.'

Tim looked quickly at his colleague and saw that George was fascinated by Robertson's story. 'I see why you're worried. Of course we'll do a thorough survey and come up with some proposals. Wouldn't it also be a good idea for you to try to find out who's trying to put the frighteners on you? I mean, you must have some sort of idea...'

Their host stood up. 'I'm a wealthy man. And I have a number of business interests. Inevitably, that means I have enemies.'

'And some of them have come to see you here? They know the layout of the castle?'

'There were no visitors here at the time of these incidents, Mr Lacy. I had a conference of business colleagues at the end of November and two days of important negotiations just before Christmas. Since then there have been no callers at Lanner. Now, I am sure you will want to start your survey or whatever it is you people do. I suggest you do outside first while you've got good weather. After dinner this evening I'll take you on a tour of the collections. In the meantime, if you need access to any parts of the buildings that are locked, Jenkins will open them up for you.' He walked to the double doors and opened them wide. 'As you will already have gathered, I have a potential son-in-law to interview.'

Tim and George walked across the wide, carpeted drawing room. At the door Tim turned. 'One more question, if I may. Why Maggie?'

Robertson stood smiling, his hand on the dog's head. 'Tenacious, uncompromising, unstoppable—just like the Iron Lady. Well, gentlemen, for now, goodbye.'

'Goodbye!' The raucous utterance startled them both.

'Goodbye! Come here, Jenkins!' The parrot sidled along its perch, fixing them with a malevolent eye.

George wandered over to the bird's corner. 'What's your name, then?'

'Goodbye! Welcome to Lanner Castle! Goodbye!'

Cautiously, George stroked the parrot's grey feathers through the wire of the cage. 'He's got quite a repertoire, Major.'

'Major!' the bird mimicked. 'Major. Goodbye!'

'Crikey, he's quick.'

Tim laughed. 'You'd better come away before you incriminate yourself, George.'

They withdrew and, minutes later, were seated in Tim's room.

'What do you make of all that, George?' Tim lay back in the deep armchair and stretched his legs out.

'We certainly get some rum 'uns, Major. It's a bit early in the day but I could do with a bracer. How about you?'

'I'm OK, but you go ahead.'

A console table beside the door was furnished with full decanters, glasses and an array of mixers. George poured himself a generous tot of whisky. 'Frankly, this whole place gives me the creeps. Can't we pass on this job, Major?'

'You're still a bit shaken by that business on the road yesterday, aren't you?'

'I don't believe in ghosts, but I do know what I saw and it certainly fits in with what the landlord told us last night.'

'Tourist tales, George. I shouldn't take them too seriously.'

'But that story about the children, it can't have been made up on the spur of the moment—and there were definitely three young kids standing in the middle of the road.'

'Well, I'm sure there's a logical explanation —one that doesn't involve ghosts.'

'And is there a logical explanation for what's been going on here?'

'Well, I've never heard of ghosts killing

dogs. Whatever Robertson's frightened of is very corporeal.'

'He didn't strike me as a frightened man. Angry, certainly, but not frightened.'

'I think he's a man used to living with fear. He shuts himself away in a place like this for years. He does everything possible to ensure that only people he knows or experts can get to him. Now, despite all these precautions, someone has broken through his defences and is threatening him in his own stronghold.'

'You believe all that stuff about the dogs then?'

Tim shrugged. 'I can't see any reason not to. We could have a quiet word with his man Jenkins, but I'll bet he confirms the story.'

'Well I reckon Robertson's mind's been turned by all these hideous pictures around the place and the sort of books he reads. You can't tell me it's healthy and rational for someone to spend his time brooding about torture and violent death.'

Tim closed his eyes and pondered the point. 'Robertson is odd—no doubt about it—but he doesn't strike me as a man who's flipped his lid or suffers from delusions. Perhaps his macabre research is a kind of self-imposed therapy: he's afraid of something or someone, so he surrounds himself with pictures of every conceivable terror, believing that if he can cope with them he can cope with the specific fear that's haunting him.'

George scowled over the rim of his glass. 'So when I see phantom children I'm imagining things, but when Robertson talks about ghostly animal-killing prowlers he makes perfect sense!'

Tim jumped up. 'Don't be daft, George. I never said you were imagining things. If you say you saw something that's good enough for me.' He walked to the window and gazed out at the brilliance of snow and sunlit water. Below, in the fenced-off area enclosing the helicopter pact a mechanic in overalls was brushing snow from the machine's rotor blades. Tim turned back to face his friend. 'Anyway, whether Robertson's fears are real or not is no concern of ours. We have a job to do, so I guess we'd better get on and do it.'

CHAPTER 4

Tim and George spent the remainder of the morning examining the external security arrangements of Lanner Castle. The island's flat surface stood nine or ten metres above the level of the loch, and on all sides the ground fell sheer away to the water. Apart from one or two drifts against the house the snow was not deep; strong winds had kept the plateau well swept. Jagged rocks made approach by boat hazardous anywhere, and in most places impossible. The only viable landing point was where the boathouse had been built out from the cliff. The entire north-western side of the castle facing Briachan rose from the island's granite edge. The wide terrace area fronting Lanner's other aspect was ring-fenced, and the helicopter pad, as well as being circuited on all outward-facing sides, was separated from the castle courtyard by another wire barrier. The gates from the boathouse and the helicopter compound were operated electrically. There were two sets of controls, one in the kitchen complex and one in Robertson's private quarters. The fence was in good condition and there was no sign of it having been breached.

At 12.30, Jenkins came to find them to say that lunch would be served in half an hour. Tim took the opportunity to quiz him.

'Ex-army, aren't you, Jenkins?'

'Ex-Marines, sir. How did you know?'

Tim smiled at the well-built, well-turned-out man who carried himself very erect. 'It takes one to know one. Most of my time was in the SAS. Mr Martin here was with me in that outfit.'

'You must have seen some interesting service, sir.'

'It had its moments. How long have you been at Lanner Castle?'

'Ever since Mr Robertson came here, over twenty years ago.'

'Mr Robertson said something I didn't quite follow about the servants being shut up at night. What did he mean?'

Jenkins automatically smoothed a wisp of his thinning hair which had been dislodged by the strengthening breeze. 'That's not quite what it sounds, sir. If you'll come over here to the middle of the terrace, I'll show you.'

The wind was swirling powdery snow into airborne whirls as the three men stood facing the castle. Jenkins explained. 'As you can see, the building is really in three sections. At the south end we have the circular bastion or keep. That has the yellow drawing room and the library on the ground floor and Mr Robertson's private quarters on the higher storeys. The central area consists of the hall, the dining room, various reception rooms and, above, the billiard room and the secretarial suite. The north range with its corner turrets has the kitchen and staff quarters on the ground floor, guest rooms immediately above them and, on the third storey, more staff bedrooms. Every night I do my final rounds and check that everything is secure. Then I throw a switch on the control panel—that's in a locked cupboard in the security room off the kitchen. That automatically locks the connecting doors between the three parts of the building.'

'What happens if there's a fire?' Tim asked.

'No problem, sir.' The butler smiled reassuringly. 'The doors I mentioned are all fire doors. They're meant to prevent the spread of a blaze. All parts of the house have their own access routes to the outside. And in any case the alarm system incorporates an automatic override on all electronic locks.'

'So that you can get everyone away from the island quickly and bring in fire fighters.'

'We could certainly evacuate the island. But the professionals wouldn't be much use to us here. We have to be self-contained. We've got a good sprinkler system and our own hoses to carry water pumped from the loch. Still, sir, I don't really like to think about that. It would be a tragedy if the second castle were to go the way of the first. Now, if you'll excuse me, gentlemen, I should be getting back to supervise the lunch.'

George and Tim went to their rooms to

freshen up. George emerged first. He was descending the staircase to the hall when Andrea came running up.

He stepped aside. 'Plenty of time,' he observed cheerfully, 'It's only ten minutes...' But the girl brushed past him. Not, however, before George noticed the tears glistening on her cheeks. At the bottom, Ben Azikwe was looking up the stairs, helpless and angry.

George felt that he should say something but did not know what. 'Trouble?' he enquired as he reached the bottom step.

Azikwe muttered, 'Any man who treats his daughter like that doesn't deserve to live.' He started up the stairs two at a time.

Campbell's force camped along the loch shore. The junior officers commandeered what was left of a hamlet called Briachan while the troops set their tents up on the flat ground around. Their arrival had been noted at the castle and three boats were despatched to meet them. The colonel saw his prisoners safely loaded aboard two of them, then sent his servant to find Ewen.

The boy came running. 'Is that Castle Huich?' His eyes were wide with wonder. He had never seen a building so large. Square and massive and bigger than the church at Kirkhill, it looked as though it

91

had grown out of the island on which it stood.

Campbell smiled at his charge's eagerness and curiosity. 'Aye, lad, that's Castle Huich, home of Alan Duncan, Duncan o'Strathfarrer. He's the laird of these lands. You'll be safe enough with him till I come back this way.'

'Where are you going?' Ewen did not like the thought of losing his protector.

'Oh, I've more Jacobites to find yet. But this sorry business will soon be over. Then we must see about getting you educated and making a Scottish gentleman out of you.'

Campbell stepped into the boat that was being held for him and Ewen eagerly jumped in to sit beside him. Throughout the short crossing he stared fixedly past the brawny shoulders of the oarsman at the approaching mass of the island. The castle's high granite walls were pierced with small windows. Soldiers were posted at intervals along its battlements. As they neared the fortress, Ewen tilted his head back to stare up at its massive bulk. Suddenly it seemed as though the sheer granite was about to topple over on to the boat, and the boy shouted out his alarm.

'Cease your noise!' Ewen felt the slap of Campbell's gauntleted hand on his bare knee. 'You've nothing to fear here.'

The boat nudged up to a flight of stone steps and the oarsman gripped an iron ring to hold the craft steady. The colonel stepped ashore and Ewen scrambled after him. The steps led directly to a gate whose wide wooden door stood open, barred by a sentry, who moved aside to let the visitors pass. Campbell obviously knew the castle, for he strode across a large courtyard, busy with soldiers, servants, horses and domestic animals, to a door in the range of buildings opposite.

The room they entered was long, high-ceilinged and lit through tall windows. A fire burned in a large hearth and round it stood a group of men. The colonel told Ewen to remain just inside the door. The boy gazed in wonder around this great enclosed space with its fine tables and cupboards of polished wood and the painted portraits round its walls. He saw a stubby, red-bearded man in an embroidered coat with gleaming buttons detach himself from the party round the carved fireplace and come forward to greet Campbell. For several minutes the gentlemen talked and laughed among themselves, ignoring Ewen, but then Campbell beckoned him over.

In the boy's own language he said, 'This is your new master, Duncan o'Strathfarrer.

Make your bow to him. He'll look after you till I return.'

Ewen doffed his head as he had seen some of the soldiers and servants in the camp do when approached by an officer. That brought a laugh from the men. As they stared down, obviously talking about him, Ewen tried hard to understand. He picked out a few words here and there.

Had he been able to comprehend fully, he would have heard the youngest observe with a sneer, 'I see you've taught the little savage some manners.'

'He's a bright lad. He learns quickly,' Campbell replied.

'There's not much of him,' another said, 'and what there is is scrawny.'

'He'd been living rough and alone on the moor for many days before we found him. He's badly shocked. He doesn't remember a thing about his family and what happened to them.'

'If it had been me, I'd have taken my sabre to him,' the younger man retorted.

Campbell scowled in his direction. 'Aye, Alistair, I've no doubt of it. We all know how fearless and brave you are when it comes to dealing with women and children.'

'You'll take that back, Campbell!' The man flashed his anger.

'Indeed, I will not. Where were you at Culloden?'

Before the young soldier could reply, Duncan held up a hand. 'Enough, Alistair. You're talking out of turn. James, of course we'll take good care of your protégé. He'll join our little nursery till you come to take them all off our hands. We'll do it out of friendship and be glad to, though I'm bound to say I agree with my son—it's a waste of time trying to inculcate finer feelings into these animals.'

'Well, Duncan, there's been enough killing—more than enough. You cannot exterminate all the clans that rose for the Stuart or failed to rally to the king's banner. Sooner or later there has to be rebuilding, populating the Highlands with loyal, educated Protestants. It's important to start with children because they haven't yet learned hatred or developed thoughts of revenge.'

Duncan shrugged. 'You may be right. Anyway, you have my word that Ewen will be fairly fed and sheltered for as long as he's here. Now, about the prisoners—how many have you brought?'

'Six have survived the march, though one is in a bad way.'

'Have they any news of the Pretender?'

Campbell frowned. 'That's for you and your special methods to determine.'

'Aye, we'll get the truth from them. His royal highness expects no less. He's vowed to take Charles Edward Stuart back to London in chains. He's due here in a few days. I want to have some good news ready for him.'

'Cumberland's coming here?'

'Aye, James, the hero of Culloden will be staying under this very roof. It's a great honour. But what was I thinking of? You'll be wanting food and drink. Alistair.' He turned to his son. 'Be so kind as to organise dinner for our guest. Take the lad with you and see that he's properly quartered.'

Young Alistair gripped Ewen by the arm and led him from the room. In a passage outside he bellowed for a servant. An elderly man came shuffling up.

Alistair pushed Ewen towards him. 'Throw this one into the tower with the other brats.'

Lunch was a sombre affair. The dining room at Lanner Castle had been built and equipped to accommodate large parties of expensively-dressed guests making sparkling conversation while working their way through seven- or eight-course meals. On this bleak winter's afternoon, four unremarkable people stared at each other across the gleaming mahogany and tried

96

to think of things to say. George and Tim attempted small talk with the university girls, but Carol and Steffy were showing signs of nervousness as the time for their interview with Robertson approached. All four lunchers were overawed by their surroundings. Automatically they spoke in subdued tones like people in church. The decor of the tall-ceilinged room certainly had about it more than a suggestion of the ecclesiastical. The Gothic arched windows carried stained-glass heraldic devices realised in deep Victorian ultramarine, crimson and saffron. The medieval revival featured in the carved panelling around the lower part of the walls, and made a not-altogether happy match with the Arts and Crafts wallpaper above. The canvases suspended on chains from an elaborate picture rail maintained the religious theme, and were scarcely conceivable as aids to digestion. They were a set of nineteenth-century genre pieces depicting Biblical incidents. Blind Samson brought the walls of the Philistine temple crashing down upon himself and his captors; a vengeful Joel drove a tent peg through the temple of Sisera, her sleeping guest; and pride of place was given to a voluptuous Salome positively drooling over the sight of John the Baptist's head on a silver salver.

The quartet had lapsed into virtual silence by the time the soup plates were cleared away. Then they heard the sound of the helicopter taking off.

'That's not our host deserting us I hope?' Tim asked.

'No, sir,' Jenkins explained. 'Mr Robertson always lunches alone. We're expecting two more guests tonight. Gunnett's going to Edinburgh to collect them.'

'Gunnett? He's the resident pilot, is he?'

'We have two men who look after all the transport, sir—Gunnett and Arvine.'

'They're new, aren't they? Mr Robertson mentioned a recent change of staff.'

'That's right, sir. You wouldn't happen to know where Miss Robertson and the African gentleman are, would you? I wonder whether I ought to send someone to find them.'

George shook his head. 'I don't think they're feeling much like lunch at the moment.'

Steffy grimaced. 'Has there been a row? Andrea wasn't exactly looking forward to seeing her old man.'

George decided on discretion. 'I shouldn't wonder, miss.'

Quiet seeped back into the atmosphere. They took coffee in a small sitting room off the hall. After only ten minutes the students withdrew to have a final briefing before their meeting with Robertson. Tim busied himself with a selection of magazines laid out on a sofa table. George opened the book Tam had lent him.

Ballads of the Great Glen by B. K. Ogilvie was a modest volume but packed with information. Among the hundred or so folk airs the author had gathered, there were thirteen songs relating to Ewen of the Glen. To most of them the academic had appended explanatory notes. George read through them quickly, looking for the one aspect of the legend that interested him. He found it in a footnote to 'A Lament for the Bairns':

This ballad exists in at least three versions, the best-known of which appeared in *Sibbald's Chronicle of Scottish Poetry* (Edinburgh, 1802). The verses printed here are from the earliest known manuscript source in the collection made by Lady Anne Lindsay around 1770. It is interesting for the light it sheds upon an otherwise obscure aspect of the aftermath of the 1745 uprising. As the Duke of Cumberland's vengeful cohorts burned and pillaged their way through the Highlands, ostensibly in pursuance of military objectives but in reality to break a proud and independent people, hundreds of innocent children suffered. Some, we know, were taken into the households of clan leaders as servants or estate workers. There are even examples of boys being adopted by great families and educated in England in order to become the building blocks of a new socio-political order. The vast majority, however, are unaccounted for. 'A Lament for the Bairns' tells of a tragedy that is unlikely to have been unique. Castle Huich, home and principal fortress of the notorious Duncan the Red, was a collecting depot for scores of displaced children. In the fire of July 1746, here and in other ballads attributed to the mysterious Ewen, several undoubtedly perished. Some escaped and wandered the countryside, a pathetic band of ragamuffin outlaws waylaying travellers and breaking into farmsteads until privation or the law caught up with them.

George read 'A Lament for the Bairns'. It described how a group of children under Ewen's leadership had overpowered Duncan the Red and his entire garrison before razing to the ground Castle Huich, 'tyranny's black emblem'. It was the last verse that George repeated to himself several times.

Duncan then and a' his crew
Have found their way to hell.
But canny Ewen's bold compeers
Gang far by hill and dale.
And wander yet where tyrant's hand
Is raised against the poor.
Nae flood, nae fire, nae death itsel,
Can hold the bairns nae mare.

He mused over the words, then looked up. 'Major?'

'Mmm!' Tim was immersed in his copy of *Country Life*.

'Do you think it's possible...' George's question dwindled away into embarrassed silence.

'Do I think what's possible?'

George snapped the book shut. 'Oh, nothing. I suppose we'd better get going.'

Tim smiled up at him. 'I guess you're right. After all,' he drained his coffee cup and tossed the magazine aside, 'we are just humble working men, not gentlemen of leisure.'

They spent most of the afternoon with Jenkins on a tour of the castle, checking the existing security arrangements. Soon after four, the helicopter returned, and minutes later, Tim happened to be passing through the hall as Jenkins welcomed the two new arrivals, a man and a woman. The latter Jenkins left briefly while he conveyed her companion straight into Robertson's presence.

At seven o'clock, showered and changed, Tim entered the yellow drawing room. Most of the company were already assembled. Tim accepted a glass of champagne from Jenkins and set about the business of mingling. Within minutes Robertson, dressed now in a dark suit and silk tie, accosted him. 'Mr Lacy, may I introduce Dr Hildegard Nefsky?'

Tim shook hands with a sallow-complexioned, middle-aged woman, enveloped in shapeless grey.

'Dr Nefsky is director of the Harman-Lederer Humanities Institute. I'm sure you're familiar with it.'

'I've never actually visited it but, of course, I know you have some fine collections, Dr Nefsky.' The Harman-Lederer Institute was an offshoot of an Anglo-American arms consortium. The company supplied tanks and assorted weapons systems to governments worldwide, including a number whose human rights records were far from clean. A proportion of their not-inconsiderable profits was very publicly diverted into various charitable activities, including the Humanities Institute in London's West End.

'One day we'll have a very significant

addition.' Dr Nefsky gestured significantly to the display of Japanese prints occupying most of one wall. They delineated in exquisite and repellant detail methods used by the shoguns to extract information from their prisoners.

'So the Harman-Lederer Institute will be the beneficiary of Mr Robertson's life's work?'

Their host interposed sharply. 'I suggest you keep our arrangement to yourself, Hildegard dear. If you go around telling stories you'll look awfully silly if—or when—I change my mind.' He drifted away to talk to other guests.

The woman looked anguished. 'Do you know who that man is—the American?' She pointed towards the swarthy, diminutive figure with whom Robertson was now talking.

Tim shook his head. 'I assumed he came with you in the chopper.'

'Oh, he did. We collected him from Edinburgh airport, but he didn't say much about himself except his name; helicopters are not very conducive to conversation. I wonder if he's...' She snapped off the sentence in order to concentrate her attention on Tim. 'Are you here representing a museum, Mr Lacy?'

'No, I represent no one but myself—Tim Lacy, Lacy Security. I'm here with my colleague to advise Mr Robertson on his...defensive shield.'

Dr Nefsky frowned. 'He's putting in more security? But that must mean...' Another sentence was axed. Distractedly, she wandered away and found a chair in the corner of the room beside the parrot's cage, now covered in a white cloth that extended to the floor.

Tim found the university girls sitting on a sofa. They had actually made the effort to appear feminine and wore dresses of passable smartness. They were altogether more subdued than they had been twenty-four hours before.

'How did you get on with the ogre?' Tim asked cheerfully.

'Don't ask.' Steffy squinted at him through lowered lids.

Her friend looked round sharply and nudged her. 'He was OK,' she added quickly. 'How are you getting on fixing security for his hideous pictures and things?'

Tim shrugged. 'I don't know that there's much more we could add. This place is already like Fort Knox.'

Carol grimaced. 'I can't imagine anyone wanting to steal any of Robertson's ghastly treasures. You have to have a sick mind to surround yourself with all this stuff.'

'I gather there's an obligatory guided

tour of the horrors after dinner,' Steffy observed. 'Good job it's not before—it would put me right off my food.'

When they took their places at table, Tim found himself between Andrea and Hildegard Nefsky and opposite the American, who immediately introduced himself as Cal Lopez from Texas.

Tim stared at him, though not, he hoped, too pointedly. 'Haven't we met somewhere?'

'I don't think so,' Lopez replied quickly —a little too quickly, Tim thought.

Throughout the meal he wrestled with memory. He was sure he had come across the American somewhere, but the connection eluded him. Lopez described himself as an antiquarian book dealer, come to do business with Robertson over an American collection currently being broken up. For no rational reason, Tim was sure the man was lying.

The meal was gastronomically excellent and socially disastrous. Tim wondered whether a convivial evening at Lanner Castle was not a contradiction in terms. Quite apart from the room's macabre decor, other pollutants poured freely into the atmosphere. Everyone except Lopez, Robertson, George and himself seemed preoccupied with their own thoughts. They ate like automata, and were about as communicative. When they looked up from their plates it was to offer monosyllabic replies to conversational openings or to cast hostile glances at the man at the head of the table. If looks could kill, Robertson would have suffered the death of a thousand cuts. The seating arrangement seemed to have been designed to exacerbate the tensions. Andrea had been placed on her father's right and her fiancé relegated to the other end of the table. Carol sat on her host's left, but Robertson spent most of the meal talking across her to Lopez, her neighbour. The American seemed oblivious to the undercurrents of fear, anxiety and hostility. He chatted eagerly about various countries he had visited. Robertson, equally well-travelled, was able to match the other's reminiscences. Tim, sitting opposite Lopez, became the third point in a triangular conversation after abortive attempts at ice-breaking with Andrea and Hildegard. The nether end of the table remained enveloped in introspective silence. When Robertson eventually rose to lead the way back to the yellow drawing room there was almost an audible sigh of collective relief.

As soon as everyone was provided with coffee the host rose to address them. 'Ladies and gentlemen, most people who come to Lanner Castle take one look around and say to themselves, "What sort of an oddball lives here?" ' Tim recognised the beginning of an oft-repeated routine. 'So to avoid someone sending for the men with the white coats I like to explain what my collection is about. For the last twenty years I've made a point of gathering together the best, the most dramatic, the most revealing examples of the dark side of human nature. There could scarcely be a more appropriate place for such an undertaking than Lanner Castle. It was the Scottish bard who coined the phrase "Man's inhumanity to man". This island was the scene of one terrible example of that inhumanity. After the Jacobite rising of 1745, several rebel prisoners were held here and tortured for information on the whereabouts of Bonnie Prince Charlie and his leading supporters. The infamous "Butcher" Cumberland himself came here, bringing the implement known as Cumberland's Cradle. A couple of years ago I was lucky enough to find what is probably the only surviving example. You'll see it when we go down to the torture chamber.

'Most people think that it's only psychopaths who are capable of inflicting deliberate pain and suffering on others. History suggests otherwise. Everyone has a dark side; everyone is capable of cruelty. There isn't a person in this room who, given the right circumstances, wouldn't torment another human being either mentally or physically. I'd like you to remember that as we make our little tour. However repelled you feel, just say to yourself, "It could be me." That's the whole purpose of my collection. I have brought these objects together in order to create a permanent exhibition. It's my little contribution towards building a better, less violent world. The more people can be made to look into their own souls the less likely they are to find scapegoats like TV violence, bad schooling and lack of parental control. Right, let's start with the pictures in this room.'

The sermonette was received in embarrassed silence. Tim was intrigued by the message and the preacher. Did Robertson really believe all that claptrap? Had he developed his theory about the cathartic effect of violence in order to erase his own obsession? No man who deliberately surrounded himself with images of lacerated flesh, bleeding torsos, twisted limbs and faces distorted in agony could be considered normal—perhaps not even fully sane.

Tim tagged on to the little procession as it moved from room to room. The guide's voice droned on but Tim thought his own thoughts. Robertson did make one concession to his guests' possible reservations: he kept his comments short. Only twice did he stop for several minutes in front of a painting to point out details. Otherwise he contented himself with general observations. Thus, chivalry was a glamorous mantle thrown over a brutal social system more accurately exemplified by Lanner Castle's array of medieval combat weapons. Mental torture was a constant of political control, as could be illustrated by pre-Renaissance images of hell and Soviet experiments with hallucinogenic drugs. The shockwaves of such bestialities as the Holocaust subsided all too rapidly, in the view of this connoisseur, who had devoted a whole room to the photographic representation of modern atrocities such as the effects of napalm in Vietnam, poison gas in Kurdistan and unrefined methods of torture in various parts of Africa.

The tour concluded with a visit to the dungeons. The series of interconnecting chambers at first sight resembled a mechanic's workshop. Floor, walls and benches were strewn with objects of wood and metal whose functions were not immediately obvious, except for those devices into which dummies had been inserted to remove any uncertainty.

In the first room, pride of place was given to a contraption of iron rings and bars that was suspended from the ceiling. 'Cumberland's Cradle,' Robertson announced, and looked round as though expecting applause. 'They say that several were made by an army blacksmith to the duke's own specifications, and installed in loyalist strongholds like this castle. It had two advantages: it was portable and remarkably effective.'

Some of the party began to move into the next cellar, but the guide had not finished what was obviously a favourite part of his commentary. 'It was the opposite of the rack: instead of stretching the prisoner's body, it compressed it. These hoops—' he demonstrated the simple mechanism, and Tim noted that it was obviously well oiled—'were fastened to the ankles, and this upper one to the neck. The connecting rods then held the victim absolutely rigidly. By means of these simple screws, which could be tightened very easily by one interrogator, the body, clamped into a foetal position, was crushed in further upon itself. The pain in the joints, the constriction of stomach and lungs...'

'I think we get the picture,' Tim said loudly. 'What's through here?' He marched into the next room.

Steffy sidled up to him. 'Thanks for that.' She slipped an arm through his and shivered. 'I can't take much more of this.'

Tim smiled reassuringly. 'Hang in there. The show's almost over.'

In fact, it came to an end sooner that he thought. They were in a central dungeon area from which several thick, iron-studded doors led to small individual cells. Robertson opened each in turn, flicking on spotlights which dramatically illuminated the exhibits within.

He pushed the second portal wide and stood looking as the light came on.

'And here...'

The sentence ended in an odd gurgling sound. Robertson stood motionless.

George, who was closest to him, peered over his shoulder. 'Good God!'

Tim stepped up beside him and looked into the cell. What was displayed here was one of the simplest of devices, the *garrucha*. The prisoner was suspended, usually by one arm, and a weight was attached to his ankle. The dummy which had been used for the display lay on the floor. In its place, the hanging chain fastened round its neck, was a grey parrot. On the floor beneath it there was a chalked symbol: 'III'.

CHAPTER 5

The place into which Ewen was thrown was the base of a round tower some ten metres in diameter. It had an earth and rock floor, and a wooden ladder in the centre led to an open trapdoor giving access to the chamber above. Five children, all, Ewen guessed, younger than himself, lay around the perimeter in various poses of listlessness.

As the door slammed behind him, Ewen gazed around, uncertain of what to do.

'Who's that?' The voice came from the open space at the top of the ladder.

Ewen stared up and saw a girl's face peering down. He advanced to the foot of the ladder.

'You're new,' the face announced. 'Come up.'

He climbed the ladder and emerged into a room identical to the one below except that it was wooden-floored and less gloomy. Three narrow windows in its circumference allowed shafts of light to intersect in a pool on the boards. Ewen found himself staring into the appraising eyes of a fair, straggle-haired girl a couple of years his senior. Her woollen dress was tattered but pinned together with twigs as improvised fastenings to cover the worse holes.

'What's your name?' the girl asked.

'Ewen.'

'And how old are you?'

He shrugged.

'Do you think you're more than ten?'

'Does it matter?'

She nodded. 'If you're over ten you sleep here with the chiefs. Otherwise your quarters are below with the clansmen.'

Ewen looked quickly around at the three other 'chiefs' who had boxes to sit on and straw to lie on. He made a swift decision. 'Eleven.'

The girl smiled. 'I'm Aileen. Come and meet my brother, Ranald. He's in charge here.'

She led the way up another ladder. The topmost chamber displayed a further improvement on the accommodation of the lower floors. Here the straw was deeper, the rough wooden boxes more numerous, and there were a couple of blankets spread out on one side of the room. Two twelve-year-old boys were seated on boxes, playing a game which involved tossing stones into a wooden bowl on the floor by the far wall. They turned to face the newcomer.

Ranald, the fairer of the two, took a

long look at Ewen. Ewen stared back, equally frankly. The first thing he noticed was that the boy's left arm was in a sling made from a piece of old rope. Then he saw the grubby, tattered shirt hanging on a gaunt, slender frame. The boy's eyes were dark and deep-set, yet they glinted with a hidden fervour. This passion and his undisputed authority were clear as soon as he spoke.

'What's your name? Where are you from? What's your clan? Did your father fight in the prince's army?'

Ewen explained, falteringly, that he could remember almost nothing of his past life.

'How did you come here, then? Do you know that?'

Ewen reported on the events of the last couple of days.

'So, Campbell's here!' Ranald's lieutenant, a small, dark lad, spat as he spoke the name.

Immediately, Ewen spoke up for the colonel. 'I like him. He gave me food and rode me on his horse.'

The boy jumped up and prodded Ewen in the chest. 'Campbell's a traitor and all his clan. My father and brothers fell at Culloden, cut down by his cavalry.'

'Sit down, Hamish,' Ranald ordered. 'If Campbell's back that means more prisoners. How many men in chains did you have with you, Ewen?'

'Six. The soldiers wouldn't let me speak to them.'

'Six.' Ranald mused. 'That means twenty-one in the cells, unless Robert Farrar has died of his wounds since yesterday.'

'They'll be running out of space,' Aileen said.

Ranald nodded thoughtfully. 'Aye, and they'll have more men to interrogate.'

Hamish added, 'So the dogs will be even more ruthless. That's bad. We must think of some way—'

'Not in front of the kid,' Ranald interrupted him. 'Aileen, take him down and explain the clan rules. But first we'll swear him.' He looked again at Ewen. 'Raise your right hand.'

Ewen did so.

'Now, repeat these words after me.' Phrase by phrase the fair-haired boy recited the following incantation: 'I, Ewen, do solemnly swear, in the name of God, Our Lady and all the saints, that Charles Stewart is my rightful king, that Ranald McCombie is my laird and that Alan Duncan is my enemy. I will obey my laird in all things, do all in my power to aid the subjects of King Charles and work for the destruction of Alan Duncan and all his red dogs.'

Ewen understood little of the words,

but the solenm intensity of the three older children communicated itself to him and he dutifully swore the oath. Afterwards Aileen took him back to the floor below. She seated herself on a box and gathered Ewen and the other 'chiefs' around her, squatting on the floor. There were two boys and two girls. She then explained, with the occasional aid of offerings from the others, the situation at Castle Huich.

The children being held by Alan the Red were, like Ewen, orphans of war, captured by the troops Butcher Cumberland had sent out to punish the kinsmen of those who had taken arms against King George. Aileen did not know what their fate was to be and it seemed that their captors were undecided on the question. Their treatment was brutal. They were made to perform a variety of menial tasks around the castle, from cleaning out pigsties to polishing uniform buttons, from scrubbing down stonework to carrying logs into the officers' quarters. They were constantly cuffed and beaten by Duncan's soldier—the 'red dogs', as they called them—and for serious offences, or simply for their captors' sport, they were subjected to whatever punishments Duncan and his cronies could dream up. These included being ducked in the loch, suspended by their feet from the castle walls, and being made to fight each other with knives. It was in such a contest that Ranald's left arm had been badly slashed. His opponent, Ranald's friend of many years, had received a fatal wound. He was one of four children who had succumbed to their treatment in the last six weeks. The girls and, sometimes, the boys were regularly taken to the officers' sleeping quarters and sexually attacked by their masters.

Ewen listened with horror and fear. He only partly understood what they were telling him, but it was obvious from the circle of drawn faces and the eyes that had forgotten how to cry that he had come into a place of torment.

'Don't worry, Ewen.' Aileen laid a hand on his shoulder. 'We'll be even with them. That's why it's important that we stick together. Ranald and Hamish make the plans and we all follow them.'

'But what can we do?' Ewen wanted to know.

'Lots of things. We pretend to be terrified of the dogs—little kids who cower in corners and do whatever we're told for fear of punishment. All the time we keep our eyes and ears open. Sometimes they say things in front of us because they think we're too stupid to understand, but some of us have learned several words of their language.'

'What sort of things do you find out?'

'The places where the soldiers are looking for King Charles. What regiments are moving in or out of the Highlands.'

'What good does that do?'

'Sometimes the dogs get us to take food to the cells where the prisoners are. We tell them what we know and they give us messages and tell us who we should try to contact. Then we organise an escape. Two boys have managed to get away from the island. One swam the loch and the other hid in an empty wine barrel. Ranald is trying to work out a way to help some of the prisoners to escape. Only that's much more difficult.'

'And much more dangerous.'

'Aye, Ewen, much more dangerous. But what have we to live for else? The Butcher's men have killed our mothers and fathers, our brothers and sisters. They treat us worse than animals. Revenge is the only thing worth living for—and dying for.'

'Whose idea of a joke is this?' Robertson turned to glare at his guests, slamming the cell door behind him.

In the moment of bewildered silence that followed, Tim stared at his host. The self-confident guide had disappeared to be replaced by a man with hunched shoulders, clenching and unclenching his hands. Tim said, 'Perhaps it would be a good idea if we retired to somewhere more comfortable.'

The company drifted back to the drawing room, but no one felt like lingering and making conversation. Robertson withdrew to his own quarters with a mumbling apology. Andrea, pallid and shaken, went straight to her room. Most of the others wandered away after a few minutes. Tim and George remained with Ben Azikwe. They sat around a well-stacked log fire drinking brandy.

George gazed moodily into the flames. 'Someone obviously wants to put the frighteners on our host. That's the third...' He caught Tim's eye and left the sentence unfinished.

'Third what?' the African said.

Tim shrugged. 'Oh well, you're virtually family so I suppose there's no reason why you shouldn't know. Two of Robertson's dogs have been killed in much the same way. Obviously it's an attempt to intimidate him.'

'Poetic justice, wouldn't you say?' Ben swirled the liquid in his glass and stared down into it.

'Meaning?' Tim asked.

'He enjoys being thoroughly unpleasant to other people. I assume all visitors to Lanner Castle are subjected to the same harrowing experience that we've been put through this evening. If someone's turning the tables on him I, for one, fully approve.'

'I get the impression that your meeting didn't go off very well.'

A look of resignation passed across Azikwe's placid features. 'References to "wogs", "ignorant savages" and "ancestors swinging through the jungle" featured rather prominently in it. But I don't mind so much what he said about me.'

'He lammed into Andrea?'

'He was absolutely vile to her. He put on the outraged parent act: after all he'd done for her—travel, best schools, private tutors, no expense spared to turn her into a highly cultured cosmopolitan woman—she throws herself away on a black man.'

George looked up. 'I thought that sort of attitude was pretty dated these days, among intelligent people, anyway.'

'Well, Robertson's doing his best to preserve it, along with all his other horrors.'

Tim said, 'I expect he'll come round. Most parents do.'

'I doubt it. He told his daughter that unless she stopped seeing me he wanted nothing more to do with her—ever. You can imagine how that upset her. The man's a weirdo, a tyrant, a monster. I'll bet when he was a boy he used to spend happy hours pulling the legs off spiders. But he is the only family Andrea's got.'

'What happened to her mother?' George asked.

'She and Robertson parted company when Andrea was a child. According to his story she died soon afterwards, but Andrea doesn't know whether to believe that.'

'That must have been about the time that Robertson came here.'

'Yes. I gather he bought the castle for a song when he came back from abroad.'

'Abroad?' Tim raised an eyebrow.

'Don't ask. All Andrea knows is that her father was in the army and left it in mid-career. He's always refused to talk to her about his former life. Oh well,' Ben shrugged, 'if he wants to sever his connection with his own flesh and blood, so be it. We've done our duty by coming here.' He drained his glass and stood up. 'I'd better go and see how Andrea is. Good-night to you both.' He moved languorously across the room and left, closing the door quietly behind him.

George broke the thoughtful silence that followed. 'So, Major, who do you reckon's behind this campaign?'

'I don't think "who" is our question. We've been hired to find out how. Someone is going to a lot of trouble to demonstrate to Robertson that he's not

121

secure—even in a ring-fenced castle in the middle of a pretty big pond.'

'Do you think whoever it is really intends to kill him or just put the wind up him?'

'I don't know, George. But whichever it is it's our job to stop him. I think we'd better go and have a good look at the dungeon now.' He stood up. 'But first...' He walked across to the draped parrot's cage and lifted the cloth. Apart from a couple of small feathers lying on its floor, the container was empty. 'Oh well, just a thought. Come on, George, let's see how our animal killer got in.'

The two men spent over half an hour prowling the nether regions of Lanner Castle. They established that Robertson's Chamber of Horrors was completely subterranean and that the only access was via the staircase from the hall. Tim spent some minutes examining the dead bird. Whoever had arranged the display had taken some trouble. He had used a loop of rope to attach the parrot's neck to the chain, obviously realising that metal would cut right through feathers, flesh and brittle bone. For much the same reason the lightest of the weights laid out on a table against the wall had been suspended from the bird's legs. Even so, one of the hip joints was already dislocated. The Roman numeral chalked on the flagged floor was drawn with clear, straight lines. Whoever had perpetrated this sick joke had had plenty of time to arrange everything precisely as he or she wanted. Perhaps it had been done during dinner.

George and Tim climbed the stone steps and looked closely at the door.

'Good lock, as mortices go, and it hasn't been forced,' George observed.

'According to Jenkins, he and his boss keep the only two keys.'

'That tells us nothing, Major. You or I could get in there in a matter of seconds. So could any experienced and well-equipped burglar.'

'We'd better recommend that this is added to the electronic locking system.'

'Yes, and they'll have to remove the main control panel. In fact, my first recommendation would be a security ops centre, manned round the clock by professionals. Then you can have cameras everywhere.'

'Concealed?'

'Preferably. And with image enhances for night-time.'

'How about a hush meter?'

'Why not? It could certainly cover all the central section of the castle—no one's supposed to be in there after the wings are locked at night.'

The hush meter was one of Lacy

Security's more recent technical developments, and had already proved popular with museums and galleries where it had been installed. It was a machine for measuring silence in empty rooms, such as exhibition galleries after closing time. It registered not only noise levels but the pattern of micro-sounds that give a particular silence its distinctive quality. Once set to that pattern the ultra-sensitive scanner detected any significant alterations to it and set off an alarm.

They made their way back to the drawing room.

'Hair of the dog, Major?' George waved the brandy decanter.

'Sure, it might help us to sleep. So, to recap—it looks as though we can make the place secure internally, even though it means subjecting everyone in the castle to almost constant surveillance.'

'If that's what the man wants, we can do it.' George handed Tim his glass, then stooped to put another log on the fire.

'What about outside?'

'Well, it shouldn't be necessary to add anything. The place is like Alcatraz already. The only way anyone could come in without being brought by Robertson's own transport is by air. That means helicopter. Hang-gliders are all very well in James Bond movies, but in reality, in a setting like this... No, chopper's the only way, and you can't get much less discreet than that.'

'Yet somebody got in.' Tim sipped his cognac thoughtfully. 'And if tonight's exhibition is part of the pattern he's still around.'

'You mean hiding in the castle somewhere?'

'There must be plenty of nooks and crannies.'

'It would be pretty difficult for someone to stay holed up here for weeks. And for what? If he was going to kill Robertson he'd have done it by now.'

'OK. But what's the alternative? Tonight's show must have been put on by a member of the castle staff or one of the guests.'

'No wonder our host was in a hurry to leave us. He must be a pretty worried man.'

'Oh, he's worried all right. That business with the parrot was a very real shock. I was standing close to him; I saw his reaction. I'll bet he's gone straight to his private suite, looked in the wardrobes and under the beds and locked himself in.'

George set his glass down and stretched his arms. 'There's nothing more we can do, is there?'

'No, we'd better get some sleep. To-morrow I want to look for some of those nooks and crannies.'

Back in his room minutes later, Tim had just begun to strip for bed when there was a light tap at his door. He threw a dressing gown round him and answered the knock. Steffy was standing there. She was still fully clothed but her dress was creased and her straight hair was tangled and tousled.

'Could I possibly come and talk to you?' Her eyes were downcast, all trace of the brash campaigner vanished.

CHAPTER 6

It took very little time for Ewen to verify what the other children had told him about conditions at Castle Huich. Apart from occasions, such as the visit of Colonel Campbell, when they were hidden away, they were kept working most of the daylight hours and locked up at night. Each morning they were brought a ration of bread, water and oatmeal which Aileen, as the oldest girl, doled out twice a day. Regular food, even though sparse, and somewhere dry to sleep meant a distinct improvement to life on the open moor, which was all Ewen could remember. But he would readily have swapped his present state for the uncertain freedom of the fugitive. The cold, grey confinement of his prison chilled his very soul. The automatic brutality of his jailers angered him. Duncan's soldiers were in no way like Campbell's. They did not talk with him or let him join in their games. On the contrary, they lashed out with fist or boot whenever he came in range.

He had his first taste of punishment during his second day on the island. He and another boy were sent to work in the soldiers' latrines, where a blockage had created a foul overflow. Ewen and a smaller lad called Will were given a bucket and a bowl and told to clear the mess. In the doorway of the room Ewen drew back, overwhelmed by the smell. Immediately a rough hand gripped his hair and dragged him, yelling, along a corridor. He was thrown into a room where a fat grey-haired soldier was sitting at a table playing cards with a colleague.

'This young rebel has just refused an order, Sergeant,' Ewen's captor announced.

The soldier was scrutinising his hand. He did not look up. 'First offence?'

'Yes, Sergeant.'

'A dozen lashes.'

Ewen was taken to the courtyard, where his custodian called out to a couple of friends to give him a hand. They marched Ewen to a low wall and stretched him across. One of the men held his arms, another pulled down Ewen's breeches. Then the first soldier took up a length of knotted rope and applied it with maximum force to the boy's buttocks. As he laid on each stroke the man provided his own incantation.. 'This...will teach...you...to do...as...you're...told...you ...scruffy...son of...a Highland...traitor.'

Ewen clenched his teeth hard as the pain shot deep into his body. Something even profounder than the anguish told him to remain silent and hold in the cry that reverberated round his head.

There was a flash of light in his mind, as though the torture had thrown wide a closed door. He had a vivid picture. A memory.

He held on to it as he stumbled away and resumed his work, and found that he could recall it at will. When not concentrating on his evil-smelling task or warily watching every soldier who came within striking or kicking distance, he explored it further. When, at day's end, he thankfully lay face-down on the straw, and eventually found the position least aggravating to his throbbing flesh, he focused his inner eye

128

on a sequence of images.

He saw a tall man with long, black hair standing over him. He held a broad leather belt in his hand, and he was saying, as the soldier had said, 'Ewen, you must learn to do as you're told.' But the words had a very different ring to them. They were not spoken with the Englishman's contempt and hatred. And the blows when they came were not as many, nor as hard. They were not laid on with the intention of inflicting the greatest possible pain. And they aroused very different feelings in Ewen. His father's punishment had provoked shame and tears of remorse. The soldier's brutal strokes drew resonances of resentful fury from the boy's psyche.

There was more in the unfolding vision. His father's explanation: 'When I set you to watch the animals I don't expect to see them away across the moor while you and your cousin wander off after rabbits.' Somewhere in the picture there was a woman, large and comforting, and a couple of older brothers and a familiar cottage interior. But people and places stubbornly refused to be allocated names. The part memories generated only an overwhelming sense of loss, and Ewen cried himself into sleep.

Tim opened the door wide for Steffy and

closed it behind her. 'Problems?'

'I hope you don't mind. I was lying in my room next door waiting for you to come up. I need to talk to someone but I can't think who. I don't suppose anyone can do anything for us.' She was clutching a large envelope nervously in both hands. 'But someone must do something about him.'

Tim led her to a chair. He poured a small brandy and held it out to her.

'Oh, I don't think...'

'Medicinal. It will help calm the nerves.' She sipped the spirit and winced.

'So, what can I do for you?'

'Well, it's not me really...it's Carol...'

'Does she know you're here?'

Steffy's eyes opened wide in alarm. 'No! And she mustn't. Promise me you won't tell her.'

'My lips are sealed. What sort of trouble is your friend in?'

She took a deep breath and began her story. 'Well, you know why we're here...'

'Last ditch effort to reach some agreement with Mr Robertson about the hydro-electric scheme.'

'That's right. Carol's masterminded the whole campaign—brilliantly. It's not easy, you know, keeping up pressure on the establishment. They have all the money and power and influence. Standing up to them—'

'I get the picture.'

'Well, fund-raising is a constant head-ache, as you can imagine. Well, about six months ago Carol received an offer of an anonymous donation of fifty thousand pounds.'

'Handy.'

'It was an absolute godsend. It came at a time when it seemed we'd have to call off the on-site action. The arrangement was that Carol was to meet a Mr Bradnish, the donor's lawyer, for lunch at a big hotel in Edinburgh. He wanted to know how we were going to use the money before he handed it over—at least, that was the story.'

'So what went wrong?'

'Absolutely nothing—then. Carol met up with this middle-aged Bradnish bloke and he seemed very charming and a bit stuffy the way lawyers are. He asked lots of questions, then said he was sure his client would be very happy that the money would be well employed. At the end of the meal he handed over a parcel containing one thousand fifty-pound notes. Carol came back to college as pleased as punch, and that evening we all went out for a celebratory drink.'

'But...there was a snag?'

'Yes, and today we found out what it was. We were a bit surprised that Robertson had asked to see us. We assumed we'd made such a nuisance of ourselves that he wanted to get us off his back.' She gave a cynical laugh. 'We couldn't have been more wrong. We were summoned to his presence this afternoon. But when we turned up, Robertson said he wanted to talk to Carol alone.'

'He didn't try to—'

'Oh, no. Nothing like that. Carol could have handled that. She teaches karate to a women's self-defence group. No, what he did was give her these.' Steffy handed over the envelope.

Tim extracted three black-and-white photographs and two letters. The prints showed Carol sitting at a table with a smartly dressed middle-aged man. In all the shots the subjects were smiling, with every suggestion of enjoying each other's company. In what was obviously the last of the short sequence the man was handing over a thick package. Tim smiled grimly. 'I think I begin to see the problem. This Bradnish character is a fake.'

'Oh, no. He's real enough. But he isn't a lawyer. He's on the board of Finian Construction, the main contractors for the hydro-electric scheme.' Steffy jumped up and stood quivering with anger. 'God, the plan was so simple and so clever. Bradnish telephoned Carol and set up a meeting. He asked her to confirm it in writing, and to tell nobody until the offer was actually confirmed. There's a copy there of Carol's letter.'

Tim read the brief, hand-written note on plain paper.

Dear Mr Bradnish,

Thank you for your telephone call and generous offer. I confirm our appointment for 12.30 on 21 June at the Royal Abbey Hotel, Edinburgh.

I look forward to discussing the situation with you then.

Yours sincerely, Caroline Sellis

Steffy continued her explanation. 'When Bradnish and his cronies received Carol's letter they concocted the reply. Of course, they never sent it. It was a complete fake.'

Tim picked up the sheet of copy paper headed with Finian Construction's logo. It was dated two days after Carol's letter.

Dear Ms Sellis,

Thank you for your letter.

I am delighted that you are amenable to a resolution of your organisation's dispute with this company, along the lines suggested in our telephone conversation.

You and your colleagues have made your protest with skill and tenacity but, as you now recognise, the time has come for pragmatic solutions. I look forward to our meeting on the 21st, when I am sure we shall be able to reach a mutually satisfactory conclusion.

Yours sincerely, J. H. Bradnish.

Tim sat back in his chair. 'As you say, simple and clever. This makes it appear that Carol was being bought off.'

'That's right. And they had someone at the hotel secretly taking pictures of Carol lunching convivially with the enemy and accepting a bundle of cash from him.'

Tim frowned. 'Hang on a moment. Presumably Carol paid the money into campaign funds.'

'Of course! Every penny!'

'Then I don't see the problem. That proves that she behaved honourably. In fact, she beat the enemy at their own game—continuing the protest with cash that they had tried to bribe her with.'

Steffy shook her head miserably and sank back into her chair. 'Oh, no. They're much too smart for that. Didn't you notice the receipt?'

Tim looked through the photographs and letters and finally discovered another sheet of paper in the envelope. It was a photocopy of a very simple typed document: 'Received with thanks from J. H. Bradnish, the sum of one hundred thousand pounds.' It was dated, and signed 'Caroline Sellis'.

'This is presumably a fake. Carol didn't really sign this?'

Steffy sighed. 'She doesn't know. She thinks she may have done.'

'What?'

'It was right at the end of the meeting. Bradnish had been very clever. He relaxed her, got her to talk about herself and her political activity. She thoroughly enjoyed the lunch. Then Bradnish handed over the money and she was euphoric. He told her she ought to check it. He made a joke of it—said it might be a bundle of old newspapers. She undid the packet and looked inside and saw lots of lovely money. While she was doing that Bradnish produced a receipt. Carol admits she didn't really look at what she was signing. Bradnish may have actually covered up the figure.'

'I see the amount is written out in full, not in numbers. Carol would have been less likely to notice the difference, I suppose.'

'She doesn't know. She thinks Bradnish may have done a swap somehow. She just can't remember. She's in a state of shock. She knew nothing about all this till today.'

'I presume Robertson waved all this at her and said, "Call off your protest or I go to the press." '

'Something like that. He insisted on seeing Carol alone. When she came out she was dazed. It took me a couple of hours to get the truth out of her.' Steffy looked at Tim imploringly. 'Can you suggest anything? Poor Carol's desperate. If she tried to tough it out and any of this stuff was published...well, it would mean the end of her university career. If she called off the campaign she'd have a lot of very difficult explaining to do.'

'And it would lend credence to the bribery allegation if it ever came out.'

Steffy's eyes opened wide in horror. 'You don't really think Robertson would publish anyway?'

Tim shrugged. 'It would be a pretty vindictive thing to do, but our host is not the most generous-minded of men.'

Steffy stumped. 'So the money men win again.'

'Possibly. If you call making enemies and going in fear of your life winning. I'd say he had more pressing things on his mind right now than persecuting your friend.'

'I suppose so. That business this evening

was horrible.' She shuddered. 'I gather it's not the first veiled threat Robertson's received.'

'You know about the others?'

'I know that a couple of his dogs were killed in similar ways.'

'How did you hear about that?'

'It's one of those bizarre tales that very quickly spreads. We have a group in Inverness who pick up any relevant information that comes to hand. I believe they got this story from someone who used to work here. All I can say is that I hope someone does bump Robertson off in his own torture chamber—odious, vicious bastard!' She shook her head. 'Wishful thinking! What do you think we ought to do, Tim?'

He stood up. 'I'll give it some thought. Perhaps I'll have a word with Robertson if I get a chance. Right now, the best thing is for everyone concerned to get some sleep.' He led Steffy to the door.

When Tim went to bed it was to slip rapidly into unconsciousness.

He was dragged from deep sleep by a roaring sound which his mind was reluctant to decode. For what seemed like several minutes he struggled, like a man underwater, to identify the noise. Was it in his head? In the room? Only when he was fully awake did he realise that it was coming from outside. At the same moment he knew what it was.

He rolled out of bed and stumbled to the window, stubbing a toe on the coffee table in the process. As he pulled back the curtain, he recoiled from the sudden glare of bright light. Lamps round the perimeter of the helicopter pad were fully on. The machine itself was already in the air. As Tim watched it climbed rapidly, turned and swung away in a southward arc across the loch.

He made his way cautiously back to bed. The digital display of his travelling clock registered 02.33. Someone was leaving at dead of night. Tim recalled George's conviction that anyone wishing harm to the owner of Lanner Castle could only come and go by helicopter. He wondered if he should check that Robertson was all right. He dismissed the thought. Everyone in the castle would have been woken by the chopper, including Jenkins. It was other people's responsibility to look after Robertson. Anyway, if someone had bumped off the Laird of Lanner...Tim slept once more.

Tim was late getting down to breakfast and found George in sole possession of the table. 'Morning, Major. You've missed all the action.'

Tim helped himself to food from covered dishes on a hotplate. 'So tell me about it.'

George came across to the sideboard. 'I suppose I'd better keep you company.' He helped himself to a second portion of bacon, sausage and scrambled egg. 'Well, Robertson's done a bunk and everyone else is following suit.'

Tim looked at his friend sharply. 'Robertson's gone? You're quite sure of that?'

'That's what Jenkins said. Apparently, his boss took off by helicopter in the wee small hours. You're not going to tell me you didn't hear the chopper take off?'

'Oh, I heard it all right. Saw it, too. But I didn't know who was in it.'

'Just Robertson, apparently, piloting himself.'

Tim sat down and started to eat, only realising as he did so how hungry he was. 'Where's he gone?'

'Jenkins either doesn't know or won't say.'

'And everyone else is leaving?'

'The majordomo delivered the news about half an hour ago. The others all decided that since our host has disappeared there wasn't much point hanging around. If you ask me, most of them couldn't get away fast enough, which is not surprising after last night's little drama.'

'Not to mention the run-ins some of them have had with Robertson.'

'You mean the engaged couple?'

'And the girls. Robertson made himself pretty unpleasant to them too.'

'I thought there was something up with them. They looked as though they hadn't slept a wink all night.'

'How are they all getting away? I haven't heard the chopper come back.'

'You obviously haven't looked outside this morning. It's been raining for several hours. Jenkins says most of the roads are clear. Staff have been laid on to get everyone to Inverness.'

'So where does that leave us?'

'Oh, we have our instructions, Major, relayed via Jenkins. We're to complete our survey and make a full report. But we're not to wait for the customer's response. He wants us to go ahead and do all the installation work without delay.'

'Regardless of cost?'

'Yes, seems we were right about him being a very worried man.'

'So, it looks as though he's gone into hiding until we can make this place virtually impregnable.' Tim got up and poured coffee from a flask on the hotplate.

'Dear God, what a life! Fancy being holed up here for the rest of your natural.'

'It's hard to believe he doesn't know who has it in for him. If someone started playing very unfunny games with me and was clever enough to get into my own home undetected I'd have a pretty shrewd idea of who it was.'

'Oh well.' George pushed away his plate and swallowed the last of his coffee. 'It's an ill wind... Friend Robertson has given us a blank cheque.'

'Then I suppose we'd better start earning our money. We've obviously got to cover every inch of this place. I suggest we start at the top and work down.'

They emerged into the hall to find the other guests assembling for departure. The students, as George had suggested, looked haggard. Tim drew Steffy to one side. He slipped a business card into her hand. 'It looks as though you've got a breathing space. I can't see Robertson doing anything about Carol for quite a while. Call me if you need any help.'

As Jenkins and the boatman collected up the luggage, Ben and Andrea came to say goodbye.

Ben held out his right hand. His left arm was firmly round his fiancée's shoulder and she looked as though she might collapse without it. 'It's been good to meet you and George. I wish we'd had more time to get to know each other.'

'Me, too. I'm afraid the last twenty-four hours have been very distressing for both of you.'

Andrea looked up at Tim. 'At least they've made me think. Sort a few things out. I've never understood him and I used to imagine that was my fault. Now I know that's not true. He doesn't want to be understood; doesn't want to be loved, admired. Doesn't want anything that I might be able to give. So there's no basis for a relationship, is there?'

George and Tim shook hands briefly with Hildegard Nefsky and Cal Lopez. Still something unidentifiable stirred in the murky depths of Tim's memory as he looked at the American. Still it refused to surface. Then the guests were gone and the security men set about their work.

They began in the attics, which covered the whole of the castle except the bastion. They were gloomy, lit by naked bulbs and littered with dust-covered clumps of long-abandoned furniture and household junk. They checked the trapdoors leading to the parapet and the doors giving access to the floors below. It was in the section of roof space at the north-east corner that they made an interesting discovery. George pointed out that the dust had been disturbed over quite a wide area.

Tim shrugged. 'Someone must have to

142

come up here sometime—plumbers if no one else.'

'Plumbers don't usually sleep on the job.' George pointed to a corner where an oblong area was virtually dust-free. He crouched beside it. 'I reckon someone's had a sleeping bag down here. And look at those.' He indicated a group of overlapping circular marks on the wooden floor, obviously made by a drinking vessel of some sort. 'Someone spent quite a time up here.'

Tim grinned. 'Well done, Sherlock.'

George ignored the taunt. 'It reminds me of that anti-terrorist stake-out we did in Kassel back in seventy-eight. The big house on the square—eight days and nights shut up in that stifling attic in the middle of summer. You must remember it.'

'Hard to forget it. We had to improvise screens hung from the rafters to keep the flies at bay. We died of thirst all day and only dared drink at night because we had to go outside to relieve ourselves. And people still think the SAS is exciting and romantic.' Tim walked over to a door in the opposite corner. 'This leads to the turret staircase, which goes right down to the kitchens and store rooms.'

'And what they laughingly call the security room. Once there, he could break into the electronic locking controls and go anywhere in the castle.'

'So we don't know how the intruder got here, but we do know how he operated once he was inside. That means we need electronic locks on all the attic doors and surveillance cameras covering them from the other side.'

'Got that, Major.' George added more notes to the clipboard he was carrying.

It took the rest of the day to check every room and corridor in the castle. Robertson's private quarters in the bastion were a further revelation of his paranoid obsession with security. They were a fortress within a fortress. Inside the two floors above the library and yellow drawing room the owner of Lanner Castle could have withstood a siege. The suite consisted of bedroom, bathroom, sitting room, gym, study and fully-equipped office, dining room and kitchen. An annexe off the gym housed a locked arms cupboard containing an impressive variety of rifles and handguns.

By dinner-time the work was almost completed, and over the meal they agreed to do a final check on the dungeon in order to be able to leave the following morning. They obtained the key from Jenkins and walked down the circular staircase.

It was only after they had spent

several minutes planning the location of surveillance cameras that Tim said, 'Something's wrong.'

George was standing on a bench and taking readings on a section of wall with a tape measure. 'How wrong, Major?' He did not look round.

'Different. Something's moved...or missing. Last night there was another contraption over here. Of course, Cumberland's Cradle! It's gone.'

George jumped down and stood beside him. Together they stared up at the steel hook in the ceiling from which the pride of the collection had been suspended.

II

DARKNESS VISIBLE

Farewell, thou fair day, thou green earth
    and ye skies
Now gay with the broad, setting sun.
Farewell loves and friendships, ye dear
    tender ties.
Our race of existence is run.

Robert Burns,
Oran an Aoig or *The Song of Death*

CHAPTER 7

February was a meteorological anticlimax. The first month of the year had raged with blizzards and storms. Hilly areas had been cut off by snow while, in other parts of Britain, low-lying regions had been coping with floods. But February began uncharacteristically mild and remained so.

Angus Logan had mixed feelings about the weather. It meant that he could keep a full complement of men and machines working on the new road, and with Finian Construction demanding daily progress reports that was vital. The reverse side of the coin was that the protestors were able to keep up their activities almost non-stop. Their numbers were never large, but they constantly changed their tactics and it was impossible to know from day to day where they would strike next. Sometimes they blocked the exit from the camp. Sometimes they packed the area where the excavators were trying to work. And there were days when they formed a chain across the junction of the Briachan road and the main A862 and turned back supply vehicles. Left to his own devices, Angus and a posse of picked men could have made short work of the long-haired, sloppy layabouts and effete liberal do-gooders, but the local news media had taken to keeping a watching brief on the Loch Huich situation. Twice some of his men had had to appear in court after running battles with the protestors, and that had led to some highly-coloured reporting in the press and on radio and television. Finian Construction had made it clear that they could do without that kind of publicity.

'All very well for them,' Angus muttered to himself as he drove his Range Rover through the camp gateway on a mid-February morning while the sun was still only a suggestion beyond the still-black hills, 'they're not pig in the middle. They want their road delivered on time but they're not prepared to help us with our problems. They won't even pay a decent share of the bill for police protection.' He replayed the mental tape of his meeting with Finian's senior management. They had assured him that they had the measure of the Save Glen Huich agitators. They spoke obliquely of behind-the-scenes action which would put a stop to the protests. That had been a couple of months ago and there was no sign of a let-up in mob intimidation. If it had not been for Mr

Robertson helping out with payments to the local constabulary, Angus knew that he would be much further behind schedule, facing penalties and bankruptcy.

Where the track petered out he headed down to the water's edge and drove towards the southern end of the loch. 'Oh, no!' From half a mile away Angus saw the glow of braziers, and knew that the troublemakers had set up pickets at the point where he wanted the graders to be working. He brought the car to a halt and grabbed up his mobile phone. He punched in a number and waited for his foreman to answer. 'Alan, hi! Change of plan! Our friends are down here. Get everyone to section three. We'll see if we can make that stretch ready for topping. Meanwhile, I'll go and talk with the great unwashed.'

Minutes later he pulled up in front of a Transit van and a battered old Ford, which had been made into a makeshift barrier across the entrance to a wide excavated area designated as the site for the dam construction offices. Wearily, Angus clambered from the vehicle.

A figure clad in a bobble hat and a shapeless knee-length sweater detached itself from the dozen or so people huddled round the brazier. 'Good morning, Angus.'

'Well, if it isn't Ms Sellis. I thought we'd

seen the last of you.'

'It takes more than your dirty tricks to get rid of me.' Carol smirked at her old antagonist.

'And just what is that supposed to mean?'

Carol gave a mocking laugh. 'Innocence doesn't suit you, Angus. I can't believe you weren't in on the machinations of your lords and masters.'

'You tell him, Carol!' A lank-haired individual of indeterminate sex shouted from the open window of the Transit.

Angus choked back the retort that came to his lips. He spoke with lowered voice. 'I don't know what you're on about and it doesn't really matter. Look...Carol...for heaven's sake let's stop these silly games and talk like intelligent grown-up human beings.'

'All I want to hear you say is that you and your men are getting into your foul-smelling lorries and going home.'

'And you know I'm not going to say it, any more than you're going to tell me you're calling off your demonstration. Look, let's—just for five minutes—drop the posturing and the insults on both sides, and talk.' He turned deliberately and walked slowly down towards the water. After a moment's hesitation Carol followed. Shapes, colours and textures were rapidly returning to the landscape as the sun surmounted the skyline. Angus stopped where a long slab of rock leaned out over the loch. Five metres below, rivulets bounced and splashed through granite channels in their haste to escape to the lower levels of the valley.

'So, what's on your mind?' Carol asked, coming up beside him.

Angus gazed moodily down into the water. 'You know perfectly well this dam will be built. The most you can hope to do is delay progress and put up costs.'

'And keep the issues of rural rape and exploitation in the public eye. Wild Britain is disappearing at an alarming rate. Someone has to tell the world about it.'

'Even the best publicity gimmick wears thin eventually. The media have got tired of Loch Huich. There hasn't been anything in the papers or on TV for weeks.'

'Oh, there will be.' Carol smiled mysteriously and stared across to the opposite shore.

'And what's that supposed to mean?'

'You'll see soon enough. You wouldn't really expect me to reveal my battle tactics in advance, would you?'

'Battle tactics, is it?' Angus scoffed. 'See yourself as some latter-day English general come across the border to put us poor Highlanders in our place, do

153

you? You come here trying to impose your crackpot ideas on people who don't want them—any more than we want the rubbish you and your scruffy so-called environmentally concerned friends leave strewn about the glen.'

Carol turned away. 'Oh, you're pathetic! Is that the best argument you can produce? We don't leave any litter. All our people are meticulous about—'

'I suppose you're going to tell me that that's not yours.'

'What?' She swung round to gaze in the direction of Angus's pointing finger. Something black and shiny was caught among the rocks below. It looked in the half-light like a large plastic sack tied round with rope.

Carol shrugged. 'Nothing to do with us.'

'Oh, really? Let's go and see, shall we?' Angus jumped from the rock and started down the heather-strewn slope.

'Oh, don't be so childish!' The young woman stood her ground for a moment or two but then reluctantly followed.

When she joined the tall man at the river's edge he was leaning out, trying to grasp the bundle. It obviously wasn't plastic: it only appeared to glisten because of the water flowing over it. Closer examination showed it to be made of cloth and girthed with thick metal rings.

'I can't get a good enough grip,' Angus muttered. 'Hold on to my belt so that I can use both hands.'

'Oh, this is ridiculous,' Carol protested, but she fastened her fingers through the leather and braced herself as Angus grasped the large, ungainly object.

It was heavy and well weighted with water, but it was also buoyed by the stream and, with a grunt, Angus was able to roll it over on to the flat rock at his feet.

The next instant he sprang back, recoiling into Carol, who almost fell.

'Good God Almighty...'

Carol stared past him. 'What is it?' For some seconds she could make no sense of the feral-bound mass of cloth, matted hair, protruding bone and decomposing flesh. Then her eyes widened and she opened her mouth in a hoarse, rasping scream.

As each miserable day at Huich Castle succeeded its equally dispiriting predecessor Ewen learned the knacks and skills of survival. He calculated the character differences of his captors; knew the soldiers to be avoided at all costs and those in whom indifference was more prevalent than malice. He kept his ears open and rapidly increased his understanding of English. His natural facility in this soon enabled him to surpass the ability of most of the children who had been longer in captivity, considerably enhancing his prestige in the tower. Ewen discovered that Duncan's men, believing the children to be mere Highland barbarians understanding nothing but their own outlandish Gaelic, would openly discuss news and gossip in their young prisoners' hearing. Ewen was thus able to pick up scraps of information, and was often summoned to the top floor to reveal intelligence gems to Ranald and Hector.

Some ten days after his arrival he had a fresh piece of news to convey. After the children had been shut in for the night he asked permission to report to the laird. The last light reached in through the narrow windows as Ewen stood in the gloaming before the dimly perceived figures of the two older boys.

'Well, what is it today?' Hector demanded, not altogether kindly. He was beginning to resent the attention this newcomer was receiving from the McCombies.

'Lots of the dogs are talking about someone important who's coming.'

Hector sneered. 'Oh, and did they happen to say who?'

Ewen wrinkled his nose in concentration.

'It's a man called "Highness" or "Cum-land".' He struggled to get his tongue round the harsh English sounds.

Hector laughed, but Ranald spoke quickly from the darkness. 'Do you mean his royal highness, the Duke of Cumberland?'

'Yes! Yes, that's it,' Ewen said eagerly. 'At least, I'm fairly sure that's it. He's the man in charge of their army, isn't he?'

'Aye.' Hector spat. 'He's the Butcher.'

Aileen's voice came out of the blackness. 'Ewen, the Duke of Cumberland is the one I told you about; the one the English king has sent here to destroy our people.'

Ranald added, 'He killed scores of our clansmen at Culloden and probably yours, too, if you could remember. And he's coming here...' He paused thoughtfully. 'Do you know when?'

'A couple of days, I think.'

'We must do something—but what?'

'Slit his throat,' Hector suggested.

'Aye, that'd be great.'

'And we'd all have our throats cut in revenge—every one of us.' Aileen came forward and sat cross-legged on the floor beside her brother.

'But we must do something,' Ranald objected. 'Father used to say that the day he found himself within a musket ball's length of Cumberland would be the

157

Butcher's last. If we're going to be that close to him we ought to do something.'

'Who says we'll get that close, Ranald? We'll be shut away here out of sight as we always are when Duncan has important visitors.'

But in this she was wrong. Two days later they were not roused for work at dawn as usual. In fact, the day was well advanced before the tower door was opened and a group of soldiers swaggered in.

'Right, strip off, the lot of you,' a red-faced sergeant ordered and, in case the children had not understood, he grabbed the nearest—a girl of eight or nine—and in one movement ripped the thin dress from her body.

When they had undressed, the soldiers tied a length of rope to the wrist of each one. The captives were led, shivering, across the courtyard and through a gateway leading to the edge of the rocks. There was a drop of some three metres to the loch. Laughing, the soldiers hurled them into the deep, cold water, keeping hold of one end of each line. They used the ropes to dip the children in and out of the lake. The younger ones spluttered, choked and gasped. Some cried out, and that only prolonged the experience. At last they were hauled out, taken back to the courtyard and ordered to run around and get dry. As they circuited the open space they were encouraged by the soldiers with the flats of their swords.

When the men had tired of their fun, the sergeant called Aileen over and thrust a bundle of clothes into her arms. 'See they're all dressed up decent. We've got company today and you're all to be on parade.' As an afterthought he added, 'And you'd better do something about their hair. Simkins!' He shouted to one of his men. 'Find a comb and some scissors.'

Back in the tower, away from the jeers and laughter, the children put on their new garments—grey-white linen smocks. Most of them were too large, but Aileen trimmed them with the scissors and used the lengths of cloth cut off to make belts. By the time she had tended their straggling locks they were transformed from grubby urchins into clean and tidy urchins.

Around the middle of the day Ewen was lying in his bed space, wondering what would happen next, when he heard raised voices from the floor above.

'I said, give me the scissors, Aileen.'

'Ranald, no! You mustn't! It's too dangerous—for all of us.'

'Don't tell me what to do, girl. I'll not have the Butcher here and not try to avenge my father's death.'

There were the sounds of a brief struggle, then Aileen came down the ladder and descended quickly to the ground floor without a word.

A little later, three red dogs came to take the children to the main building. They were put into a small sitting room and made to stand in a line. Within minutes Duncan himself came to inspect them. He moved along the rank, prodding and tweaking. Then he stood facing them and spoke through an interpreter.

'Today you're to have a privilege you don't deserve. His royal highness, the Duke of Cumberland, the victor of Culloden, has asked to see you for himself. Since you little savages know nothing of the civilised world I'll explain to you just who this great man is: he is the son of George the Second, by the grace of God King of England, Ireland, Wales and Scotland—*your* king. You will, therefore, pay his royal highness the respect you would give to the king himself. If he asks you about your treatment here you will tell him that you are well looked after. If you don't you'll suffer for it later. Remember that his royal highness will decide what's to become of you, so it will pay you to try to behave like civilised, Christian human beings.'

After Duncan the Red had left, the children had another long wait. The light beyond the window panes steadily weakened. Through the door could be heard the muffled sounds of men's voices talking and laughing, the clink and rattle of silver and glass. Ewen and his companions sat around, hungry and listless. Three of the younger ones curled up together in a corner and slept.

At last the door opened. The red-faced sergeant ordered them to get to their feet.

He lined them up and peered at each in turn. He was followed by two soldiers who draped strips of tartan cloth round each young shoulder and thrust wooden swords and round shields fashioned from wood and paper into the children's hands.

They were led into the hall where Ewen had first seen Duncan o'Strathfarrar. Now a long trestle table had been set up, running most of the length of the room. Duncan's officers ranged along each side in their scarlet braided uniforms and powdered wigs. The remains of the meal they had enjoyed still littered the board but were being rapidly cleared by servants. At the head of the table sat a fat, perspiring man in his mid-twenties who Ewen realised must be Butcher Cumberland.

Duncan, seated at his right hand, called for silence. 'And now, your Highness, I'd like to present all that remains of the army of Charles Edward Stuart.'

He gave a signal, and one at a time the children were lifted on to the table and instructed to parade along its length. They shuffled forward while the men on either side laughed, clapped and prodded them with knives to keep them on the move.

Cumberland roared his appreciation of the joke. 'My, what a fearsome body of warriors! I declare I quake in my boots, Alan.'

Duncan led the laughter at the royal jest. 'I warrant you're safe enough from this rabble, your Highness. They've not the stomach for another Culloden.'

'I've heard the Highlanders are great dancers,' the duke observed. 'Will Bonnie Prince Charlie's men not give us a dance?'

'Aye, that they will, your Highness. Come on, you heathen scum, dance for his royal highness.'

One of Duncan's aides translated the order, and all along the table the officers beat with their fists on the oak and chanted, 'Dance, dance, dance!'

Awkwardly and self-consciously the boys and girls hopped and skipped an unco-ordinated jig, while their laughing audience shouted, 'Faster! Higher!'

Ewen noticed that Ranald and Hector were working their way towards the top of the table. They reached a point little more than a couple of metres from the guest of honour. Then Ranald shouted, 'Now!'

The boys tugged up the hems of their smocks. Ewen saw that each had one blade of the dismantled scissors strapped to his leg. They grabbed these improvised knives, and with screams of rage leaped at Cumberland.

George Martin heard about the discovery of Robertson's body when he went to the Briachan Inn for lunch. Two-and-a-half weeks after he and Tim had completed their initial survey and gone back to their Wiltshire base, he and a team of three from Lacy Security returned to Lanner Castle to carry out the installation of new equipment. His men had even less stomach than he for Robertson's macabre collections, and took every opportunity to get away. They had quickly fallen into the habit of slipping across to the mainland in the middle of the day for a pint and one of Mary's generous pub lunches. Though for Johnny Price, one of the firm's young computer whiz-kids, the cook was a greater attraction than the food.

It was Johnny who, on this Wednesday lunchtime when the launch was half-way to the shore, pointed to the cluster of buildings ahead. 'Something seems to be up.'

Several people were gathered in groups and three police vehicles were drawn up in front of the hotel. When the visitors entered the bar they found it well filled with locals and strangers, some of them in police uniforms. The atmosphere was that unique mix of hushed shock, excitement and curiosity that pervades crowds at road accidents and fires. George looked round for someone to question. Tam was at one end of the bar holding forth to a cluster of open-mouthed tourists in hiking gear. Angus was deep in conversation with a police sergeant, and there were half a dozen other members of the construction gang. George was surprised to see Carol and Steffy sitting at a corner table with a couple of uniformed women, one of whom seemed to be taking down a statement.

He saw the landlord's daughter enter the room through a doorway behind the bar and hurried across to her, his colleagues following. 'What's up?'

'Oh, George, it's terrible, terrible! Mr Robertson...he's been...killed.'

'Killed? How?'

'They found him this morning. Well, Angus and Carol did, in the loch.'

George brushed aside the incongruity of the construction boss and his declared enemy being together. 'He was drowned, then?'

Mary shook her head firmly. 'No, no... That's what makes it so awful. He was...well...trussed up. He was in one of those dreadful torture things. Apparently he was rolled up like a bundle of laundry...all pressed together.' She shuddered. 'Oh, it must have been horrible.'

George stared at her, images rushing through his mind. 'Do you mean they found him in the Cumberland's Cradle?'

'That's what Carol seemed to think— only, she's so badly shocked she could be wrong.'

George looked thoughtful. 'Well, that figures. The cradle was stolen from the castle last time we were here.'

Mary's eyes opened wide. 'Stolen? I didn't know. No one knew. Are you sure?'

'Oh yes. It was after Robertson had taken off suddenly in the middle of the night. At least, I suppose... Well, we—the Major and I—we found it missing and told Jenkins. Beyond that, it was none of our business.'

'It must have been a terrible shock.' Johnny gazed sympathetically into Mary's eyes and casually placed a hand over hers as it rested on the counter.

She smiled faintly at him and did not shrink from the advance. 'It would be hypocritical to say that I liked the man. I never really knew him. No one round here did. But to die...like that. Father says he's not surprised. Three people claim to have seen the lost ones recently. He believes that spells doom. In my opinion it spells too much whisky. Oh, George, who can have done such a thing?'

'Presumably, whoever stole the cradle.'

'Yes, of course. Yes, it must have been. George, you ought to tell Inspector Thompson about that.'

'He's in charge of things, is he?'

'That's right. He's the one with the beard over in the corner, talking to two other plain-clothes men.'

'Right you are. Well, if Johnny here can let go of you long enough for you to pull me a pint, I'll go and have a word.'

Mary blushed and drew her hand away as though someone had poured scalding water over it.

When George had his beer he made his way across the crowded room to the group standing by the outer door. Thompson was a short man who exuded energy. He was rattling off instructions to two subordinates who were having trouble keeping up with him. George waited for a pause in the flow and then introduced himself.

The inspector scanned him with dark eyes that probed from beneath an over-hanging thatch of thick brows. When he spoke it was with a Tyneside accent. 'Got

166

something for me then, Mr Martin?'

'Possibly. Well, it might help you build up a picture. I gather Mr Robertson was found inside one of his own torture implements; something known as Cumberland's Cradle.'

Thompson remained poker-faced. 'We haven't released details yet. We haven't even identified the body officially. Suppose you just tell me what you know.'

'OK. I was staying at Lanner Castle when Robertson did a bunk.'

'Did what?'

'Well, let's just say he made a speedy and unscheduled departure in the middle of the night, since when he hasn't been in touch with his people at the castle. At the same time that he left, Cumberland's Cradle went missing from his collection. Either he took it with him, or—'

'Exactly when was this?' Thompson fastened terrier-like on the new evidence.

'The end of last month. To be precise, Robertson took off in the small hours of the twenty-ninth. We discovered the torture implement missing the following evening.'

'You said you were here upgrading the deceased's security system. I take it from that that he was concerned about the protection of himself and his property.'

'Not concerned, Inspector—obsessed.'

'Did he give you the impression that he thought someone was out to kill him?'

'He certainly believed he was being threatened. And he put on a convincing Howard Hughes act. He made it very difficult for anyone to get to him. Even his own daughter was here by appointment. And there was a lot he wasn't telling us. Oh, and one more thing—despite all Robertson's precautions, someone unauthorised did get into the castle.'

'Who was that?'

George shrugged. 'Search me. Me and the Major found evidence in the attic.'

'Major?'

'My boss, Major Lacy'

'Well, Mr Martin, this all sounds very interesting. You'd better make a full statement. I'll get someone to take it down. Charlie...' He turned to one of his subordinates. 'See to that, will you?' Directing his attention back to George, he said, 'I'd better have a word with Major Lacy, too. Is he here?'

'No, he's back at HQ in Wiltshire. I'll give you his number and warn him you'll be calling.'

'I'd be grateful if you would.'

'No problem. I'll have to call him anyway, to let him know we no longer have a client.'

'OK, but only give him the bare facts. I don't want this story getting out till I'm ready with the official version. This is the sort of case the media dirt-dishers and sensation-mongers just love: "The Body in the Loch; Millionaire Recluse in Torture Drama; Murder Visits Jinxed Dam Site". They'll soon be here writing their crack-brained copy and trying to dig out every bizarre detail.' He suddenly raised his voice and called for everyone's attention. 'I won't have anyone talking to the media. Is that understood?' He glared round the room. 'They'll be here soon, swarming all over the place, asking for interviews, flattering you with their attentions, pointing cameras and microphones at you, waving chequebooks for all I know. Well, you keep quiet and you refer them to me. That goes particularly for those of you who are looking for publicity.' He stared at the little group gathered round Carol. 'This is police business and police business only. I won't have it fouled up by anyone with a private agenda or a passion for seeing himself on the telly. Thank you, ladies and gentlemen.' He turned back to his companions, muttering under his breath, 'Not that that little speech will do any good. This thing will be all over the media by tonight and on the front page in every national paper tomorrow.'

He was wrong.

CHAPTER 8

The odd thing about what happened next was that nothing happened next.

By early afternoon the police seemed to have completed their scene-of-crime investigations. The body had been taken away and most of the official vehicles left Briachan. Thompson commandeered one of the castle launches and crossed to the island. He interviewed Jenkins and set some of his men to go painstakingly through all Robertson's papers. He inspected the dungeon and it was as he was emerging again into the hall that he met George.

'Right, Mr Martin, I'm ready now to have a look at this find you made in the attic.'

They set off up the stairs, but at that moment Jenkins appeared. 'Telephone call for you, Inspector. You can take it in the library.'

George waited in the hall. He waited a long time. When Thompson did reappear his whole body was throbbing with anger. 'Carter!' he bellowed. The roar brought a young man running from an adjacent room. 'Carter, round everyone up. We're

170

leaving—now!'

The inspector stood in the middle of the hall, hands thrust deep into overcoat pockets, breathing heavily.

'Problems?' George ventured.

'Don't ask. I'll probably say something I shouldn't.'

George ignored the instruction. 'You're interrupting your investigation here, then?'

Thompson glowered back silently but eventually could not contain himself. 'Not interrupting—cancelling. Apparently, the local constabulary is not deemed competent enough to handle this case. "Too sensitive"—that's the expression my lords and masters choose to use. You know what that means, don't you? Politics. The mysterious Mr Robertson had friends, associates, interests that someone doesn't want us to know about. Mr Plod is all very well for probing the deaths of toms, pushers and assorted low life, but when it comes to victims with contacts in high places up go the "Keep off the Grass" signs. My God...' The murmur of voices indicated the approach of the inspector's colleagues. Without another word he strode from the castle.

Minutes later, George phoned Farrans Court to report the latest development to his boss.

Tim received the news stoically. 'There's

no point hanging around there, George. We've wasted enough man-hours at Lanner Castle. Best pack up everything and make your way back home.'

The Lacy Security team arrived at Farrans the following evening.

Tim was annoyed. A project he had never wanted to get involved in had turned out to be a complete waste of time. And money. There was no guarantee that the firm would be compensated for the hours of work put in or the aborted order. Through Jenkins, Tim obtained the name of Robertson's Edinburgh solicitor, a Mr Macrae. He was polite, understanding—and vague. If Mr Lacy would submit his account to the executors—his firm—it would be considered when their late client's estate was settled. No, he could not say when that was likely to be. Mr Robertson had died a wealthy man with a variety of business interests. Setting everything in order would, inevitably, take time.

Yet what aggravated Tim more than the 'law's delay' was the knowledge that Cumberland's Cradle had been stolen under his very nose. It was embarrassing that, while the leading executives of Lacy Security had actually been on the spot, engaged in upgrading the protection of the castle's contents, a valuable and rare item had gone missing. It was possible—probable—that Robertson himself had taken it, though Jenkins was adamant that he had made no mention of doing so, and that it was uncharacteristic of him to remove anything from the collection without informing staff concerned. Even so, the incident had to go down in the files as unfinished business. And Tim Lacy hated loose ends.

For several days he searched the papers and watched TV newscasts in the hope of learning more about the murder investigation, but the passing of Mr Robertson, Laird of Lanner, received not the slightest mention. There could only be one explanation for the failure of such a bizarre, sensational, circulation-boosting homicide to receive media coverage. As Thompson had indicated, the story was being suppressed for political reasons. Slight confirmation of that came from Johnny Price. His feelings for Mary McFadden were strong and seemingly reciprocated. Most evenings they spoke to each other on the phone. Johnny relayed the information that the police had not been back, but that there had been several helicopters going to and from the castle. None of the visitors had called at the inn. Most of the staff had been dismissed with generous severance pay, but the Jenkinses were staying on for the time being. No one knew what was going to happen to the castle. Since many people in Briachan and nearby villages were dependent on the estate in one way or another, there was considerable local concern.

Other events and preoccupations gradually pushed the unpleasant Scottish business to the back of Tim's mind. It was a week after Easter when it was brought to the fore again. He had spent a couple of days in Portugal with a new client and was going through his messages with Sally, his secretary.

'Andrea Robertson phoned yesterday morning,' she said.

Tim looked blank. 'Who?'

'Andrea Robertson—the Scottish fiasco.'

'Oh, yes, of course. What did she want?'

'She wondered whether you could meet her in London next time you're there. She seemed very anxious to see you. I said you'd call.'

'Better do it now, then. Find out what she wants.'

But when Andrea came on the line she was determinedly uninformative. 'Thank you very much for calling, Tim. I hope you don't mind me getting in touch. I couldn't think of anyone else to turn to.'

'What's the problem?'

'I don't want to talk about it over the

phone. Could we meet? Lunch, perhaps?'

Tim consulted his diary and they made an appointment.

Two days later they met in an Italian restaurant close to Andrea's Whitehall office. Tim arrived to find her sitting at a quiet corner table, which because of the geography of the room was separated from its more crowded neighbours. She was dressed in efficient, well-tailored navy blue, which emphasised her pallor.

As he sat down Tim said, 'I'm terribly sorry about your father. It must have been a horrible shock for you.'

Andrea nodded gloomily 'It would be silly to pretend that we were close or that we parted on good terms. You were there, Tim. You know we had a dreadful row. That's what makes it worse. He was horribly rude to Ben and I lost my temper with him and we both said things we didn't mean. It ended up with him disowning me. We'd had arguments before—though never as bad as that one—but we'd always patched them up. I know he'd have come round in time. But he never had time, did he?' She lowered her eyes and quickly tugged a handkerchief from her jacket pocket.

'It'll take a while but you'll get over it.' Tim could think of nothing better to say. Counselling the grief-stricken was not his forte.

'But I can't get over it. They won't let me!' Andrea almost sobbed the words.

A waiter appeared and they ordered food. The interruption gave the sophisticated young civil servant a chance to recover her composure.

'Look, perhaps we ought to talk about something else,' Tim offered. 'It's not good to brood.'

Andrea responded abruptly, her dark curls catching the light as she looked up. 'No, we must discuss this wretched business. That's why I wanted to see you.'

'OK. You said "they" wouldn't let you get over your father's death. Who did you mean?'

'I'd better start at the beginning. The first thing that happened was that I received a phone call at work late one afternoon. I know now that it was the day my father's body was discovered. The caller gave his name as Hatherton and asked me to come and see him straight away in the Foreign Office building. I walked round there, assuming that he wanted to discuss some inter-departmental matter. There were two of them in the office when I got there—Hatherton, who was elderly, tall and grey-haired, and a younger, rather smarmy man called Smythe. Hatherton broke the news to me. He was very kind and sensitive. He said that my father had died, quite suddenly. When I asked how, he said the doctors hadn't decided yet, but without actually saying so he intimated that it was a heart attack or something like that.'

'He obviously wanted to spare your feelings. He knew the truth would be too much of a shock.'

'That's what Ben said. He was in Nigeria, and I told him about it as soon as he got back. But I don't think Hatherton and Smythe had my best interests at heart. They wanted information, and they were trying to make sure I wasn't too distressed to provide it coherently.'

'What sort of information?'

'They started firing questions at me. What did I know about my father's business? How much had he told me about his earlier life? Did I remember anything about my mother? They wanted to know pretty well everything about our relationship. While they were doing that I was trying to find out about the practicalities of the situation—funeral arrangements, that sort of thing.'

'And I suppose they said they would take care of all those details.' Tim was beginning to see a pattern that was not altogether unfamiliar.

'Not exactly. They said they'd let me know when I could go to Scotland to organise things. And that's the last I heard from them. When I got on to the FO a few days later they denied all knowledge of Hatherton and Smythe. That was when I began to panic. I called everyone I could think of. Jenkins at the castle was politely unhelpful. Father's solicitors couldn't or wouldn't tell me anything I wanted to know. They hinted at "slight problems" over probate, but assured me that everything would be sorted out in time and that, as the principal beneficiary, I would be "a very rich young woman"—as if I give a damn about that.' She paused as the waiter returned with their food.

'So, are you saying that you still don't know the circumstances of your father's death?'

Andrea shook her head. 'No. Eventually I got on to the McFaddens, the people at the inn. Mary was horrified that I hadn't been told the facts but she couldn't bring herself to tell me over the phone. She wrote me a long letter explaining everything—or as much as she knew. You can imagine what a shock that was—my father murdered, and in such a way. I keep seeing that wretched contraption hanging in the dungeon and hearing him explain how it was used...trying to imagine...'

'Don't try to imagine such horrors. It doesn't do any good.'

'I can't help it!' She pushed her plate away, the food virtually untasted. 'If I stop myself thinking about it I only wake up in the small hours with the most ghastly nightmares. Ben is sweet, but I know he's getting fed up with what he calls my "obsession". It's affecting our relationship. But, Tim, what can I do?' Andrea sobbed the question and pressed her handkerchief to her eyes. 'What was my father involved in? What sort of a man was he? Why did someone hate him enough to kill him...like that? Who killed him? It's the not knowing, the mystery, the shadows, the horrors that may still lurk in that godawful, gloomy castle. How can I even begin to grieve...?'

Tim watched her fighting back the tears. 'Unfinished business,' he muttered.

'That's right.' She looked up with glistening eyes. 'You will help me, won't you? I racked my brains to think of someone who might be able to get at the truth. Then I remembered that evening at the Briachan Inn, and you and George talking about unofficial investigations you've been involved in. You know people in high places...and low places. People who'll tell you things they won't tell me.'

Tim leaned across the table to hold the distraught woman's hand. 'I'll do whatever I can—on one condition.'

'What's that?'

'That you eat your lunch.'

Andrea managed a weak smile. 'You *will* help? You'll find out—'

'I said I'll do whatever I can. But I don't want you building up too much hope. If powerful people are putting out a smokescreen, my chances of penetrating it are not very good. All I can say is that I'll give it my best shot.'

She gave his hand a squeeze. 'Oh, thank you so much, Tim. I feel better already.'

'Good.' Tim smiled encouragingly. And wondered if he had done the right thing.

Cumberland threw up an arm to shield himself from the attack. He deflected Hector's blow, which grazed his bulbous neck and drew blood. Twisting sideways, he toppled from his chair and lay sprawled on his back like a helpless beetle. Ranald, unbalanced by his useless arm, stumbled as he jumped down to get close enough to strike and was gripped by powerful hands.

Duncan was on his feet, shouting in incoherent rage. All the children were pulled from the table and held firmly. Duncan and his son helped the duke

180

to his chair and fussed around him, but Cumberland waved them aside. Alistair handed him his wig, which had fallen off, and the prince arranged it carefully over his cropped hair.

'It seems that treason is in the very blood of these Highlanders, Alan,' he said slowly, regaining his composure.

'Yes, your Highness. There's only one way of dealing with them; only one thing they understand.'

'So I have found, so I have found.' Cumberland dabbed a kerchief at the blood oozing from the scratch on his neck. 'Who are these two would-be assassins?'

Duncan provided the names and explained that their fathers had both fallen at Culloden. 'They'd have been there, too, if they'd been old enough, make no mistake.' Alistair intervened. 'There are those, like James Campbell, who believe these young louts can be reformed civilised, turned into Scottish gentlemen. Your Highness has now seen for yourself that they're animals. That's true of them all, every one of them. I say we get shot of them, dump them all in the loch.'

'Whisht, Alistair.' His father silenced the bellicose youth. 'His royal highness needs no advice from us.' He turned to Cumberland. 'My apologies for this murderous attack. What are your orders?'

The duke sat back, arms folded in front of him, his pose of judicial solemnity marred by the red stain spreading along his neckband. 'I've much sympathy with your son, Alan, but as you know I'm a man inclined to mercy. I'd rather use this incident to teach these children a lesson. The king requires loyal subjects, not dead ones. In the morning we'll string up these two assassins in front of their friends. That should deter them from future treason.'

'A wise decision, your Highness.' Duncan was intensely relieved that reprisals were to fall upon the perpetrators and that he was not to be taken to task for his failure to protect his general.

The duke nodded. 'Have one of your men explain my decision to the brats in their own outlandish tongue.'

The verdict was recited in Gaelic.

'No!' Aileen broke away from the soldier holding her. Cumberland shrank back in his chair as the girl threw herself at his feet. She struggled to find the English words she needed. 'Highnesss...Highness...please! They...boys...stupid boys. Not kill them... please, Highness...*please!*'

'Who is that creature?' the Duke demanded as Aileen was dragged away.

'She is the fair-haired boy's sister.' Duncan replied.

'Same murderous brood, eh? Well, you'd

182

better hang her too. The sooner that line comes to an end the better.'

Hector and the McCombies were dragged away to the cells. The other children were returned to the tower.

Ewen slept little that night. He burrowed himself into the straw, faced the wall, and tried to close his ears to the whimpering and sobbing coming up from the floor below.

At first light they were all dragged outside and marched into the courtyard between two lines of armed soldiers. Mist-laden air rolling across the loch curled clammy fingers around Ewen's bare arms and legs, but it was not the cold that made him shiver. The scaffold at one end of the courtyard was a permanent structure. The remaining three sides were fronted by troops. The whole garrison had been turned out to witness the execution, though of the Duncans and the duke there was no sign.

Somewhere out of sight a side drum began a slow beat. A corner door opened and another double file of soldiers emerged. Between them Ewen saw his three friends. They stumbled out into the open, manacled to each other by chains fastened to rings round their ankles. But these restraints alone did not explain their unsteady steps. The white garments they still wore from the night before were streaked with blood. Ewen realised what that meant. For Duncan the Red, death was not enough. Three children had severely embarrassed him, and for that they had had to pay.

Ewen was terrified by what he was witnessing, yet curious too. He was impatient at the preliminaries, which seemed to take a long time. The prisoners had their fetters removed and were pushed up the ladder to the platform. There, the red-faced sergeant was in charge. He spent what seemed several unnecessary minutes adjusting the nooses and making sure that the condemned were standing in exactly the right place. Then he climbed down and marched across to report to the duty officer.

The latter raised his sword and the monotonous drumbeat changed to a roll. Ewen looked at the girl who had befriended him in this dreadful place. She stood, head erect, staring straight before her, lips moving in what was probably a prayer. Ranald, whom Ewen had called laird, sagged, head lowered. Only Hector gazed around him, defiant to the last. 'God for King Charles!' he shouted in the last moment of his life. Then the sword flashed downwards. There was a thud as a soldier behind the platform pulled the lever operating the trapdoor. The three bodies jerked into space, writhed for a few seconds, then hung limp, swaying gently to and fro.

And that sight battered down the last guardian door of memory. Suddenly, with sickening clarity, Ewen knew exactly who he was and how his journey to this place had begun.

The Lacys kept a small Westminster flat in a road off Great Smith Street, and it was from there that Tim made a call straight after his lunch with Andrea Robertson.

'Hello, Tiger. I'm in town for the day and I seem to recall you boasting about knocking spots off me at squash. Do you want to put your racquet where your mouth is?'

His friend laughed. 'Any time, though I do feel a bit guilty about humiliating older men. My club, six-thirty? I'll book a court.'

When he and Aubrey Maximian met for their game that evening Tim, while not exactly letting his opponent win, certainly made it easier for him to do so. He wanted Tiger in as cheerful and relaxed a mood as possible. By the time they had showered and downed a couple of whiskies in the club bar the younger man was well mellowed. They sat beside a simulated log fire on well-worn leather chairs as the room filled with dark-suited men just escaped from their boardrooms and counting houses.

Tim eased the conversation in the intended direction. 'That Scottish job your boss set up for me at the end of last year turned out to be a dud: the customer died on me before he could pay his bill.'

'Yes, I did hear something of the sort.' The young politician was deliberately vague. 'Rotten luck.'

'You'll have to do better than that.' Tim stared unblinkingly at his companion. 'You've indirectly caused me a lot of expense and a lot of aggro, and all you can say is "rotten luck"?'

Aubrey looked uncomfortable. 'What more do you want me to say?'

'Some sort of explanation would be a good start. You nearly bust a gut getting me to take on the odious Mr Robertson. Why was it so important to your boss? If I could be persuaded that my sacrifice was in the national interest I might feel a bit less sore about it.'

'It was just a favour for a friend of the minister. I thought I'd explained that.'

'You did, Tiger, you did. I didn't believe you then and I sure as hell don't believe you now.'

'That's not very nice, Tim...'

'What you did to me wasn't very nice. But leaving that aside, I'll give you five reasons why your explanation won't wash. Number one: I met Jack Robertson and I very much doubt whether he had friends, ministerial or otherwise. Number two: the man was an illicit arms dealer.'

'No! Impossible!' Maximian looked genuinely shocked.

'Yes, very possible. While my colleague and I were there Robertson had a visitor, a man calling himself Cal Lopez. His face was familiar but I couldn't place it. It haunted me for weeks. Recently I was looking through an old file and there he was, his photograph in a cutting from an American newspaper. Only the name in the caption wasn't Lopez—it was Lombardo, Carlos Lombardo. Then it all came back to me. I had some brief dealings with him six years ago. He wanted Lacy Security to set up systems in a prestigious museum of national heritage he was sponsoring. I turned him down. I didn't fancy being paid with money that had come from arms and drug trafficking.'

'How did you know...'

'That Lombardo was an international criminal? I make it my business to find out. A lot of the money that gets invested in the world's most precious and beautiful things—the sort of things I'm hired to

187

protect—has dubious origins. I like to know who I'm dealing with. If I took on every millionaire who approaches me I could find myself involved with stolen art, money laundering, high-level fraud, to mention but a few. You can take it from me, Lombardo is a wrong 'un.

'So, on to number three: Robertson was murdered—in a particularly gruesome way. And before you ask me how I know, I'll tell you: my men were working at Lanner Castle when the body was found. Number four: when the body *was* found the local police were warned off within hours. Now doesn't all that suggest to you that something out of the ordinary is going on?'

'Not necessarily. There could be—there is—a perfectly simple reason for each of these facts you seem to find so sinister.' Ostentatiously, Tiger looked across at the imposing long-case clock in the corner of the room. 'Well, I really must be going.' He stood up. 'Thanks for the game, Tim. You'll have to get some practice in before the return match.' He began to steer a course between the groups of chairs.

Tim called out, 'Why is Special Branch involved?'

Maximian stopped dead as though he had walked into a glass wall. He turned and returned quickly to his seat. 'For

God's sake keep your voice down, man. What on earth are you talking about?'

'I said I had five reasons for disbelieving the official version of events. Number five: Special Branch—in the guise of two non-existent FO civil servants—have been making themselves unpleasant to Robertson's daughter.'

'What makes you think they were Special Branch?'

Tim's patience gave way. 'Oh, for goodness sake, Tiger, let's stop this ridiculous cat and mouse game! Something pretty unsavoury is going on and I've got caught up in it. So has Andrea Robertson, and it's ruining her life. Now either you know what all this is about or you know a man who does!'

'Do stop making such a row, Tim.' Aubrey glanced around at the quizzical and disapproving faces turned in their direction. 'Your bloodhound instinct will be the death of you. Once you've got your teeth into something you don't let go, do you?'

'That's what terriers do, not blood-hounds.'

'Don't be bloody facetious!' Maximian's brow was moist with anger and anxiety. 'I'll tell you enough to warn you off, Tim, and if you don't take the hint...' He left the threat unfinished. 'Yes, we were interested in Robertson's activities.'

'Interested enough to put a stop to them—permanently?'

'Don't be stupid! The Foreign Office don't go round staging bizarre assassinations.'

'But you know the sort of people who do?'

'We don't know who murdered Robertson but we're trying to find out. And we don't need other people getting in the way. We will find the people responsible, and when we do we'll take the appropriate action. Then Miss Robertson will be able to sleep easy in her bed.'

'Are you suggesting she's in some kind of danger?'

'We can't rule out that possibility. But she is under discreet observation.'

'Well I hope it is discreet. If she realised she was being followed and watched she'd go totally to pieces. Look, what the poor kid wants right now is to be able to bury her father. Is that too much to ask? Surely you can release the body.'

Maximian sat back, eyes closed, thinking hard. 'I suppose I could have a word in the appropriate quarter.' He opened his eyes and stared fiercely at his friend. 'But if I do manage to sort something out you've got to promise to walk away from this business.

The people in charge know what they're doing. Trust me.'

Tim laughed. 'When a politician says "Trust me" I reach for my gun.'

CHAPTER 9

The funeral of Jack Robertson was a bleak, meaningless affair. Twenty or so people, most of whom had scarcely known the deceased, gathered in a village church five miles from Lanner Castle on a bright spring morning, to take part in a Presbyterian service with which they were unfamiliar and which would have meant nothing to the man in the coffin during his lifetime. The minister seemed embarrassed about the brevity of his eulogy, but it reflected all that could positively be said about the secretive Jack Robertson. When the officiant confidently outlined the joys of heaven for which our brother had exchanged the trials of earthly existence, some of the mourners could not help thinking of the monstrous images of hell, temporal and eternal, with which the deceased had surrounded himself. The brief ceremony over, the congregation shuffled out to the tiny churchyard to watch

191

all that was left of the Laird of Lanner lowered into obscurity. Those who had seen him in death or were possessed of vivid imaginations envisaged the crushed and bloodless corpse to which they were paying their last respects. Then each person present joined an embarrassed procession to file past the dead man's daughter, trying to find some words of regret and condolence which had at least a passing acquaintance with sincerity. All were grateful to regain the familiar cocoon of their motor cars for the short drive to the Briachan Inn.

The McFaddens had laid out a cold lunch on the long dining table and the guests helped themselves enthusiastically. Eating and talking reasserted normality after the enforced solemnity of the morning. Tim looked around with curiosity at the odd assemblage of people who had come together to bid farewell to a man whom few if any of them would profess to have liked. Mr and Mrs Jenkins were there with two other members of the castle staff. There were half a dozen villagers and some other locals—presumably estate workers—whom Tim had never seen. Angus Logan was present, representing his construction workers. Hildegard Nefsky had made the journey from London, presumably to strengthen her museum's claim to the Robertson collections. Andrea was supported, as was to be expected, by Ben Azikwe, who looked even more imposing than usual in his immaculate dark suit. There were three other smartly-dressed men standing apart from everyone else, engaged in their own conversation. Business associates of Robertson's or Special Branch men? Tim thought probably the former. Heterogeneous though the company was, everyone had a reason, declared or covert, for being here.

Tim considered his own motives. He had come, basically, because he thought Andrea might take some comfort from the presence of people from her own metropolitan world in this remote place where she knew almost no one. He had brought Johnny Price along to share the driving and because the lovesick young man was desperate for a reunion with his Mary. Those, at least, were the reasons he had given his secretary and Catherine, his wife. He was not, he told himself, investigating a murder. Who killed Robertson and why was not his concern. Yes, he empathised with Andrea. Yes, he resented being manipulated by Maximian's superiors and then told to mind his own business. But he knew his limitations. Blundering around in the murky terrain where crime and politics meet did not lie within them. Still, no one could possibly object to his attending a late client's funeral. If people chose to tell him things he could not stop them, and the fact that he was accompanied by the one member of his staff best qualified to plug into local gossip was purely coincidental.

As he gazed around the room, chewing a chicken drumstick, he saw one person whose presence did surprise. Steffy looked strangely demure in a plain white blouse and dark skirt. She was standing with a couple of denim-clad young men who had certainly not been at the funeral. Oh well, Tim thought, might as well start with her.

'Hello again.'

'Tim, hi!' She returned his smile. 'You've come a long way.'

'Robertson was a valued customer. What's your excuse?'

Steffy grimaced. 'Demonstration,' she said firmly.

'Of what?'

'Of the fact that we wished the man no harm.'

'Last time we spoke you didn't wish him much good.'

She looked up, suddenly anxious. 'We ought to talk.' She said 'excuse me' to her two companions and drew Tim away to the other end of the table. When she spoke again it was in a lowered voice.

'Tim, you must never say a word about what we discussed before—promise!'

'I wouldn't dream of it. Why has it suddenly become so important?'

'They're spreading disgusting stories about us.'

' "They" being the enemy, I presume—Angus Logan and Co.'

Steffy shook her head and an inexpertly gathered coil of hair unravelled itself. 'The calumnies come from higher up.'

'What sort of calumnies?'

'They're saying that we, the Save Glen Huich campaigners, murdered Robertson.'

'What?' Tim was stunned. 'You're not serious!'

'Deadly.'

'But what could you possibly have to gain? It's so...illogical.'

'Logic isn't really the point. It's a smear campaign. We're not exactly popular round here. Some of the locals support the dam project, and those that don't have been bought off by Finian Construction. Naturally everyone's shocked by Robertson's death and no one knows who's responsible. So it's dead easy for the builders to point the finger at "those long-haired, pot-smoking, coke-sniffing, fornicating foreigners". We're the obvious scapegoats. So you see, that's why you've got to keep quiet, Tim. If the enemy knew what had passed between Carol and Robertson they'd have some devastating ammunition.'

'Yes, I see.' Tim sipped his whisky thoughtfully and put his empty plate down on the table. 'It was Carol who found the body, I understand.'

'She and Angus Logan together. She was terribly shaken. How anyone could possibly imagine—'

'Tim, Steffy, what a sad reunion.' Ben Azikwe had silently appeared beside them. 'It was very good of you both to come. Andrea appreciates your support enormously.'

'How is she?' Steffy craned her neck to look up at the tall Nigerian.

'Rather badly stressed, but I think she'll be better once she's got today out of the way.'

'I'll go and have a word. I haven't really had a chance yet.' Steffy made her way across the room.

Ben popped a tiny vol-au-vent into his mouth and managed to make the gesture appear elegant—a talent acquired, Tim supposed, after years of diplomatic receptions. 'I wanted to add my thanks to Andrea's. We're both very grateful to you for getting the powers that be to release her father's body.'

'I can't honestly claim the credit. I

did have a word in a certain ear but I don't know whether that really affected the decision.'

'You're being modest, Tim. I've been hearing quite a bit about you since we last met. You have a formidable reputation.'

'Who's been talking?'

'Oh, two or three people—all highly placed and very intelligent. You are a man of many parts and well respected for all of them.'

Tim changed the subject. 'Is Andrea really OK?'

'It'll take time, but I'm doing all I can to help her put this ghastly business behind her. I do, at least, understand what it's like to be an orphan.'

'Oh, I didn't realise...'

'I never knew either of my parents. I am a child of the mission school. So, we only have each other. It makes for a particularly strong bond. Once Andrea can start planning for the wedding she'll have other things on her mind.'

'When's that to be?'

'We had arranged it for June, but now I think—I hope—September.'

'I'm sure things will turn out well for you both. Of course, she is going to have another problem.'

'Oh, what's that?'

'Money.' Tim looked straight at the

African as he spoke. 'She is obviously going to be a very wealthy young woman, and she may not find that the easiest thing in the world to handle.'

Azikwe's eyelids flickered almost imperceptibly, and he was not ready with a quick reply. Eventually he responded, 'You could well be right. Perhaps I should encourage her to take up some expensive hobbles.'

'Where will you live? I suppose you'll be called back to Nigeria eventually.'

'Not for several years, I hope. I'm angling for a Washington posting. I think Andrea would enjoy a spell at the real centre of world power. Putting a few thousand miles of ocean between herself and Britain should finally sever the link with the horrors of the last few weeks.'

'I doubt whether that'll really happen until her father's murderer is brought to book. Such a bizarre and horrible death has to be explained. Otherwise it could go on haunting her for years.'

'Oh, I don't think so.' Ben's alarm was genuine. 'For one thing they may never discover the truth. I think it would be wrong to encourage the hope of an early solution. I know she talks about wanting to get at the facts, but her best chance for recovery lies in burying mystery and uncertainty along with her father. That's what I shall be helping her to do.' There was an element of challenge in the frank gaze which accompanied these words. 'And now, I suppose I'd better circulate. Are you staying overnight?'

'Yes.'

'See you later, then.'

Mary was dispensing coffee from a point near the other end of the long table, helped—unnecessarily—by Johnny. Tim collected a cup, then attached himself to the group of businessmen who had now been joined by Hildegard Nefsky. He introduced himself and noted the wariness with which the men looked at him. 'Quite an odd assortment of people here,' he offered. 'We have a diplomat, a road-builder, a clutch of university students, a civil servant, Dr Nefsky is a museum curator and I'm in the security business. How about you gentlemen?'

'Finance and investment,' a tall, military-looking man stated and did not elaborate.

Hildegard hastened to fill the conversational gap. 'Carl Lehmberg and Peter Hovenden are directors of Harman-Lederer. Miles Quartermain,' she indicated the tall man, 'is with a merchant bank that has a major stake in the Humanities Institute.'

They all shook hands.

Tim said, 'Securing the Robertson collection must have been a major coup.'

Hovenden—rubicund, bald and peering through thick glasses—agreed. 'Not that we wanted to acquire it this way, of course. It's obscene, what happened to Robertson, quite obscene.'

They all agreed. Quartermain added, 'The sooner they catch the pervert responsible the better. He's obviously a dangerous man to be on the loose.'

Hildegard shuddered. 'I don't even like to think about it. What sort of a person could do that?'

'Obviously a nutter,' the banker suggested.

Tim sipped his coffee thoughtfully. 'I wonder.'

'You don't seriously think any rational person could commit such an outrage?' Hovenden peered at him through the circular lenses as though he were an aberrant laboratory specimen.

'My guess is that the murderer is certainly rational within his own terms of reference. He was sufficiently obsessed to plan an elaborate killing and to make it a demonstration.'

'A demonstration of what?' Quartermain demanded.

'I suppose if we knew that we'd be a long way towards identifying the killer. There are people who feel strongly about lots of things. I talked with an artist once who felt no shame whatsoever at having gone into a gallery and thrown acid over a priceless Van Dyck. For months there have been protestors up here campaigning against the dam project. You gentlemen must have encountered people fanatically opposed to the arms industry. What Robertson had done to upset the murderer I don't know. Someone may have objected to his preoccupation with human cruelty. Then again, he was consorting with criminals like Carlos Lombardo and that's a dangerous thing to do. Whatever it was...' Tim rambled casually on, pretending not to notice the effect the name had had on his audience. Dr Nefsky's mouth dropped open. Lehmberg spilled some of his coffee. The others displayed more controlled reflexes. '...the killer felt very strongly about it. He dealt out retribution in such a way that poor Robertson was left in no doubt what sins he was being made to pay for and then, instead of quietly disposing of the body, he made sure that the world would see that justice had been done.'

After a strained silence Quartermain observed brusquely, 'I don't go much on this criminal psychology stuff. In my view we ought to devote more time and money to catching and punishing offenders then trying to understand them.'

Tim deliberately changed the subject. 'I guess the Robertson collection is going to present quite a storage problem.'

'We certainly hadn't planned to have to house it yet,' Hildegard agreed. 'We shall have to build a substantial annexe on to our existing premises. I'm hoping to show my colleagues around the castle later on, so that they can appreciate just what it is we shall be acquiring.' She found it hard to contain her excitement.

Tim smiled disarmingly. 'And to think that you almost came within an ace of losing it, because Robertson was considering bids from other museums. Well, nice to have met you, gentlemen, Dr Nefsky.' Before they could react he drifted away.

He set down his empty cup and went outside. The view of castle, loch and hills beyond was dramatically different from the winter landscape he had last seen. The island, with its battlemented Victorian pile set in a shimmering, silvered expanse of water, now looked the setting for a fairy-tale princess rather than the sinister abode of an evil sorcerer. The jagged skyline was softened by a haze, and the sun-warmed breeze was fresh with the scent of growing things. Tim filled his lungs with the wholesome air. A few tables had been set out in anticipation of summer tourists, and at one of them a solitary figure sat.

Tim went over to her. 'Good afternoon, Mrs Jenkins. May I?' In response to her faint smile he pulled out a chair and seated himself opposite her. 'Are you, like me, not much of a one for parties?'

'I always find small talk very difficult.' Eleanor Jenkins was lumpy and practical-looking, with little overt femininity; the sort of woman about whom the word 'capable' sprang most readily to mind. Tim had observed many examples of her unobtrusive efficiency at Lanner Castle.

'This has been a shocking business,' Tim ventured.

'Mr Robertson was not the sort of man to die quietly in his bed.' The verdict was delivered evenly, without emotion.

'You didn't care for him much.'

She stared out across the water, weighing her answer. 'He was a fair employer.'

'But a very odd man. I mean, all those gory pictures...'

'I always thought it was his way of coming to terms with a violent past. It's called catharsis. I learned about it in an Open University psychology course.' Then, by way of further explanation, she added, 'There's not much to do in the evenings here.'

'What did you mean by Mr Robertson's violent past?'

'Only that he was in the army and was involved in some pretty nasty operations. As a service wife I know how men can react to brutality. Some go to pieces. Some repress their anger and revulsion. Some become thoroughly brutalised.'

'Did your husband know him in his army days?'

'No. He and Graham had both put military life behind them when they came together.'

'And you've no idea who would want to kill your boss?'

Eleanor laughed. 'I can think of several. Very few people got on with Mr Robertson. Over the years Graham and I have listened to some furious arguments, really...' She stopped, struck by a sudden thought. 'It's interesting you should ask that question. It's the one thing the others didn't ask.'

'Others?'

'The castle was swarming with the men in grey suits for days. They went through all Mr Robertson's papers and took crates of stuff away. They scoured the place from attic to dungeon. It took us a week to get the castle straight again. And they grilled all of us. But they never asked if we knew who might have done the dreadful deed. Odd that, isn't it?' She turned shrewd grey eyes towards Tim. Her gaze was distinctly unnerving.

He looked away towards the island. 'I see there's a helicopter over there now. Does that mean some of the supersleuths are still here?'

'No, that's the castle helicopter.'

'But how did it get back?'

Eleanor hunched her shoulders. 'Brought back courtesy of MI5 or Special Branch or whoever they are.'

The door behind Tim opened and closed and a tall figure passed on his way to the car park.

Tim called out, 'Are you off now, Angus?'

The burly construction worker turned. He looked as uncomfortable as doubtless he felt in his tight-fitting suit. 'Yes, we've got to get the last of the heavy vehicles away today.'

'You're leaving?'

'You mean you haven't heard, Mr Lacy?'

'Heard what?'

'You'd better go back in there and ask the great unwashed. They're gloating.' He resumed his brisk walk to where the vehicles were drawn up on the gravel.

Tim jumped up and hurried after him. 'I'd rather hear it from you.'

Angus stopped with his hand on the door catch of his Range Rover. 'I underestimated them. I never thought they'd go as far as murder.'

'You really believe it was the Save Glen Huich brigade who killed Robertson?'

He spun round, glowering angrily. 'I know it. And I told the police. Much good that did.'

'So, you have proof?'

'Listen!' Angus prodded his finger into Tim's chest. 'I found the body. It had been dumped in the loch less than a stone's throw from where the hairy ones were staked out with their decrepit vehicles. There was no one else around. The body had not been there long, and it must have been carried in a van of some sort—like their clapped-out Ford Transit.'

'The police would need more than that for a conviction.'

'Well, how about this, then? That bloody woman, Carol, the ringleader, she was there and she was gloating. She said she had something big planned. Something that would put her campaign back on the front page of every newspaper in the country. She actually took me to the spot where I would be sure to see the body.'

Tim wrestled with this new information. 'But what would be the point of killing Robertson? How would that help the antis' campaign?'

Angus opened the door and swung himself into the driving seat. 'It now seems that there were still a few contractual

206

details to be sorted out between Robertson and Finian Construction. They'd agreed everything but the lawyers had been dragging their feet. I don't know all the details, but what I do know is that Robertson's death has put the whole project on hold. The builders have got to open fresh negotiations with the new owner of the estate. That means Finian lay off their sub-contractors. So, instead of having another seven months' work lined up I have to go scrambling round looking for clients.' The car's engine roared into life. 'And if you think that's easy in the current economic climate, just try it!' He slammed the door and let in the clutch fiercely, and the Range Rover skidded away in a cloud of dust and gravel.

Ewen assumed command in the tower and no one challenged him. He moved to the top floor, taking one chosen lieutenant with him, a boy of about the same age called Tom Lennox. Subdued by suffering, Tom was a lad of few words, but he had a good thinking head on him and Ewen trusted him to be firm but gentle with the younger children.

As firm, gentle and intelligent, perhaps, as his own father had been. Ewen now remembered everything clearly. William M'Ewen had brought up his three sons to be honest, open-hearted farmers, taking a pride in the land they held from their laird. When Charles Edward Stuart had sent his agents through the glens to recruit the chiefs to his banner, William's clan was among those who would have nothing to do with him. When other men from the area willingly or reluctantly obeyed their lairds and went off to the muster point, William had remained quietly at home tending his land and his beasts. He had explained carefully to his three sons that this quarrel between the Stuarts and Hanovers was none of theirs. 'I was young Ewen's age when this prince's father made a bid for the crown in 1715,' he told them. 'No good came of that, and nothing but misery and grief will come of this.' Despite his words, Ewen's elder brother, Andrew, had gone off as a volunteer to fight for the man their father dismissed contemptuously as a 'little Italian adventurer'. Weeks later, news had reached Ardnabreachy of Andrew's death in battle at a place called Prestonpans. Ewen's mother had died soon after. She had been ill for some time, but William insisted that it was a broken heart that had carried her to her grave.

Ewen could now recall the events of the following months without difficulty. The house that had once been a place of bustle and laughter had fallen silent. William had gone about his work in a lacklustre way, caring little for matters he had always been very particular about before. Meals had been quiet events at which the only news for discussion had been about the rising. Scarcely a week passed in which they did not hear of the death of another erstwhile friend or neighbour.

Then a day of excited activity had arrived. Charlie Stuart's agents had once more appeared in the village. The prince's army was only a few miles away, and he had need of every able-bodied man for a great and deciding confrontation with Butcher Cumberland. One of the Jacobite officers had visited William M'Ewen and been civilly received. Ewen had listened enthralled to the man's stories of battles and victories and treacheries and defeats. But he and his colleagues had left Ardnabreachy with no fresh enlistees.

It was a week later that the countryside around the village had filled up with wounded and frightened men fleeing from a battle at a place called Culloden, the other side of Inverness. William had lodged a few of these pitiable creatures in his barn for a couple of nights. They had scarcely moved on when the Butcher's men arrived. Ewen came back to the cottage one afternoon to see a group of redcoats in the roadway. Instinctively, he crept round the back of the buildings. Peering in at a window, he saw his father and brother arguing with two soldiers who were shouting words he could not understand. William noticed his son and stepped across to the open window. 'Run, boy. Run for your life.'

Ewen had never seen his father so agitated. Not understanding, he turned and fled towards the wall between his family's ground and the moor. He heard a shout behind him but he carried on. As he reached the low stone barrier and scrambled over it there was a loud crack and something whined past his ear. He reached the shelter of the far side and crouched down, heart pounding. For a moment he listened intently but there were no sounds of pursuit. Nevertheless, he made his way diagonally across the moor to his secret place, a tumble of boulders he could squeeze inside.

He lay on the earth floor of the small cavity and peered out through a chink between the rocks. He could see red uniforms among the houses and outbuildings, but no one was climbing the hill towards him. He watched intently, anxious to miss nothing. The soldiers were obviously searching, presumably for Prince Charles' men who had passed through recently. When they had finished they would march away. But why were they pushing all the people out into the road? Why were they shooting the sheep and the cows? What were they doing with lighted torches? Horrified and scarcely believing what he saw, Ewen watched his father and brother and all their neighbours forced into their own carts, then driven eastwards out of the village surrounded by soldiers. Then he saw the redcoats left behind setting fire to every building. Flame and smoke rapidly engulfed the whole of Ardnabreachy. The smell of burning thatch reached Ewen's hiding place. Through the rolling clouds of fume he saw the troops form up in two files and march away up the road behind their colleagues.

Ewen bounded down the hillside. He tried to get into his blazing home but the heat was too intense. He stood staring round helplessly. Not a building, not a creature had been spared. Ewen's family, his friends, his home, his whole life had disappeared in a matter of minutes. He was the only living thing in Ardnabreachy, a place which would soon be no more than a jumble of blackened stones.

The frightened, bewildered lad had done the only thing he could think of to do. He had followed at a safe distance the column of soldiers and their prisoners.

A three-hour, non-stop march had taken them to Inverness. There, in the crowded streets, no one paid any attention to Ewen. It was not difficult to find the town jail where the people from Ardnabreachy were being held, because the building was surrounded by redcoats, but Ewen could not get near enough to see inside. Night came, and he slept in a barrel in a cooper's yard.

Up early the next morning, he had wandered around aimlessly for a couple of hours. Then he had joined a crowd assembling in the town square. From snatches of conversation he overheard he realised that the people were congregating to witness a hanging. He burrowed his way through to the front. A redcoat officer was standing on the scaffold addressing the people of Inverness with the aid of an interpreter, who translated his tirade into Gaelic, phrase by phrase.

'We are determined to find the papist invader, Charles Edward Stuart, and all his followers. Those who help us will be rewarded. Those who hamper us will be punished. We will have no mercy on those who shield the pretender and his men, no mercy whatsoever. You are now going to witness a demonstration of that. Yesterday we discovered a village near here which had given succour to the pretender's troops fleeing after their total defeat at Culloden. They refused to help us track down these traitors. You will now see what happens to such disloyal subjects of King George.'

The officer was the man Ewen now recognised as Alistair Duncan. He had the people of Ardnabreachy—men, women and children—brought out in groups of five. The second batch to be hanged included Ewen's father and brother.

How he had got away from Inverness or how long he had wandered on the moor Ewen could still not remember. What mattered was that now he had an identity. An identity and a purpose—to take vengeance on the Duncans.

CHAPTER 10

'Oh, there you are.' Tim stepped into the kitchen of the Briachan Inn and saw Johnny at the sink scraping new potatoes at the rate of about one every three minutes.

Mary was standing at the stove stirring something in a saucepan. She turned and smiled at the newcomer. 'Hello, Tim. If you want any dinner tonight you'd better take this laddie out of here.'

Johnny protested. 'I thought I was helping.'

She grinned. 'In that case my best advice to you is not to give up the day job.'

'She's right,' Tim agreed. 'You've got a lot more training to do before you qualify as the new man. Come on, we're going for a brisk walk to work up an appetite.'

Tim set a rapid pace along the shore of the loch. As they cleared the village he asked his young companion, 'What have you got to report?'

'What about, Major?'

'You know perfectly well what about. I told you to keep your eyes and ears open, and not just for Bonnie Mary's sighs and blushes. What are people saying about the murder?'

'Most of the locals are pretty pissed off about it by all accounts.'

'They don't like homicide in their back yard?'

'That's right, and they don't like their own police being pulled off the case and having a bunch of know-alls from London throwing their weight around.'

'Anyone running a book on whodunit?'

'The students—the protestors—seem to be top of the poll. But that's probably because they're pretty unpopular anyway. Folk round here are very conservative, from what I can make out. They reckon people who don't wipe their boots on the doormat and go screwing about in the heather are quite capable of murder.'

'Anyone else on the list?'

'They don't care much for the idea of a black man as Laird of Lanner. Some people reckon his plan was to bump off the old man and then marry the daughter for her money. But that's just prejudice. What do you think, Major?'

'I think it's a hell of a lot more complicated than that. There's too much going on. It's a bit like one of those three-dimensional pictures—just a jumble of shapes and colours until you manage to focus your eyes properly.'

They walked for a few moments in silence, then Tim said, 'Let me see if I can set the facts out in the right order. You might spot something I've missed.'

'OK, Major. Fire away.'

'Well, the first thing that seems to happen is that someone gets into the castle—heaven alone knows how—at the back end of last year. He camps in the attic and manages to avoid discovery.'

'Was that the murderer?'

'I hope so. It must have been him or someone he was in league with.'

'Was it right—what George said—that he butchered Robertson's two pet dogs?'

'Yes. And he chalked Roman numerals

215

beside each one, and he intimated that Robertson would be number three.'

'Only he wasn't, was he?'

'Wasn't what?'

'Robertson wasn't number three. That was the parrot, wasn't it? Strictly speaking, Robertson was number four.'

'That's jumping ahead. Let's try to stick as close as we can to the actual running order. A very worried Robertson asks his friends in government circles to recommend a good security firm, and no less a person than the foreign secretary puts him on to us.'

'So what's the political connection?'

'As far as I can piece it together at the moment, the powers that be are keeping a very careful watch on our friend Robertson. He has close connections with the arms trade—probably both legal and illegal. They know or suspect him of having dealings with international scum like Carlos Lombardo.'

'So why don't they pull the rug?'

'The arms industry is incredibly sensitive. It's a massive export earner. That means the government doesn't want to upset it. So, as often as not they turn a blind eye to shady deals. That's how British weapons end up in the hands of foreign tyrants and are sometimes even used against British troops.'

'Nice.'

'Very. Let's suppose Robertson is some kind of international fixer. He can bring dealers and foreign government representatives to his Highland hideaway. They come and go by helicopter and no one is any the wiser. That's guesswork, of course—but he must have been involved in some pretty big commercial deals to live like he did and scour the world for items for his bizarre collection.'

They spent the next couple of minutes negotiating a tumble of boulders which extended to the water's edge. When they regained the flat, Johnny said, 'So we've got to the point where you and George came here, haven't we?'

'Yes... No. Damn, I've left a whole strand out of the story—the building project and the Save Glen Huich agitators. The power authority gets government approval for a hydro-electric scheme to supplement the electricity supply for the national grid. Finian Construction gets the contract and negotiates with the relevant landowners. The biggest of those is Robertson.'

'Then the protestors turn up and try to put a spoke in the wheels.'

'That's right and they make a sufficient nuisance of themselves for Finian and Robertson to stoop to some pretty dirty tricks.' Tim explained the way Carol

Sellis had been duped by Bradnish and threatened by Robertson.

'Bastards!' Johnny kicked at a pile of stones and sent them skittering into the water. 'I'd be furious if that happened to me!'

'Furious enough to take pretty drastic revenge?'

'Why not? I mean, it's the classic example of the establishment ganging up against the little man—or little woman in this case. They want to make money. Carol gets in the way. So Carol must be crushed. Yeah, if I were her I'd certainly feel like hitting back.'

Tim looked around the skyline. The scenery really was magnificent. Britain, he thought, had few prospects more spectacular than Glen Huich. He tried to envisage a concrete barrier stretched across the valley and the lower part of the glen flooded to raise the water level and double the size of the loch. 'I guess the personality profile fits. Carol is a woman with a personal grievance. She's intelligent. But over and above all she has a cause, and people with causes are dangerous. They believe little evils are justified by the greater good. Carol could easily persuade herself that she wasn't acting out of personal malice; she was simply determined to preserve all this. But could she have done it? Do the logistics work out?'

'She couldn't have done it by herself, that's for sure.'

'Right enough. Lugging a dead body around is a harder job than most people realise. When it's parcel-wrapped in solid steel it takes a lot of strength. Let's get back to the events of January. George and I turn up here at the same time as Andrea, her boyfriend, Carol, Steffy, Dr Nefsky and Carlos Lombardo, travelling under an alias. During the course of our visit, Robertson manages to upset just about everyone. He threatens to sever all relations with his daughter if she doesn't break her engagement. He tries to blackmail Carol into abandoning her protest. And he tells Hildegard not to bank on her institute getting his collections.'

'Plenty of motives there, then.'

'But who had the opportunity to stage the little demonstration that evening? I learned from Jenkins that he covered the parrot's cage just before six. Everyone assembled for dinner around seven.'

'So there was plenty of time for someone to snaffle the bird, throttle it and string it up in the dungeon. Anyone could have done it.'

'No, not anyone. Only someone who was involved in the earlier demonstrations or, at least, knew about them. The killing of the dogs wasn't a very well-kept secret. The girls had heard the story. And, of course, the Jenkinses and probably the other servants were familiar with it. As for Andrea, it's not the sort of intimate detail her father would have shared with her, and Azikwe didn't know until I told him.'

'That narrows the field a bit...unless...'

Tim looked round eagerly. 'What is it, Johnny? Have you spotted something I've missed?'

'I was wondering about the bloke in the attic. If he did for the dogs, he most likely disposed of the parrot.'

'No, that won't work. He was long gone. When George and I discovered his hideyhole it was obvious he hadn't been there for quite a time.'

'That puts Carol and her crowd pretty firmly in the frame, then. One of her chums gets into the castle last year, does the biz with the dogs, and Carol and Steff bump off the parrot.'

'Why? What was their motive?'

'To show the enemy that they weren't the only ones capable of dirty tricks?'

'But Carol didn't know anything about the plot against her until she got to the castle.'

'Ah, but you've only got Steffy's word for that,' Johnny pointed out triumphantly. He was warming to his theme. 'Now, suppose they intended all along to murder Robertson. It might be a bit risky to try it in the castle. They have to smoke him out. So they kill the dogs. That doesn't work. Then Robertson plays into their hands—he invites Carol and Steffy to the castle. They do for poor Polly, and that's the final straw. Robertson does a bunk, they track him, and wallop!'

Tim considered his young colleague's reconstruction. 'It's certainly a theory worth considering.' He pointed to a large outcrop of rock just ahead. 'That must be the point from which Angus and Carol spotted the body.'

They hurried forward and climbed up on to the jutting slab of granite. Below them a tumble of rocks formed a sieve at the point where water gushed out of the loch and cascaded through narrows into the valley.

'Any large floating object would get caught here,' Johnny observed.

'But Robertson's body wouldn't be floating, not with all that metalware around it.'

'You reckon it was dumped here deliberately, Major?'

'Must have been.'

'Why?'

'So that it would be discovered by the road-builders, presumably. I can't think of any other reason.'

'In that case,' Johnny said, turning round, 'it can only have been brought down the track made by the construction teams.'

Heavy vehicles had ripped the vegetation away to scour a wide path leading to the brow of the hill above them.

'That would take them straight over to the main road, and that means they could have brought Robertson here from anywhere. Where the hell did he go when he left the castle?' Tim looked at his watch. 'We'd better start back.'

'You're sure it was him?' Johnny asked as he jumped down to the springy moorland grass and heather. 'It couldn't have been one of his men taking the chopper away in the middle of the night?'

'George and I went through the castle from top to bottom and side to side the next day. Robertson couldn't have been skulking there. But let's pick up our train of events. We all had dinner together that night, and afterwards Robertson takes us on a tour of his revolting exhibits. We end up in the dungeon. When he sees the parrot and the number chalked on the floor he's very badly shaken. He goes back to his own rooms and the party breaks up quickly. Jenkins locks up about eleven-thirty, electronically isolating the three sections of the castle. At two o'clock the next morning he is woken by his boss telephoning him to say he's leaving the castle for an indefinite period. Half an hour later Robertson takes off, destination unknown. Some time during the night Cumberland's Cradle disappears from the dungeon.'

'Robertson could have taken it with him.'

'Yes, I'd thought of that. It's quite possible, although I can't imagine why someone on the run from an unknown assassin would want to encumber himself with a load of old metal.'

'Well, someone reunited Robertson and his prize exhibit.'

'Yes. Wherever he was hiding, the murderer tracked him down, presumably rendered him unconscious and clamped him into that diabolical machine, and enjoyed watching him slowly being crushed, impacted. The murderer listened to his victim's groans and cries for mercy and took cruel pleasure from ignoring them. He—or she—heard bones crack, watched blood spurt, and gloated over Robertson right up to the moment when the last vestige of life was squeezed from him.'

'You don't reckon your imagination's going a bit over the top there, Major?'

'No, it's vital to try to understand the murderer's mentality. Anyone who could kill in that way must have really hated his victim. It wasn't enough just to murder Robertson. He had to inflict pain, and he wanted Robertson to know what it was like to die like the subject of one of his own pictures. Robertson was writing a history of torture. The murderer must have known about it. I'm sure that's significant.'

They surmounted a small rise and Briachan came into view. Johnny patted his stomach. 'Well, I don't know if this has helped you sort out your thoughts, Major, but it's certainly given me an appetite. I'm looking forward to another taste of Mary's cooking. Game soup and Aberdeen Angus steaks tonight.'

As they completed their walk in silence, Tim's mind re-ran the sequence of events he had outlined to his colleague. Something lurked among the untidy jumble of facts, ideas and rumours; something that held the clue to their intelligent rearrangement. It was something that Johnny had said. Try as he might, he could not identify it.

For three or four weeks after Cumberland's visit the bestial violence visited upon Ewen M'Ewen and his charges bordered on the intolerable. But gradually life at Castle Huich returned to its normal level of unpleasantness. The greatest challenge to Ewen and Tom during the difficult days was maintaining morale in the tower. But somehow the young prisoners survived; in fact, their shared hardships fused them into a real unit. They became what they had never been before, a band of youngsters with an identity, with martyrs to revere, leaders to respect and follow, and a solemn cause—the destruction of the Duncans—to work for.

The first need was for training. Every evening Ewen and Tom gathered the clansmen together to teach them English. This led on to a more organised pooling of intelligence: the better the children understood their captors the more information they were able to contribute to the store of knowledge in the tower.

There were moments of triumph and of disappointment. One of the girls, taking rubbish to the tip outside the walls, found an old, rusty iron key and brought it back, hidden in the sleeve of her dress. Perhaps it would fit the lock of the tower door, she suggested. That night the children waited until all was quiet in the castle. Then Tom took the key and inserted it in the lock from the inside. It slipped in easily and a ripple of excitement went round the circle of watchers. But when Tom tried to turn it nothing happened. Tom kept the key anyway.

More hopeful was the accumulation of a

supply of oil. In a little-frequented corner of the kitchens stood a tapped barrel of lamp oil. Sometimes it was possible for one of the children working in that part of the castle to run off some of the fluid into a discarded beer flagon Ewen had picked up in a corner of the courtyard, and smuggled back to the tower where it was stored in a chipped pottery pitcher stolen from a kitchen cupboard. Tom guarded the supply carefully. If ever they needed lamps, he explained, they could now improvise them—if they found some means of lighting them. Such little triumphs brought some brightness into the children's dismal days.

It was Tom who coordinated this activity. As soon as a clear picture began to emerge of how the castle was run, Ewen's lieutenant was able to identify the gaps in their understanding of Duncan's organisation and set members of the group to try to fill these gaps. In order for this espionage to succeed it was necessary to catch the enemy off guard. Ewen stressed that all the clansmen were to concentrate hard on giving no offence to the dogs; the children were to do as they were ordered with cowering subservience, giving the impression that the execution of Ranald, Hector and Aileen had broken their spirit.

Within two months of that tragedy, Tom had gathered a mass of statistics about the numerical strength of the garrison, the times when the guard was changed, where the keys were kept, how many boats were in service, the names and locations of most of the prisoners, the methods Duncan used for interrogation and the relative effectiveness of those methods.

There was much talk among the soldiers about the value of the latest torture implement, the crushing gyves. It had apparently been brought to Huich by the duke, who was growing desperate for reliable information about the whereabouts of Charles Stuart, and the dogs had christened it 'Cumberland's Cradle'. Some were in favour of it because it imposed maximum pain on the victim with minimum effort by his tormentors. Others thought it too cruel, and insisted that it was no more effective than the rack and other conventional instruments of torment. They argued that once a prisoner had decided to endure physical pain it made no difference what was done to him; he simply would not talk. The more Ewen heard about Cumberland's Cradle the more he longed to see Alistair Duncan clamped within its metallic embrace. Although he had not seen the implement, he tried to envisage it and his exultation at seeing his enemy's body crushed by it. He dismissed the dream as unrealistic, but it frequently returned unbidden.

The step from gathering information to using it was long and difficult to the point of impossibility. Night after night Ewen and Tom lay in the darkness discussing and dismissing plans, defining their objectives with precision. They wanted to achieve three things: to free the prisoners, escape from the island, and punish the Duncans and their red dogs. Tom insisted that they should do nothing until they had a carefully worked out plan. If they tried something and failed there would be no second chance; the Duncans' retaliation would be swift and total. Yet what could a few children achieve against a garrison of forty armed men and the Duncans' fifteen personal servants? And how could they escape from a securely guarded castle in the middle of a loch? It was only their determination and their growing hatred of their captors that kept the boys turning over these problems.

Access to the prisoners was the biggest difficulty they faced. Even if they were to work out a plan that stood a chance of succeeding it had to be conveyed to the men in the dungeons. Neither Ewen nor Tom had ever been down there. Two of the younger children were sometimes employed to carry food or other supplies to the jailers, but none of their seniors were trusted near the prisoners. Time and again Tom quizzed the eight-year-olds about what they saw on these visits. He made them draw out plans of the dungeon layout on the tower's earth floor, but they were not very good at it and he did not regard their information as reliable.

It was Alistair Duncan who inadvertently played into the plotters' hands. He decided to put Ewen and Tom to torture.

The evening passed quietly but for one strange event.

Apart from Andrea and Ben, Tim and Johnny were the only members of the funeral party staying overnight at the Briachan Inn. The heiress had no desire to sleep in the castle but there were various formalities to attend to and the family lawyer, Mr Macrae, was coming up from Edinburgh to steer her through them. The four of them sat down to dinner at eight o'clock, together with the McFaddens and three other visitors, retired ladies from Sussex on a tour of the Highlands. The conversation was general and Tam was in his usual good form as a purveyor of local folklore.

The company had just disposed of a thick and meaty game soup when the barmaid, a girl from the village, peered round the door. 'Tam, could you come a moment?'

When the landlord returned five minutes later he was leading a small, bespectacled man for whom the word 'dapper' might have been invented. The stranger was clearly in some distress. He held a briefcase in one hand and clasped a tot of Tam's whisky firmly in the other. He allowed himself to be led to a seat at the table.

McFadden made the introduction. 'Andrea, this is Mr Macrae from Edinburgh. I'm afraid he's had a wee bit of a shock.'

The lawyer took another gulp of spirit and struggled to regain his composure. 'Miss Robertson, I'm so sorry I'm late. There was a mix up over the hire car in Inverness. I suppose I was driving faster than I should have done, not concentrating properly. If I hadn't been in such a hurry...'

Mary set a bowl of soup before the newcomer. 'Well you're here now, Mr Macrae. Just you eat this nice and slowly. We hadn't long started and we shan't mind pausing while you catch us up.' As the lawyer applied himself thankfully to the food, Mary glared at her father.

He refused to catch her eye. 'Poor Mr Macrae was telling me that he's just had a very disturbing experience on the road.

He thought he'd run someone down away on the hill.'

Macrae nodded. 'I'd just come over the brow and I found myself suddenly where the trees overhang. What with it being dusk and the light poor...'

'He saw someone in the road right in front of him,' Tam finished dramatically.

The Sussex ladies gasped and muttered 'Oh poor you!' and 'How terrible!'

The little man looked up at the faces —sympathetic and eager for detail—and responded. 'It was a young lad. I saw him as plainly as I see you.'

On this occasion Mary McFadden was firm. 'The evening light can play strange tricks at this time of year, *isn't that so, Father?*' She went over to Tam's chair and laid a hand purposefully on his shoulder. 'Now, will you be helping me to serve while Mr Macrae finishes his soup in peace?'

After the meal Andrea and her fiancé spent the rest of the evening with the lawyer. Tim went to bed with a book and was up early in order to get to Inverness in good time for the mid-morning Heathrow flight. After a quick breakfast he left Johnny to say a lingering farewell to their hostess while he put their bags in the car.

He had just started the engine when Andrea came running up. 'Tim, I'm so sorry we haven't had a real chance to chat. Yesterday was a bit of an ordeal, and then Mr Macrae wanted me to look at reams of papers.'

'That's OK, you've had a lot on your plate. I hope things work out for you now. I'm sure they will. You will let me know when the wedding is, won't you?'

She looked crestfallen. 'Oh, I don't want to think about that yet. I want to know about the other business. How are your investigations going?'

Tim climbed out of the car. 'Andrea, Ben thinks you ought to let go of the past—and I agree with him... You've got everything ahead of you—a good man, no financial worries, an interesting life. Ben tells me he hopes to get transferred to Washington...'

'I can't just forget it! I can't! Ben refuses to accept that. He keeps saying, "You'll get over it," but I won't. I have to know!'

'The case has been taken up by Special Branch, as you're aware. They'll sort it out.'

'Will they? I wonder. Do they really want to see justice done or are they only concerned to hush everything up? I don't know much about the security services, but I do know they only get involved when there are political issues at stake. So what on earth was my father mixed up in? I've a right to know!' Suddenly she threw herself into his arms and sank her head on his shoulder.

Briefly Tim hugged her, then he held her away. 'Yes, you have a right to know, and I hope that right is respected.'

'You promised,' she sobbed.

'I said I'd do whatever I could and I kept my word. I spoke to someone pretty high up, and as a result you were able to bury your father. That's about the extent of my influence. I'm not a private detective, and even if I were I could hammer from now till kingdom come on the firmly locked doors of the establishment and never get any response.'

Andrea turned away. 'So I really am all alone.'

'No, of course you're not. You feel absolutely rotten about things now, but—'

'I'll get over it?' She laughed bitterly. 'Now where have I heard that before?' She walked slowly back to the hotel. And Tim could only let her go.

Twenty minutes later, as he twisted the car along the narrow road that wound over hill and through forest to the main highway, Tim was angry. Angry with himself for letting Andrea down; angry with the situation which prevented him doing any more to help her; and angry with Andrea for not appreciating how helpless he was. How was it that women had this ability to make a man feel like a louse when he knew perfectly well that he had done nothing wrong?

As he brought the car carefully round a hairpin bend and changed up into third for a straight stretch of downhill road he caught a fleeting glimpse of a vehicle in a driveway on his right. Seconds later he picked it up in his rear mirror—a green Land Rover, rather old. The driver flashed his lights.

'You'll have to wait, chum,' Tim muttered. 'There's no room to get by along here.' The road, emerging from a belt of trees, was a scant two cars' width with occasional passing places. It descended along the side of a valley to join the A862 a mile or so ahead. To the right the land rose steadily towards a craggy summit. To the left it fell steeply away. The vehicle behind was still coming on, swinging out to the right as though determined to pass.

Johnny twisted round in his seat. 'Impatient sod! What the hell does he think he's playing at?'

The next moment he was jerked forward against his seat belt. With a grinding crump the Land Rover had struck the car's offside rear wing and lurched towards the road's edge.

Tim gripped the wheel tight. 'I think he

knows exactly what he's playing at.'

He pressed down on the accelerator. The car careered fast—too fast—down the incline. A gap opened between the two vehicles, but only momentarily. Tim wrestled with the steering as another thud threw the car against the bank on a slight curve.

'Bloody hell, Major. What—'

'Brace yourself,' Tim shouted.

He had spotted a grassy track less than a hundred yards ahead, running up the hillside. He kept the car in the centre of the road. It took another two blows from the Land Rover's bumper but stayed on course. At the last moment Tim swung the wheel to the right. The suspension crunched as the car hit the track's uneven surface. Tim slewed it to a halt, jammed on the hand-brake and, in the same motion, unfastened his seat belt.

By the time he was out of the car the Land Rover was streaking down the road. He looked for the number plate. It was either covered or missing.

Johnny walked round the car from the other side and angrily inspected the crumpled boot and smashed light fittings. 'Bastards!' he shouted after the fast-disappearing vehicle.

Tim was no less incensed but more controlled. 'Come on,' he said. 'We've got a plane to catch.' He backed the car on to the road. As it gathered speed down the hill he glared through the windscreen. 'I just changed my mind about something.'

CHAPTER 11

A couple of days after his return from Scotland, Tim phoned Andrea. He intended to begin by apologising for being unsympathetic, but the young heiress forestalled him.

'Tim, I'm so glad you called. I've been feeling awfully guilty about the way I spoke to you the other day. I'm so sorry.'

'There's nothing to be sorry for.'

'Yes there is. You've done a lot for me—much more than I had any right to ask—and all I could do was grumble at you for not doing more. It was terribly rude, as though I expected you to be at my beck and call. Perhaps I take after my father more than I realise.'

'Don't give it another thought. You've every right to know as much as anyone else knows about your father's death. I phoned to tell you that I'll find out whatever I can.'

'Oh, Tim, do you really mean that?' He

could hear the relief in her voice. 'I've no right to expect it and you must be very busy...'

'I'll find some time. I don't promise that I'll be able to discover anything of any value, but I will try.'

'Tim, you're a real friend. Look, you must keep a note of the time you spend so that I can pay you properly.'

'Andrea, there's no need—'

She cut in quickly. 'I insist. My father has made me a wealthy woman. The least I can do is spend some of the money finding out who killed him.'

Tim did not pursue the matter. 'How did you get on with the lawyer?'

'OK. The will was very straightforward. My father told me that he'd checked everything was in order a while back, when the dogs were killed. So the will was quite up to date. The collection goes to the museum that Nefsky women runs, which suits me excellently; I didn't want to have anything to do with all those awful pictures and torture implements. There was a generous—a very generous—bequest to Mr and Mrs Jenkins. That was a relief I wasn't looking forward to having to pension them off. Jobs are hard to find nowadays. Fortunately, they won't have to work again if they don't want to.'

'That generous?'

'Yes, they'll be pretty comfortably off, which is no less than they deserve. Looking after my father in that dreary castle must have been sheer hell at times.'

'You're definitely closing the place up?'

'Definitely. I don't want ever to set foot in it again. Mr Macrae will take care of the sale of the estate and the castle contents as soon as we get probate, though heaven knows when that'll be.'

'What's the hold-up?'

'Mr Macrae can't deal with it through the normal legal channels. Because the Home Office and the Scottish office have taken an interest, all the papers have to be referred to Whitehall mandarins. Oh, these wretched delays! They just make matters worse.'

'So, apart from you, the Jenkinses and the museum, no one benefits financially from your father's death?'

'You're looking for a possible motive?'

'One has to start somewhere...'

'Yes, I realise that. The money motive doesn't get us very far, does it? Jenkins wouldn't have killed his boss, and I can't imagine Dr Nefsky—'

'Your father was contemplating writing her institute out of his will.' Tim did not add that the late Laird of Lanner had also threatened to disinherit his daughter.

There was a gasp at the other end of the

238

line. 'Really? Gosh, you don't think...'

'I really don't know. All I can say is that Nefsky and her chums were extremely keen to get their hands on the collection. What's more, they do have some pretty unsavoury business associates.'

'So we do have a possible lead, then?'

'That's certainly one avenue to explore. Then there's the pro- and anti-dam people. I gather there's a problem about the scheme going ahead.'

'Oh yes,' Andrea sighed. 'Macrae went into that in tedious detail. It seems my father hadn't finally assigned all the necessary rights to Finian's, the main contractor. I have to sign various documents—which of course I can't do till probate is given.'

'And will you do it then?'

She groaned. 'Oh, I suppose so. I really don't have the energy to go into all the moral pros and cons. I've had screeds of propaganda from the antis, and Steffy was bending my ear after the funeral. Oh Tim, it's depressing having all that responsibility. I don't want to see the Highlands spoiled but if people need the jobs and the electricity... Oh, I don't know!'

'Well, you don't have to rush into a decision. You might even be able to sell the estate before the matter is resolved and let someone else have the headache.

Did Macrae say anything else that might be helpful?'

Andrea hesitated. 'There was something that shook me...well, more surprised me, really. It can't have any relevance to my father's death, though.'

'Tell me anyway.'

'It seems that Robertson is not my real name, or not my father's original name. He changed it by deed poll. Before that he was John Rycote.'

'When did that happen?'

'That's what I asked Macrae, of course. I got the distinct impression he didn't want to tell me. I saw the name on an old document and questioned him about it and he went all, sort of, evasive. He couldn't actually refuse to tell me, and when I pressed him he said that my father changed his name about twenty years ago, at the time he bought the castle.'

'Hm...interesting.'

'You think so? Surely it can't have any bearing on his death. It was a long time ago.'

Tim replied quickly, reassuringly. 'I expect you're right. Well, let me know if anything else occurs to you. I'll get back to you if and when I have anything to report.'

As soon as he had ended the call Tim picked up the internal phone, buzzed

George Martin's office and asked his assistant to pop along the corridor. When the burly ex-sergeant had lowered himself into a chair Tim said, 'Do you still have any contact with that old drinking companion of yours who works in army records at Aldershot?'

'Nipper Beal? We exchange Christmas cards. He and his missus looked in last summer on their way to their holiday in Cornwall.'

'Would he do you a favour?'

George gazed across the desk suspiciously. 'What's this all about, Major?'

'It's the Scottish business.'

George looked disapproving. 'I was afraid we hadn't heard the last of that. That run in with the Land Rover caught you on the raw, didn't it?'

'When people kill other people I can be fairly relaxed about it, but I do tend to react badly when people try to kill me.'

'Even when they're trying to stop you sticking your nose into something that doesn't concern you?'

'Especially when they're trying to do that.'

'OK, what is it you want to know?'

Tim explained about Robertson/Rycote. 'I'd like to see his military record.'

'You really think that might be relevant?'

Tim tilted his executive chair backwards

241

and stared up at the beamed ceiling of his office in what had once been the stable block of Farrans Court. 'What do we know about Robertson?'

'Sweet FA.'

'Exactly. We don't know what business he was involved in, where his money came from, or what he did before he buried himself in the Highlands. Now it appears he changed his name from Rycote, which is pretty distinctive—distinguished even, compared with the comparative anonymity of Robertson. What does that suggest to you?'

'Something to hide?'

'Yeah, me too.'

'Well, I'll see what I can get Nipper to turn up. What have we got to go on?'

'Apart from the name, almost nothing. But there can't have been many John Rycotes who left the service prematurely around twenty years ago in their early to mid-thirties.'

'OK, Major, leave it with me.' George walked solidly from the room, and Tim knew that within a couple of days he would have the information he wanted or, at least, whatever was available.

Moments later a phone call came through from Dr Hildegard Nefsky. Since Tim had been kind enough to express an interest in the Harman-Lederer Institute, would he like to have a personally guided tour?

The tower inhabitants had warning of Alistair Duncan's change of tactics. Two of the boys were carrying logs into the great hall and heard the heir to Castle Huich boasting to his cronies about his latest brainwave.

'He said time was running out and they weren't getting any useful information from the prisoners,' the young clansman reported that evening.

His partner nodded. 'He said the stubborn Highlanders didn't care about pain. Then he said, "But they might change their minds if they see children being punished for their obstinacy".'

'Yes, he said he was going away for a couple of days, and when he got back he'd put some of the Highland brats to torture...starting with the two eldest.' The boy looked sadly at Ewen.

Ewen glanced at Tom. 'A couple of days. Then we don't have much time. We must talk.'

He dismissed the clansmen. After that, the two of them sat late into the night working out a plan and going over it again and again. When they eventually lay down to sleep Tom muttered, 'There are so many things that could go wrong.'

'Aye, but it is the chance or half-chance we've been waiting for. We'll maybe never get another.'

Early the next morning, Tom assembled the clansmen and told them part of the plan. He avoided the details that the children would not understand, and he underplayed the risks that might frighten them.

The first step was to get a message to the prisoners. Ewen tutored those most likely to be sent to the dungeon, and that evening checked on their progress. A bright girl called Jenny made a very clear report. She and her companion had taken food to the jailers. She had gone into the main dungeon with a jug of ale. Her colleague, descending the staircase with a basket of bread, had deliberately dropped it and the loaves had rolled down the dusty steps. Cursing, the two guards had rushed out to retrieve the bread and administer a sound thrashing to the clumsy child. Jenny had taken the opportunity to go to the nearest cell door and have a whispered conversation with the inmate.

'What did you tell him?' Ewen demanded urgently.

Jenny remembered her message word for word: 'Two of the children are going to be tortured to make you talk. Try to get a few moments alone with them. They have a plan to get you out.'

'Well done, Jenny.' Ewen smiled at her. 'All we can do now is wait.'

The waiting process lasted less than two days.

Early in the afternoon, Tom and Ewen were marched into the castle hall to see Alistair Duncan. Although the day was warm he stood with his back to a large log fire. His Gaelic interpreter stood beside him. He leered at the boys. 'Right, you'll be pleased to hear that you are to have an opportunity to serve your king and country. You're going to help me gather some vital information. My men will take you from here to the dungeon where we keep the king's enemies. We also keep down there some amazing toys. I expect your little friends have told you about them. My men are going to let you play with them. They're going to hang one of you in chains and put the other in a special new toy brought by his royal highness. And do you know what that's going to do to you? It's going to crush you. It's going to fold you up like a twig. Of course, that will hurt. It will hurt a great deal. You will feel like crying out with the pain. That's quite all right. In fact, the more you cry out the better. Because the only thing that will stop the pain is when the prisoners tell me what I want to know. So, you see, the more noise you make, the better it will be for you—and, of course, for me.' He laughed and ordered the soldiers to take the boys away.

Ewen recognised the dungeon layout from the descriptions the clansmen had given. There was a large central area where the jailers sat and where the various torture implements were laid out. Around the perimeter of this space were ten cells with stout oaken doors with iron grilles set in them. Ewen looked around intently, registering every small detail that he could. He noted the cell keys attached to a ring hanging on a hook just inside the door. He saw the three unshaven faces of prisoners watching from their places of confinement. He noted that there was only one jailer in the room.

Then it was time to act the part of surprised and terrified victim. He struggled and screamed as two dogs dragged him over to an apparatus hanging by the wall. 'Please, please, don't hurt me!' he gibbered as they clamped steel rings round his wrists, ankles, chest and thighs.

Tom also shouted out as the jailer bound his hands together above his head and slipped a hanging hook through the cords. He worked a pulley to lift him clear of the floor, then attached weights to his ankles and hoisted him higher.

'For the love of God,' a voice shouted from one of the cells, 'has Duncan no shame that he must go tormenting children?'

One of the guards turned to him. 'The brats will be freed as soon as you tell us what we want to know.'

The soldiers left the chamber and the boys were at the mercy of the jailer—a brawny man whose profession was cruelty. He turned a wheel which contracted the implement's frame and began to apply pressure to Ewen's joints. Beside him Tom groaned, face contorted with pain. Ewen decided it was time to go into the act. There was, yet, only a dull ache in various parts of his body but, as the jailer applied slightly more pressure to the wheel, he yelled, 'No! Stop! Oh, please, stop!'

Tom added his screams.

The jailer laughed. 'You haven't felt nothing yet, dearies.'

The boys ignored him, continuing to yelp with simulated fear and pain.

'Stop it!' The voice came from one of the cells. 'I'll talk. Let the boys go and I'll talk.'

The jailer turned to him. 'That soon loosened your tongue, didn't it?' He sounded disappointed. 'Right then, you know the questions we want answered.'

'I'll answer to Duncan and no one else.

Let the boys go and fetch Duncan.'

The jailer went over and grimaced at his prisoner through the grille. 'Do you think I'm stupid? I free the boys, fetch Duncan. Then you go all silent again and I get the edge of Duncan's tongue. Oh, no. The brats stay here till we've got the information we want. I'll go and report to the master.' He crossed the room. At the foot of the staircase he stopped and looked back. 'Don't go away,' he called out, and laughed at his own joke.

As soon as he was out of earshot the man in the cell said, 'We got your message. What's afoot?'

Ewen turned his head and could just see the speaker. 'We think we can get you out, sir. At least, we'll try. How many of you could make it to the boats?'

'Six, I think. The others are too far gone, poor devils. But how can you possibly—'

'No time to explain, but sometime in the next couple of days we'll make our move. Be ready. When Duncan comes down, can you tell him something that'll make him let us go?'

'Aye, I'll spin him a convincing yarn. One that'll take several days in the checking. Perhaps, by then...'

'I hope so, sir. We'll do our best.'

'You're brave lads, both of you.'

'It's not just us...'

They were interrupted by footsteps on the stair. The jailer returned, running down the steps, followed more sedately by Alistair Duncan, a self-satisfied smile on his lips.

The prisoner shouted out, 'What are you doing here, Alistair Duncan? I sent for the fox not his cub.'

'Hold your tongue, Cameron! If you've anything to say you'll say it to me—or these urchins get a taste of real anguish.' He pushed Tom's body and set it swinging so that the boy cried out in real agony.

'Very well, enough! Loosen them and I'll tell you where the prince is headed.'

'Tell me first and I'll release them afterwards.'

'Oh, no, you evil bastard. I don't trust you. You're as likely to get what you want from me, then torture the lads for sheer sadistic pleasure.'

Duncan thought hard, then nodded. 'Very well. But remember, I can bring them back here any time I want, and if I have to do that I'll really hurt them. Get that one down,' he ordered the jailer.

The man slackened the pulley and lowered Tom to the floor. Duncan turned to the cradle and laid his hand to the wheel. He twisted it and Ewen screamed in genuine distress. Duncan laughed. 'Oops! It must be the other way.' He slackened the pressure and Ewen thankfully stretched his legs.

When the jailer had released their bonds, both boys stood for some moments getting the feeling back into their limbs.

'Right, take yourselves off,' Duncan ordered. 'You know what's in store for you if I have to bring you back here.'

Like old men feeling their failing joints, Ewen and Tom staggered up the winding stone steps. Back in the open air Tom grinned. 'Stage one complete.'

The Harman-Lederer Humanities Institute was housed in an imposing neo-classical building in a quiet street off Park Lane. It had once been the town mansion of Viscount Sandby, a Georgian courtier and property speculator. Later generations of property speculators had long since encroached on his lordship's pleasure grounds and the house, crudely jostled by rows of more modest dwellings, had fallen into considerable decay. That was when the international arms company had come to the rescue. Now the gleaming stonework, crisply carved Corinthian columns and the writhing figures of the tympanum once more gazed down on their meaner neighbours with haughty condescension.

Hildegard Nefsky met Tim in the marble-floored atrium. 'Tim, how good of you to come.' Her handshake was firm and masculine.

'Very kind of you to invite me. Meeting you in Scotland certainly aroused my curiosity, so I'm pleased to have the opportunity to explore your treasures thoroughly.'

'Well, of course, you'll need more than one visit to appreciate what we're trying to do here but at least I can offer you a quick overview.' She led the way into the first of a series of interconnecting ground-floor galleries.

'What exactly is the philosophy behind your collections?' Tim gazed around the room, which displayed primitive decorative items from amulets of bone and wood to silver and gilt pectorals and vivid textiles.

'Pascal described mankind as "the glory and the scum of the earth". You could say that that was the motto of the Harman-Lederer Institute. We aim to show what the human spirit can aspire to, largely in terms of the visual and decorative arts, and also the depths to which it can sink. We believe and hope that by bringing together under one roof evidence of man's soaring with the angels and crawling with the brutish beasts, we can give our visitors a vivid experience and, hopefully, inspire them to reach for the best and highest.'

Tim smiled. 'A noble aim. But I imagine

you wouldn't want to be too successful.'

Hildegard stopped abruptly in the doorway of Gallery II. 'What do you mean?'

Tim peered into the room, which was obviously meant to counterpoise the one illustrating the artistic accomplishments of primitive peoples. A hologram display in the centre enacted and re-enacted an Aztec human sacrifice, and there were static models demonstrating the use of early weapons. 'Only that, as we can see here, tribes and nations have been fighting each other since the year dot. If they ever stopped, armament manufacturers like Harman-Lederer would go out of business and your funding would disappear.'

She smiled an uncertain smile. 'I suppose, in that happy situation, they would find something else to sell—beat their swords into ploughshares or computers or whatever the market demanded.'

'Still, joking apart,' Tim said as pleasantly as he could, 'I presume the institute is really a sop to conscience—rather like Alfred Nobel getting fabulously wealthy through supplying explosives to the world's armies and then funding a peace prize.'

Dr Nefsky stiffened and marched forward with awkward, angular movements. 'I don't think that's at all an appropriate comparison, as you'd know if you'd ever met Freiderich Lederer, the founder of

252

the firm. He resigned from the board of Krupps in 1938 and fled to South America because he would not be a party to the build-up of the Nazi war machine. He spent several years in Argentina, Peru and Mexico studying the native societies. He never took a university degree, but he became one of the leading anthropologists of his age.'

'That didn't stop him going back into the arms business.'

'It was the only business he knew; the only way he could raise enough money to realise his dream of founding the Humanities Institute. All his personal fortune and most of his energies went into creating this place. It was opened just three months before he died.'

'I imagine you must regard it as something of a sacred trust.'

'That wouldn't be putting too strongly. The institute does a lot of good works. Besides the exhibition, we organise courses and international seminars. Then, as you probably know, there are the Harman-Lederer scholarships, to Oxford, Harvard and Heidelberg.'

Hildegard pointed out various artefacts as they continued their tour of the ground-floor exhibitions. It was as they emerged once more into the vast entrance hall and began their ascent of a wide double staircase that Tim asked nonchalantly, 'You've presumably been in this sort of work quite a long time. Where were you before you came here?'

She shook her head. 'I had no previous museum experience. I've been with Harman-Lederer all my working life, including nine years as Mr Lederer's personal assistant. It was his wish that I should run this place.'

'Acquiring the Robertson collection must be an enormous feather in your cap. How did you hear about it? Robertson was a very secretive person.'

'I can't really claim much credit. Jack Robertson was an associate of Mr Lederer. They often talked about their mutual interests. It was they who agreed to the eventual merger of the collections. All I did was get the arrangement made legal.'

'I suppose it was quite a shock to discover that a couple of rival museums were in the running.'

Dr Nefsky brushed the suggestion away with an airy wave. 'Oh, that was just Robertson's way of applying pressure. He never really intended to leave his collection to another public institution.'

'So there was nothing urgent about your travelling to the castle in the depths of winter?' Tim asked the question in a throwaway manner as he turned to examine a display of crossbows. He was aware of a long, calculating pause before his guide replied.

'You seem very interested in our connection with Jack Robertson's life and death, Tim. Have you a particular reason?'

He smiled. 'It's not every day one is involved in a murder, especially such a bizarre and grisly murder. Aren't you just as curious about it as I am? Or perhaps you know more about it than I do.'

'No, of course I don't!' Hildegard responded brusquely. 'There was a little problem that needed ironing out, and that was why I had to make a flying visit to Lanner Castle. Robertson stipulated that his treasures should be shown *en bloc* in special rooms. We would have preferred to integrate them with our own exhibits and to have set aside some for travelling displays. Keeping them all together will, in fact, involve us in adding to the existing building and raising finance over and above what we receive from the company.'

'How did your discussions go?'

'Jack Robertson was a very stubborn man. He had the whip hand and he knew it. We had to agree to his terms. But,' she added quickly, 'our meeting was perfectly amicable.'

Tim recalled the doctor's glum, self-absorbed silence at the Lanner Castle

255

dinner table. 'So there was no serious disagreement, no suggestion that Robertson might change the terms of his will in a fit of pique?'

'And give me a motive for murder? Certainly not. The idea is preposterous.'

They wandered on through chronologically arranged galleries, and Tim found himself impressed by the juxtaposition of beauty and bestiality, displays devoted to the arts of peace and war. Tim was careful to keep his observations and questions on neutral ground. He asked about the proposed annexe. When would it be built and opened? Dr Nefsky replied that delicate negotiations were currently in train over funding and planning permission. Decisions had, as Tim would realise, been forced upon everyone concerned because of the unexpected way that the institute had come into its legacy. Eventually they returned to the director's ground-floor office, where Dr Nefsky offered her guest tea and gave him a copy of the institute's thick, heavily illustrated catalogue.

After glancing through it for some moments, Tim dropped it beside his deep armchair. 'So what do you think really happened to Robertson?' he asked.

Hildegard clenched her eyes shut momentarily and shuddered. 'I try not to think about it. Jack was a visionary. He was rather like a medieval hermit, cutting himself off from the world in order to contemplate its follies with detachment. That someone could hunt him down and... It just proves what we're trying to say here, doesn't it? However civillsed man becomes, he's still capable of...things like that.'

'Someone must have really had it in for him. Who can it have been? You obviously knew him as well as anyone and better than most. Did he never mention fanatical enemies, people who might be capable of planning an elaborate and painful execution?'

'Execution?' She jumped at the word.

'Well, that's surely what it was, wasn't it? As I suggested after the funeral, someone warned Robertson that they were going to kill him and how they were going to kill him. He took the warnings very seriously—even fled, presumably to some hideaway he thought would be safer than the castle. But the murderer tracked him down and then carried out his gruesome threat. Instead of shooting Robertson or battering him to death in an outburst of insane rage, he drugged or stunned him, locked him into one of his own torture implements and...well, I need not elaborate. To my mind that suggests a premeditated campaign of punishment, a perverted sense of visiting justice on an offender who has broken some law, violated some code.'

'All it suggests to me is the activities of a madman.'

'You could be right, but we mustn't overlook one uncomfortable fact.'

'What's that?' Hildegard looked at him warily.

'The murderer or his accomplice was in the castle the night we stayed there.'

'Well, yes, of course, that had occurred to me. That business with the parrot...'

'Not to mention stealing Cumberland's Cradle. I wonder how on earth they got that off the island.'

'It must have been one of the servants. They knew the castle better than any of us. One of the boatmen, perhaps; he could easily have bundled the thing up and brought it across to the mainland.'

'Do you think so?' Tim paused and gave every appearance of weighing the opinion carefully. 'No, my money's still on Lombardo. I mean, the man does have a criminal record.'

Dr Nefsky assumed a puzzled frown. 'Lombardo—that was the name you mentioned last week, in Scotland. Were you referring to the American...Cal Lopez?'

'Yes—that wasn't his real name. He is Carlos Lombardo, Mexican by birth, although he now has an American passport.

He has been investigated by the FBI on suspicion of illicit dealings in arms and drugs. They've brought some of his associates to book, but Lombardo has always slipped through their fingers.'

Hildegard stared horrified across the broad expanse of her desk. 'You must be mistaken.'

'No. I met Lombardo once, briefly, and had occasion to check him out. I discovered that he was heavily into syndicated crime in California...'

'I can't believe it. To think that we were actually sitting at the same table as such a man. It's horrible!'

'But it does tie up with Robertson's death, doesn't it? Being murdered in that way—a kind of public execution—it has all the hallmarks of a gangland killing.'

Hildegard made no reply. After some moments Tim said in a brighter voice, 'Sorry. I'm afraid I've been dwelling on the morbid and unwholesome, and that's a poor way to repay your hospitality. What plans do you have for the new annexe—or is that a closely guarded secret?'

They chatted for another quarter of an hour, and then Tim got up to take his leave. He leaned across the desk and shook the director's hand. He read relief in her face. 'Please don't bother to show me out. I've taken up enough of your time already.

Thank you so much for the tour. It's been fascinating.'

He crossed to the door and, with a final smile to Hildegard Nefsky, left the office. But he was careful not to pull the door completely shut behind him. He was testing out a theory—or, more accurately, a guess. Dr Nefsky was not all she seemed—of that he was sure. It was just possible that he might be able to prove it. He walked as far as the marble hall, stopped, retraced his steps along the corridor, and came to a halt outside her office door.

He could hear Hildegard's voice, and he bent his ear to the crack to understand her words.

'...knows all about Lombardo... No, I don't think so, but we shouldn't bank on it... Yes, I'm sure that would be wise...'

Tim knocked loudly on the door and pushed it open in the same movement. He crossed the room quickly. 'Don't let me disturb you,' he half whispered. 'Forgot the catalogue.' He bent quickly and picked up the glossy volume from the floor. He flashed a quick smile and hurried from the room.

'Gotcha!' he muttered as he walked down the broad front steps of Sandby House.

CHAPTER 12

When Tim entered his office the morning after his session with Hildegard Nefsky he found George Martin comfortably ensconced in an armchair, reading the *Daily Mail*.

'Morning, George.'

'Morning, Major.' He peered over the top of his tabloid. 'Did we oversleep, then?'

'Had to run the boys to school. Catherine's in Gloucester organising an exhibition. What can I do for you? Problems?'

'Not mine, Major. I thought you'd want to know what I've got on Robertson/Rycote.'

'Did your friend Nipper Beal come up trumps?'

'Yeah, cost me a pub lunch—which I'm putting down to expenses.'

Tim grinned. 'It'd better be worth it, then.'

'It's certainly interesting, though I'm not sure how much further it gets us.' George folded his paper carefully and laid it on the desk, took out a notebook, licked his finger and flicked over the pages. 'Nipper was a bit bothered about data protection and wouldn't put anything in writing, so I had to scribble down info as best I could. Still, I think I got the gist of it. Right, here we go.' He read. 'There were only two Rycotes who left the service at the time we're interested in. One was invalided out—wheelchair case. We can forget him. The other was John Chaloner Hastings Rycote—what a mouthful! Military family. Posh school. Commissioned in the Guards, no less. Ten years in the service. Tours of duty in Kenya—that must have been the tail-end of the Mau-Mau troubles—Cyprus, Germany and Northern Ireland. Never made it above captain. Poor disciplinary record. Dishonourable discharge for conduct unbecoming—that was twenty-three years ago.'

'Not what you'd call a model officer. What had he been up to?'

George closed his notebook. 'Nipper didn't know. Court-martial records are handled by another department and guarded very closely. He doesn't have security clearance.'

'Pity. It would be interesting to know what he got up to and what he did between leaving the army and going to Scotland.'

'Do you really reckon all this is relevant? Sounds like ancient history to me.'

'Well, he was obviously up to no good all those years ago. Subsequently he got involved with the Mafia, and somewhere along the line he made a great deal of money. Add to all that the fact that he was a sadist, obsessed by cruelty and violence, and you have the sort of man who makes enemies.' He closed his eyes, frowning in concentration. 'I wonder if there's anyone else who can tell us about John Chaloner Hastings Rycote. There must be some family somewhere.'

'You could try the ancestral home.' George laboriously reopened his notebook. 'Rycote Hall, Compton Marney, near Petersfield, Hants.'

Tim raised his eyebrows. 'Impressive. Master Jack really did come from the quality, then. It begins to look as though he was the black sheep of a very white family.'

'So, what do you reckon he was up to, then?'

Tim sat back, running a finger thoughtfully along the bridge of his nose. 'Well, there's one element that keeps cropping up in everything we know about Rycote/Robertson—military hardware. He came from an army family, so he was familiar with guns and other weapons from an early age. He had ten years in the service, some of it front-line duty.

I discovered yesterday that he was a close friend of Friederich Lederer, the arms king.'

'Lederer.' George frowned. 'Why does that name ring a bell? Wasn't he one of the blokes some of those Israeli Nazi hunters were after back in the seventies?'

'I don't know, George. According to Hildegard Nefsky, he left Germany before the war.'

'Yes, it's coming back to me now. The Israelis reckoned Lederer was involved in setting up concentration camps, but he claimed he was in South America somewhere. They said he'd obviously fixed himself up with an elaborate alibi but they were never able to prove it.'

'Well, that could be another piece of the jigsaw. The Latin-American connection may be significant. Robertson had dealings with Carlos Lombardo and we know that he's an illicit arms dealer. Moreover, I confirmed yesterday what I suspected before, that Lombardo and Harman-Lederer are hand-in-glove. As soon as I left the fair Hildegard she was on the phone to her colleagues in the company to let them know what I'd sussed out about the little mafioso.'

'So what do you reckon—they had a falling out with Robertson and dealt with him in traditional gangland fashion?'

'That's certainly one scenario.'

'Your snooping around after the funeral must have put the wind up them—hence their attempt to run you and Johnny off the road.'

'Maybe. They had time to organise an impromptu accident. They could check the number of our car and find out what time we were leaving. It would take some arranging, but given an efficient criminal organisation it could be done.'

'Then, when they muffed it, they got the Nefsky woman to find out exactly what you do know.'

'Possibly.'

'So, what did you tell her?'

'I didn't pull any punches. I wanted to see what her reaction would be. I gave her a pretty detailed dossier on Lombardo.'

George exhaled breath noisily. 'You want your head examined!'

'Why's that?'

'If you've nearly been stung by a wasp, you don't go and poke a stick in the nest. These people have tried to kill you once and you've just given them an excellent reason to have another bash.'

'Call it a calculated risk, George. The only way we're going to find out anything is, as you say, to poke a stick in the nest and see what flies out.'

George stood up and went over to the

door. He looked back at his friend and boss. 'Well, OK, but promise me one thing.'

'What's that?'

'Remember me in your will.'

As the door closed Tim picked up the phone and buzzed his secretary. 'Morning, Sally. We'd better get down to the labours of the day. Can you bring in the post please?'

'Tim, there are two gentlemen here to see you. They say they have urgent business to discuss.'

'Who are they?'

'A Mr Hatherton and a Mr Smythe.'

The morning after Ewen and Tom had been tortured, Duncan the Red left Huich Castle with an escort of a dozen men.

'He'll be going personally to report to the Butcher on the information he's had from the prisoners,' Ewen said to his friend as they watched from a corner of the courtyard.

Tom nodded. 'Aye, so the garrison will be less than thirty for a couple of days. There's no better time. It will have to be tomorrow.'

'But how are we going to get the fire? We haven't worked that out yet.'

'I don't know, but we must get it somehow. Everything depends on it. By the time Duncan gets back it'll be too late and he'll know he's been tricked.'

Throughout the day they both pondered the problem. Neither had come up with an answer by the time the children were shut in for the night. Despite that, Ewen called everyone together. When they were seated in a ring around him he announced, 'We're leaving here tomorrow.' Over the murmurs and gasps he went on: 'We have a plan. We've already told you part of it. Now we'll tell you it all. Everyone will have a job to do and success depends on each person doing the right thing at the right time. So listen carefully.'

Tom went over the details and repeated them again and again until he was sure that each boy and girl knew exactly what was supposed to happen on the morrow. When the clansmen had been dismissed he and Ewen retired to their bed spaces. After a while Tom said, 'I think the fire will have to come from the great hall.'

'That's risky. Duncan's son or some of his officers might be there.'

'There's nowhere else. And I think I can see how we could do it.'

Ewen listened to his friend's scheme. It had flaws. It could fail at two or three points, and if it failed then everything else would fail. But, as Tom said, there was nowhere else to find fire. Neither of them slept that night.

In the morning they joined the others on the ground floor. Ewen checked that no one had any questions about what he or she had to do. He wished them all luck. Tom said, 'It'll be around the middle of the day, when the soldiers have their food. Be in the courtyard. Watch out for Ewen and me and take your cue from us.' Then they waited for the morning routine.

Every day was the same. The elderly soldier appointed as their guardian brought them breakfast and came back about half an hour later to collect the dishes and lock them out of the tower for the day. When he arrived on this occasion he found the children unusually boisterous, and when he returned three of the younger ones were quarrelling. Roughly he thrust them all outside, picked up the bowls, closed the door and locked it. That was the moment at which two little boys, arms locked round each other in combat, crashed into him and sent him sprawling. He struggled to his feet, shouting imprecations and trying to grab hold of his assailants. While this was happening Tom slipped behind him, removed the key from the lock and replaced it with the one found on the rubbish dump. He sauntered away round the corner of the next building. Jenny was waiting. She took the key from him, tied it to a piece of string and hung it round her neck beneath her dress.

The children went about their morning tasks but their minds were not on their work. Each was thinking of what lay ahead, and the part he or she had to play in it. When the sun had passed its highest point Tom and Ewen met up near the side gate of the courtyard. Just inside was the pile of logs which were stacked here when they arrived from the mainland. The solitary guard paid no attention when the boys began filling one of the large wicker baskets beside the heap; they often came to collect fuel for the big fire in the great hall.

Tom and Ewen crossed the courtyard carrying their burden between them and looking around for the others. Three were sitting near the main gate polishing a pile of boots. In the far corner Jenny nodded and slipped around the side of the building towards the tower. The rest were in their appointed locations and looking busy.

The two boys entered the great hall. Two officers standing just inside the door glanced at them briefly and then carried on with their conversation. Tim and Ewen walked the length of the room and began unloading the logs on one side of the large fireplace.

Tom whispered, 'We can't do anything

while they're here,' indicating the soldiers still talking and laughing.

'Well, just take your time. Perhaps they'll go.'

They reached the bottom of the basket and stayed where they were, crouched in the hearth.

'Hey you!' One of the men was calling to them. He sauntered down the hall towards them. 'Get a move on, you lazy Highland brats!' He stood towering over them. 'I suppose you're trying to make a simple job last all day. Well, just for that you can bring another basketful.'

Ewen and Tom looked puzzled. The man cuffed them and swore, and then indicated by sign language that they were to fetch more logs. They hurried from the room. As they almost ran across the courtyard, Ewen looked around at the other children and quickly shook his head. When they returned to the hall with their second load the room was empty.

Quickly they emptied the basket of all but a couple of small pieces of wood. Then Ewen, wrapping the sleeves of his shirt round his hands, lifted a glowing ember from the fire and placed it carefully on top of the wood. A couple more logs were added to buttress the burning brand. Then Ewen said, 'Quickly, before it goes out.'

They hurried back into the sunlight. As

they emerged, Ewen nodded to the others who were waiting for a sign. From the corner of his eye he saw Jenny walk slightly stiffly across the corner of the yard towards a low building separate from the others. Tom and Ewen made for the same spot, the garrison's powder magazine.

The two men who came into the office were dark-suited and sombre. The taller one whipped out an identity warrant with a well-practised gesture, and was about to put it away again when Tim held out his hand for it. He took the wallet and read the information printed beside the postage-stamp-sized photograph: 'Metropolitan Police Force. Detective Chief Superintendent Bernard Hatherton'.

Tim returned the documents. 'Special Branch top brass—what have I done to merit such an honour?'

Unbidden, the two policemen sat down. Hatherton stared with grey eyes fixed in a face devoid of expression. 'Not to put too fine a point on it, Mr Lacy, you've been getting in the way.'

Tim came round the desk and perched on its edge, looking down at his unwanted guests. 'You'll have to spell that out for me.'

'Don't frig around with us! You know

271

damned well...' Smythe burst out, but was motioned to silence by his superior.

Tim looked at the younger man and recognised the type—the junior officer given to bluster, hiding inadequacy behind rank and power.

Hatherton was cooler, restrained, enigmatic, potentially more dangerous. 'You know we're Special Branch, Mr Lacy, and that we're investigating the death of Mr John Robertson. Being an intelligent and well-informed man, you will realise that the death is of more than purely local significance. We don't concern ourselves with every eccentric millionaire who gets himself murdered.'

'Sure.' Tim agreed cautiously. 'Somehow Robertson's assassination touches matters of national security, government interest or international relations.'

'Exactly. That means it has to be handled with great sensitivity. Now, that's our forte. We happen to be well trained in carrying out this kind of investigation. You, on the other hand, are not.'

'I have done—'

'The state some service?' Hatherton suggested. 'That is a matter of record—of impressive record. Some of my colleagues speak glowingly of help you have given in matters relating to stolen art and antiques. Your contacts and expertise have been very useful. But we're not dealing here with purloined Picassos or faked Fragonards.'

'I was going to say,' Tim observed, 'that I have done nothing wrong—unless talking with people about a particularly unpleasant murder has become a criminal offence.'

Smythe could not contain himself. ' "Talking with people", as you innocently put it in your smart-arse way, could put the murderer on his guard and bugger up our attempts to trap him.'

Tim raised an eyebrow and spoke to Hatherton. 'I see what you mean by sensitivity.'

Hatherton pinched the crease in his immaculately pressed trousers. 'My colleague has a direct way of putting things, but what he says is substantially correct.'

'Then you won't mind if I am equally direct, though perhaps a little less offensive. I don't think you're very concerned about catching Robertson's murderer. And I have a whole string of reasons for reaching that decision. A colleague and I were at Lanner Castle the night Robertson vanished. Before that he told us all about the threats he had been receiving. Yet no one from your department has approached either of us for a statement. Some of my men were working at the castle when Robertson's body was discovered. Not one of them has been interviewed. There were other people staying there during these events. Several I have spoken to have not been asked for any evidence. What have you and your men done?' Tim checked the items off on his fingers. 'You grabbed the body. You hushed up the inquest. If you hadn't come under pressure from cabinet level you'd have put off the funeral even longer. You confiscated all Robertson's papers. You've told the dead man's daughter nothing about the progress of your enquiry. That doesn't sound to me like an investigation. Do you know what it does sound like?' He took a few paces round the room. 'It sounds like a cover-up.'

'Watch it!' Smythe blurted.

Tim continued to ignore him. 'You were good enough to call me intelligent and well-informed. So I assume you might be interested to hear my intelligent and well-informed analysis of this wretched business.'

Hatherton nodded almost imperceptibly. 'You've gathered every scrap of evidence in order to destroy it. You've failed to interview witnesses so that the whole business will die down. Because I'm not disposed to let it die down you've come here to throw your weight around. And you're doing that because you failed to get me killed in a staged accident.'

'What on earth are you talking about?' It was the elder policeman's turn to protest.

'Are you suggesting that it wasn't your boys who tried to run me off the road in Scotland the day after the funeral?'

Hatherton exchanged a quick glance with his underling, who shook his head. 'Tell me about it,' he said.

Briefly Tim related his tussle with the Land Rover.

Hatherton frowned. 'You have my assurance that that had nothing to do with us. We don't operate that way.'

'Maybe not, but you know people who do—Department A3 at MI5, isn't it?'

The blank expression returned to Hatherton's face. 'I'm interested in this conspiracy theory of yours. What, in your opinion, lies behind all our cunning subterfuge?'

Tim resumed his position leaning against the desk. He looked straight at Hatherton. 'I'd say it has something to do with dodgy arms deals.'

'Go on.'

'The only thing that connects Robertson with Harman-Lederer *and* with a particularly unpleasant American citizen by the

275

name of Carlos Lombardo is the sale of weapons. I think the government was surreptitiously facilitating certain sordid negotiations. Harman-Lederer was having to supply weapons to an objectionable foreign regime. I think the company was using Robertson and Lombardo in those negotiations and that they had a falling out, which proved fatal to Robertson. The last thing our political lords and masters can allow is for any of this to get out. So it's up to MI5 and their chums in Special Branch to sweep everything firmly under the mat.'

'And I suppose you regard yourself as a lone knight errant sallying forth to topple the giants of corporate greed and political corruption.' Hatherton permitted himself a cynical smile. 'What I see is a Quixote, tilting against windmills. This imaginative scenario you have projected is no more than that. You have not stumbled upon a British Watergate. There is no elaborate cover-up orchestrated by Number Ten. The prime minister is not quaking in his shoes for fear of what Mr Timothy Lacy may discover. No SIS hit squads are roaming the country with a contract on your life.'

'So, if there are no matters of national importance at stake, why this visit?'

'I didn't say that. We are investigating

certain people and events. I will go so far as to tell you that we have Carlos Lombardo under surveillance and are piecing together his dealings with the late Jack Robertson. But these matters are no concern of yours.'

For the first time Tim allowed his anger to surface. 'That's exactly the kind of statement that makes my gorge rise. You think you can make your own rules. A bunch of people become involved in a bizarre and upsetting murder. I nearly get tumbled down a Scottish mountainside. A young woman is traumatized because her father has been methodically and terrifyingly done to death. She wants to know who and why and what on earth her father has been mixed up in. She needs answers—we all do. And you come along and tell her, "This isn't your business. Leave it with us. We—the Establishment, Big Brother—know best." God, but you're so bloody arrogant!'

Smythe struggled out of his armchair. 'You watch what you're—'

'Oh, shut up!' Tim placed a foot on the young man's chest and pushed, so that Smythe fell back with a gasp and a scowl. 'And all that's before we get down to things like justice. Whoever killed Robertson—or Rycote, or whatever his name is—has to be brought to book.

277

Andrea deserves it. Society deserves it. Justice isn't a card in the government's hand to be played or not according to the state of some political game.'

Hatherton stared back in silence for some seconds and Tim could almost hear his mental cogs whirling. Eventually he stood up. 'I think we've just had what, in diplomatic circles, is known as a full and frank exchange of views, Mr Lacy. I hope we will all profit from it. For the moment I don't think there's any more that can usefully be said.'

He turned and left the office. Smythe gave Tim the benefit of a glare full of malicious promise, then followed.

For some moments Tim stood motionless, thinking hard. Then he shouted, 'Damn! Lacy you're an idiot!' He picked up the internal phone and put a call through to George's office.

'George, can you drop what you're doing for the rest of the morning?'

'No.'

'Good. Meet me in the garage in five minutes.'

'What've you been up to now?'

'Stirring up another wasps' nest.'

'So what's new! Where are we going in such a hurry?'

'Rycote Hall, Compton Marney, near Petersfield, Hants.'

CHAPTER 13

As George slipped into the BMW's passenger seat Tim handed him a road atlas. 'Take me the fastest route to Petersfield.' He let in the clutch and eased the car out of Farrans Court's stable yard and on to the long drive through parkland to the main road.

'I'm never going to get any paperwork done at this rate. Why all this ruddy blush?'

'Because I let something slip to a rather smart policeman and I don't think he'll waste any time before he follows it up.' Tim reported his conversation with Hatherton. 'Like an idiot I revealed that we knew Robertson's other name. I saw him prick up his ears.'

'And you reckon he'll be off hotfoot to put the frighteners on Rycote's family?'

'He's in the business of closing loopholes and plugging leaks. If he didn't follow up this lead he wouldn't be doing his job. My guess is that he'll make a detour to Compton Marney on his way back to London.'

'Well,' George consulted his maps, 'it's

279

the best part of sixty miles cross-country and he's got a head start.'

'I'm banking rather heavily on two things: we know the roads better than he does, and he may not see any reason to be in a tearing hurry.' Tim nursed the 525i round a long right-hand bend, then accelerated towards Stibb Green and the A338.

They drove into Compton Marney as the dashboard clock registered 10.52. Assembling clouds that had threatened rain were now being dispersed by the sun. Referring to an Ordnance Survey map, George had already located Rycote Hall. In the middle of the village's only street Tim turned the BMW in through tall stone pillars that had once supported gates. A pockmarked drive ran between fields where sheep ambled and lambs gambolled. It turned left past a deciduous copse, hazed with the fresh green of new foliage, and ended abruptly in a circle of tarmac before the house. Rycote Hall was a more modest residence than Tim had expected. Square and three-storeyed, built of red brick with stone architraves to the door and windows, it was Queen Anne in style, though, he guessed, no older than the nineteen-twenties or thirties.

Tim brought the car to a gentle halt. He and George climbed out and approached the front door. He rang the bell. The woman who after a few moments opened the door wide and stood like a warrior guarding the pass at Thermopylae was tall, or perhaps gave that impression by her erect bearing and the upward tilt of her chin. She was in her mid-sixties and wore a greyish-mauve woollen dress. Her hair was granite-coloured and her long, well-boned face might have been carved from that stone.

'Mrs Rycote?' Tim ventured.

'My name is Chaloner,' the *femme formidable* declared. 'I do not buy from itinerant salesmen, and if you are Jehovah's Witnesses all I have to say is that I have been Church of England all my life and have no intention of changing now.'

The door began to close and Tim thought quickly. 'You're quite right to be wary of Jehovah's Witnesses, Mrs Chaloner. There are a couple working their way through the village today. I'm glad to say we're nothing to do with them. May I present my card?'

She took the rectangle of pasteboard he offered and held it at arm's length to read it. 'Security installations? What would I want with one of them?'

'No home today should be without adequate protection from the criminal fraternity, Mrs Chaloner.'

281

'Mr...' She squinted again at the card. '...Lacy, I no longer have anything worth stealing, and I certainly cannot afford security installations—whatever they may be.'

'Sadly, burglary isn't just a matter of theft. There's damage to property and the distress of having strangers going through your belongings. We also have to consider personal violence. But I don't want to pester you. Perhaps you'd like to think over the possibility of securing your property and give me a ring if you'd like me to call and explain what my company can do.'

Mrs Chaloner gave a gracious, almost royal, nod.

Tim began to walk away, then, as if suddenly remembering something, turned back. 'Oh, I wonder if you could help me. I understood that a Mr and Mrs Rycote lived here. I was obviously mistaken...'

'Not so much mistaken as thirteen years out of date, Mr Lacy. My parents were Mr and Mrs Rycote.' She pronounced the word 'Ricott'. I am the last of the line. My married name, as I've told you, is Chaloner. Good-day to you.'

'Goodbye and thank you, Mrs Chaloner. And watch out for those Jehovah's Witnesses.'

Back in the car Tim chuckled. 'I do

hope Hatherton and Smythe turn up here today.'

'Well, if they have a wasted journey they won't be the first ones,' George grumbled.

Tim took the rough drive at a sedate pace. 'Oh, I wouldn't say that it was wasted. Did you get a good look into the hall?'

'Oh yes. Lots of very military portraits. That certainly chimes in with what Nipper told me. What relation do you reckon that old biddy is to our Jack Rycote?'

Tim turned the car into the village street. 'At a guess I'd say elder sister, wouldn't you? Her parents presumably left her the ancestral home.'

'Where does that leave Jack?'

Tim parked the car behind a Land Rover and horsebox. 'Disowned, I suppose. Proud military dynasty. Son gets himself cashiered and brings shame on the family. They'd find that very hard to forgive.'

'So you reckon they cut him off without a shilling and told him never to darken the door of Rycote Hall again?'

'Well, that's as good a working hypothesis as any. I'm going to have a snoop around the village. Why don't you wait for me in the pub? See if you can find some old codger ready to dish the local dirt in exchange for a pint.'

While George made for the Rycote Arms, Tim crossed the road to the post office-cum-general store. He squeezed between racks of packaged foods and detergents to a less cramped corner, where he browsed through a rack of postcards. As soon as the shop's only other customer had left, Tim carried a selection to the counter.

'Lovely village,' he observed to the middle-aged postmistress.

'It's quiet and off the beaten track,' she agreed. 'Are you on holiday?'

'Not really. I'm actually doing some historical research—leading families of the nineteenth century, that sort of thing. I suppose the Rycotes were the biggest landowners round here then.'

'One pound fifty-eight, please.' The woman slipped the cards into a little paper bag. 'I suppose they must have been, what with the hall and the pub being named after them.'

'Are there any of the family left?'

She shook her head. 'No one of that name hereabouts now. You'll have been up to the church, of course, and seen all the memorials round the walls.'

'I'm on my way there now. Thank you for the cards.'

The small, squat-towered church stood on a small rise above the village at the end of a path running between overarching yews. After a few seconds inside it was obvious to Tim that Saints Philip and James, Compton Marney, was a treasure house of funerary sculpture. Generations of local worthies had donated carved figures, incised tablets and elaborate tombs to remind God and man of their importance. A book rack just inside the door contained a display of dog-eared devotional paperbacks and piles of guide books whose pristine condition suggested a more rapid turnover. One of the latter attracted Tim's attention. It was a pamphlet of some dozen or so pages, priced at twenty pence and entitled, *The Rycote Family and their Memorials*. He picked up a copy and slipped a pound coin through an aperture in the wall, which a faded notice on yellowing card designated as the appropriate posting box for 'donations'.

He spent the next few minutes touring the building and locating the monuments, under the guidance of the author, Major-General Hastings Rycote, whose pamphlet outlined the brief lives of members of a family prominent in the locality from the mid-eighteenth century. The soldier was surprisingly lively and occasionally scurrilous in detailing the doings of his ancestors. But he had nothing whatever to say about one inscription. Beside the south door a small slab of black marble was let into the wall. Its incised and gilded lettering conveyed a simple message:

Near this spot are deposited the ashes of
CAPTAIN JOHN CHALONER HASTINGS
RYCOTE
1940–1975
'There is joy in Heaven over one sinner that repenteth'

Outside the powder store Tom and Ewen found Jenny on her knees. She had taken the pitcher of lamp oil and was pouring it beneath the door. When she had finished she concealed the container again beneath her dress and walked nonchalantly away. The boys knelt in her place. They were concealed from view by a haycart a couple of paces away. While Tom tipped out the logs Ewen, grabbed a handful of dry hay. He held it to the smouldering ember. Both boys blew fiercely upon it. It smoked. It threw off sparks. But it would not ignite the tinder.

'Come on! Come on!' Ewen was sweating.

Tom, outwardly calmer, blew more fiercely. At last there was a flicker of flame. He held the torch to the pool of oil. It caught and flared up. As soon as the fire had spread to the other side of the door Ewen stamped on the flames outside

286

so that there was no indication of anything amiss. Then they walked steadily back to the side gate with the basket.

'Do you think it'll catch?' Tom asked.

'I saw some sacks just inside the door a few days ago. They'll burn very readily.' But he was not as confident as he sounded.

They replaced the basket and walked slowly towards the entrance to the dungeon, trying not to look across the courtyard.

Tom muttered, 'I was wrong. It was a rotten plan. It's not going to—'

They felt a sudden blast of hot air followed instantly by a dull roar. Instinctively they drew back against the wall. Fragments of wood and stone spattered around them. They stared open-mouthed at the place where they had been moments before. The cart had disintegrated. Clumps of burning hay were floating down all around the courtyard. The building beyond was hidden by a dense smoke cloud, but only momentarily. Another flash illuminated it from the inside. The accompanying explosion tore it apart. Others followed.

There was pandemonium. A soldier slumped against the wall beside the boys, holding his hand to a gashed face which spouted blood. Others were rushing around. Officers emerged from doorways, shouting orders to which no one listened. There were cries of 'Water!' Guards threw open the main gates and men rushed out to fill buckets from the loch. Ewen saw three smaller figures follow them. He stood mesmerised by the chaos he had caused. Then from the door a few paces away two jailers came running, and he recalled that there was still work to be done.

He and Tom darted down the dungeon steps. He grabbed the keys and began opening the cell doors. Prisoners stumbled forth. 'This way, please,' Ewen shouted, and started up the steps. He came face to face with the point of a sword.

Alistair Duncan descended the staircase holding his sabre before him. His jacket was open, his cravat awry and he wore no wig. 'I was right!' He stared wildly round. 'I knew I could smell treachery.'

Ewen backed away as Duncan moved to the centre of the room.

'Right, you scum, back into your cells.' He brandished his sword.

Behind him Tom emerged from the shadow by the staircase. Carefully he took hold of the heavy chain hanging from the ceiling, then swung it with all his might. It caught Duncan in the small of the back and sent him sprawling against the rack. His sabre clattered on the flagstones. The nearest prisoner picked it up and in a single movement plunged it into Duncan's chest.

Ewen stared as the stricken man staggered, arms twitching and clutching for support, then sagged to the floor.

'Come along,' the man called Cameron shouted. 'Don't waste time on him. Where to now, boy?'

'The boats,' Ewen cried and ran up the steps.

When they emerged into the courtyard he saw that other buildings were already on fire and people were rushing to and fro in total confusion. No one stopped the escapees as they ran through the main gateway and down the steps to the water. The other children were waiting, holding three boats. Everyone scrambled into them. Tom and Ewen grabbed up the oars of the first and began pulling away. Two of the prisoners rowed the others and were swift to follow.

After a few strokes Cameron called out, 'Steer away from the village, boys. They may not be friendly.'

Tom and Ewen headed for a spot on the coast half a mile further up the loch. They were concentrating so hard on making a landfall that the sound of musket-fire took them completely by surprise. Looking back they saw a boatload of soldiers leaving the island in pursuit. Some were loosening off their weapons as they came. There was nothing the escapees could do but row faster.

Ewen and Tom landed first, nosing their boat into a place where bracken and bushes came down to the water's edge. They helped everyone else ashore then led the scramble up the bank. Two of the prisoners, weakened by torture, were slow and had to be pushed and pulled up the slope by their companions. Their pursuers were getting closer and they had no cover to shield them from the sporadic gunfire. One of the girls screamed as a ball struck her in the leg. Tom stopped to grab her. He swung her on to his shoulders and continued scrambling upwards.

At last they reached the road which wound up the hill from Briachan. The party made their way along it, the children and four of the prisoners moving rapidly but the others panting and stumbling badly.

Tom stopped. 'They're not going to manage it, Ewen.'

'We can't let the soldiers catch them. Not after all this.'

'No. Look, you lead them across country. I'll take a couple of the clansmen up the road and get the dogs to follow us. We'll easily outrun them. Here, look after this one.' He swung the wounded girl from his shoulder.

There was no time to argue. Ewen called to most of the party to follow him and led them into deep bracken on the other side of the road. They struck across the flank of the hill to a belt of woodland and stopped to rest in its cover. Ewen climbed a tree to get a view of the road. He saw Tom and his two companions reach the top of the hill. Further down the road the soldiers were pursuing at the double. The children stopped to look back and Ewen knew Tom was making sure they were being followed. The dogs stopped, too. They raised their muskets, took steady aim and fired. Then they reloaded and fired again. As Ewen watched, horrified and helpless, his friends crumpled and fell to the roadway.

While Tim was making his discoveries in the church of Saints Philip and James, Compton Marney, George was propped up against one corner of the lounge bar in the Rycote Arms. The hour was early and only two other members of the pub's lunchtime clientele had arrived. George found that the landlord, a man of about his own age, was only too happy to talk.

He laughed when the visitor mentioned that he had just been up to the hall. 'I don't suppose you got much change out of the general's daughter.'

'Not much,' George admitted ruefully.

'I thought not. She's a pillar of the Church and just about as hard. Her husband got fed up with her—and with the struggle to make the estate pay. He took off about six years ago.'

'I suppose that's what comes of being the last of a long line of soldiers.'

The landlord shrugged. 'Her father—the old general—he was all right. Many's the evening he sat in here spinning yarns about army life. Went a bit ga-ga at the end, poor old chap, but that was probably his son's fault.'

'Oh, how was that?' George tried not to sound too eager for information.

'Morning, Harry.' The man moved to the other end of the bar to serve a new arrival. He was soon involved in an argument about a big fight shown on television the previous evening.

It was several minutes before he came back and George had to prompt him. 'You were saying, about the general and his son...'

'Oh, yes. Sad business. Of course, it was a long time ago now. My father had the pub then. That was before he bought it from the brewery. Took every penny he could scrape together, but it was well worth it in the long run. The way some of these brewing conglomerates treat their licensees today you wouldn't believe.'

He took a pull at his pint of bitter and George grasped the opportunity to grab the conversational steering wheel. 'What went wrong between the general and his son?'

'The old boy pinned all his hopes on the son and heir. He had Jack's life planned out for him—military career, marriage to the right kind of girl, lots of sons to carry on the army tradition. But Jack had other ideas. He was a real tearaway. I ought to know: as often as not I was one of his partners in crime. His father was always bailing him out when he got into scrapes. But when he managed to have himself thrown out of the army the general told him enough's enough. We never saw no more of the lad after that. I say "lad", but he would have been the same age as me.'

'Would have been?' George fastened on the words. 'What happened to him?'

'I don't think anyone rightly knows. He got involved in some unsavoury business overseas—Africa I think it was, but I could be wrong. Anyway, it was one escapade too many. He fell foul of the sort of police force that shoots first and asks questions later.'

'You mean he was killed?'

'Yes. That destroyed the general good and proper. He'd have come round in time and welcomed the prodigal back. But he never got the chance because his only son—the last of the Rycotes—was gunned down in a shoot-out... So, like I say, he went to pieces. He was dead within a twelvemonth.'

'So his daughter inherited the hall?'

'That's right. She'd married a cousin, so I suppose there was some chance of keeping the family going. But they had no kids. Knowing the general's daughter I suppose you can't wonder at it. OK, Edgar, I'm not deaf.' That to a regular noisily demanding service.

The landlord went about his duties and soon afterwards Tim came in. The two men ordered ploughman's lunches and sat at a corner table to wait for the food.

'I've just discovered something that'll raise your eyebrows.' George opined.

'Me too. You go first.'

'Well, according to local legend, Jack Rycote died a long time ago.'

'Snap! Only my version is a bit more substantial than village gossip.'

They compared notes.

'So, if Jack Rycote was bumped off in some seedy outpost of the empire over twenty years ago, who have they just buried in Scotland?' George asked, pausing in his enthusiastic ingestion of crusty bread and fresh cheddar.

Tim shook his head. 'This thing gets murkier the deeper we go... And talking about murky depths,' he lowered his head rapidly, 'don't look round: the Gestapo has just walked in.' From beneath lowered lids he looked across to where Hatherton and Smythe were standing at the bar.

The room was filling now and several people were between him and the policemen, but it could only be a matter of time before they saw him.

'I'd rather not be recognised right now,' Tim muttered.

George shrugged. 'If they're any good as coppers they'll find out we've been here.'

'Very probably, but we're not in the business of making their job any easier. Besides, right now Hatherton needs to find out how much we know. The more we can keep him guessing the more likely he is to be a bit more co-operative.'

'What's the plan then, Major?'

'Diversionary tactic. They don't know you. See if you can distract them long enough for me to get out the back way.'

George raised his eyes heavenward. 'The things I do for England!' He took a last, large mouthful of bread and cheese, then piled up the plates and glasses. 'Ready?' he asked through half-masticated food.

'Ready.'

George got to his feet, picked up the pile

of crockery and glass and weaved his way towards the counter where the two Special Branch men stood.

Seconds later there was a splintering crash. While everyone in the bar turned towards the noise and a red-faced George Martin staring down at the debris, Tim slipped out of his seat and went through a door marked 'Gentlemen'. As he had guessed, the rear premises of the Rycote Arms included an external door giving on to the pub's small car park. He went straight to the BMW.

Three minutes later George joined him. 'That's another fiver the firm owes me,' he grumbled as he sank into the passenger seat. 'Now can we go home?'

On the return journey they discussed the relationship between Rycote and Robertson, but could only agree that their discoveries in Compton Marney had made everything more complicated.

'I reckon we ought to pass on this one,' George suggested. 'We're never going to get to the bottom of it.'

Tim scowled at the Mini in front, which was doing a sedate 25 m.p.h. and was being driven by an elderly man who was hunched over the steering wheel and seemed to be peering at the road ahead with considerable difficulty. 'Can't do that, George—not yet, anyway. I can't stomach the way governments and their secretive agencies muck up the lives of ordinary people. Take the "death" of Jack Rycote. All we know is the story that was fed to his family. Now, supposing the truth is that he was actually killed while working for the British government, or even that they got him out of a potentially embarrassing situation and wanted people to believe that he was dead. Do you reckon they'd tell his parents that? Would they hell! They'd be much more likely to cover their tracks with some story about the black sheep of the family being involved in a sordid deal that went wrong. What do they care if that drives a proud old soldier into an early grave?'

Tim roared the BMW past the Mini and accelerated along a stretch of empty road. When he spoke again he was in a reflective mood. ' "There is joy in Heaven over one sinner that repenteth"—that's what it says on Jack Rycote's memorial. I find that incredibly sad.'

'Why's that?'

'The plaque must have been put there by his sister. She could ill afford it, but she had to do it. Jack was the last of the Rycotes. He had to have his memorial along with all his illustrious ancestors. But given what she'd been told about his death, what could she say about him? "There is joy in Heaven over one sinner that repenteth"—words that reflect pious hope rather than knowledge. She grieves as best she can for her kid brother, believing the worst but hoping for the best. And all the time the truth could be very different.'

'We don't know that, Major. From all I heard about Jack from one of his old mates he was always likely to end up like that.'

'So why don't Special Branch want us nosing about in the Rycote family history? What's the connection with Robertson? Why are they hushing up the real fact of his death? No, George, I don't buy it. What's happening now is a rerun of what happened after Rycote's death. They had no respect for his next of kin then and they've none for Robertson's now. All that matters is saving the establishment's face. God, that makes me angry!'

After a few silent miles had passed, George said, 'Oh, by the way, I've fixed my holiday. First two weeks in September—Maureen and I are doing a tour of the Highlands.'

Tim laughed. 'All this romantic Jacobite stuff has really got to you, hasn't it?'

'Yeah, why not? It's like making a new discovery. We had all that stuff about the forty-five and Bonnie Prince Charlie crammed into our heads at school and I thought it was all dead boring. But when you actually get close to the story, see the places where things happened, hear about the ordinary people who were involved...well, it comes to life, doesn't it!'

'Not to mention meeting up with phantom children,' Tim suggested mischievously.

'You can scoff all you like, Major. When you come up with a convincing, rational explanation for what I saw I'll be more than happy to believe. Till then I'm keeping an open mind. Anyway,' he added triumphantly, 'according to Johnny, the Robertsons' lawyer had an identical experience on the same stretch of road.'

'Apparently.'

'There you are then.' George's tone suggested that the case for the defence had been proved beyond a shadow of doubt. 'As a matter of fact,' he went on, 'I've just been reading a novel about the events of 1746 at Castle Huich. It's an old book; I got the library to track down a copy. The language is a bit flowery. It's called *Children of the Glen* by Flora McAlister. She describes how these kids were shut up in the castle and brutalised by their captors. Eventually they rose against them and extracted a terrible revenge. After that they formed themselves into an outlaw band.'

'Sounds a bit like modern street gangs.'

'Exactly the same thought struck me, Major. She gives an idealised picture of these deprived and maltreated Scottish kids, but basically it rings true. From what I read in proper history books, Highland society was totally disrupted for a couple of generations. There was a programme on telly the other night about juvenile crime in a very respectable London suburb, and someone said, "If you want to create a violent society the best way of doing it is to abuse children." It all ties up, doesn't it?'

'Churchill said that those who neglect their past are destined to repeat it.'

'Did he, now? Well, in my book, Churchill was right about most things.'

When they arrived back in the office Sally had a message for Tim. 'There's an Eleanor Jenkins been trying to contact you. She wouldn't leave a number; said it was "difficult" and she'd phone again this afternoon.'

CHAPTER 14

When Mrs Jenkins came on the line again, it was to ask Tim for a 'private' meeting. She and Graham had left the castle and were spending a few days in London before taking up a new appointment. It required little reading between the lines to realise that she wanted to see Tim without her husband knowing. He arranged to meet her the following afternoon at the London flat.

She arrived precisely on time, accepted a cup of tea and, as soon as Tim had seated himself on a chair opposite, explained her visit without any preliminaries. 'It will be obvious to you, Mr Lacy—'

'Tim,' he interrupted with a smile of encouragement.

'I'm sorry, but I'm happier with "Mr Lacy", if you don't mind. I know informality is the fashion these days, but after years in service I find it difficult to change my thought forms.'

'Whatever you feel more comfortable with. Please carry on.'

'I was remarking that it would be obvious to you that I shouldn't be here. If anyone found out it could get Graham—both of us—into very serious trouble.'

'Who with?'

She held up a hand. 'No questions, please, Mr Lacy. I've considered very carefully what to tell you. It will only be part of what I know, but it's as much as I dare say without it becoming obvious where your information came from. I'm telling you because I know you're trying

301

to help young Andrea. Although I've seen little of her over the last decade, I'm very fond of her. She's the nearest I've ever had to a child of my own. Most years she came once or twice to stay at the castle and she always spent the greater part of her time with me. It was like watching someone else's life in instalments. Every time she'd grown up a bit in different ways. Still.' She brushed the thoughts away. 'My sentimental reminiscences are neither here nor there. If what I have to say enables Andrea to come to terms with her father's death I shall be happy.'

'I understand, and I assure you that anything you tell me will be in confidence.'

'That's all right, Mr Lacy. I know I can trust you, otherwise I wouldn't be here. I'm going to give you two addresses. The first is 29 Inchferry Road, Edinburgh. That's where Mr Robertson went on the night he left the castle.'

'So, he had another bolt-hole he could run to?'

Eleanor Jenkins shook her head and Tim knew it was useless to press her further.

'The second address is Madame Jeanne Picard, Relais St Pierre, Charleville-sur-Seine, near Rouen, France.'

Tim raised a questioning eyebrow.

'That's Andrea's mother.'

'But I thought—'

'That she died when Andrea was a child? That's the official story. Jeanne was supposed to be as good as dead to her daughter. That never seemed right to me, so I stayed in touch on-and-off. I thought the time might come when Andrea would need her mother. I haven't heard from her in over two years now, but she was at that address then, helping her second husband to run a small hotel.'

Eleanor Jenkins stood up. The meeting was over. Tim helped her on with her coat. 'Thank you for telling me this. I appreciate that it wasn't an easy decision to confide in me.'

At the door she smiled as she shook hands. 'Clashing loyalties can make life very uncomfortable. I've had to live with them for twenty years. Goodbye, Mr Lacy. Please, help Andrea all you can.'

The government's deliberate destruction of the clan system and the laying waste of Highland settlements ensured that the chaos of war in Scotland was succeeded by the chaos of peace. Dispossessed crofters and tenant farmers were driven from the land by lairds encouraged to develop new methods of agriculture and estate management. Thousands fled across the border or beyond the seas from the fearful spectre of beggary. Some found other ways to keep their bellies full...

On a summer's evening in 1749 Dr George Hamilton rode homeward, attended by a single servant, after a long day treating Falkirk's sick. He had a fashionable practice and could, therefore, afford a sizeable house overlooking the Forth and built in the neo-classical style now fashionable in England. But Hamilton was a man of warm heart and cool principle. He religiously set aside fifty per cent of his time to working among the town's poor and supporting the free hospital.

The affable forty-year-old doctor was tired. He let his mare amble homeward at her own pace and had less conversation than usual to share with his man. He was looking forward to a quiet supper and the company of his wife and children. It was when he reached 'The Bend' that he was shaken from his comfortable lethargy. He and Anne, his wife, called this turn in the highway 'The Bend' because they regarded it almost proprietorally as a special, personal place. It was the first point on the road from which one obtained a clear view of Drumnaree, their beautiful, much-loved home. As he emerged from a belt of woodland where the road inclined sharply to the left he looked expectantly across the shallow valley.

'Good God!' He reined in, a look of horror on his face.

Drumnaree's gleaming and symmetrical façade stood out against a background of flame and smoke.

He prodded his horse into a canter and took the road, the winding lane and finally the carriage drive at a speed he had never used before. As he leaped from the saddle he realised that the fire was not in the main house but behind it. He ran around the building. The stable block was well ablaze. A group of estate workers were frantically breaking up the roof at the end of the range where it abutted the mansion to stop the flames spreading. Apart from them the entire household was occupied in a chain conveying buckets of water from the well to the conflagration. Hamilton and his manservant hurried to join the firefighters.

It was two hours before they brought the blaze under control. Then Hamilton set the servants to the work of extinguishing the last embers and seeing what, if anything could be salvaged from the ruin, while he put an arm around his drooping wife and helped her into the house. Anne's dark hair straggled all over her grimed face. Her silk dress was torn and wet.

She clung to him, whimpering, 'Oh, George, George, it was terrible.'

'Hush, my dear. Tell me about it later.' He summoned his wife's maid and gave instructions that Anne was to be undressed and put to bed.

Then he went to his own room, washed and changed. Half an hour later he entered Anne's chamber with a glass of brandy. She was wearing a clean day dress and lying on top of the coverlet. As she smiled up at him he congratulated himself, not for the first time, that he had married a woman who was as level-headed as she was beautiful, and did not have a fit of the vapours at the slightest domestic upheaval nor even a major crisis such as this.

'Here, my dear, drink this.'

Anne sniffed the spirit and winced. 'George, you know I—'

'A few sips, please. It will calm you.' He sat on the side of the bed. 'God be praised it was only the stable. Do you know how the fire broke out?'

She stared up at him, anger colouring her cheeks. 'It didn't break out—it was started.'

'What! By whom?'

'Let me tell you quickly, George, in my own way. You'll have to send into Falkirk for the constable and his men. They must get after the ruffians with the least possible delay.' She took another sip of the brandy, discovering that she needed it after all if she was to keep a hold on her anger and revulsion. 'It was outlaws, George. There were a dozen or more of them—some of them little more than children. They were led by a tall, dark, bearded man. He had a cockade in his hat and a plaid sash around his jerkin as a belt for his sword and pistol.'

'A forbidden tartan?'

'Yes.'

'One of these accursed Jacobites, then.'

'Yes. They forced their way in and demanded money and jewellery. One of them tore off my locket.' She put a hand to her throat. 'George, they were the most evil-looking, terrifying...and so young. I was more afraid for our children than anything else. The two little ones were safe upstairs. Only Becky was with me in the drawing room.' She trembled and sipped more brandy. 'Oh, poor Becky.'

'What happened? What did they—'

Anne held up a hand. 'I must tell it to you in order or it will all be horribly jumbled. Two of them—the man and a lad, fourteen or fifteen at most, who seemed to be his adjutant—held us in the drawing room. They both had pistols. They sent the others through the house to round up the servants and children and brought them all down to the same room. They went everywhere, taking whatever they fancied and bringing it to their leader who had a large sack. All I could think was, "For God's sake help yourself to whatever you want and go," but they weren't in the slightest hurry. They were so arrogant, sure of themselves, cocky.'

Anne paused. She took several deep breaths before she was able to continue. 'Then, the eldest boy—I think I heard one of the others call him Ewen—sat down on the sofa beside Becky and started stroking her hair. Of course, she was terrified. I asked him to stop but he just laughed. "Your daughter is very pretty," he said. "How old is she?" I told him she was just thirteen. He laughed again. "Old enough" he said. He grabbed her hand and pulled her towards the door. She screamed and old Rowly tried to help her...and that cowardly brute of a Jacobite pig shot him.'

'Killed him?'

'Praise God, no. But you'll need to tend him, dear. The ball took him in the shoulder but did not lodge. I went to see to him and while I was tearing open his shirt the boy dragged Becky upstairs.'

'Did he...?'

'Yes. I'm afraid she's in a terrible state, but what with the fire and Rowly I haven't been able to do anything for her.'

'I must go to her!'

'No, dear, I'll see to her directly. Marie's with her at the moment.'

George stood up and paced the room. 'The bastards! The lawless, bestial, Jacobite bastards! They'll pay for this. I suppose the fire was a final gesture of defiance.'

'When the boy—Ewen—had finished, the man said they must sadly deprive us of their company. But first they had something else to do. They were in need of fresh horses and, in case we had any ideas about sending for help, they would take everything in the stables and give us something else to think about into the bargain. They left two children—about ten years old—pointing their pistols at us while they went to carry out what they had threatened. They seemed very organised...almost military. When they left we rushed out to find the stables already blazing. This was about an hour before you came home.'

Anne moved to a sitting position on the bed. Her husband dropped beside her and held her close. 'Dearest, I'm so sorry I wasn't here. It's been a harrowing ordeal for you—for all of you. You're right. We must send to Falkirk straight away and alert the constable, though I fear the blackguards will be far away by now. Children, you say?'

'Yes, almost all of them.'

George sighed. 'I heard, some months ago, of a similar incident up near Perth. Well, children or no children, they'll swing. Sooner or later, they'll swing.'

'We do have a business to run.' Catherine Lacy threw the words at her husband across the boardroom table—and they hurt. At the monthly senior staff meeting of Lacy Enterprises the six participants were accustomed to speaking their mind. In terms of personnel theirs was a small business. Everyone knew everyone else. Most of the executives had been with Tim and Catherine from the early days. They had worked hard for and shared the success of this very successful two-sided operation. Tim had always encouraged frankness within the management team, but being challenged by his own wife in front of the others came as a shock.

Catherine, a forthright New Englander by upbringing, continued her attack, which was in no way softened by her laconic drawl. 'Emma and I are working our butts off getting the summer exhibition together. Added to that I'm doing daily battle with the builders to be finished and have their scaffolding away from the south front by preview day. George, as he's told us, has a stack of new installations to organise and is making a plea for more staff. We've got a team of four away all week at the Birmingham trade exhibition. I'm trying to make space for a few days in Germany and Austria to look at a batch of promising new artists—heaven knows whether I'll manage it. It doesn't look too good, Tim, when the boss is taking time off to play private detective.'

The outburst was followed by an embarrassed silence and downcast eyes.

Tim glowered round the table. 'Do I take it that vote of no-confidence is carried nem. con.?'

George met his gaze. 'Come off it, Major. You know Catherine didn't mean that. It's just that with business pressure as it is at the moment, extracurricular activities are a bit of a luxury.'

Tim thought hard. The others had inescapable logic on their side. Yet his gut feeling—that gut feeling that was Lacy Enterprises' biggest asset—was that they were wrong. 'Thanks for bringing the Scottish business up, Catherine. Let me try to explain how I see it. I can't justify my involvement in terms of pounds and pence or man hours. I never wanted to be an unlicensed PI. I certainly never planned for Lacy Enterprises to get involved in criminal investigations. But, as you know, over the years that's happened on a number of occasions. And it hasn't done the firm any harm. It's given us a higher public profile, earned us the respect of the police, brought us friends in high places. We've acquired a certain reputation, and people tend to come to us with their problems—especially when they've nowhere else to turn. I'm the first to admit that this particular baby has grown into a troublesome, attention-demanding adolescent, but we're stuck with it.'

'We could try saying no,' someone muttered.

'It's difficult to see any advantage for Lacy's in this Scottish business,' George added.

'I can't disagree with that but, as you're aware, all this started with what could have been a very lucrative contract and one which had useful government connections. By the time it all turned sour we were already heavily involved. Since then its complexities have reached almost Byzantine proportions.'

'My point exactly.' Catherine's bobbed blonde hair bounced as she nodded vigorously. 'This thing's gotten too big for us. We don't have the resources to follow up all the leads.'

Tim rubbed a finger along the bridge of his nose. 'Yes and no. The reason it's so complicated is that almost everyone involved has something to hide. Government,

construction companies, arms manufacturers, protest groups—they're all frightened of skeletons getting out of cupboards.
And Robertson's whole life, as we now
know, was one massive deception obviously
being used for a cover-up campaign.
With so many interested, powerful parties
involved, the chances of the truth coming
out are pretty slim. The only fly in all this
conspiratorial ointment is Lacy Enterprises.
George and I were there when the victim
was forced out of his secure stronghold
into the open, where the murderer could
strike quite safely. All the answers are in
the events of those few hours we spent in
the castle. We've got the truth in our grasp
if only we can unravel it. That's why we've
been warned off.'

'Not to mention nearly killed off.'
Despite the fact that Johnny had been
sworn to secrecy over the brush with the
Land Rover, Catherine had got to hear
about it and she had not been pleased.

'What it comes down to,' Tim hurried
on, 'is that someone killed the parrot and
stole Cumberland's Cradle. That someone
either murdered Robertson or was an
accomplice. Once we can figure out how
those things were done we'll know who
did them, and once we know that all
the secrecy and subterfuge will just fall
apart.'

'And then?' Catherine demanded.

'Then we'll have made life a little bit easier for a certain poor little rich girl. Already we're in a position to put her in touch with a mother she didn't know she had. Whatever else happens, that must be worthwhile. Also we'll have administered a kick in the backside to secrecy-obsessed establishments. I don't know about anyone else, but that certainly makes me feel good. As to what's in it for Lacy Enterprises —well, that's imponderable. It should be good PR. For example, Azikwe's in the diplomatic corps. Embassy security would certainly be a good market to break into.'

Tim looked around at five faces registering scepticism. 'OK. Compromise: I'll run with this for another week. If we're still not getting anywhere by then I'll tell Andrea Robertson that I've done all I can...'

A high-pitched squeak came from his pager. He picked it up and heard Sally's voice. 'Mr Hatherton on the line. I told him you were in a meeting but he doesn't seem prepared to take no for an answer.'

'OK. I'll come through. We're just about finished anyway.' He folded the phone and slipped it into a pocket. 'I think that about winds it up for this month, folks.'

'Saved by the bell,' Catherine muttered

as she gathered her papers together.

Moments later, Tim was back in his office listening to DCS Hatherton's precise diction. 'Since we last spoke I've consulted with some of my superiors and with colleagues who have been able to fill in more details about your record. The consensus seems to be that the best way to get you off my back is to be candid with you.'

'I certainly tend to hit back if I think someone's messing me about.'

'So I discovered at Rycote Hall, Mr Lacy. Very amusing. I propose another meeting, not because I want or need any help but because this business is important and I haven't the time or energy to waste on running battles on the sidelines. My office, eleven o'clock tomorrow morning.' An order, not a request.

Tim reflected that the man probably did not know the meaning of the word 'please'. He said, 'OK, but this time leave your pit bull terrier in his kennel.' He disconnected.

When Tim presented himself at New Scotland Yard Hatherton came down to the front desk. 'It's such a fine day I thought we might take a stroll in the park.' He led the way at a brisk pace out of the building, elegant in a brown-grey suit and a trilby. A couple of minutes later he slowed as they crossed Birdcage Walk and took the path leading towards the lake. The last daffodils still starred the sward of St James's Park, standing among patches of taller grass carefully avoided by the mowers. Ducks and geese congregated by the bridge, squabbling over the unending bounty showered by regular feeders and tourists.

As they emerged from the cover of tall trees the sun struck warm upon their backs. Hatherton opened the bidding. 'What I suggest is that we pool information, Mr Lacy.'

'OK. You go first.'

A spasm of irritation shivered Hatherton's upper body. 'I could take you in for questioning and sit you in a very bare room with the pit bull terrier and a tape recorder.'

'And you can guess how productive that would be.' Tim tried sweet reasonableness. If he was going to learn anything he would have to avoid antagonising the policeman. 'I simply thought it would save time if you outlined the important facts. You know much more than I do. All I can hope to do is fill in a few gaps, if that.'

After a thoughtful pause Hatherton launched without introduction into his version of carefully selected excerpts from the Robertson file. 'Several years ago, in the long period of post-independence chaos, the tiny African state of Doalamba was in the throes of typical internecine conflict. Tribal gangs were at each other's throats. Rival chiefs were deliberately encouraged and resourced by ideologues from East and West who wanted a base in the region—British, French and American multinationals protecting valuable mineral rights, and the usual crop of drop-outs from civilisation who saw the chance of making a quick buck out of other people's misfortune. One of these undesirables was an ex-army captain by name John Rycote. He was military adviser to the head of state, King Lasadi-Boma.'

'A mercenary leader.'

'Precisely. He and a small group of cronies organised the royal army and provided a force of white crack troops. They were also in charge of providing military hardware. That was where Robertson came in. He was a businessman operating in the country. He was clever and unscrupulous; with manufacturers, dealers and governments falling over themselves to supply arms, he became adept at playing off one against the other.'

'Was that when his contact with Harman-Lederer started?'

Hatherton nodded. 'It was just E.

Harman Inc. then; the merger with Lederer came later. But you'll be interested to know that their on-the-spot negotiator was a young man called Carlos Lombardo. He'd learned his dubious trade as go-between with guerilla armies in Central America, so Harman's trusted him with the Doalamba deal—more fool them.'

'Lombardo started ripping them off?'

'Rycote, Robertson and Lombardo were as unholy a triumvirate as it's possible to imagine. They were in business for one reason and one only, and they didn't give a damn for anything or anyone else. They were in a position to mint money. They took hefty bribes from all sides. They committed every fraud in the book. They were masters of the double-cross.'

'A dangerous game to play with powerful commercial and political interests.'

'They were safe enough. As long as they had the king's support no one could touch them. And Lasadi-Boma was just about the worst kind of fat, self-indulgent, corrupt African tyrant. All he cared about was cars, women, flashy clothes and a big yacht which was permanently moored in Lamba harbour. It was a simple deal: the crooks protected him from the three insurgent forces vying to topple him from power, and he protected them.'

'So, what went wrong?'

'They didn't expect it to last for ever, but like most greedy men they didn't know when to say "when". The profits were pouring in faster than they could be converted into gem stones and negotiable securities. Then, one fateful day, a lone assassin got lucky. He managed to plant a bomb on the royal yacht. It went off when Lasadi-Boma was hosting a diplomatic reception. All hell was let loose: full civil war; fighting in the capital; three changes of government in as many weeks. Anyway, the important point is that our three villains tried to do a bunk and only one of them made it. Rycote was killed. Lombardo must have soon wished he had been, too—he was thrown into prison and subjected to some very unrefined torture.'

'And Robertson?'

'He got away with the lion's share of the spoils—a considerable cache of diamonds. We'll never know all the details, but it seems he made contact with a group of loyal troops and posed as Rycote. They'd never seen the man who was their leader, and probably one white man looked much the same as another. They managed to get across the border. Robertson made his way back to this country and immediately went to ground. You know where.'

'He obviously had good reason to hide

himself away. But all that was twenty years ago. Why all the cloak and dagger stuff now?'

Hatherton indicated a bench beside the path which flanked the water. 'Shall we?'

When they were seated he went on, 'If it was all a matter of ancient history I couldn't care less who got to Robertson. But the trouble is he couldn't leave well alone. Either he was bored or he needed money for that diabolical collection of his. After a few years he was back in the arms business, reactivating his old contacts and setting himself up as an international fixer. We know he had dealings with the criminal fraternities of several countries but, though we kept a close watch, we could never pin anything on him. Eventually he tried for a racket too far.' He paused. 'Now, Mr Lacy, from all this it must be pretty obvious to you why this investigation has to be carried out as quietly as possible. The other day you accused my colleague and me of not being interested in catching Robertson's killer. That was hysterical nonsense, but I will admit that my top priority is not getting a murderer convicted. Robertson's death enabled us to access his records. I've got teams of officers working through boxfuls of paper and accumulating evidence on illicit traffic—drugs as well as arms—in half a dozen countries. I've no doubt that during the course of all this we'll come up with Robertson's murderer, but I'm sure even you would agree that closing down some of the trade routes of bastards who traffic in human misery is even more important.'

Tim watched a flotilla of yellow ducklings following their mother in line astern. 'From what you've told me I'd have thought Lombardo was a pretty obvious suspect. If Robertson went off with his share of the loot all those years ago and left him to the not-so-tender mercies of his African captors he had a pretty good reason to harbour a grudge. That would certainly explain the manner of Robertson's death *and* why Lombardo got into the castle under an assumed name.'

Hatherton removed his hat and put it on the seat beside him. He sat back, legs stretched out. 'We certainly have our eyes on that gentleman, but he seems to have kissed and made up with Robertson a long time ago. He got out of Doalamba during one of the many changes of regime, re-ingratiated himself with Harman's—by then Harman-Lederer and, three years later, set himself up as an independent arms dealer. The rest of his grimy career you can get out of any cuttings agency. Lombardo rose to the top of his murky pool; his sort always do. He now operates out of bases in the States and Switzerland and is a very wealthy man. We don't know whether he and Robertson had actually met up again before this January, but they had certainly corresponded and done business together.'

'If they had patched up their old quarrels, why was he travelling under a false identity?'

'I don't think we need read anything unusually sinister into that. To our knowledge, Lombardo has at least three passports all under different names. Anyway, I've told you the salient facts. What can you add?'

'A few details and quite a bit of guesswork. You know, presumably, that there was an interloper living in the castle attic for several weeks at the end of last year.'

Hatherton raised his eyebrows. 'I've obviously underestimated you, Mr Lacy What do you conclude from that?'

'Obviously it was part of a well-planned operation. It reminds me of a surveillance exercise I did once in the SAS. On that occasion we put a well-trained operative in at night by helicopter. Now, several of Robertson's business associates arrived by air. It would be easy for a chopper coming in to land to hover over the house for a few seconds—long enough for someone to be lowered to the roof'

'Would he have got out the same way?'

'Possibly, but not necessarily. Leaving wouldn't be a problem. There are no security cameras or fences on the west side of the castle. There's no need for them; it's a sheer drop to the loch. A trained man could abseil down in a wet suit and swim across to the shore.'

'And make his way to a pre-arranged pick-up point? It all sounds very elaborate.' The brief comment was loaded with criticism.

'Not really. It just needed planning with military precision.'

'But what was the object?'

'To put the frighteners on Robertson, I suppose—killing his dogs, leaving cryptic messages.'

'A real-life equivalent of the black spot?'

'Yes, I suppose so.' Tim scanned his childhood memories of *Treasure Island:* gang retribution, the old sea-dog at the Admiral Benbow receiving the sinister symbol from his grasping and vengeful associates, then a swift return to find the treasure map. Suddenly, he saw the flaw in his own reasoning.

'Then it only takes a co-conspirator,' Hatherton continued, 'to give the screw a final turn for Robertson to panic and flee his no-longer-secure castle?'

'Yes,' Tim said. But his mind insisted 'No'. Rapidly it accessed the database of memory. Johnny had put his finger on the broken link in the conspiracy theory. Robertson's two Alsatians were slaughtered and displayed in the dungeon, and he was warned that he would be number three. 'Only he wasn't, was he?' Tim heard again Johnny's objection, the objection he had brushed aside. But Johnny had been right. The business with the parrot did not fit. It looked like an afterthought, an improvisation, contrasting markedly with the cunningly conceived campaign. Putting an intruder into the castle had taken inside knowledge, careful planning, not to mention financial resources. But the plotters had not followed up their threats as Stevenson's pirates had followed up the black spot. They could have done; Tim realised now that the kind of highly skilled operator capable of wandering about Lanner Castle undetected could certainly have despatched Robertson and got clean away. So, had murder never been intended?

Tim was aware that Hatherton was looking at him quizzically. 'Sorry, I went off at a tangent. What did you say?'

'I said, have you any idea where Robertson fled to? That was presumably where he was killed.'

'I suppose that's the sixty-four-thousand-dollar question, isn't it? If we knew the answer to that we'd have a whole new field of enquiry to explore.'

'We?' Hatherton stood up, replacing his trilby as he did so and adjusting its angle carefully. 'No, Mr Lacy. I've told you enough—more than enough—for you to realise that this is a matter for the professionals.' He began retracing his steps along the lakeside path. 'From this point on I want you to forget all about the death of Jack Robertson—unless, that is, you still have some more information for me.'

'Forget about it? Just like that? Look, Mr Hatherton, when someone tries to kill me I tend to take a serious personal interest in the course of events.'

'Ah, yes, the business with the Land Rover. Leave that with me.' After a pause he added, 'Have you had any more contact with those anti-dam protestors?'

'No, I—'

'Well don't!'

Tim noted the change of tone but did not pursue the matter. 'There's another thing,' he said. 'You realise, of course, that my company is a lot of money out of pocket over this business. We didn't ask to get involved.'

'I'll see to it that you are properly compensated.'

Tim dropped this piece of information into the whirl of ideas which were tumbling around in his head like numbers in a lottery wheel.

'What do you know about Robertson's relations with Harman-Lederer?' the policeman asked.

'I gather he was thick with old Friederich Lederer. They shared a taste in morbid art.'

'I suppose that's why the collection was left to that funny museum the company finances just up the road.'

'Dr Nefsky seemed to think Robertson was under an obligation to bequeath his ghoulish *objets d'art* to her institute, but he told me quite categorically that he was thinking of making alternative arrangements.'

'Really?' Hatherton seemed genuinely surprised. 'I don't suppose that pleased her bosses.'

'She went hotfoot to Scotland to talk him round. Perhaps Lombardo was only there to add weight to her arguments.'

'I suppose the collection must be extremely valuable?'

'All together it must run into millions.'

'Well, there's a good enough motive for murder there. And I imagine the African bloke, young Andrea's boyfriend, has a financial stake in Robertson's death.'

Tim shrugged. 'There were eight guests at the castle that night in January. One of us arranged the demonstration with the parrot and stole Cumberland's Cradle. That person must have been implicated in the murder. If you can work out how that was done you're most of the way home.'

'Aren't you forgetting the servants?'

'Most of them were very new and had been carefully vetted by Robertson. The Jenkinses had been with him for years. I can't see why they would suddenly turn against their employer.'

'Still,' Hatherton mused, 'I suppose it might be useful to probe their background —that is, unless you've already saved me the trouble.'

Tim shook his head. 'All I know is that he was in the Marines and that they've been at the castle for twenty years.'

They reached the bridge. Tim said, 'I'm going this way, to Westminster. Thanks for being so frank with me.'

'Co-operation is usually better than confrontation.'

'Perhaps you could give your pet hound some lessons.'

Hatherton ignored the taunt. 'Goodbye, Mr Lacy. I hope we don't meet again. If we do it will be because you've ignored my advice about keeping out of this business.

327

Under those circumstances you would see a very different side of my nature.' He turned and strode across the bridge.

Tim almost ran back to the flat. There he poured himself a large armagnac, grabbed up a writing pad and took out a pen. He lay full length on the sofa and began scribbling down ideas. After three-quarters of an hour the floor beside him was littered with sheets of paper. Then he tried to arrange them in some sort of order. Several minutes were spent sorting the notes like cards in a poker hand. Then he lay back, drained his glass and smiled.

III

TO DISCOVER SIGHTS
OF WOE

There's a hope for every woe,
And a balm for every pain,
But the first joys of our heart
Come never back again.
There's a track upon the deep,
And a path across the sea,
But the weary ne'er return
To their ain countrie.

Oh Why Left I My Home?
traditional Scottish air

CHAPTER 15

The next day two invitations arrived at Farrans Court. The directors of Harman-Lederer Inc. requested the pleasure of Mr and Mrs T. Lacy at a reception to be held at the Harman-Lederer Humanities Institute to mark the acquisition of the very important Jack Robertson Collection. Selected new exhibits would be on display, together with a model of the proposed new gallery to house the fresh acquisitions.

Tim showed the heavily-embossed card to his wife over a hurried sandwich lunch in their flat in the manor house's east wing. 'They haven't wasted any time.'

Catherine shook her head in puzzled disbelief. 'Having architects' plans drawn up and approved by the planners takes forever. How come they've fixed all that in a few months?'

'Friends in high places.'

'Yeah, even so...'

'What intrigues me is why the rush.'

'It's a massive coup for the institute. I can understand them wanting to trumpet it from the rooftops.'

Tim collected the empty plates and

coffee mugs and carried them through to the kitchen. 'My devious mind suggests a different motivation.'

'What's that?' Catherine stood in front of the sitting-room mirror making quick adjustments to hair and make-up in preparation for her return to the office.

'I wonder if it's not all been laid on for my benefit.'

Catherine laughed. 'You don't think that's being just the teeniest bit big-headed?'

Tim was not abashed. 'They're desperate to find out what I know. Hildegard did her best to pump me. That was the whole point of my conducted tour of the institute. But she didn't handle it very well, so her bosses have got to find some other way of pumping me—without, of course, appearing to do so.'

Catherine picked up her handbag and headed for the front door. 'Well, after all you've told me, I'm certainly intrigued to see what all the fuss is about. I assume we're accepting?'

'Oh, yeah!'

The other invitation was couched less formally. Andrea Robertson and Ben Azikwe were to be married in Lagos on 17 June. Before leaving London early in the month they were throwing a party, and would love Tim and Catherine to join them. Tim decided to reply by phone.

'Congratulations, Andrea. I see you've named the day.'

'Yes, Ben's been taking a very firm line with me. He says we've not to put things off any longer. He says the sooner I'm concentrating on looking after a home and husband and children the better.' She seemed much more relaxed.

Tim laughed. 'That sounds like a very sexist attitude but I'm sure he's right.'

'Me, too. It was silly of me to get so worked up about my father's death. I see that now. I mean, we may never know the truth, and to go on worrying...well, apart from anything else, it wasn't fair on you. You're not a private eye and I shouldn't have talked you into it. You are coming to our party, aren't you?'

'Yes, please.'

'Oh good. Well, look, I want you to promise that you'll bring your bill with you. I absolutely insist on paying for all your time.'

'Well, we'll see. Meanwhile, there's one thing you could do for me.'

'Of course.'

'Could you write to your lawyer, Macrae, and authorise him to talk to me about your father's affairs?'

'Are you on to something, Tim?'

'Maybe, maybe not. You're not to build

up your hopes. Ben is right and you must be guided by him. Look forward, not back. But it is just possible that I could have a wedding present for you.'

At lunchtime, Tim surprised Catherine and George by hustling them into the BMW and running them down to the Crown and Anvil in Little Farrans. They sat at an outside table on the lawn running from the ancient inn down to the shallow, slow-running Merebrook.

When their food arrived Tim explained, 'I want to fly a few theories about this Scottish business and I need a couple of old sceptics on hand to shoot them down.'

'Hey, what's with this "old"?' Catherine grinned as she attacked her salad enthusiastically.

'Old as in experienced; old as in wise; old as in well balanced,' Tim elucidated with mock solemnity.

'OK, fire away, Major.' George took a long pull at his pint before starting the demolition of a huge Cornish pasty.

'As you know, I had a session with Hatherton recently. He's good. A leisurely walk in the spring sunshine; a detailed account of all Robertson's past life; a readiness to answer questions. The man almost had me believing that he has a heart, that he's genuinely interested in real people and cares about truth. I had to mentally make the sign of the cross to prevent him sinking his fangs into me. I kept telling myself, "This man is a creature of the political establishment who exists to protect the powerful from the powerless. It's his job to put together a menu of official lies and ambiguities labelled 'truth'." Hatherton had two objectives at our meeting: to feed me disinformation and to find out how much I already knew. Straight afterwards I spent a long time debriefing myself. I reckoned that if I could get hold of what Hatherton wanted me to think and what he wanted to find out I'd get a lot closer to the heart of this business.'

'Sounds like a reasonable theory,' Catherine observed. 'What do the men in grey suits want us to believe?'

'That Robertson and Rycote were *not* one and the same person; that Robertson's death was the result of a falling-out of criminal colleagues; that the murder was a carefully planned and executed revenge killing.' Tim gave a précis of Hatherton's information.

'I thought we'd already decided that all that business of torturing Robertson to death and dumping him back virtually on his own doorstep was a typical bit of Mafia-style barbarism,' George objected.

'Absolutely right, and if Special Branch hadn't wanted us to go on thinking that I wouldn't have seriously questioned it. But when I did I re-examined the whole sequence of events at Lanner Castle and came up with a different answer. See what you think of it. Obviously, a sophisticated operation was set up at the end of last year. An agent was put into the castle. He killed the dogs and left dramatic threats. That put the wind up Robertson; so much so that he sacked most of his staff and called us in to update his security. People in high places were very concerned that we should accept the contract. About the same time the secret operator was pulled out. Now, what does that suggest to you?'

Catherine stared across the table thoughtfully, fork in mid air. 'That his job was done?'

'Exactly! I don't believe the bizarre theatricals with the dead dogs in the dungeon were part of a plot on Robertson's life at all.'

'Then what...'

'What was the point, George? To force him into making himself more secure. He thought he was safe in his island fortress. Other people knew he wasn't and set out to prove it.'

Catherine frowned and shook her head. 'Hey, I don't like what I'm hearing here.

You're suggesting that this whole business is political—that our lords and masters not only knew about Robertson's shady dealings but were involved in them and were desperate to keep him safe.'

'Something like that. It explains why we were subjected to high-level pressure first to get involved and then to quit.'

Tim's wife sat back from the table. 'In that case I'm with Hatherton. The sooner we distance ourselves from this cloak and dagger stuff the better.'

George showed no sign of being put off his food. 'So Hatherton's paymasters knew that someone was gunning for Robertson, and that if they got to him the manure would hit the fan.'

'Yes. Investigative journalists, questions in the House, demands for a public enquiry—we all know how sensitive the government is about anything connected with arms contracts.'

George gulped down the last of his bitter. 'Someone high up must have known or suspected who the potential murderer was.'

Tim shrugged. 'I don't know. And Hatherton sure as hell isn't going to say. But let's see if we can make some guesses. We all have a pretty good idea how these things work. SIS has obviously kept a file on Robertson for years. They've monitored his contacts and kept themselves informed about his activities. They pick up some worrying vibes. They warn him, he takes no notice. They stage a demonstration and that shakes him. Not only does he take thought for his own protection; being a cold, methodical sort of man he sets his affairs in order. He reconsiders the fate of his collection—whether to leave it to Harman-Lederer as planned, or to some more deserving institution. He decides to sort out the Save Glen Huich brigade once and for all. He invites Andrea and her fiancé to the castle, and—perhaps rather uncharacteristically—he actually conveys to her something of his apprehension.'

'So he gets a whole batch of people to the castle one snowy January day, not realising that one of them is his assassin?'

'That's how it looks to me, George. We both saw how shaken Robertson was when he discovered the third demonstration in the dungeon. I'd swear on oath that he hadn't the faintest idea until that moment that the killer was right there, just a few paces away. He went and locked himself in his private rooms, and as soon as he thought it was safe to move he went to the helicopter and flew to Edinburgh where he maintained a secret bolt-hole for precisely such an eventuality.'

'Only it wasn't very secret,' Catherine commented.

'No, someone knew more about Robertson than he realised. That someone was a jump ahead of him and probably a jump ahead of the intelligence services, too.'

'It must have been a very nasty shock for them when Robertson's mangled remains showed up.' George got to his feet. 'Another drink, Catherine? Major?'

Catherine opted for coffee and Tim followed suit.

When George had strolled back into the pub, Catherine reached across the table for her husband's hand. 'Darling, I know how you feel about all this. You're concerned for Andrea and you're sore about being used and deceived by the establishment—but can't you, just this once, walk away?'

Tim squeezed her hand and tried to look reassuring. 'We agreed that if I hadn't come up with anything in seven days I'd do precisely that.'

'That was before Hatherton warned you off, very firmly.'

'It was also before Hatherton spun me a whole web of lies.'

Catherine frowned. 'You're pretty convinced about that. Are you sure you're not just being paranoid?'

'Absolutely. He knew we were on to the Rycote connection. That worried him a hell of a lot. That's why he set off straight away for Compton Marney. Fortunately we were too quick for him. That's the only reason he had a "change of heart" and made out he was letting me in on highly privileged information. What he was really handing out was bullshit.'

'To convince you that Rycote was long dead and suggest a plausible reason for Robertson at some stage having used his name as an alias?'

'Yes. Absolute cobblers! I'm sure that Robertson *was* Rycote. What makes me so furious is his total indifference to the lives of innocent people. Hatherton and Co. are determined to keep the truth from Andrea. The poor kid thinks she has no one in the world apart from Ben, no relatives, no identity, no roots. She's about to quit Britain—perhaps for good—hoping to find or create some meaning for her life. And all the time she belongs to an ancient and distinguished family. She has an aunt who would love to take her under her wing and spend her declining years telling her stories about her grandparents, browsing with her through old family albums. Above all, if Eleanor Jenkins is to be believed, Andrea has a mother.'

Catherine watched swallows swooping and soaring above the woods beyond the river. 'You'll tell her all this?'

'Wouldn't you?'

Catherine sighed and nodded. 'Do be careful, Tim.'

'I'll be as careful as I can. You can depend on that. Hatherton is utterly ruthless and he has considerable resources, courtesy of the British taxpayer. I still haven't acquitted him of that incident in Scotland, and I sure as hell don't intend to wave a red rag in front of him just for the fun of it. But, dear God, Catherine, he has no right to take away someone's history!'

'You'll have to be very careful how you break the news to Andrea.'

'Don't I know it. I could end up just getting her more confused than ever. I shan't say a thing to her until I've checked out some details with the family lawyer. I need to be absolutely sure of my facts.'

George returned with a tray and set it down on the table. 'I've been thinking,' he said as they all helped themselves to drinks. 'There must be an easier way of narrowing the field of real suspects.'

'Amen to that!' Tim added sugar to his black coffee. 'What have you in mind?'

'Well, whoever bumped off Robertson knew three things: he knew about the business with the dogs; he knew how to smuggle that torture contraption off the island, and he knew where his victim would run to. Now I reckon that, of all the people with us at the castle, there can't have been more than one who had all that information.'

'OK. Let's take those points one at a time. The Aberdeen students certainly knew about the earlier threats. They said so. So did Andrea and, presumably, Ben. As far as we know Nefsky and Lombardo hadn't heard the story, but we could be wrong. So we can't exclude anyone on that count.'

'How do you reckon Cumberland's Cradle got across to the mainland?'

Tim shook his head. 'I don't. It certainly didn't travel in someone's luggage—much too bulky and heavy, even if it was completely dismantled.'

George smiled knowingly. 'Well, as it happens, I've come up with the answer to that one.'

'OK, maestro, no need to pause for effect.'

'Well, Major, I don't reckon it was taken across the loch.'

Tim frowned. 'You're not suggesting Robertson was murdered in the castle.'

'No, of course not. What I reckon is that he was murdered in a substitute instrument. Anyone who knew about Cumberland's Cradle could easily knock up a copy.'

'According to Robertson his was unique.'

'He could have been wrong. Anyway, there are probably old drawings. The murderers had already made a replica. All they had to do was get rid of the original, and there was nothing hard about that: go down to the dungeon, dismantle the implement, take the bits back to one of their bedrooms and chuck them out of the window.'

'You used the plural—"murderers".'

'Well, as I see it, Major, it would take a couple of people to get the job done quickly and efficiently.'

'Who had you in mind?'

'That's obvious, isn't it? The Nefsky woman could easily have come up with all the information about Cumberland's Cradle. She was the brains behind the scheme. Lombardo provided the muscle. That explains why they made out they'd never met before. We know that was a lie,' George concluded triumphantly.

Tim considered this new reconstruction in silence for some moments. 'OK, that's certainly possible. But when it comes to point number three we're completely stymied. No one was aware that Robertson had a house in Edinburgh, as far as we can tell.'

George stuck to his guns. 'Well, the murderers are certainly not going to let on if they did know. I mean, the whole object of the exercise was to get Robertson to Edinburgh.'

Catherine, who had been following. this exchange with a look of increasing bewilderment, intervened. 'You guys are overlooking the obvious. There were two people with you at the castle who *do* meet your three-part test.'

The others stared at her quizzically.

'Mr and Mrs Jenkins.'

'Oh, but that's—'

'There could be no possible reason—'

Catherine scowled. 'I'm just applying male logic. The Jenkinses knew all about the business with the dogs; they knew about the Edinburgh house; and they certainly could have either got rid of or hidden the torture implement.'

'But what was their motive?' Tim objected.

'They've done pretty well out of Robertson's will. It seems to me, the more I think about it, that they had an A1 motive. They'd been cooped up in a ghastly castle for twenty years with a pretty unpleasant employer. When they looked into the future all they could see was several more dreary years of the same. Can't you imagine them grabbing the opportunity to start living a little now?'

Tim turned the idea over. 'Hatherton

was certainly keen to discover what I know about the Jenkinses... But there's one big objection to this theory: Eleanor Jenkins made a point of telling me about the Edinburgh house. She had absolutely no need to do that.'

Catherine shrugged. 'No hypothesis is absolutely watertight, but I still reckon this is the best one we've got.'

Gratefully Tim registered the use of the word 'we'. He drained his cup. 'Well, I guess we'd better be getting back. Thanks for talking this through. It's been a great help.'

Duncan the Red was more accurately Duncan the White. The death of his son and the loss of his castle at Huich came as an almost fatal shock to the Laird of Strathfarrar. His hair blanched overnight and his ruddy features became pallid and drawn. Days after the fire, which completely gutted the castle, he received a letter from the Duke of Cumberland stripping him of his command and castigating him at length for the escape of the prisoners and the loss of a valuable stronghold. He withdrew to his estate near Drymen at the southern end of Loch Lomond a broken man. There, a year to the day after the conflagration, he had a stroke which left him partially paralysed.

In May of 1751 he was fifty-five years of age and looked seventy. His life had contracted to a routine of mundane activities—eating, sleeping, sitting in his library window and being driven round his estate in a carriage. Most of these pastimes required the assistance of at least two servants to accomplish.

Alan Duncan had two attendants with him on the breezy May afternoon when he drove into hell. They were a coachman and a body servant. Having, with difficulty made no easier by long practice, man-oeuvred their master into the plush interior, they took up their places on the box, cramming their hats well on to their heads to protect them from the threatened rain. The driver cracked his whip. The well-matched pair set off at a sedate pace from the front of the house, trotted down the drive, turned left on to the public way and travelled a little under two miles before taking a climbing track through trees and emerging on a rise providing a clear view of the loch. Here they slowed to a halt. They would almost certainly have followed the regular drill without a human being holding the reins. They knew that the carriage would rest here for five minutes before making the steeper descent the other side of the hill.

But on this day the treadmill of tedious

routine was broken, shattered.

A tall grey gelding stepped carefully from the edge of the trees. Astride sat a young man of some sixteen or seventeen years. His black riding coat was of good cloth; the tricorn set on his light brown hair drawn back in a pigtail was silk-trimmed. In his hands he held a brace of elegant, long-barrelled flintlocks. When he spoke it was in clearly-enunciated English, with a Highland accent.

'Stand down, gentlemen, if you please.'

The servants raised their hands and, eyes fixed on the pistols, clambered from their seat.

'Lie down over here, on the ground.'

When they had complied, the horseman dismounted. Quickly and expertly he bound the men's hands behind them and fastened their ankles together.

Ewen M'Ewen ambled across to the carriage and opened the nearest door. He removed his hat, climbed in and sat opposite Duncan o'Strathfarrar.

'What do you mean by this? If it's robbery, you're out of luck. I've no money or jewellery about me.' The words came slurred from Duncan's twisted face.

Ewen sneered back. 'You're slobbering, you disgusting wretch. I'd hardly have recognised you, and I'll wager you've no idea who I am.'

The older man leaned forward, peering. 'I need my eye-glass.' He fumbled in a waistcoat pocket with his good hand, eventually contriving to extricate a single lens through which he squinted at Ewen. 'Don't know you from Adam,' he dribbled.

'I'll not trouble you with my name, Duncan o'Strathfarrar. When a man has a catalogue of victims as long as yours the individual entries mean nothing. I'll just tell you that I am the Highland brat you made dance on your table for the amusement of Butcher Cumberland. I'm the Highland brat whose father and brother were hanged by order of Alistair Duncan. I'm the Highland brat whose home and village were wiped from the face of the earth, also by order of your son. I'm the Highland brat who watched your men murder children.' He leaned forward. 'More importantly, I'm the one who razed Castle Huich to the ground, who saw Alistair Duncan cut down like the cur he was. And I am the one who will kill you before this day is much older.'

Alan Duncan sank back against the cushions. 'I might have guessed—a damned Jacobite.'

Ewen shook his head. 'No. I'm no supporter of the Italian lap-dog. Stuart is as guilty of spilling Scottish blood as your lot. My father told me that. He was no Jacobite. He never said a word against King George. Yet your son murdered him. I've learned a lot about you and your ilk these last few years. You were never worried by supporters of the Stuart cause. Your interest was in destroying your clan enemies and grabbing their land. If Cumberland was the Butcher, you were just one of the dogs snuffling round him to gorge themselves on the offal.'

'You're mad!' Duncan shrugged.

Ewen nodded. 'I heard a minister a couple of years ago who said revenge was a sickness of the mind, so you may well be right. But revenge I will have—for all the ills done me and mine and for all the lives ruined by the Duncans and their master. Your son is accounted for. Today is your turn. Soon it will be the Butcher.'

Duncan smiled a wry smile. 'Well shoot me if you will, but I can rob you of any satisfaction that may bring you. Look at me. As you say, I'm a disgusting wretch, half a man, not even half. Do you suppose death would not be welcome?'

Ewen gazed out of the window. When he spoke it was almost to himself. 'When I lay at nights in the tower at Castle Huich I used to dream of seeing Alan and Alistair Duncan in their own dungeon, fastened to their own instruments of torture. I imagined myself turning the screw, tightening the gyves. That vision stayed with me, even though I knew I could never make it a reality. It spurred me on. It gave me a motive, an objective. These last few years I've been working towards that objective. I've travelled with a band of friends. We've made ourselves quite wealthy. I have accumulated enough to gain freedom: the freedom to come and go as I please, to seek out my enemies.' He shook his head. 'No matter that I cannot impose on you the torture you inflicted on others without a second thought. I've done what I can to eradicate your family and your home as completely as you eradicated mine. You see that smoke?' He pointed to a grey haze lying over the woods a mile or so away. 'That's your house. I set the fire before I came to meet you. It will destroy your smart mansion just as it destroyed your castle; just as it destroyed my father's cottage.'

He opened the door and stepped down from the carriage.

Duncan sneered. 'Not a change of heart, surely?'

'No, just a determination to make your last moments as unpleasant as possible. I'll not shoot you. That would be too merciful. Goodbye, Duncan o'Strathfarrar.'

He slammed the door. He took down the whip from its rest by the driver's seat and cracked it across the flank of the nearer horse. With a yelp the beast leaped forward, dragging its partner into motion. They cantered down the steep uneven track. The carriage bounced and jolted. It went faster and faster, totally out of control. Ewen saw it reach a slight bend and disappear from view. He heard the crash which followed immediately.

CHAPTER 16

The offices of Macrae, Bannock and Macrae occupied two adjacent houses in one of the old, narrow streets hugging the foot of Edinburgh's Castle Hill. Tim negotiated a creaking staircase to reach the first-floor suite of rooms occupied by the senior partner and his secretary. Some attempt had been made to accommodate the ancient premises to late-twentieth-century standards of comfort. Macrae's spacious sanctum was an amalgam of two rooms whose dividing wall had been removed. Yet, somehow, each half of the resulting space preserved its distinct identity. In one the lawyer's desk and adjacent shelves overflowed with books and documents. In the other a chintz-covered three-piece suite was arranged around a wide coffee table on which stood a tastefully arranged bowl of fresh flowers—contributed, Tim guessed, by the young woman who announced his presence and then retreated to her PC console.

'What a pleasant surprise to meet you again, Mr Lacy. Come and sit down. I've asked Jean to bring tea. Will that be all right?' The little lawyer settled his guest in an armchair and perched on its companion opposite. 'I have Miss Robertson's written instructions to assist you in any way I can, so I am at your disposal. May I ask the purpose of your enquiries?'

Tim had prepared his approach carefully. 'Miss Robertson—Andrea—is obviously anxious to discover all she can about her father and any other relatives he might have, however distant. As you doubtless know, her visits to Lanner Castle were very sporadic. She had always intended, one day, to tackle her father about his family. Now, tragically, that opportunity no longer exists.'

Macrae shook his head, a professional expression of sympathy adorning his rather pinched features. 'And your interest, Mr Lacy? I recall that when you first contacted me it was in connection with payment for your professional services.'

'My office is merely that of a friend. My

business entails quite a bit of travelling. Andrea, by contrast, lacks that freedom of movement at the moment. I said I would talk with you on her behalf when I was next in these parts.'

'I see. Well, I hope your visit is not going to be wasted. I know very little about my late client's background.'

There was a pause while Jean set down tea in china cups and placed a plate of assorted biscuits on the table. Tim was aware during the interval that he was being scrutinized closely through Macrae's thick-lensed glasses.

As the secretary withdrew he decided to plunge straight in. 'Andrea tells me that her father changed his name by deed poll from Rycote. Is that so?'

Macrae's brow creased in an anxious frown. 'You place me in an unenviable position, Mr Lacy. There were certain facts that Mr Robertson wished to be concealed even from his daughter. Unfortunately, in going through various papers with her the name Rycote cropped up. It was my mistake, but once made it could not be reversed. I hope you won't embarrass me further by pressing me for details.'

'I assure you I only want to establish the truth of the matter. I take it that you undertook all the legal arrangements over the change of name.'

The lawyer nodded.

'You were obviously completely satisfied about Mr Rycote's identity. There were documents—birth certificates, that sort of thing?'

'I recall we had to organise archival searches, but my client had a passport and sworn affidavits confirming his identity. There was no problem.'

'When did all this take place?'

Macrae crossed to his desk and returned with a thick file. He thumbed through it for a few moments. 'Hm, yes...that would be, let me see, almost exactly nineteen years ago.'

'And he never mentioned any other relatives?'

'Never. I had the impression either that there was no family or that he was estranged from them.'

'What about his wife, Andrea's mother?'

'Dead—some three or four years earlier, I understand.'

'And there were no other children—legitimate or otherwise?'

Macrae closed the file firmly. 'All I can tell you is that my late client settled all his outstanding business and personal affairs at that time. He intended to make a completely fresh start and he was adamant that his daughter, for her own sake, should not be encouraged or assisted in any attempt to uncover the past. I cannot satisfy either her or your curiosity any further.'

Tim smiled. 'I quite understand. It seems to me to be very hard on Andrea, but I will explain your position to her. On another matter, I understand that she was the principal beneficiary under Mr Robertson's will, after the art collection had been bestowed and certain bequests had been made to staff.'

'That is so.'

'So she, presumably, inherits the house here in Edinburgh?'

'House in Edinburgh?' Macrae appeared genuinely puzzled. 'Mr Robertson had no property in the city, or anywhere else apart from the Glen Huich estate.'

'Are you telling me that 29 Inchferry Road does not form part of the late Mr Robertson's estate?'

'Categorically. As his executor I have no doubt about that whatsoever.'

'Can he have been renting the house?'

Macrae shook his head. 'Any such agreement would be on his file and the payment would be a charge against the estate. Besides, what would he have wanted with a house in Edinburgh? On the very rare occasions that he stayed here overnight he booked into the Royal Stuart Hotel.'

'Odd. You wouldn't have an Edinburgh street plan, would you?'

'Yes, of course.' Macrae went into the secretary's office and returned, moments later, with a well-thumbed city gazetteer.

Tim checked the entry for Inchferry Road and located it on the map. 'I see it's on the edge of the city, near the coast.'

Macrae peered over his shoulder. 'Ah yes, I thought the name rang a bell. I can visualise it now. It's out towards Cramond.'

'What sort of an area is that?'

'Pleasant, well-to-do suburb. It was very fashionable between the wars; quite a few large properties were built then. The R. L. Stevenson connection probably helped: our famous son grew up around Cramond and Leith. Then the development of Turnhouse—the airport—took some of the gilt off the gingerbread. There is a bit of a noise problem but, yes, by and large an attractive enough area. May I ask what connection all this has with my client?'

Tim closed the book and dropped it on the table, annoyed at having drawn a blank. 'Probably none at all. I've obviously been misinformed.' He stood up. 'I mustn't take up any more of your time, Mr Macrae.' He shook the lawyer's hand. 'Thank you so much for your help.'

Five minutes later, in the back of a

taxi heading north, he asked himself what Eleanor Jenkins was playing at. Surely she had not contacted him out of the blue just to tell him a pack of lies. But if Robertson had not owned the Edinburgh house, why was she so convinced that it was his secret refuge? A mistress? That was the answer that sprang most readily to mind. Even a cold fish like Robertson must have had a libido somewhere. Well, useless to speculate. There was an easy way to find out. Tim sat back as the car made steady progress through streets of imposing granite façades softened by the irregular outline of trees and shrubs.

Inchferry Road consisted of three-storey, nineteen-thirties houses set in rather small plots, high-hedged for maximum privacy. Number 29 occupied a corner site. Tim asked the cab driver to wait. He crossed the pavement, pushed open a well-oiled wrought-iron gate and walked along the short, weed-free gravel drive. The front garden consisted solely of a lawn rectangle. Tim noticed that the grass, though ready for a cut, was obviously tended fairly regularly. He climbed three broad steps to a front door flanked by decorative pilasters. He heard the bell ring deep in the interior. There was no other sound. After three attempts Tim retraced his steps to the gateway.

He walked to the corner of Inchferry Road. The street with which it intersected was broader and busier. Diagonally opposite there was a row of four shops. Tim crossed. He selected a small newsagent-cum-general store with the name S. Shah over the door. In the overstocked interior he picked up a copy of the *Scotsman* and a couple of bars of chocolate. A middle-aged woman in a sari took the note he proffered and, with an air of bored efficiency, opened the till.

'I was wondering,' Tim said tentatively, 'do you supply papers to the house on the corner of Inchferry Road—number 29? They seem to be away.'

The woman looked at him suspiciously as she dropped a pile of change into his hand. 'No, we don't supply them.' She obviously had no intention of elaborating.

Tim cursed inwardly. He was having a totally wasted day. He smiled what he hoped was a disarming smile. 'Pity. I've travelled quite a distance to see them.' He turned to leave the shop.

The woman relented far enough to offer another piece of unhelpful information. 'My son looks after the grounds over there but he's out.'

Tim left the shop. He was about to recross the road when a plain white van with a ladder clamped to the top pulled up almost beside him. A young Asian man in jeans and a check shirt jumped out.

Tim reacted quickly. 'Mr Shah?'

'Yes.' The man eyed the stranger warily.

'A brief word, if I may. It's about number 29, opposite.'

Anxiety flickered over the other's face. 'I'm going to cut the grass tomorrow, sir.' His Lowlands accent indicated that he had been raised in the area.

Tim's mind jumped to take advantage of the situation. If Shah mistook him for someone in authority he might learn more by encouraging the error. 'Please see that you do. It's looking a bit ragged. We don't want to have to make other arrangements.'

'No, no, I promise.' The young man brought his hands together almost in a gesture of supplication. 'Tomorrow without fail. I was going to do it last week but, of course, I couldn't.'

'Why not?'

'You know, sir, I'm not allowed in the grounds when your people are there. There were cars on the drive for four days.'

'Ah, yes, of course.'

'It's very difficult, sir, not knowing when your conferences are going to be held.'

'I realise that but it can't be helped.' Tim thought quickly. Was there any more he could learn without arousing Shah's

359

suspicion? 'About payment...is everything satisfactory?'

Shah's eyes lit up. 'Well, sir, petrol's gone up and I've had to get a new machine since we fixed the contract at fifteen hundred.'

'Well I'll see if we can't do something about making your next cheque a bit bigger.'

'Cheque?' The young man showed genuine alarm. 'I'd much prefer cash, as usual.'

Tim hurried to cover the gaffe. 'I can probably swing that. It's just that our accounts people are having one of their occasional bouts of jitters. Well, I'll tell them that you're doing a good job, Mr Shah. But you will see to that grass a.s.a.p., won't you?' He strode briskly across the road. He climbed back into the taxi and told the driver to head for the airport.

He sank back into the upholstery and closed his eyes to think. Not a wasted day after all. Inchferry Road was never owned by Robertson, nor was it used for love trysts. It was apparently for clandestine business meetings. Robertson had gone there because he believed it was safe. The address was known only to a few associates he felt he could trust. He had been wrong.

No wonder Hildegard Nefsky's superiors

were desperate to find out how much Tim knew.

From *The York Gazette*,
16 September 1753:

We have received intelligence of an encounter between a troop of the North Yorkshire Militia and the dangerous criminal known popularly as the Black Boy on account of his youth and his habitual distinctive attire. This North Briton is sought by justices on both sides of the border in connection with highway robbery, arson and a particularly vicious murder two years ago in the region of Dumbarton. Various eye-witnesses have reported this desperado to be of less than twenty years of age, appointed in all particulars like a gentleman in black riding coat and hat, and mounted on a spirited grey. Sightings and incidents early in the summer around Catterick and Richmond suggested that the blackguard was either operating from a base in that area or using the Great North Road as a means of easy access to and from his hideaway.

The placing of a price of one hundred guineas upon his head by certain justices in the county resulted in several informations being laid by persons hopeful of qualifying for the reward. We understand that it was an erstwhile associate of the brigand who, on or about the twelfth of this month, drew the attention of the authorities to the Black Boy's 'fence', as criminals refer to the depositories where thieves secrete their booty. Search of the premises, a secluded house near Easingwold, did, indeed, yield a rich result. A quantity of cash, jewellery and plate was recovered. The militia were alerted and it remained only for them to lie in wait for the tenant when he should return.

Thus matters stood on the night of the fourteenth, when, had it not been for an unhappy mischance, the villain would certainly have been apprehended. Captain Ettrick had set up his headquarters at the sign of the Cock in Easingwold, whither he resorted around midnight, having satisfied himself that a vigilant guard had been posted at the house. The Black Boy, happening to return about the same time, observed the captain upon the highway with his escort and was thereby placed upon his guard. Dismounting and approaching the fence with a greater degree of caution than he would otherwise have displayed, he gained cognisance of the intended ambush. It would, doubtless, have been his intention to steal quietly away. In this he was thwarted by a sharp-eyed, or rather sharp-eared (the night was moonless and black) militiaman, who challenged the miscreant. There followed an exchange of pistol shots during which the trooper was mortally wounded. Colleagues hastening to his aid engaged the fleeing wretch. They observed him to fall stricken at least twice, once in the leg and a second time in the head or neck. However, the Black Boy was able to regain his mount and made off in the direction of Stillington.

Captain Ettrick assures us that, in consideration of the injuries inflicted by his men, it can only be a matter of time before this ruthless and audacious young criminal is brought to the gallows.

The reception at Sandby House was a lavish affair. Guests were directed up the right-hand wing of the wide, curved staircase to the central first-floor gallery, which had been transformed for the occasion. Metre-wide strips of blue and gold silk radiated to the walls from a point in the high ceiling above the massive central chandelier, to give the impression of an indoor pavilion. Five of Robertson's larger and more important paintings were arranged around the room. The centrepiece was a vigorous bronze group depicting two warriors locked in combat. Other exhibits were arranged on velvet-draped plinths. A smaller gallery to one side housed a large perspex model of the proposed extension as well as a dramatic selection from the Lanner Castle collection of war photographs. Adjacent areas were sprinkled with tables and chairs and still more of Jack Robertson's carefully gathered examples of human savagery.

Catherine was filled with professional admiration for the way the exhibition had been arranged at short notice. She skimmed through the lavish catalogue, which described the institute's latest bequest and was illustrated with colour pictures of items not yet removed from Scotland, and gave her husband a sardonic smile. 'You still reckon all this was laid on for your benefit?'

Before Tim could offer an answer he was swooped upon by the arts correspondent of one of the leading broadsheets, a well-built woman whose low-cut dress was a triumph of faith over gravity. As the evening progressed the Lacys met several more friends and acquaintances. Harman-Lederer had succeeded in attracting the leading luminaries of London's artistic *demi-monde*—critics, dealers, curators, collectors, members of arts boards and councils; satellites who glistened ostentatiously but only with reflected brilliance.

Tim and Catherine made their separate ways through the steadily densening throng, until Tim spotted the arrival of Andrea and Ben. He found his wife and led her towards the main doorway where the new arrivals were being greeted by Hildegard Nefsky and a couple whose poise and elegance made them stand out from the crowd. The woman—forty but looking ten years younger—might have stepped straight out of a fashion plate. Catherine admired the sheath dress and the choker of diamonds and emeralds that blazed around the long neck. Tim reflected that there were only a handful of tailors in Europe who could have cut the man's three-piece suit, and few wearers who could have shown it off to better advantage. The stranger carried not a gram of unnecessary flesh. He was slim and muscular, a man who took care of his body and, to judge from his complexion, spent much of the year in sunnier climes.

Dr Nefsky fussed. 'Tim, how lovely! May I present Mr and Mrs Samuel Harman. Mr Harman is chairman and chief executive of Harman-Lederer Inc.'

'Sam and Georgey,' the American insisted with a well-practised smile as he shook hands.

Tim realised that Harman's swept-back dark hair showed just enough grey to appear distinguished and not enough to suggest age. He introduced Catherine.

The Harman smile broadened. 'Hey, I detect a fellow New Englander. We have to have an exile-to-exile chat before the evening's out. Isn't that so, honey?' Deftly he passed the conversational baton to his wife, who began talking Americana with Catherine. He turned to his other guest. 'Tim, I guess you know Andrea Robertson and her charming beau. Andrea, we're so glad you could come. Your father's generosity means an immense amount to us. We're real proud to house his collection. But I wouldn't want you to think for a single moment that we're gloating over all these wonderful things. We would rather have waited many years to stage this little party than have inherited under such tragic circumstances.'

Andrea smiled and Tim was pleased to see that it was a deep, relaxed smile. 'Thank you, Sam. Dr Nefsky and others have warmly expressed your company's condolences on other occasions. To be perfectly honest I'm delighted that you're taking all these objects off my hands. I wouldn't have known how to begin disposing of them.'

'Rest assured, Andrea, we'll display these wonderful treasures just as your father wanted. He was a remarkable man. I can't think of anyone else who could have put together a themed collection of such quality. His knowledge, his enthusiasm, his industry...'

Andrea interrupted. 'You know, you people at Harman-Lederer really knew him better than I did.'

'Oh, I can't believe—'

'No, it's true. I only saw him in short spells—school and university holidays mostly. Poor man; he didn't really know how to relate to a child or a teenager. He was always tied up in his deals and his research. What was he like to do business with? I've always imagined he must have been a very tough negotiator.'

'Your dad was a pro. We all had a deep respect for him. I'll tell you some stories about him—that's a promise. Right now I have to go make a speech and introduce your British heritage minister and look generally pompous. But later on we're getting together a little impromptu party. We have a couple of boxes at Covent Garden. They're doing *Otello* tonight. You like opera? Good. You must come. You, too, Tim. I insist. It'll be a chance to get to know each other,' he dropped his voice to a conspiratorial whisper, 'away from all these stuffed shirts.'

Tim turned to Catherine with a broad smile that said 'I told you so'.

It was impossible not to be moved. Shakespeare's dark plot, Verdi's tense music, and the superb interpretation of both by three principals drawn from the world's top singers made a stirring combination. Tim was totally absorbed by the drama. The interval brought him back to the present and to real-life tragedy.

There were ten in the Harmans' party, and the two wide boxes were comfortably full. During the intervals the hosts organised an array of champagne, spirits and soft drinks and the company split up into conversational groups.

After act two, Tim found himself leaning against the plush balustrade and chatting with Ben Azikwe. 'You must look at *Otello* from a very different perspective,' he suggested.

'Because I'm black?'

'Because you come from a very different cultural background.'

The African gazed out over the half-full auditorium, where people were talking or making their way towards the bars. 'Jealousy, revenge, hypocrisy—they're universals, are they not?'

'Obviously, but I don't suppose any of

your authors have written about the abuse of a white man in black society.'

Ben laughed. 'No, I don't suppose that would be considered politically correct in the present climate.'

'Do you find adjustment and readjustment difficult as you move backwards and forwards between Lagos and London?'

Azikwe shrugged. 'It's a problem that goes with the territory. As a diplomat one is trained to cope with it.'

'Do you think Andrea will cope?'

'She thinks she can.' The reply was casual.

'But you must be concerned about how she will adapt to your lifestyle.'

'Not as concerned as you are, apparently.'

'In other words, "Mind your own business"?'

Ben's smile as he turned to face Tim was relaxed and friendly. 'Would a diplomat ever say such a thing?'

At that moment Andrea appeared in the doorway at the back of the box. She was laughing as she came and sat between them.

'Private joke?' Ben asked.

'Oh, it's just Sam. He's very amusing. He's been telling me about the sort of things my father sometimes got up to to clinch major international deals. It seems my dear old dad actually had a sense of humour, although I never saw any evidence of it.'

'Tell us about his pranks,' Tim encouraged.

'Well, there was this time that Harman-Lederer were in fierce competition with a French company...'

'Will you excuse me?' Ben stood up. 'Time and bladder wait for no man.' He smiled before turning to leave the box but Tim noted the anxious glance Andrea directed at his retreating figure.

He would have put the incident from his mind had it not been for something else that happened a little later. The tragedy on stage moved to its dreadful climax. The Moor entered the room where Desdemona lay sleeping. She awoke and sat up in the bed, arms held out in welcome. Outlined in the doorway Otello ordered her to fall to her prayers in preparation for death. All eyes were fixed upon the hero and heroine, puppets manipulated by a relentless nemesis. Everyone was caught up in the menace of the music.

'Confess your sins!'

'My sin is love!'

'For that you die!'

At that moment Tim chanced to glance at Ben Azikwe. He was staring straight at Andrea. In the darkness of the theatre Tim could not read his expression.

After the performance Sam Harman insisted that everyone come to his Dorchester suite for supper. He had arranged limousines and it was as they were waiting briefly on the pavement outside the opera house that Catherine linked her arm through Tim's.

'You're very quiet.'

Tim turned to his wife, his face solemn. 'Andrea and Ben.'

'What about them?'

'Are they in love?'

Sam Harman bustled up as a long, sleek Mercedes prowled alongside. 'Here we are then.' He handed Catherine and Georgey into the car, then climbed in with Tim.

As they settled in the interior darkness Catherine said quietly to her husband, 'I'll need notice of that question. Ask me again later.'

At the Dorchester the party spirit continued unabated, encouraged by the enthusiastic master of ceremonies. The group was augmented by half a dozen corporate executives and their wives, among whom Tim recognised the tubby figure of Peter Hovenden. More food and drink circulated. Tim decided the time had come to stick to coffee.

It was after about twenty minutes that Harman eased his way across the room to

Tim's side. 'I wonder if we might have a brief word in private?'

'I wondered when we were going to get down to business.' Tim matched the other man's smile.

Harman led the way to an adjacent room, fitted out for formal dining or board meetings. Two others were already seated at the circular teak table—Hovenden, and a man with the face and physique of an ex-boxer or a Soho club doorman. Sam introduced him as 'Barry Duff, our head of security on this side of the water'.

The large man leaned across the table to shake Tim's hand. 'Nice to meet you, Tim. Lacy Security has an impressive record. We ought to do business.'

'I don't think guarding armaments factories is quite in our line.' He sank on to a swivelling leather chair.

Harman opened the formal proceedings. 'Tim, you're an ex-army man. You know the importance of reliable military equipment. I don't need to tell you about the pace of technical development, the complexities of international relations, the cant and hypocrisy of politicians who want to tie the defence industry hand and foot while being protected by the very weapons they denounce.'

Tim held up a hand. 'Sam, we could have a very long debate about the ethics of your business but it's already late and we all know that's not what we're here for.'

Harman nodded. 'Right, since we obviously understand each other, let's cut the crap and get down to cases. We'd like to hire you to find out who killed Jack Robertson.'

CHAPTER 17

Letter from Miss Cecily Bainbridge to her brother, Captain Jonathan Bainbridge, Lord Trensham's Dragoon:

Harrowdene Manor, St Albans,
9 June 1755.

Dearest Jon,

I had not meant to write to you quite so soon after leaving London, but I am bursting to relate the adventure which befell Hetty and me upon the road.

The weather was quite appalling for June and the carriage had to stop three times between Hampstead and Barnet for the men to free it from the mud. On one occasion we were even obliged to dismount—in the rain! I declare it was quite too bad and utterly vindicated my vexation at being packed off to the country. I am sure that Papa is completely wrong about your friend, Captain Vincent, and it was so unfair of him to oblige me to leave town without the opportunity for explanations. I am a woman of seventeen and not a porcelain figurine to be set on a mantel and admired but never touched for fear of breaking. I enclose a letter for Captain Vincent. I beg you to convey it to him—and never a word to Papa or Mama.

You may imagine that I was not in the best of humours even though the rain eased in the afternoon and the sun made an apologetic appearance. I vowed it would serve Papa right if Hetty and I took a chill upon the road and died of it. The fun of it is that something far worse happened—or I am sure that Papa will think it far worse and may speedily repent of subjecting his daughter to the dangers of travel upon the public highway.

We had left the Great North Road and advanced, I suppose, some two or three miles along the turnpike. We cannot have been far from the Shearmans' place. Of course, that is all shut up and the dowdy Caroline Shearman is with her parents in Hanover Square enjoying all the delights of the season! The owners of that section of road have been most derelict in their duty. It is appallingly rutted and potholed. We were so badly rolled and shaken about I declare I should have been happy had we stuck fast once more and the passengers been obliged to dismount into a puddle.

Well, Jon, my wish was granted but it had nothing to do with the mud. The carriage came to a very sudden halt. It woke Miss Medlar, who had somehow contrived to fall into a doze, with a start. Neither of the men came to the door to explain the delay, and when I let down the window to berate them what do you suppose I saw? A highwayman! He was an ugly, fearsome brute. His coat was patched and his hat, though once obviously fashionable, was very battered. No doubt he had it from some gentleman he had robbed well in the past. But the most fearsome thing about him was his face. I should say he was not very old but he wore a patch over his left eye and was severely scarred along the same cheek. I suppose he was a veteran of the French war. Should you not think that likely? His poor horse, a large grey, looked as though he, too, had seen better days. This dreadful man shouted at us to leave the carriage and bring all our valuables with us. As soon as I heard his voice I knew he was a North Briton. He spoke in that same, odd way that Doctor Ferguson speaks only, naturally, more coarse. Do you not think it clever of me to have observed that?

So we, all three of us, stepped down into the road. Miss Medlar took one look at the two pistols the rogue was pointing at us and fainted—right there, beside the carriage. The men virtually had to drag her across to the covering of a great tree where the grass was not quite so wet. Hetty was hysterical. She clung to my arm and refused to let go. The servants were quite useless. Someone had to take charge so I decided it should be me. Can you imagine me being so brave and cool, looking down the barrel of a gun? I suspect not, but did I not always tell you that I should make a good soldier?

I accosted the fellow. What sort of a man was it, I demanded, who rather than earn an honest living, preferred to make cowardly attacks on helpless women? His response was really rather extraordinary. He seemed not the least annoyed and certainly not shamed. He smiled—at least, I suppose his twisted grimace was meant to be a smile. 'We are what the world makes us,' he said, 'and the world has made you and I so different that I doubt either of us could ever understand the other, though we might stand here discussing such matters from now until the day of doom.' It seems my highwayman was also a philosopher.

There is little more to tell. When the ruffian was satisfied that he had despoiled us of everything of value that was readily portable he stowed his booty in a saddle-bag, pocketed his pistols and rode away across country. We climbed back aboard and reached Harrowdene without further incident. As soon as Cousin Beatrice received us you can imagine how Miss Medlar waxed eloquent about what she called our 'encounter with an emissary of Satan'. She transformed the whole incident into a three-act Drury Lane tragedy—which was very inventive of her considering that throughout most of the confrontation she was unconscious.

This episode is the only interesting thing that is likely to happen to me for weeks, and I suppose I must now resign myself to aeons of rural boredom, unless, of course, Papa can be convinced that the unknown terrors into which he has precipitately propelled his daughter far exceed any misfortune that might befall her in the company of a certain captain of dragoons.

Dearest Jon, do try your best to visit us soon before I die of ennui. And do bring a reply from Captain Vincent.

Your loving, Cissy.

Sam Harman's bold proposal stunned Tim into temporary silence.

The American expanded his statement. 'We know that you've taken an interest in poor Jack's death. We also know that your government wants to keep the whole affair under wraps. That's OK by us; we don't want the world and his wife in on this business. But we do want to know what's going on. Whoever killed Jack came damned close to lousing up some very delicate negotiations. We managed to salvage a contract worth hundreds of millions—and that's pounds sterling, not dollars—just! But if whoever was responsible strikes again...well, that simply mustn't happen. So, you see, Tim, it's in our interests to pay handsomely for whatever information you have and for you to continue your enquiries.'

Tim looked slowly round the table, gathering his thoughts. 'If you gentlemen are so keen to enlist my services why did you try to assassinate me?'

'What the hell...' Sam's outburst matched

the astonished looks on the faces of his colleagues.

'Oh, come off it!' Tim's patience slipped a cog. 'Don't pretend you know nothing about a certain Land Rover playing bumper cars and trying to topple me down a Scottish mountain back in February!'

Harman glanced at Duff, who shook his head firmly and said, 'I haven't the foggiest idea what you're talking about—and believe me, if any of our people was responsible I'd know. What exactly happened, Tim?'

Tim glared back. 'Squeaky clean doesn't suit you, but I'll let it pass. If you want my help let's start with some honest answers to a few straight questions. Robertson, I presume, was a freelance negotiator employed by Harman-Lederer over many years.'

Sam nodded. 'We and Jack go back a long way. His contacts and expertise were invaluable.'

'What about Carlos Lombardo? Where does he fit into the picture?'

Harman glanced quickly at his associates, then nodded. 'OK, it's cards on the table time. Sure, we had dealings with Lombardo. The guy's a crook—we all know that. But that doesn't mean that everything he does is crooked. Our dealings with him have been absolutely on the green baize.'

'He's another of your independent fixers,

I presume. What was his relationship with Robertson? I gather there was bad blood between them.'

Sam laughed. 'Who's been feeding you that crap? Jack and Carlos have been friends for years.'

'What happened in Doalamba?'

'I didn't know you had an interest in ancient history, Tim. That was over twenty years ago. What happened was that my company burned its fingers very badly. It was in my father's time as chairman. Jack and Carlos were fronting a deal for us with the government. A large sum of money was involved in sweeteners and expenses. There was a coup, and Jack got out by the skin of his teeth. Carlos wasn't quite as lucky, but he eventually made it home in one piece and was soon back in favour. In the chaos the cash disappeared—or so Jack said.'

'You didn't altogether trust him?'

'Well, he wasn't exactly destitute when he returned to civilisation. He and Carlos had enough capital to set up several lucrative deals.'

'So why go on doing business with them?'

'They had a lot of important friends in West Africa and among political exiles. We reckoned that if we went on being nice to these people and waited for the political wheel to take another whirl we'd be back in business. And that's how it turned out. We did good business with Doalamba. That led to negotiations with some of their allies and eventually with several other countries north and south of the Sahara. Jack and Carlos were involved in most of these deals. Their contacts throughout the continent were impressive—unique.'

'What you're telling me then is that Harman-Lederer are pure as mother's milk; your dealings with Robertson and Lombardo were all totally legitimate; Robertson's murder took you completely by surprise; and you haven't the remotest idea who was responsible.' Tim brayed a cynical laugh. 'Do me a favour: stop underrating my intelligence.'

Harman was not to be fazed. 'Tim, there's no way we down-value you. It seems to me that you underrate our integrity. Supposing you tell us what it is you think we're up to.'

'I can't pretend to have all the details, but in outline it goes something like this: twenty-three years ago Captain John Rycote was thrown out of the British army. He got together a bunch of misfits—failed soldiers and failed civilians who couldn't get their minds out of khaki—and formed his own little group of mercenaries. They propped up the corrupt regime of King Lasadi-Boma and lined their pockets with pay, loot, bribes, and the profits on crooked deals. They lost no opportunity to exploit the people and resources of a poor African country. And they made money out of other vested interests who also wanted to exploit Doalamba—like companies trying to grab mineral rights or sell weapons of destruction to the government. Harman-Lederer were in there, wrestling in the mud with all the others. Your man on the spot was Carlos Lombardo, a low life who already had a reputation as a vicious and unscrupulous operator—just the sort of representative you needed in a tough situation. Then there was a political upheaval and all your plans fell apart.

'Someone took advantage of the chaos. I don't know who double-crossed whom. All I do know is that Rycote had to disappear. The mercenary leader "died" in the insurrection and, lo and behold, a few months later, a wealthy recluse by the name of Jack Robertson appeared in Scotland. He shut himself away in an impregnable castle where enemies and cheated associates could not get at him. In the fullness of time he made his peace with some of his ex-colleagues. There were still rich pickings to be had selling arms to oppressive third-world regimes and it made sense for all concerned to swallow their pride and draw a veil over past quarrels.

But there could never be the same degree of trust that had existed before.

'Then, recently, something went wrong, something that reopened old wounds. Did Robertson get greedy over a deal? Or was it his threat to leave his valuable collection to another museum? That must have seemed like a piece of treachery on a par with his double-dealing in Doalamba all those years ago. Hildegard Nefsky was despatched to Lanner Castle to talk him round. Carlos Lombardo was there to reason with him. They both failed; Robertson was a stubborn man. So it was time for Plan B. That involved getting him out of the castle. If anything happened to him there it would be pretty obvious who was responsible. He had to be scared out.

'Time and again I've puzzled over what happened in those following, dark hours. Robertson was badly shaken. He had to get away to safety and he had to get his enemies off his back. Where could he go? Who could he talk to? My guess is that he turned to an associate he could trust. Someone at Harman-Lederer, perhaps someone in this room. What did he say, "Let's meet up somewhere in secret, talk things over, come to an arrangement"? I don't know the question, but the answer was, "Go to the Edinburgh house. Someone will meet you there." ' Tim looked around with a grim smile. 'Someone certainly did—but not to talk.'

There was a long pause. Then Harman swivelled his chair and looked straight at Tim. 'That's a very Machiavellian scenario, Tim. I'm impressed by the mental effort that's gone into putting it together. The only thing wrong with it is that it's way off beam.'

'Convince me!' Tim stared frankly back.

'Well, for one thing, what's with this Edinburgh house?'

Tim shook his head. 'It's no good denying it, Sam. I've been there. I've seen the nondescript, anonymous suburban house you use for very discreet meetings.'

'Well I don't know who your informant was, but he got it wrong. We have no house in Edinburgh, do we, Pete?' He turned to Hovenden for confirmation.

The fat man was forthright. 'Certainly not! We have a conference centre in Buckinghamshire. That has all the facilities we need for what you call "very discreet meetings".'

Sam looked thoughtful. 'So, Tim, you reckon you've located the place where Jack was actually murdered. That's great. If you can get in there and turn up some evidence, we should be able to nail the sadistic bastard.'

'No way! What I know goes to the

police. They can take it from here.'

Those words lowered the temperature almost physically.

Harman applied gentle pressure. 'Tim, I have to tell you we wouldn't be happy with that—not at this point in time.'

'I'll bet you wouldn't. You're scared...'

Sam raised his voice, his New England drawl hardening into authoritativeness. 'Hear me out, Tim. There are some things you need to know. Let's take your version of events and put one or two things straight. You're right about Rycote. Back in the days of Lasadi-Boma he was in charge of military operations—the obvious man for us to do business with. When the king was overthrown, our agent Lombardo did a stretch in a Doalamba prison—not a nice experience. Rycote we thought was dead, and—yes—we were very sore about the money we lost in the fiasco. We washed our hands of the whole region. Then, a couple of years later, Jack got back in touch. Now his name was Robertson. Several of his friends had returned to power and he suggested we reopen the shop. We took some convincing. We sounded out Lombardo, who had made it back to the States. I was actually in the office when he came in. I've seen some pretty angry men in my time but, boy, what Carlos reckoned he was going to do to Jack Robertson was stomach-churning. It was Friederich Lederer who brought them together and persuaded them that it was in everyone's interest to smoke the peace pipe.

'Since then neither of them has ever mentioned the past in my hearing. They were businessmen. They didn't let personal feelings interfere with making a profit.'

'But they weren't exactly the best of buddies?'

'OK, perhaps I did exaggerate a little there. But I can categorically say that Carlos was not harbouring thoughts of revenge.'

'As far as you know.'

Sam acknowledged the comment with an irritated nod of the head. 'Sure—as far as I know. But you can take it from me, if you've fixed your sights on Carlos as the murderer you're looking way in the wrong direction.'

'So what was he doing at Lanner Castle the night Robertson made a hurried exit?'

Sam Harman delivered the answer slowly and deliberately. 'He was warning Jack that his life was in danger.'

Tim shook his head sceptically. 'Really? You're going to have to spell it out in capital letters if you want me to believe that.'

Harman stood abruptly. He gestured to his colleagues. To Tim he said, 'Excuse us a moment,' as he led them into an adjacent bedroom.

They were gone three minutes. When they returned to their places at the table Sam's self-assurance was showing signs of fraying at the edges. 'Look, what I'm going to tell you now is absolutely confidential. If it gets out it will damage Harman-Lederer badly—very badly. You have to promise not to repeat it.'

Tim shook his head. 'I don't write blank cheques. I'm not going to go around blabbing your company secrets, but if I come to the conclusion that my silence is protecting a killer I go straight to the police.'

Harman nodded. 'I guess that's the best deal we're going to get. For over a year we've been working damned hard to secure a contract with a certain government that isn't exactly flavour of the month with several Western countries. The potential for future sales is immense, so international competition is vicious. We can handle that, but there are other problems. For one thing, we can't rely on any overt support from Washington or Westminster. There are political sensitivities. We're dealing with a friendly power, to which there are no restrictions on the export of arms. But the regime is unpopular in the West, and after the fiascos over defence contracts with Iran and Iraq no government minister is prepared to head up trade delegations or give us open support. But the real trouble comes from two groups of people who are utterly determined to sabotage the negotiations. There's a well-funded underground opposition operating from a base in this country. And there's ASHRA—the Association for Securing Human Rights in Africa.'

Tim shook his head. 'Never heard of them.'

'That doesn't surprise me. Unlike other protest groups, they don't advertise themselves much. Their political wing goes in for protest notes and petitions rather than banner-waving. Most of their money is used to support their action group—a bunch of antis and anarchists who enjoy violence for its own sake; psychos who'll take up any cause from immigration to save the bunny rabbits if it provides opportunities for mob violence, arson and even murder. Now, these two organisations have been working together in both Africa and the UK. We've had attempted break-ins at two of our factories, there was a serious fire at one of our component suppliers, and some of our staff have had threatening phone-calls.'

Tim listened intently—and critically. 'You've reported all these incidents to the police?'

388

'No, that would lead to media involvement and I'm not going to give these goddamn lefties a single column inch of free publicity. Besides, any publicity is bad for PR and it makes our customers very jittery. They got a whiff of trouble a few months back and it took days of hard talking to keep them on board. So, for lots of reasons, we prefer to do our own private policing. Barry has been doing a good job and has come up with some interesting facts.' He handed over to the bulky security chief.

'We've assembled a whole library of videos and still photos of most of the ASHRA activists. When we got wind that they were targeting Jack Robertson I sent a couple of my men up to Scotland to have a look-see. They ran into the Save Glen Huich brigade, and guess what.'

'They spotted some familiar faces?' Tim suggested.

'Hole in one, squire. No less than three ASHRA leading lights showed up there within the space of a couple of weeks.'

Tim shrugged. 'Lots of these rent-a-mobbers move from one protest to another.'

'Granted, Tim. They're anti-establishment yobs looking for a punch-up, and they don't much care who they have it with. But these weren't ordinary foot soldiers. We know that two of them, at least, are members of the ASHRA high command.' Barny opened a file on the table before him and slid a batch of photographs across the polished surface. 'Recognise anyone?'

Tim did. 'I think I've seen that young man in the bar at Briachan. But there's no doubt about the women. Are you sure you haven't made a mistake? Their names are Carol and Steffy and they were guests at the castle the night Robertson received the black spot.'

'The what?'

'Never mind. What you're telling me is that you knew, or believed, these girls to be fanatical human rights activists out to stop your deal by fair means or foul. Yet you let them get really close to Robertson.'

'We didn't know about it till afterwards. I had Dr Nefsky go through our rogues gallery and she picked that pair out straight away.'

Tim sat back with a groan. 'God, this is getting complicated. How many layers are there to this particular onion?'

Barny said, 'Forget about the girls for a moment, Tim. Take a close took at the other picture. You see what that bloke's standing in front of?'

'Looks like a pretty ancient Land Rover.'

'That's right. I've got a tenner here that

says that's your would-be assassin.'

Tim was aware of three pairs of eyes fixed upon him, three men waiting for his response. After a long pause he said, 'You seem to be doing your own investigating pretty successfully. I don't see why you need my help.'

'There are at least three reasons why you can find out or work out the truth more easily than we can,' Sam explained. 'You were up there in Scotland when it all happened. You met the people who, one way or another, are tied up in this business.'

'And the third reason?' Tim prompted.

'You haven't asked what country we're negotiating this crucial deal with.'

'I didn't think you'd tell me.'

'When I do you'll realise that you have a vital line of enquiry that isn't open to us. Our customers are the government of Nigeria.'

CHAPTER 18

Sam Harman organised a fleet of company limos to convey his guests to their respective homes. It wasn't until the Lacys had been dropped at their flat—shortly after two in the morning—and were preparing for bed that they were able to discuss the evening's events.

'That question you asked me—about Andrea and Ben,' Catherine began as she sat at the dressing table, removing her make-up.

'Yes, what's your considered opinion?' Tim emerged from the bathroom, towelling himself down after a shower.

'You wanted to know whether they were really in love. I don't think it's as simple as that. I chatted to them both while you were closeted with Sam Harman and his cronies. I'd say they had a pretty unstable relationship. Each is looking for something in the other that probably isn't there.'

'That sounds very profound.' Tim stood behind his wife, hands on her shoulders, speaking to her reflection.

'Don't mock.' She leaned back against him. 'It was you who asked.'

'I'm not mocking. I trust your instinct in these things. What do you reckon Andrea wants out of the relationship?'

'I guess, basically, a father figure. She never really had any parents, poor kid. Her dad kept her at arm's length all those years. All the vital signs that children pick up in the home about how to relate to the opposite sex—they just weren't there. She needs so many things—protection, guidance, a set of values to take as a starting point for forming her own, a male image to measure all men against... She's the original little girl lost.'

'More like the original poor little rich girl. Do you reckon Ben is exploiting her inexperience?'

Catherine deftly applied a tissue to her eyelids. She answered cautiously. 'I don't think so—not deliberately, anyway. He's in much the same boat—he has no memory of either of his parents—but he did grow up on a mission station. That gave him a stable and loving environment and a set of standards. It also gave him a very good start in life, otherwise he wouldn't be one of Nigeria's élite.'

'Isn't he what someone would call a black European—so immersed in white culture and values as to have a real identity problem? He told me once that he hoped not to be recalled to Nigeria.'

'You could have a point. A person's earliest impressions are the strongest he ever forms. Ben's attitude towards whites was developed when he was a child. If they were the people who gave him love and fostered his self-worth, he might now find it easier to relate to them than to his own kith.'

'Hence his desire to marry a white woman?'

'Could be.' Catherine wandered into the bathroom.

'Not exactly the best emotional basis for a marriage.' Tim raised his voice above the sound of running tap water. He slipped thankfully beneath the duvet and relaxed all his muscles. When Catherine entered the bed beside him minutes later, he asked, 'You wouldn't say there was anything sinister about Ben's interest in Andrea?'

'What do you mean by sinister?'

'Sam as good as hinted that Ben could have been somehow involved in Robertson's death.'

Catherine scoffed. 'Why on earth would Ben kill his fiancée's father?'

'They had a very unpleasant row the first and only time they met, as George and I know—but that wasn't what Sam was on about. He reckons the murder is all tied up with Nigerian politics.' Tim outlined his discussion with the Harman-Lederer top brass.

Catherine was unimpressed. 'What it comes down to is coincidence, and a pretty tenuous one at that: Robertson *may* have been killed to stop him completing a Nigerian arms deal; Ben Azikwe is Nigerian; ergo Ben Azikwe is the murderer.'

'To be fair, Sam didn't actually accuse

Ben. He suggested he might be able to shed some light. Do you know what exactly Ben does at the embassy?'

'I did ask him but he wasn't very forthcoming. He said he was in the immigration office, dealing with what he called "boring" things such as passports and work permits. Anyway, you haven't told me the outcome of your clandestine meeting.'

'Sam Harman wanted to hire me to find Robertson's murderer.'

'You refused, of course.'

'Yes and no.'

'Tim!' Catherine sat up in bed and glared at her husband.

'It's OK, darling. I didn't agree to go on the Harman-Lederer payroll. But I thought I might as well use their resources for a couple of things I want to check on.'

'Such as?'

'I must go and talk to Jeanne Picard.'

'Andrea's supposed mother?'

'Yes. I owe that to Andrea. And I also want to have another word with Carol Sellis. If her friends were responsible for trying to run Johnny and me off the road I want to know. Sam's offered to put one of the company jets at my disposal, to have his security chief work closely with me, and to cover all my expenses.'

'Haven't you had enough of this business yet?'

Tim yawned. 'Yes, more than enough. You were quite right; this isn't our scene. I hate the topsy-turvy, cloak-and-dagger world where men brandish smoking secrets and file away tanks under "Confidential". I'll find out what I can about Andrea's family... It's up to her to decide what she wants to do about it... If I can get my hands...joker in the Land Rover...I'll...but, right now, I...'

Seconds later he was asleep.

On 15 April 1756 William Augustus, Duke of Cumberland, celebrated his thirty-fifth birthday with a dinner at St James's Palace. The event had been planned as a banquet but had had to be scaled down when several invitees sent their regrets. It was eventually attended largely by place seekers, court hangers-on and those—like Lord Sandwich and Henry Fox—who had political reasons for attaching themselves to the prince's entourage. Of real friends Cumberland had few. In the army the commander-in-chief was criticised for being more German than English, for being tyrannical with his officers and harsh with his men. In the country at large, 'Stinking Billy' was lampooned for his obesity and suspected of wishing to usurp the royal succession from his nephew. The ecstatic popularity that in 1746 had greeted the 'conquering hero'—and had been marked by Handel in the oratorio *Judas Maccabaeus*—had evaporated within months. It was not only the Scots who dubbed him the Butcher. News of his excessive brutality in suppressing the Jacobite uprising sickened the public and dismayed the political pragmatists—who understood that a nation facing repeated crises in Europe, the American colonies and India could ill afford disaffection at home. As the post-Culloden years unrolled, increasing reports came in from justices and corporations throughout the country of Scottish vagrants—individuals, groups, families—wandering from town to town seeking succour, shelter and employment. Cumberland had quelled a rebellion, subjected a people, crushed a culture, and created a problem.

Not that he was without solutions to the problem. 'If they require money to feed their families let them fight for it, I say.' The duke, buttoned tightly into the uniform of Colonel-in-Chief of the Coldstream Guards, stared along the gilt-littered table at the thirty guests ranged along both sides. 'The army is in want of new blood. I say raise some regiments in the Highlands. Let the ex-Jacobites do themselves some good and prove their loyalty to the crown. What do you Scots gentlemen say to that?'

He directed the question in a booming voice at two guests seated at the lower end of the table. James Campbell had put military life behind him and was now a member of parliament for the county of Inverness, in which capacity he spent much of his time in London where he championed Scottish interests, largely through his friendship with Henry Fox, the government leader in the Commons. Opposite Campbell sat Simon Fraser, a young lawyer, recently arrived in the capital and paraded by the government as the outstanding example of Scottish acquiescence in the Hanoverian regime. Fraser had fought for the Stuart cause in 1745–6. His father, Lord Lovat, had been beheaded on Tower Hill after the rebellion, and thousands of Londoners had flocked to witness the end of so celebrated a traitor. Afterwards, Simon Fraser had made his peace with the regime and was anxious to demonstrate the fact on every possible occasion. That explained why he eagerly courted Campbell and others close to the duke's party.

'Your Highness, as usual, strikes to the heart of the problem. There are many brave lads among my own tenantry who would leap at the chance to defend the nation's interests abroad.'

'Spoken like a loyal subject, Fraser. What do you say to that, Campbell?'

All eyes turned on the older Scot to see how he would respond to Cumberland's question. Campbell was known to be no enthusiast for the rivalry with France which was swallowing up vast quantities of manpower and treasure.

He cleared his throat and spoke in measured tones. 'My people are eager to serve their king and country in many capacities, Your Highness. Farmers, soldiers, lawyers, doctors, tradesmen—they ask only equal opportunity with those born south of the border to develop their skills and to put them at the disposal of their fellow countrymen.'

Silence greeted this judicious answer. Then someone asked the duke whether he gave any credence to the rumours of French preparations for a cross-Channel invasion and the conversation revived.

At 11.00 the following morning the Duke of Cumberland set out by carriage for parliament. It was a fine day and several ladies and gentlemen of quality were taking the air on foot, on horseback or by sedan. Some doffed hats or nodded as the Butcher drove past. Others pointedly did not.

The well-known equipage had travelled half-way along Pall Mall when a man on a white horse spurred out from a side street. As he drew level with the carriage he released the reins and swung a pistol butt against the door glass, shattering it. He discharged the gun into the interior, then did the same with its partner, and wheeled his grey around, setting it into a canter towards St James's. The assassin would have escaped, so sudden had been the assault, had it not been for the panic of a servant holding the back end of a sedan chair. His mistress, inside the conveyance, chanced to witness the incident. She screamed lustily—so lustily that her man let go the handles. The chair toppled into the road right in the path of the fleeing gunman. The horse reared and the rider fell. Momentarily he was winded. When he picked himself up he saw several men running towards the scene of the attack. His mount had skittered off and there was no time to call it back. The Black Boy took to his heels.

He was captured in the Hay Market.

Three days later he was conveyed in an open cart with two other felons from Newgate prison to Tyburn. The vehicle rumbled and jolted its way along Holborn attended by a mounted escort of dragoons. Watched over by two guards, the prisoners lay chained together on the wagon's floor beside the rough, elm coffins that would carry them on their return journey. They did not speak to each other. They did not respond to the jeers from the citizens along the route.

A young clergyman clung to the swaying side boards with one hand and held his book open with the other. With what dignity he could muster he incanted formulae that were already a hundred years old: 'Lord, now lettest Thou Thy servant depart in peace according to Thy word, for mine eyes have seen Thy salvation which Thou hast prepared...'

Once, when he came to a longer than usual pause and was fumbling to find his new page, the one-eyed prisoner asked, 'It is true, sir, is it not—that we are what the world makes us?'

Eager to air his theology, the minister responded quickly. 'My son, we are what God makes us. It is the world that mars us—that and our own sinful nature.'

'And does God take account of the world's work in us?'

'God looks on the heart. No man fathoms His judgement.'

That seemed to satisfy the prisoner, for he spoke no further word throughout the rest of the journey, nor upon the scaffold. The ranks of open galleries around the gibbet were quite full despite the light rain which had set in. Ewen barely noticed the spectators. He was locked up in his own thoughts. He saw other deaths, which had always seemed more important than his own and which still seemed so—mother, father, brothers, Ranald, Hector, Aileen, Tom.

Only when the rope had been placed around his neck and priest and executioner had left the platform did he look over the heads of the watchers. Suddenly he saw a familiar face. Two gentlemen on horseback had stopped to watch. One he knew. He opened his mouth to call but the jolt of the noose cut off any sound.

James Campbell and Simon Fraser were returning from exercising in Hyde Park. They reined in briefly to watch the execution.

Fraser said, 'The one-eyed wretch is the man who tried to kill the duke, so I'm told.'

'Doubtless he had reason which seemed good to him.'

'Come, James—you don't condone such barbaric behaviour, surely.'

'There are many things I don't condone, Simon, and Cumberland has committed more of them, I'll warrant, than that poor Highlander.'

'You knew him, then.'

'Like you, I listen to gossip. I never saw him before in my life.' Campbell sighed. 'Yet I pity him.'

He tapped his heels to the mare's flanks and trotted on into Oxford Street.

Carol Sellis proved surprisingly difficult to track down. The university secretariat informed Tim that she was no longer on their student roll. When he asked for her home address he was curtly informed that the university was legally inhibited from divulging such information. If Mr Lacy cared to write to Miss Sellis, care of the university, they would see that his letter was forwarded. Tim preferred to pass the problem to Barny Duff. Within hours he received a fax bearing a simple message: 'Caroline Sellis, Enderby Lodge, Briar Lane, Ashcot Green, nr Guildford'. He decided to call unannounced and use the element of surprise.

Briar Lane, when Tim's BMW cruised along it around noon two days later, turned out to be a privately maintained road, bordered on one side by a golf course and on the other by a dozen or so exclusive detached houses each set in grounds of about an acre. There were four expensive cars on the drive of Enderby Lodge. Tim parked just inside the gate and walked up to the house, a long, low, Lutyensesque building in 1930s brick. He was about to ring the bell beside the studded-oak front door when he heard approaching voices.

Six ladies engrossed in animated conversation appeared round the side of the house. They were casually but expensively and, Tim guessed, competitively dressed. Noticing him, they came to a halt. Tim was acutely aware of six pairs of appraising eyes.

'Ooh, company, darling!' a tall woman in white slacks and waistcoat over a polka-dot shirt announced suggestively. 'We must make ourselves scarce.' Her friends giggled.

There was a flurry of hugging and cheek-pecking before the guests sauntered back towards their cars, offering Tim wan smiles and stares of frank curiosity as they passed.

'Can I help you?' The lady of the house was a dyed blonde, mid-forties, dressed in a loose top of ice-blue silk over multi-coloured Bermuda shorts.

'Mrs Sellis? Actually I was hoping to see Carol.'

The woman held a hand over her eyes theatrically. 'Oh my God, what's the stupid bitch done this time? You'd better come round.' She turned and led the way towards the back of the house.

Tim saw a wide terrace overlooking a

sloping lawn. Garden tables, chairs and umbrellas were set out and a maid was collecting up plates, cups and saucers. Through sliding glass panels along the side of the house Tim saw an indoor swimming pool.

'Coffee?' the woman asked, waving Tim to a wicker chair. 'I'll get Rose to make up some fresh.'

'That's very kind, Mrs Sellis. I don't want to put you to any trouble.' Tim donned his most charming manner.

'Trouble!' The hostess grimaced as she sat opposite. 'That madam is seldom anything else. Rose, leave that and bring us a fresh pot,' she snapped at the servant. Turning back to Tim, she said, 'My name's Maggie Peverill. Sellis is my maiden name. Carol adopted it after my ex walked out on us. So what is it this time? Illegal substances? Damage to property? Obstructing the highway? I thought her new job would settle her down. Seems I was wrong.'

Tim smiled reassuringly. 'No, Mrs Peverill, nothing like that, I assure you. My name's Tim Lacy. I met Carol earlier in the year in the Scottish Highlands in rather...unfortunate circumstances.'

'Oh, my God! You were there when that poor man was...' She shuddered. 'That shook Carol badly. She reckons she's as

405

tough as old boots but that really got to her. She had to come back here for several weeks and was on the brink of a nervous breakdown. But, being Carol, she bounced back.'

'She's not here any longer?'

'No, her father fixed her up with a flat in town and a job. She screwed every penny she could out of the bastard and good luck to her. Keeping the pressure on Mark Kenley is about the only thing she and I agree on.' The coffee arrived and Mrs Peverill busied herself pouring it into elegant cups.

'Most youngsters go through a wild phase,' Tim suggested. 'Carol's obviously a very intelligent young woman. I'm sure she'll settle down.'

'Oh, she's bright all right. She'd have got a very good degree if she'd stuck to her studies instead of getting involved with all those protest groups.'

'I expect she'll put all that behind her now that she's a working girl.'

'I hope to God you're right. I've had it up to here with that young lady. I still get phone calls and visits from her weird associates. That doesn't please Simon—my husband. He's tried to get on with Carol—heaven knows he's tried—but he doesn't take kindly to long-haired layabouts and blacks wandering in here. One of them turned up at the weekend, black as your hat but well spoken and polite. Said he represented some organisation called Ash...something or other.'

'ASHRA?'

'That's it. You've heard of them? Well, poor Simon blew his top and ran him off the premises. Very image conscious is Simon—and just a little prejudiced.'

Tim noted the confirmation of Harman's identification of Carol as an ASHRA activist. 'So, what's your daughter doing now?'

'At this moment she's on holiday somewhere—Greece or Crete, I think— with some of her disreputable friends. But she's supposed to be back at the weekend in order to start work in her father's company, Finian Construction.'

Tim almost choked over his coffee. 'Finian Construction?'

'Yes. Mark is the top dog—a hard man in a hard business. When I was young and green I admired his macho image, but he also had a soft, gentle side in those days. It pretty soon disappeared. Now he's a money-making machine—nothing more, nothing less. Although Carol hates him she's definitely his daughter.'

'In Scotland she was leading a campaign against one of Finian's major projects.'

'Yes. That proves my point, doesn't it?

Carol's never forgiven her father for what he did to us. She reckoned he owed us and was rich enough to pay. She reckoned that if she punished him by attacking his Scottish dam, he'd have to buy her off eventually—and she was right. Finian Construction have created a new department for her. She's supposed to be assessing the environmental implications of every proposed new project.'

Tim re-examined his mental image of the ardent student campaigner. 'You reckon she's not really an idealist at all; that she's calculating her own personal advantage in these causes she supports?'

Mrs Peverill shrugged. 'Why ask me? I'm only her mother. What was it you wanted to see her about, Mr Lacy?'

'It was nothing very much. I was hoping she could put me in touch with one of her associates. We met in Scotland but I didn't make a note of his name.'

'Well, I'm not sure that I ought to hand over Carol's address. Nothing personal, Mr Lacy, but, well, you can't be too careful these days, can you?'

'Quite right, Mrs Peverill. In fact, all I really need is her phone number. Do you think it would be safe to divulge that?'

She laughed. 'Oh, I'm sure I can trust you that far. Now, you will stay for a bite of lunch won't you? Nothing wonderful,

408

I'm afraid, but I can offer you paté and a glass of Chablis.'

Tim declined, although Maggie Peverill pressed him hard to reconsider. He had no desire to become the object of speculation over the coffee cups of Surrey's bored stockbroker-belt wives. He spent the drive back to Farrans Court reassessing the principal characters in the affair of Jack Robertson deceased. Robertson, Lombardo, Nefsky, Hatherton, Harman, and now Carol Sellis—dear God, was everyone play acting; did no one know the meaning of the word 'truth'? Carol, the lank-haired idealist—living proof that we should never stereotype people. She might have rebelled against the establishment her parents represented, but she carried in abundance their ruthless, money-grubbing genes.

Twenty-four hours after his alfresco meeting with Maggie Peverill, Tim was sitting at another open-air table. The Relais St Pierre was backed by sloping ground, part lawn, part orchard, that bordered the Seine. Tim alone enjoyed the sunshine; the hotel's few other lunchtime customers had elected to eat in the intimate, timbered dining room. He enjoyed a simple meal, cooked to perfection and served by an attentive young waiter, and wondered how he could gain a few minutes alone with the proprietress, and what he would say to her when he did. He was still undecided when the young man brought his coffee.

On a sudden impulse he produced a business card from his wallet. 'Would you, please, give this to Madame Picard and ask if she would be kind enough to join me for a cognac?' Before he handed over the card he wrote on its back one word: 'Andrea'.

Moments later he was aware of being scrutinised from the kitchen window but he did not turn to face the house. For several minutes after that nothing happened. Then the waiter returned to his table and, without comment, set down a tray bearing a bottle and two glasses.

Another long wait. Tim gazed across to the broad river. A pair of swans lazed haughtily on its mirrored surface. What was it they said about swans—that they were totally monogamous, mating once and for life? A pity humans couldn't learn the trick.

'M'sieur?'

He had not heard her approach. He jumped up and stared into the face of a diminutive, tidy woman. Her brown eyes returned his gaze steadily, but the hands tightly clasped in front of her betrayed her nervousness.

'Madame Picard, it was good of you to

agree to meet a perfect stranger.'

'No customer of the Relais St Pierre is a stranger, Mr Lacy.'

They sat, and Tim poured brandy into the two glasses. The action filled time and the void he could still find no words to occupy. For unreal moments he and Jeanne Picard sipped their drinks. Then she placed Tim's card on the table, reverse side up, and looked at him with a quizzically raised eyebrow.

'I'm a friend of Andrea's,' he began tentatively.

'Has something happened to her?' The question slipped through tightly compressed lips.

'Not at all. She's very well. In fact she's about to be married.'

Tim was unprepared for the effect of this statement. Tears spilled from the woman's eyes. She fumbled in her skirt pocket for a handkerchief and pressed it hurriedly to her face.

'I'm sorry,' she muttered, struggling for composure. 'But it's very difficult. For years you people tell me nothing about my little girl. Then you arrive unannounced and tell me that she is a girl no more. That she's going to...' She took deep breaths to control her emotions. 'This is cruel. You know I would want to be at the wedding and yet you won't let me.'

Tim was alarmed, puzzled. 'Madame Picard, I have no power to prevent you doing anything you wish to do. You must be confusing me with someone else.'

'Do you think I have forgotten how you people work?' Bitterness staunched the flow of tears. 'Your card calls you a security expert. Security, intelligence—they all amount to the same thing.'

'Madame Picard, I assure you that what I said is true. I am a friend of your daughter.'

'No, Mr Lacy.' She shook her head firmly. 'My daughter does not know that I exist. She was told years ago that I was dead. You are from the British government. If you are not here simply to torment me, please tell me quickly why you have come—and then leave.'

'I'm sorry if I've distressed you. I realise that all this is stirring up unhappy memories. The reason for my visit is to reunite you with Andrea, if that is what you both want. If you will permit me to explain how I came to know your daughter I think everything will become clear. Perhaps we might walk a little by the river.'

As they strolled beneath the trees and then along a path beside the water, Tim presented a carefully-censored version of the events of the last six months. He explained how he had met Andrea and

Ben at the castle and how Robertson had died soon afterwards. He made no mention of murder. He referred to Macrae's slip which had led to Andrea discovering her father's former identity. He glossed over the facts surrounding his own discovery of Mme Picard's name and address.

When he had finished, Jeanne released a long shuddering sigh. 'Well, I thank you for the trouble you have taken to find me and tell me all this, Mr Lacy, but it makes no difference. They will never let us see each other or be together.'

'I think you're wrong,' Tim suggested gently. 'Now that Jack is dead, what reason can they possibly have for keeping you apart?'

'Reason?' She laughed bitterly. 'Why, the most compelling reason of all—what we French call *raison d'etat*. Individuals don't matter, life and death don't matter—not when it comes to governments saving face.'

'Could you tell me what happened all those years ago?'

'No, Mr Lacy. I was sworn to secrecy on pain of the most dire consequences. If you knew these people you would realise that they are perfectly capable of carrying out their threats.'

They stopped, and Tim turned to face her. He looked straight into her eyes and spoke with all the sincerity he could muster. 'I do know these people, and your assessment of them is absolutely correct. But this secret is already too old. It is going rotten and poisoning more and more lives. We must put a stop to it. If I know the truth I can put a stop to it. That I promise. I can't give you and Andrea back the lost years, but I can make sure that the misery, loneliness, the anger and the violence end here.'

'Oh, if only I could believe that.' She seemed to shrink within herself.

'Try to believe it—for Andrea's sake. I didn't want to say this because I had no wish to alarm you, but I suspect that she may be planning to marry the wrong man or, at least, for the wrong reason. Most of her life she's had no real love or security. She wants those things desperately—we all do—but she may be looking to someone who cannot supply them. You're the only person who could possibly get her to see that.'

'Heaven forbid that she should make the same mistake I made.' Jeanne Picard turned and began walking back to the hotel. 'I met Jack Rycote in Cyprus. I was on holiday there. Jack was with the army. Oh, he was a wild one; not at all an English stuffed-shirt. He was full of fun, very sure of himself, very determined to get what he wanted from life. What chance did a convent-reared eighteen-year-old girl stand? We were married within six weeks of meeting. A year later Andrea arrived. By then things had already begun to go wrong. Jack had appalling moods. Sometimes he was ice cold. No one could talk to him or approach him. Then he would suddenly become violent and start lashing out with his fists. Once he threw me across the kitchen and broke my arm. He was just as unpredictable at work. Eventually he was court-martialled for physical abuse to men under his command. That turned out to be a blessing for me. We set up home in England, but Jack couldn't live an ordinary civilian life. He had to have organised violence—guns, knives, war games. He was always going off with groups of other unstable young men to play at killing. But that wasn't enough. He formed his own little mercenary army and went off to Africa. Andrea and I were left in peace. For two or three years we were very happy. We lived partly in England and partly in France with my parents.'

'Are your parents still alive?'

'My father, yes. My mother died of cancer three years ago.'

'Any other family?'

'Oh, yes, I am one of five children. You

are wondering, I suppose, what relatives Andrea has?'

'Yes.'

'One uncle, three aunts, several cousins and two half-brothers. They would all love to see her.'

'What happened next?'

'Jack was in his element in—what was the name of the country?—Doalamba. He was paid handsomely to do what he most enjoyed—killing and maiming. He could do exactly what he liked. There were no laws or senior officers to restrain him. He was responsible for several atrocities. He used to come home and boast about them—how he and his men relentlessly tracked down guerilla bands and slaughtered them, how he only took prisoners in order to torture them, how he ordered the destruction of whole villages. I didn't want to listen to his stories but he got a thrill every time he told them. The fact that I tried to stop my ears made his pleasure all the greater.'

'But eventually he failed.'

She nodded. 'There was a coup and Jack Rycote became the most wanted man in Doalamba. He would have been lynched if the British government hadn't launched an expensive operation to get him out.'

'Why would they want to do that?'

'Oh, it was all tied up with politics. Jack told me about it. He reckoned he had been enormously clever and I suppose he had. He knew Britain had been secretly supplying arms and funds to the Doalamba regime. There was a lot of British investment in the country and so there was pressure on the government to maintain their influence in the area. Jack knew all this, and he was prepared to trade names and details with the new rulers in return for his safety.'

'So, he demanded a rescue mission and a complete change of identity. And you were not to be part of the new image?'

'No. That suited me. The deal was that I was to be paid off to get out of Jack's life and stay out. It was wonderful. Release. Freedom. The chance to start over again. Until I heard Jack's one condition.'

'Andrea.'

'Yes. He didn't want her, of course. He did it to punish me. At first I refused, but your SIS made it brutally clear what would happen if I failed to co-operate.'

'Whew! No wonder they wanted to keep all this under wraps.'

They turned to walk up through the orchard. 'Jack didn't get things all his own way. The intelligence people made it clear they were going to keep a very close watch on him.'

'Mr and Mrs Jenkins!'

'Pardon?'

'Sorry, just thinking aloud.'

They reached the inn buildings and lingered on the grass outside.

'So, Mr Lacy.' Jeanne looked up at him anxiously. 'What happens now?'

'With your permission, I will tell Andrea what you have told me—the relevant bits, anyway—and I'll give her your address.'

'Do you think she'll want to know me—the mother who abandoned her?'

'I'm sure she will, but you'll obviously have to give her time to get over the shock.'

Tim did not prolong his stay. Jeanne Picard would have a lot of thinking to do and there was no more he could tell her that might help. They parted, Tim assuring Andrea's mother that he would keep in touch.

The jet took him from Rouen to Bristol. During the short flight Tim took advantage of the comfort and solitude to rearrange his thoughts. He now knew as much as he was ever likely to know about the death of Jack Robertson. Most of the trig points were in place on his mental map. It remained only to connect them. When he did so, they all intersected in one place—Carol Sellis. That calculating young lady was a leading light in ASHRA, and ASHRA, doubtless, had a file on Rycote/Robertson. The

418

man had never been as discreet as his SIS minders would have liked. A dedicated snoop would have made the connection. Then there was the Save Glen Huich outfit, set up by Carol Sellis to keep an eye on Robertson and also to hit back at her father. Carol had managed to get inside the defences of the unsuspecting Laird of Lanner Castle, and had been perfectly capable of the jiggery-pokery in the dungeons—perhaps with the help of her henchwoman, Steffy. Both of them were art students and could have made design drawings of Cumberland's Cradle. She was on hand to register suitable horror when the body was discovered. How clever she must have thought herself when everything had gone according to plan. Then had come the panic when SGH came under suspicion. No wonder she got a fit of the trembles and packed in her university course—running back to Mummy and the comforting affluence of Surrey's executive-owned acres. Finally there was the young man in the Land Rover. Had Ms Sellis been behind that piece of murderous stupidity? Tim imagined the desperate phone call from Briachan to Ashcot Green when 'that Mr Lacy' turned up asking awkward questions. He could hear Carol opting for the easy solution, and ordering her co-conspirators to 'get rid of him'.

Tim accepted tea and pastries from a smiling hostess. The question was what to do now. He gazed through the cabin window. Beneath wisps of light cloud, England's green and pleasant land was spread out like the page of an atlas. What chance was there of seeing Carol and her cronies brought to trial? Tell Hatherton? The policeman would not thank him for interfering, and certainly would not put the culprits up in open court. Report back to Harman? He would probably have his own way of settling scores. Leak the whole sordid story to the press? The thought of stripping away the seven veils of secrecy from the extremely unalluring body of undercover arms dealing had immense attractions. But innocent people would get hurt. The Wapping truffle-hounds would be sniffing around Andrea, Ben and Jeanne. That was not an acceptable option. The plane tilted over, beginning its circuit over Bristol. Tim reminded himself that Carol was out of the country until the weekend. Perhaps by then he would have decided on an appropriate course of action.

In the event, the decision was made for him.

CHAPTER 19

Andrea Robertson was sparkling. She wore a linen suit of lemon yellow with a wide hat to match, and was enjoying being the centre of attention. She and Ben stood on a wide terrace receiving their guests, and responding with cheerful modesty to the congratulations proffered by the procession of elegantly dressed men and women—some in western clothes and some in bright, loose-draped robes—who, once received, made their way down on to the lawn.

Ben's high commission had made available for the 'little' pre-nuptial party a house it owned on the Thames near Henley. Three striped marquees with open sides formed a wide courtyard, at the centre of which a fountain plumed water into an oval pool where goldfish lazed.

'This is all very grand,' Catherine observed when their turn in the queue arrived.

Andrea laughed. 'Ben insists we do everything properly. I'd have been happy with a few friends and a Chinese takeaway.'

'If your man wants to make a fuss of you,

let him,' Catherine insisted. 'That phase soon passes. We've brought you something for your new home.' She handed over a package wrapped in gold paper.

'Goodness, everyone's being so kind.' An attendant took the present and added it to the pile on an already heaped table.

'And here's the gift I promised.' Tim held out a long envelope.

Andrea's face registered a mix of delight and apprehension. 'Have you discovered who...?'

'I've discovered something much more important than that. Read it later, when all this is over. I think you'll be pleased.'

Tim and Catherine moved on to shake hands with Ben and then walked down broad steps to the lawn.

'She looks fine,' Catherine said. 'I'm sure she can face it.'

'I hope so.'

'You left all the nasty bits out. In fact, I think you worded it very well; it was remarkably sensitive.'

Tim grinned. 'Less of the remarkable. I told her what she most needs to know: that she has family and how she can go about contacting them.'

They collected champagne and food from the trestles set out in one of the marquees, and sat at a small table to eat. After a few minutes a strikingly beautiful

Nigerian woman in turban and tribal costume came across. 'May I join you?' she asked. She sat down and introduced herself as Nana Aminu, a colleague of Ben Azikwe.

'You work in the same department? Immigration, isn't it?'

'That's right,' she sighed, and the flesh over her high cheekbones glistened in the sunlight slanting in beneath the canvas canopy. 'Forms, forms, forms. Are you in the diplomatic racket?'

Catherine laughed. 'No, neither of us possesses the tact and patience necessary for your profession.' She explained how they came to be there.

'Oh, then you don't really know anybody. You must let me introduce you to some people.'

They made small talk as they ate, and afterwards Nana set them on their conversational circuits. The afternoon slid past pleasantly in meeting new people, enjoying the warm sun, smelling the scent of flowers and watching the varied craft on the river. Drinks were served continuously, and while Tim stuck to the excellent champagne, Catherine, who had opted to drive home, restricted herself to fruit juice.

The occasion reached the stage when guests began looking surreptitiously at their watches. Tim was with three members of the American embassy sharing reminiscences about various parts of their large country when he heard Andrea's voice behind him.

'Tim, there you are. I was afraid you might have left.' She smiled at the rest of the group. 'If you don't mind, I'm going to steal this wonderful man away from you.' She took Tim by the hand and led him, almost running, across the lawn to a natural arbour formed by a horseshoe of laurels.

There she threw her arms round him in a hug which dislodged her hat and almost rocked Tim backwards into the shrubs. 'Oh, Tim, thank you, thank you, thank you! What a fabulous present—a whole family!'

Tim kissed her forehead and then gently detached her. 'Hey, you weren't supposed to read it until later.'

'I couldn't stop myself. Now, you've got to tell me everything you can think of. Tell me about my mother. What's she like? Will she want to see me after all this time? What stopped her getting in touch?'

Tim held up his hands. 'Oh, no, I'm not going to say anything, except yes, of course, she's longing to see you. I don't want to colour your judgement in any way. You're going to have to discover each other and there's no place for anyone else in that process.'

'Yes, you're right, of course. It's just that I'm so excited I can't think straight. I'll call her this evening as soon as all this is over. I can go over to France straight away. We don't leave for Lagos till Friday. We can have three or four days to start getting to know each other—and, of course, she must come to the wedding. After that...'

Loud voices from the other side of the laurels broke in.

'Let go or I'll scream the place down!' A woman's agitated tones.

'Oh, come on, you lovely little spy, don't hold out on me.' The man's voice was slurred.

'Let me go!'

'Ouch! You bitch! I'll teach you.'

Tim pulled a face. 'Oh, dear. Sounds like trouble. Excuse me.'

He strode quickly round the screen of bushes, where he saw a Nigerian woman and a white man struggling perilously close to the river bank.

Tim walked over and took a firm hold on the man's shoulders. 'The lady's saying no.'

The assailant loosed his hold and swung round, flailing a fist as he did so. 'Who the hell...?'

Tim easily ducked the uncoordinated

blow, then grabbed the man's wrist and twisted his arm behind him.

'Hey, that hurts!' the drunk yelled.

Tim moved his prisoner a few paces away from the woman, who he now saw was Nana Aminu. 'I don't want to hurt you any more than necessary but that's entirely up to you.' Tim breathed the words into the man's ear. 'You've had a bit too much to drink. Now, I suggest you sit down quietly and contemplate the river for a while until you're fit for company.'

'Sod off! Ouch!' Belligerence vanished as Tim increased pressure.

He forced the man to his knees and then into a sitting position. When he was sure that what little fight the drunk possessed had gone out of him, he released him and stepped across to where Nana had been joined by Andrea. 'Are you all right?'

The Nigerian gave him a slightly tense smile. 'I'm fine. Thank you so much for coming to my rescue, Tim.'

Andrea laughed. 'Oh, that's second nature to him. Damsels in distress are his speciality, aren't they, Tim?'

'Come on, let's go back to the house.' With a woman on each arm, Tim made his way to the main lawn. 'Who is that creep? Is he likely to give you any more grief?'

Nana made light of the incident. 'He's

426

just a Whitehall Romeo. I've met him a couple of times, purely professionally. He won't try anything on because if he does I can make a lot of trouble for him.'

They reached the terrace and Tim said, 'Now that I've done my good deed for the day I ought to find my wife and set out for home.'

Andrea squeezed his arm. 'You've done more than one good deed. I can't begin to tell you how grateful I am.'

'Well, have a great time in France, and be sure to let us know how you get on.'

'Oh, I will. That's a promise.'

Tim found Catherine and they went in search of Ben to offer their formal thanks and farewells.

'I wonder how he'll take the news,' Catherine said as they walked back to where the car was parked.

'He ought to be delighted with anything that makes his wife happier.'

'It's going to be a bit of a shock for him, though—discovering that he's suddenly acquired a whole posse of in-laws.'

For the journey home Tim tilted back the passenger seat and refocused his mind on the problem of Carol Sellis. Could he be sure he was right about her? Should he, at least, give her a chance to try to explain away the facts which seemed ever clearer the more he thought about them? Yet again he turned them over in his mind: Carol at Lanner Castle; Carol finding the body; Carol using protest groups for her own personal ambitions and vendettas...Carol...'

'OK, Buster. Beauty sleep over.'

Tim's eyes jerked open as Catherine brought the BMW to rest in the stable yard at Farrans Court. 'Sorry, I must have dozed off for a moment.'

Catherine laughed. 'Several hundred moments to be a bit more precise. For that you can cook the supper while I sort the boys out.'

It was much later that evening, after the family rituals of eating and reading a story to Timothy and Rupert, that Tim had the chance to bring his mind back to the problem of Jack Robertson's murderer. He now knew what he would do: he would phone Carol and offer her the choice between meeting him and explaining herself to the police. He went to his office and put a call through to the number Maggie Peverill had given him.

Carol answered almost instantly, her voice agitated. 'Thank God you've called! You got my message on your answerphone? I called half a dozen times. Look, things are going very wrong. You've got to get me out of...' She stopped abruptly. 'Who is that?'

'Carol, it's Tim Lacy here. I think we ought...'

There was a gasp at the other end and a click as the line went dead. When Tim tried the number again there was no reply. He sighed and sat back in his chair. Now there was only one thing to do. Carol had been warned. Doubtless her mother had told her about his visit to Enderby Lodge. Now she was panicking, planning with her associates to make a run for it. Only the police could stop them.

He drove into Marlborough, found a phone box and put a call through to the duty desk at Scotland Yard. He succinctly informed the officer who answered that a Ms Carol Sellis at a telephone number which he quoted had vital information about a recent murder, and that the police should go to her flat straight away before she had a chance to abscond. The message took less than fifteen seconds to deliver and Tim cleared the line immediately.

And that's that, he thought as he drove back through the twilit lanes to Farrans Court. He tried to convince himself that he was relieved it was all over, but his overwhelming feeling was a mixture of anticlimax and disappointment.

That night he lay awake long after Catherine had gone to sleep. He spent what seemed hours trying to wrangle with niggling anxieties which in the darkness swelled into bloated fears. Something was wrong, the unconscious insisted. No, reason argued, he had gathered all the necessary scraps of information and sewn them into a garment of pure logic. Anyway, right or wrong, his brain clamoured as he wrestled with uncooperative pillows and wiped sweat from his brow, he had done all he could. He had worried away at the truth while others had tried to distract him with lies and self-interested part truths. Now he had set the police on the right trail and could walk away with an easy mind and a clear conscience. When half-sleep came it was filled with images of frustration. Tim saw himself trying to pull on a jacket several sizes too small, and close a door against an unseen force which was ever so slightly stronger than he was.

Sunday breakfast was one of the few meals of the week that the Lacys were often able to keep as family time. Not this week. The boys were probably no more than usually boisterous, but their antics were aggravating Tim. He yelled at them to keep quiet. That made Timothy sulk, brought Rupert to the edge of tears and drew from Catherine a look that would have seared leather. Eventually Tim strode out of the kitchen announcing pointedly that he was going to his office for some peace and quiet.

He played with some paperwork and switched on a portable radio for background noise. He was only half listening when a mid-morning newscast came on. It was the third item that exploded his mind into complete attention. The body of a young woman found murdered in a flat in Kensington had been identified as being that of Carol Sellis. She had been the victim of a brutal assault around ten o'clock on Saturday night. The police had arrived on the scene soon after the killing, and were particularly anxious to interview a man who had telephoned them shortly before.

Tim slumped in the chair, his brain a courtroom where prosecution and defence counsels shrieked hysterically at each other.

'You as good as killed her!'

'Rubbish! It was one of her associates—probably the nutcase with the Land Rover.'

'But if you hadn't been hounding them it wouldn't have happened.'

'Nonsense! They'd have fallen out sooner or later. Anyway, no one else was doing anything about Robertson's murder. Hatherton won't be able to keep everything locked in the closet now.'

'That's your justification for the death of another human being, is it?'

'If it's the only way of turning the spotlight on a disgusting trade in arms that's killing thousands every year, yes. Yes!'

'Major?'

Tim was suddenly aware that George was standing in the doorway. 'Sorry, George. Miles away.'

The burly ex-soldier, clad in off-duty sweater and jeans, took a couple of paces into the room. 'Catherine said I'd find you here. It's Johnny's birthday. Me and the lads are taking him down to the Crown and Anvil. Care to join us?'

'Thanks, George. Nice thought, but...'

'Catherine reckoned you could do with a break. By the look of you, she was right.'

Tim relaxed a fraction. 'She usually is. OK, let's go.'

'Families,' George announced as they crossed the stable yard. 'Wonderful things, but we'd go mad if we didn't escape from them sometimes.'

They walked over the fields to Stonegallows Top, then strode down the hill into the village. The dozen Lacy's men were gathered at one end of the bar. Pete Cole raised his glass in salute. 'What'll it be, Major, brandy? I'm in the chair.'

Tim held up a hand. 'Don't tempt me, Pete. I had a heavy alcohol intake

432

yesterday. Make it a bitter, please.' Tim received his glass and raised it in salute to the young man seated at a table by the wall. 'Happy twenty-first, Johnny. By the way, how's that long-distance romance of yours progressing?'

The wideness of Johnny's smile suggested that he was already falling under the influence of his colleagues' generosity. 'Fine thanks, Major. Mary's coming down for a few days next week.'

'Oho, your bachelor days are numbered, Johnny boy!' someone called out. 'She'll soon have you dancing a reel all the way to the altar.'

The leg-pulling continued on a Scottish theme for some minutes at Johnny's expense, then Pete said, 'But he's not the only one who's lost his heart in the Highlands, is he, George?'

George shook his head. 'There's nothing new about it. Me and the wife have often said we'd like to explore Scotland. Well, now that the family's off our hands and we can please ourselves we're going to do just that.'

'Going ghost-hunting are you, George?' A chorus of laughter greeted the retort from one of the younger men.

'You scoff as much as you like.' George stood up to the taunt. 'I know what I saw. If you'd been to that place you wouldn't dismiss the supernatural so readily. Isn't that so, Major?'

'There's certainly an atmosphere about the castle and the loch,' Tim agreed.

'It's evil,' George insisted. 'You can sense it in the air—a sort of accumulation of negative energy from all the terrible things that have happened there.'

'Have you found out any more about your young hero, Ewen the Brave?' Tim asked.

The older man shook his close-cropped head. 'I don't suppose we'll ever know what happened to him in the end. There are three theories. Some say he went to London intending to assassinate Butcher Cumberland and was caught and hanged. Others believe he fled abroad and lived and died as a mercenary soldier somewhere in Europe. And those who love happy endings see him settling down on some remote croft and living the rest of his life in peace.'

'That reminds me,' Johnny intervened. 'In her last letter Mary sent a message for you, George.' He fumbled in his pockets, produced an envelope and painstakingly extracted one sheet of paper from the others. He peered at it.

'Better make sure it's the right page, Johnny. You don't want to make George blush.'

George squinted at the careful writing. 'Looks like a poem.'

Johnny nodded. 'That's right. Mary says it's a ballad that her dad found among some old papers.'

'Give us a song then, George,' Pete demanded.

'Do you want to hear it or not?' George growled.

'Yes, come on. Don't leave us in suspense.'

Several other voices echoed the plea, so George cleared his throat. 'It's called "The Last Song of Ewen", and it goes like this:

'Farewell Strathconan's craggy shank
And Beauly's winding, timbered bank.
Farewell brave clansmen of the fell.
Farewell my friends, my foes farewell.

My heart I leave here in the glen,
Safe kept by honest Highland men,
And take the road that has no bend:
Vengeance runs straight unto its end.

Not danger fills my eyes with tears.
I quake not at the unknown fears
That cluster round my southward path.
I weep for my abandoned hearth.

Nor well-loved sight, nor smiling face,

435

Nor fireside tale, nor warm embrace,
Nor comradeship against the foe
Accompany where I must go.

The hunter now has left the moor.
The scattered coneys meet secure.
My tyrant quarry shall not rest
Save with my skean-dhu in his breast.

Vengeance alone is sacred more
Than homestead's ever-open door.
With unpaid wrongs I cannot dwell,
And so, my land, farewell, farewell.'

A round of ribald applause followed the recitation.

Tim said, 'Well, if that's genuine, or at least very early, I suppose it clinches the matter: Ewen, at some stage, decided to take on his people's arch-enemy, the Butcher himself I suppose—'

The barmaid called his name. 'Tim! Phone for you.'

At the other end of the bar he picked up the receiver. 'Hello?'

'Tim.' It was Catherine's voice. 'Sorry to break in on the party but there's something I thought you'd like to know straight away.'

'Go on.'

'I've just had Andrea Robertson on the phone. She's in an absolute state, poor kid. She said she had to talk to someone and we were the only ones she could think of.'

'What's the matter?'

'Apparently Ben's insisting that they go to Lagos now, today. He's made her pack in a hurry and booked them on the two o'clock flight. She was literally on the point of leaving when she phoned. Ben had just taken the bags down in the lift.'

'Why? What's the panic?'

'He says he met someone last night who gave him a message from Nigeria. He's needed there urgently.'

'Does Andrea believe him?'

'I don't think so. She reckons it's got something to do with finding out about her mother. She told him after the party yesterday and his mood changed drastically. He covered it up but Andrea thinks he wasn't at all pleased at the idea of having a white family.'

Family—that word again. Family. Vengeance. Not arms deals. Not human rights. 'Oh, my God. I've got it wrong, horribly wrong.'

'Tim, what's the matter?'

'Can you bring the BMW now and collect me? We've got to get to Heathrow and stop them.'

'Heathrow! Tim! We—'

'Darling, we have to. Andrea's in danger.'

He put the phone down, made his excuses and went outside to wait for the car.

Ten minutes later, as Catherine jumped out of the driving seat to let Tim in, she said, 'You'd better have some pretty convincing arguments. I can't make any sense of all this.'

'I have. I'm almost certain...'

'Almost!'

'I'll talk it through with you as we go along.' Tim threw the BMW into gear, turned in the pub forecourt and pointed it up the hill out of Little Farrans. 'First of all, see if you can get hold of Hatherton. I haven't got his extension number but the switchboard will put you through.'

Catherine picked up the mobile phone and punched in the number. She spoke with an operator and then with a bored young man on another line. 'He says Chief Superintendent Hatherton isn't in today.'

Tim took the handset from her. 'My name is Lacy and it is vital I speak with DCS Hatherton immediately.'

'He's off duty, I'm afraid, sir. I'll transfer you to—'

'You'll do no such thing. Phone Hatherton and give him my name and mobile number.'

The policeman made an effort to remain civil. 'Sorry, sir, more than my job's worth to disturb—'

'Officer, I give you my guarantee that if you don't pass my message to Chief Superintendent Hatherton, by this time tomorrow you won't have a job. I am on my way to create a diplomatic incident and Hatherton is the only one who can stop me. Now, take down my number.' He dictated the digits and clipped the receiver back in its holder.

It was twelve minutes later that Hatherton rang.

'All right, Lacy. What precisely is going on?' His tone was level but there was an angry edge to his words.

Tim spoke equally deliberately. 'Some facts about Benjamin Azikwe. You don't have to confirm or deny them, but if I've got them right you have to act p.d.q.'

'Look here, Lacy—'

'There's no time for striking attitudes. Just listen.' He added, as an afterthought, 'Please. The facts, as I see them, are these: Azikwe is with Nigerian Intelligence. As a result of co-operation with his British counterparts he knows of the existence of a certain safe house operated by SIS in Edinburgh. He has murdered two British subjects and, unless we can stop him, he will kill a third. He and his fiancée are on

439

their way to Heathrow. They're booked on the two o'clock flight to Lagos. I'm *en route* to the airport, ETA about one-fifteen. I don't know whether I can get to him before boarding or what I can do, anyway. But there must be all sorts of things you can do—hold up the flight or something.'

'I can't charge in and start harassing an accredited diplomat. Nor can you!'

'You can prevent the abduction of a British subject.'

'Not if she's going with her fiancé of her own free will.'

'That's why we have to talk to them before they get airborne.'

'Good God, Lacy You don't know what you've blundered into!'

'I've got a pretty good idea.'

'I'll see you at the airport!' The line went dead.

Tim came off the intersection on to the M4 at speed.

Catherine glowered at her husband. 'Now, would some kind of explanation be too much to ask for?'

'Sorry to bounce you like this, darling. Yes, I'll try to get everything into some sort of order. I have to get things clear in my own mind before I confront Ben Azikwe. Let's go back to what we were saying about the three qualifications for Robertson's murderer: he'd have to know

440

about the incidents with the dogs, and how to get the Cumberland's Cradle off the island, and that Robertson would go to the house in Edinburgh. You suggested that Jenkins was the only one who fitted the bill and, as far as we know, you were right. But Jenkins was Robertson's minder. He was installed by SIS to keep their troublesome protégé safe and under control.'

'Which, given Robertson's record and his character, was a pretty tall order.'

'Absolutely. And that was the heart of the problem. I reckon Intelligence got wind of a plot on Robertson's life. They knew someone was after him but they didn't know who. So they told him to move. But Robertson was bloody minded. He was ensconced in Lanner Castle and saw no reason to budge.'

'Hence the business with the dogs?'

'I'm sure that's right. SIS were the only people who could have put an operative into the castle. With Jenkins' help it would be dead easy to knock off the only creatures Robertson really cared about. That, they hoped, would shake him into quitting the castle for some other hideaway. It very nearly worked—but not quite.'

'I can see that Ben heard about the dog incidents from Andrea, but what makes you think he knew where Robertson would bolt to if he was really scared?'

'That, of course, was the big stumbling block. Once I realised where the Jenkinses fitted into the picture, I knew the Inchferry Road house had to belong to SIS. It's an ideal location for all sorts of purposes: undistinguished, close to the airport and the docks. They could meet discreetly there with foreigners, people leaving the country or arriving; it's perfect for briefings and debriefings.'

'Or for hiding someone.'

'Precisely.'

'Yes, but how did Ben...'

'OK, this bit is guesswork, but Hatherton just confirmed it by not rubbishing my suggestion that Ben was in a position to know about the place. You remember at the party yesterday we met that woman, Nana Aminu, and she said she worked with Ben? Later, when she was being molested by that drunken slob, he called her a "lovely little spy".'

'An inebriated attempt at endearment?'

'I don't think so. Officially, Nana and Ben work in the immigration department. That's a pretty typical cover for Intelligence. So he could have known about the Edinburgh house. He certainly knew about ASHRA; Nigerian Intelligence keeps very close tabs on such organisations and their links with dissident groups back home.

And that means that he knew all about Carol.'

'So basically what you're saying is that Ben used his diplomatic contacts to ferret out the truth about Rycote-Robertson?'

'Yes, with all the single-mindedness of a Jewish zealot relentlessly pursuing Nazi war criminals.'

'And he deliberately sought out Andrea?'

'It was the only way of getting inside Lanner Castle. But once there he needed an accomplice. What he had in mind couldn't be done single-handed. So he made contact with the eminently-corruptible Carol.'

'Surely he didn't tell her he intended murdering Robertson.'

'No, when she realised, too late, what she'd got herself involved in she went into genuine shock. When I started nosing around she panicked totally—hence the Land Rover incident. I expect she had thought she was just helping Ben put the fear of God into Robertson. Once she'd got her appointment at the castle, all Azikwe had to do was make sure he was there the same day. Between them they were easily able to manage all the business in the dungeon.'

'Then all he had to do was tell Andrea he'd been called back to Lagos and calmly make his way to Edinburgh. Do you think

Hatherton's had his eyes on Azikwe all the time?'

'He knew that the murder had to be tied up with someone in the intelligence business. That's one reason why he didn't want me prying into Robertson's death. That and things like dodgy arms deals, secret government support for tyrannical regimes, international civil rights organisations. There were just too many worms in this particular can. I almost feel sorry for him trying to keep the lid on.'

Catherine was silent for a few moments. Then she said, 'What's Hatherton going to do now?'

'I'm sure that question is giving him a headache even as we speak. He'll be trying to calculate just how much damage limitation he can achieve. And that's going to depend on how much I know and how much I can be persuaded to keep under my hat.'

Catherine scarcely dared to put her next thought into words. 'There's one way of ensuring your silence.'

Tim moved the BMW into the outside lane and eased the speed smoothly up to ninety-five. 'That idea will certainly have occurred to him, but I think—I hope—he'll realise that things have got too complicated for simple solutions. Robertson's murder he managed to cover up. Carol's took him by surprise and the media have got hold of it. Another death and people will start making connections. Hatherton has to play his hand very carefully. So does Azikwe. And the stakes are high. Ben's playing for his freedom, perhaps his life—his government doesn't like being embarrassed. Hatherton's job could well be on the line; certainly his promotion prospects are. If even a fraction of the truth gets out heads are going to roll.'

'And Tim Lacy? What stakes is he playing for?'

'Boring old justice, I suppose. I want to see Azikwe pay for his crimes.'

'What was his motive in all this?'

'I've got my ideas about that, but nothing I can prove.'

They reached Terminal 4 at Heathrow at 1.13 p.m. By the time they had parked the car and hurried into the building it was almost half past. Catherine, running to keep up, said, 'They've probably already boarded by now.'

'No.' Tim stopped to scan one of the departure screens. 'Either Hatherton's done his stuff or the gods are on our side.' The Lagos flight was shown as being 'delayed'. No take-off time was indicated.

Tim and Catherine walked briskly towards the departure lounge.

'What now?' Catherine whispered.

'Frontal assault.' Tim walked straight up to the official at the desk. 'I have an urgent message for a passenger on the Lagos flight, a Miss Andrea Robertson.'

The man gave him a professional scrutiny. 'And your name, sir?'

'Lacy.'

The official nodded to a sandy-haired man standing a few paces away, and said to Tim, 'This gentleman will look after you, sir.'

The other approached with the faintest of smiles. 'Mr and Mrs Lacy? Come with me, please.'

'That depends where we're going and who you are.'

'Airport security, Mr Lacy. I have instructions to convey you to the VIP lounge. I understand you have business with a couple of passengers.' He pushed open a door marked 'Private' and ushered them through.

After leading them along a mini-maze of corridors, their guide showed them into a room where lights were dimmed, colours muted and sounds hushed. The atmosphere of restful opulence was a triumph of the interior decorator's art. A dozen or so first-class passengers sat in deep armchairs enjoying free drinks and refreshments and, where necessary, being soothed by attentive staff apologising for the delay.

Andrea saw them immediately. She and Ben were seated by the wide window overlooking the runways. 'Tim! Catherine!' She jumped up and took a step towards them.

Immediately Ben was on his feet beside her, a hand gripping her arm. 'What are you doing here? Please leave! Steward!' He called to one of the uniformed staff. 'Remove these people!'

Andrea turned to him, horrified. 'Ben, don't be silly.'

'You're not to talk to them. I forbid it!'

She shook herself free. 'What on earth's got into you, darling?' She rushed across the expanse of deep carpet and embraced Catherine. 'What a lovely surprise.'

Tim exchanged quick glances with his wife and stepped over to the tall Nigerian. 'It's over, Ben. And don't insult my intelligence by saying you've no idea what I'm talking about.'

Azikwe resumed his seat, crossed his legs with elaborate care and pinched the creases in his trousers. 'You realise your police can't touch me.'

'Diplomatic immunity? You're stretching it a bit if you think that covers murder.'

'We'll see. It wasn't murder, you know. It was justice—delayed for many years, but justice nevertheless.'

'What was it that you had against Robertson?'

'Enough. He wiped out my entire family.'

'In Doalamba?'

'Yes. You worked that out, did you?'

'Not worked out. Guessed. Were you taken to Nigeria by the missionaries?'

'Not even the mission station was safe from the Butcher's men. That's what we called Robertson, or Rycote as he was then—the Butcher. There's a fine irony for you, Tim! The Smithsons—they were American evangelicals—had to flee across the border with as many children as they could get to safety. By that time, at least one of those children was scarred for life. Shall I tell you what the Butcher and his savages did to me? They slaughtered my father and three uncles in what they were pleased to call a battle. It was no fight, just a flushing out of 'resistance' with helicopter gunships, gas canisters and flame-throwers. Then they worked their way up into the hills systematically, moving from village to village. When they attacked ours they killed everyone they could find—women, children, old men. It was a massacre. That was when I lost the rest of my family. All except my baby sister. I got away with her and we took refuge in another village. But not for long. The soldiers turned up there a few nights later. Again I ran, somehow carrying the tiny bundle that was my sister. I got as far as the river.'

He stopped, choking on the words. Tim saw him clench his eyes to keep back the tears. He took a deep breath. 'I put her down while I found a shallow place to cross. When I returned, a soldier was standing over her. As I watched he fired his rifle into her. She was nine months old and that bastard filled her little body with bullets. Then he laughed. It was the last sound he ever uttered. I sprang at him and he went into the river—where it was fast and deep. So, do you see what Robertson did to me? He took away all my family and he turned me into a killer. It wasn't innocence that died in me that day; I doubt I ever had much of that. It was humanity. That's what Robertson did to me. Now you tell me, Tim, did such a man deserve to live?'

A shriek sawed through the stillness. 'No! No, it isn't true!' Andrea had been talking quietly with Catherine on the other side of the room. Now she jumped up and ran across to her fiancé. 'Ben, they're saying horrible things about you. Tell them they're not true!' She sank on to the chair beside him and threw her arms around him—protective, possessive.

Gently Ben detached her. 'Go with

Catherine, darling, please. Just for now. We'll talk later.'

She stared at him, uncomprehending and unwilling to comprehend. 'But all you have to do is tell them that they're making a ghastly mistake!'

'Andrea, please.' He stood and lifted her to her feet. 'Just for a few minutes.'

The other VIP travellers had been watching the drama attentively, but now a tannoy announcement declared that the Lagos flight was ready for boarding. They collected their bags and newspapers and began moving to the exit. Catherine led Andrea gently away in the opposite direction, to the other door. Only Tim and Ben Azikwe were left standing in the middle of the room.

Tim said, 'I think I could have forgiven you for Robertson. But not for using others. Carol Sellis—you exploited her greed and vanity and perverted idealism. You made her an accessory to murder. Then, as soon as she became a liability, you killed her. And what about Andrea? You needed her to get to her father. What would have happened when her usefulness ran out? Would she have disappeared somewhere in Nigeria? You certainly couldn't let her meet her mother, could you? She might have learned the truth about Rycote and Doalamba, and that might have led—'

'Well, it's all academic anyway, isn't it?' Azikwe straightened his tie—a gesture of defiant nonchalance. 'As I said, the British authorities can't touch me.'

'They can hold you while they make a request to your high commission for the lifting of diplomatic immunity.'

'What, and put me on trial? And have the whole sordid story of Rycote-Robertson and his relations with your government come out in open court? I don't think so. Now, if you'll excuse me, I have a plane to catch.' He moved towards the exit.

Before he reached it Hatherton appeared in the doorway with Smythe at his elbow. 'Excuse me, sir. I wonder if we might have a word with you.'

Tim breathed a sigh of relief. 'He's all yours, Superintendent. He's as good as confessed already.' He turned away and went in search of his wife and a betrayed and broken-hearted Andrea Robertson.

The sandy-haired young man was outside the door. He conducted Tim to an office where the two women were waiting. Andrea was sitting rigid, in shock, a steaming mug clenched tightly in her hands. As Tim entered she looked up, expressionless. 'Where's Ben? I must go to him.'

'He's with the police at the moment.'

'Police?' She shook her head. 'But it can't be true! It simply can't!'

Catherine put an arm round her but she remained stiff and upright. After several moments silence she said to Tim, 'You're supposed to know all about it. Tell me everything—now!'

Tim shook his head and sat down opposite her. 'A bit later, perhaps, when you've had a chance—'

'No, now!' Andrea shouted. 'Everyone knows everything except me. I want to know. I've a right to know!' She slumped as the tears gushed forth. 'Tell me...please.'

'OK.' Tim told the story as simply as he could, keeping to the bare essentials. Even so it took him almost half an hour.

Andrea listened, questionless, her eyes hardly ever moving from Tim's face. When he had finished, she said, 'I don't understand all of that...but I understand enough to realise that it must be true. My father...my fiancé...I don't seem to be very lucky with my men, do I? What do I do now?'

Catherine gripped her hand. 'Well, you certainly mustn't be alone. Why don't you come back with us? A few days in the country? Then, as soon as you feel up to it, I should do what you were planning to do yesterday—go and see your mother. You wouldn't know it, but that's what mums are for.'

The door opened wide enough to reveal

Hatherton's gaunt figure. 'A few words, Mr Lacy, if I may.'

In the corridor outside, Tim asked, 'Have you taken him into custody?'

Hatherton looked squarely at him. 'I've escorted him to his plane and I've told him that he is *persona non grata* in this country. In doing that I exceeded my authority, but I'm sure that my superiors will back my decision.'

Tim sneered. 'Yes, I'll bet they will. Azikwe was right. Murder we can wink at, but embarrassing the government, making difficulties for the arms industry, shaking public confidence in our lords and masters, risking the loss of a few thousand votes—those are serious matters to be avoided at all costs.'

'The important thing is that the case is closed.'

'Ah but you don't know that, do you? You don't know what I'm going to do. It's a great story. All the newspaper editors would fall over themselves for an exclusive.'

'I do hope you're not going to be silly, Mr Lacy. Look, on my way here I had a phone call with no less a person than the foreign secretary. Your name featured very prominently in our conversation.'

Tim laughed. 'Really? What's coming now, a bribe or a threat?'

'He asked me to convey his personal thanks—for your help...and discretion. I'd like to be able to tell him that he can continue relying on that discretion.'

'What you can tell the foreign secretary is...' Tim shook his head. 'No, you wouldn't have the guts to pass the message on.'

He turned abruptly and went back into the office where Catherine and Andrea were waiting.

EPILOGUE

It was on a whim that, driving home from London on a clear winter's afternoon, Tim made a wide detour that took him through Compton Marney. It was more than a year since the visit to Lanner Castle which had set in motion so bizarre a trail of events, and over five months had passed since he and Catherine had heard anything of Andrea Robertson. Following the disappearance of Ben Azikwe the confused young woman had spent a few days at Farrans Court. As best they could, the Lacys had eased her through the delayed shock and the ensuing emotional upheaval. Then she had gone to France to discover her mother, to study the past of which she had been deprived, to explore the possibility of a future. There had been an ebullient letter cataloguing her first impressions of the Relais St Pierre and her French relatives. Then nothing. Tim was anxious and slightly annoyed that Andrea seemed to have forgotten them but Catherine insisted that it was a good sign, evidence that she was healthily busy in a novel environment.

Tim's tidy mind was less tolerant of loose ends. It was his reluctance to live with impatient questions rather than any hope of finding specific answers that brought him into Compton Marney's almost deserted village street. He parked at the top end, by the church path. Buttoning his top coat against a scalpel-sharp east wind he hurried, head down, up the slope to the shelter of the porch. He pushed on the heavy door and stepped into the ecclesiastical interior with its characteristic odour of polish and must. Low sunlight through windows largely devoid of stained glass reflected from whitewashed walls and stout Norman pillars. There was no sound save the faint rustling of a lady adjusting the flower arrangements in the sanctuary.

Automatically Tim turned to the right to look at the black tablet with its familiar gilt lettering on the wall beside the door. Yes, there it was...and yet it was not. A discreet rectangle of marble occupied the space, but it was not the same piece of stone. The crisp, gold script was in the identical style, but the legend was different. It now read:

In memory of
CAPTAIN JOHN CHALONER HASTINGS
RYCOTE
1940–1995

'Christ Jesus came into the world
to save sinners'

So, the truth, or some of it, had filtered
through to Jack Robertson's surviving
family. Tim nodded his approval. One
less loose end.

'Mr Lacy, isn't it?'

He turned to see an erect figure carrying
a small watering can and a trug basket
containing faded blooms and strands of
discarded foliage. 'Mrs Chaloner, how
clever of you to remember me.'

'I noticed you as soon as you came in.
We don't get many visitors, especially at
this time of year. In fact, if I hadn't
been doing the flowers you wouldn't have
been able to get in. We've taken to
keeping the church locked in the winter
months—vandals, you know.'

Tim pointed to the inscription. 'I see
you've changed your brother's memorial.'

'I had to. The other was blasphemous—
well, sacrilegious.' She glowered angrily.

'I don't quite see...'

'The other tablet was a lie. I was furious
when I heard about it—and the vicar was
none too pleased. To think that Jack could
do such a despicable thing, fobbing us off
with some other poor wretch's ashes. It was
a terrible problem when we discovered the
truth. We had to consult the archdeacon

457

to see whether the original urn should be disinterred. Very embarrassing.'

'May I ask how you discovered the truth?'

'Tea?' Mrs Chaloner questioned imperiously. 'The last time we met I seem to recall I gave you rather short shrift. You must permit me to make amends.'

'Thank you. I'd like that.'

Tim took her encumbrances from her, helped her down the path and into his car, and headed for Rycote Hall.

Twenty minutes later he was sitting before a log fire and sipping Earl Grey from Rockingham china, in a south-facing room whose lime-painted panelling emphasized the intensity of the winter sunlight. Mrs Chaloner proffered a slice of Victoria sponge, lush with cream and strawberry jam. 'Last time you called here,' she said accusingly, 'you were masquerading as a burglar-alarm salesman.'

Tim laughed. 'I *am* a burglar-alarm salesman.'

'But that was not the purpose of your visit. You were probing the history of my brother, Jack.'

'I confess it. But how—'

'How did an old biddy like me manage to put two and two together? Well, I haven't yet fallen victim to senile dementia—not quite, anyway.'

'I wouldn't suspect it for a moment. You are obviously...'

With an impatient gesture the general's daughter cut off the proffered flattery. 'I certainly couldn't have worked out the truth for myself. Twenty years ago my family became the victims of a monstrous and cruel deception, a very clever deception. It worked extremely well. So much so that it killed my father. Twenty years...' She shook her head. 'It's a long time to wait to be disabused. Then, when the truth came out, it was even worse than the lie I had come to live with.'

'But, how—'

Mrs Chaloner's frown silenced the interruption. 'Last September I received a letter from someone claiming to be Jack's daughter.'

'That must have been a shock.'

'Yes, it was rather. I hadn't seen Andrea since she was tiny. The family never knew what had happened to her and her mother after Jack's reported death. My first reaction was to dismiss the letter as the work of an imposter—you know, a sort of Anastasia. But the more I thought about it the more it seemed to me that there was no motive for fraud, no Rycote millions for an unscrupulous gold-digger to batten upon. The house and estate are all that's left, and they're mortgaged up to the hilt.'

'So you agreed to see her?'

'Yes. She came here—sat where you're sitting now—and we talked for hours. It was a remarkably...moving experience. I'm not readily given to tears but I don't mind admitting we both wept buckets. She's a charming gal—far nicer than Jack deserves. She told me what had really happened to her father and how a certain Tim Lacy had helped to piece the story together. The name rang a bell. I rummaged around and found your card—I'm a terrible hoarder, I'm afraid, never throw anything away. Two or three times since Andrea's visit I've been on the point of contacting you, but I could never think quite what to say. And today you turn up out of the blue. Kismet, Mr Lacy, wouldn't you say?' She held out her hand to take his cup and refilled it from a Georgian silver pot.

Tim smiled. 'I'm glad you met up with Andrea. She's taken a lot of hard knocks. She needs all the support she can find.'

'Well, I'll do whatever I can. She's a very agreeable young lady and she is a Rycote.'

'I'm sure anything that enables her to discover her real identity will be valuable. But now, how can I help you, Mrs Chaloner?'

She sat back in her armchair with a long sigh and seemed almost to shrink against the faded chintz. 'Oh, I don't know. Reassurance, I suppose. What he did to us—his family—is difficult to forgive, but I'd love you to be able to tell me that Jack wasn't all bad, that he had some redeeming features.'

'I only met him once, and then very briefly.'

'But you've spoken to lots of people who knew him.'

Tim searched for some words that might bring comfort to the old lady. 'I'd say that your brother had a very acute conscience. He shut himself up in a grim old castle and he filled it with symbols of human cruelty. He spent several years writing a history of torture. Some people regarded that as an unhealthy obsession. Perhaps it would be truer to say that it was a self-imposed penance.'

'I'd like to think that he felt some guilt, some shame. We are a military family, Mr Lacy. Generations of Rycotes have put service to crown and country above everything else. Yet the last Rycote was nothing better than a penny-in-the-slot killing machine.'

'Families,' Tim muttered and shook his head.

'I beg your pardon?'

'I was just reflecting that families are what this whole tragic sequence of events is about. It was only when I realised that that I saw the truth of things. There's an old Scottish legend connected with Jack's castle. It's all about a boy who exacted a terrible vengeance on those responsible for killing members of his clan. The family is a powerful thing, as you know well, Mrs Chaloner, and as Jack discovered to his cost. He abandoned his family. He deprived Andrea of her family. He was responsible for destroying hundreds of families in Doalamba. Retribution was slow—but terribly sure.'

The light outside was fading, but his hostess did not immediately press the switch on the table lamp beside her. For several minutes they sat in silence, the glow from the fire painting their faces in vivid chiaroscuro.

The publishers hope that this book has given you enjoyable reading. Large Print Books are especially designed to be as easy to see and hold as possible. If you wish a complete list of our books, please ask at your local library or write directly to: Magna Large Print Books, Long Preston, North Yorkshire, BD23 4ND, England.

This Large Print Book for the Partially sighted, who cannot read normal print, is published under the auspices of

THE ULVERSCROFT FOUNDATION

THE ULVERSCROFT FOUNDATION

. . . we hope that you have enjoyed this Large Print Book. Please think for a moment about those people who have worse eyesight problems than you . . . and are unable to even read or enjoy Large Print, without great difficulty.

You can help them by sending a donation, large or small to:

**The Ulverscroft Foundation,
1, The Green, Bradgate Road,
Anstey, Leicestershire, LE7 7FU,
England.**
or request a copy of our brochure for more details.

The Foundation will use all your help to assist those people who are handicapped by various sight problems and need special attention.

Thank you very much for your help.